MASTER WOLSEY

A HISTORICAL NOVEL OF THE TUDOR COURT

LAURA DOWERS

BLUE LAUREL PRESS

ISBN (Paperback): 978-1-912968-14-5

ISBN (Large Print Paperback): 978-1-912968-15-2

ISBN (MOBI): 978-1-912968-16-9

ISBN (EPUB): 978-1-912968-17-6

ACKNOWLEDGMENTS

I would like to thank my Advance Reader Team for taking the time to read this book and provide feedback. Your comments were greatly appreciated.

I would also like to thank my copyeditor, Jessica Cale of Historical Editorial, for her editing of my manuscript.

THE RED DRAGON AND THE
WHITE BOAR

BOSWORTH, 1485

The red dragon flapped noisily above his head, the brightly painted canvas catching every gust of wind that blew on that summer day.

All the years of waiting, all the moving from one place to another, never staying long enough to call anywhere home, had come down to this moment. His mother had always told him it would end thus, with he and his army on one side of an English field and his enemy on the other. She had also assured him God would be by his side on that day and that he would be victorious. Henry Tudor wished he had his mother's faith in the battle's outcome.

His prematurely lined eyes flicked down to the man standing by his foot. John de Vere, the Earl of Oxford, was stroking the neck of Henry's horse, his expert hand soothing the animal made nervous by the noise of thousands of men in armour. 'How many men does Richard have?' Henry asked.

'We counted ten thousand,' Oxford said, looking back across the field to where King Richard's white boar standard flew.

Henry winced. 'And we have but half that number.'

'Aye, but all good soldiers, my lord. Our men know how to fight. Richard's army may be large, but it is untrained. 'Tis skill that matters in battle.'

'I trust you are right.' Henry looked up at the sky. The sun had risen at five that morning and chased away the mist that draped the field. There would never be a better time to begin, and besides, he wanted it over. He knew he had no choice but to fight to win the crown, but he did not relish the task. 'Take up your position. Order the advance as soon as your lines are ready. It is time to bring the tyrant down.'

'Yes, my lord,' Oxford strode away, his armour clanking.

The horse missed Oxford's touch and whinnied. Henry leant forward to pat the mare's neck, wondering who he was really trying to calm, the horse or himself. Like every man of his rank, he knew how to fight, and he could remember clearly the first time he held a sword. He had been a very young boy, no more than five years, and the sword had been heavy. He could remember the steel glinting in the sunlight and how he had enjoyed slashing at poles stuck into the ground by his master of arms to represent opponents. It had all seemed so much fun back then, but now he had to use his sword against flesh and bone. The prospect was not exciting; it was terrifying. He had the skill, he knew, but did he have the courage to fight?

'I shall find out,' he murmured to himself.

He watched as Oxford raised his sword in the field below and gave the order to advance. As the line moved off, Henry shifted his gaze to the opposite side of the field. Richard's front line was on the move too. Those soldiers wore no armour, and most of them only had padded gambesons to protect their torsos. The luckier ones might have tunics of chain mail beneath the fabric, but even those would prove ineffective against the arrows that began to rain down on both sides. Men fell like ninepins.

And then the York cannons boomed.

Henry's plan had been to remain at his vantage point longer, to let the mercenaries he was paying fight most of the battle for him. But then he saw the white boar standard move and Richard, easy to spot with a gold circlet surmounting his helmet, spur his horse forward. Richard was charging to fight, and Henry knew he would have to do the same if he was to command any respect amongst his men. He slid his visor down and raised his sword arm. Yelling 'For Tudor,' he kicked his mare's sides and galloped towards the fight.

All he could hear in his close-fitting helmet was the reverberation of his horse's hooves and those of his personal bodyguard who rode with him. They thundered across the field. Men scattered before the horses, all save those who were too slow and became trampled into the mud. Henry knew he was the man the enemy soldiers would want to attack most, seeking the honour of killing the rebel Henry Tudor, but his bodyguard were doing an admirable job of keeping him safe. Indeed, he was so safe, Henry had leisure to look about him.

And through the narrow slit of his visor, Henry saw Richard heading straight for him.

'This day, I will die as king or win,' Richard promised as their eyes met across the battle.

He means to kill me himself, Henry realised. *Come on then, you devil.*

But Richard was not allowed to reach Henry unhindered. Sir William Brandon saw the danger Henry was in. Still holding the red dragon standard high, he turned his horse towards the king. His sword out straight, already badly dented and soiled, he aimed for Richard's breast. But before it could reach its mark, Richard's long lance knocked Brandon's sword away and continued its inexorable path to pierce Brandon's armour and his heart. Brandon's scream was terrible but mercifully brief. The force of Richard's thrust drove him out of the saddle. Henry stared, aghast, as Brandon fell, the dragon standard disappearing with him.

Before Henry could move or cry out, the standard was up again. Henry's fellow countryman, Rhys Fawr ap Maredudd, a giant of a man, had dragged it from the mud and was holding it high, swinging his sword at any man who dared to come near. The dragon breathed yet.

And so did Richard. His lance still stuck in Brandon, Richard abandoned it and put all his power into his mace instead. Sir John Cheney, another of Henry's personal bodyguard, succeeded in blocking the terrible weapon again and again, but Richard was determined. With one mighty swing, he pounded Cheney from his saddle. Richard pulled on his reins and steered his horse towards Henry.

Henry held himself ready to receive Richard's blows. But suddenly, Richard was gone, hidden behind a mass of red livery. With enormous relief, Henry realised that his stepfather, Lord Stanley, had at last come to his aid. Part of Henry wanted to shout at Stanley's men that Richard was his to kill, but he lacked conviction, and the words never came. Besides, there was no opportunity. Stanley's men appeared frenzied, mad with bloodlust, and Henry could only watch as Richard fell beneath their blows. He did not get up again.

'Stand back there,' a shout came, and Henry turned in his saddle to see Lord Stanley drawing his horse alongside his. Stanley said nothing to Henry, scarcely even glanced at him. Instead, he dismounted, and his men, sated, stepped back to allow him access to the prostrate king. The gorge rose in Henry's throat as he looked down on the thing in the mud. He watched as Stanley bent over the broken body, and he could bear to be silent no longer.

'Is he dead?' he called, hearing the anxiety in his voice.

Stanley prodded Richard with his foot. Richard did not move. The attack on him had been so savage that his helmet had been bashed into his skull. The gold circlet was gone, nowhere to be seen.

Stanley straightened and looked up at Henry. 'The tyrant is dead. The day is yours.'

Henry shivered despite the sweat running down his neck. 'Where is the crown?'

Stanley ordered his men to look for the gold circlet, and it was found yards away beneath a bush. With the crown in his hands, Stanley told Henry to follow, leading him to the edge of the field where an ancient oak stood. Stanley had chosen the spot deliberately; it was a place of higher ground, and they could be clearly seen by all.

'Kneel,' Stanley instructed, nodding at the dirt.

His legs shaking, Henry knelt and removed his helmet, wincing as the metal raked his skin. With his chin-length, dark brown hair sticking to his scalp, his armour dented and smeared with mud and blood, he held his breath as Stanley lowered the gold circlet onto his head.

It was probably just his fancy, but when the metal made contact with his skull, Henry could have sworn he felt a surge of warmth course through his body. The sensation passed in a heartbeat.

Then all he could hear was the shout of 'God save King Henry.'

∼

'Well, we came through that remarkably unscathed,'

Stanley said as he followed Henry into his tent. 'I shall be covered in bruises when I get this armour off, I warrant, but no wounds to speak of. How did you fare, Henry?'

'The same, I believe.' Henry reverently removed the circlet of gold and studied it for a moment, hardly daring to believe it was his. He felt Stanley's eyes upon him and hurried to put the crown on the table at the side of his tent.

'I'll have some of that.' Stanley pointed to the jug of wine on the table.

Through old habit, Henry reached for the jug, then he paused and drew back. He was king now, and kings did not pour drinks for their inferiors. 'You may help yourself.'

He did not want to see Stanley's knowing smile, so he turned his back, crossing to the rear of the tent and holding his arms out so his squire could begin removing his armour. Out of the corner of his eye, he saw Stanley move to the table and pour two cups of wine. Armour removed, Henry waved the squire away, and Stanley pressed one of the cups into his hand.

Stanley raised his cup. 'To victory.'

Henry echoed the gesture. 'I think I owe my victory to you,' he said quietly.

Stanley licked his lips. 'In some small measure.'

'I think you are being modest. Although, I must confess I doubted whether you would fight with me at all. You certainly left it to the last moment.'

'Nonsense, Henry, I timed it perfectly.'

'Still – '

'How could you doubt me?' Stanley stared at him, eyes narrowed. 'Your mother would never forgive me if I had not ridden to your aid.'

'No,' Henry agreed, 'I do not think she would.'

And yet the doubt of Stanley's loyalty still lingered. Henry had never been sure of his mother's fourth husband. When he had learnt that his mother, Lady Margaret Beaufort, had wed Thomas Stanley, Henry had not queried his mother's sagacity in marrying one of England's richest nobles, but he had challenged her assessment of Stanley's character. His mother had written of Lord Stanley's respectful conduct towards her, of his sound political understanding and sense of duty to his wife and stepson, but as far as Henry could tell, Stanley was loyal to one person only, and that person was himself.

'I must write to my mother and tell her the news,' he said, setting down his cup.

'Your mother can wait,' Stanley said. 'You must decide what is to be done with the king's body.'

Henry raised an eyebrow. 'Whose body?'

Stanley's smile was tight and swift. 'Richard's body,' he corrected. 'My men have him under guard at present, but he should be moved from the field soon, if only to escape the looters. I can send to his camp for suitable transport.'

Henry cupped his hands into the bowl of hot water his squire had prepared and brought the steaming liquid up to his face, closing his eyes as he rubbed away the dirt of the battlefield. 'We have carts enough of our own, do we not?'

Stanley frowned. 'A cart? Our carts are being used for the common men, the damned mercenaries you hired. We cannot heap Richard on top of them.'

Henry wiped his face with a towel and nodded. 'Yes, you speak true. He cannot be borne away like the others. He must be shown to be dead. Have the body stripped and tied to his horse, then taken to Greyfriars in Leicester.'

Stanley set his cup down on the table with a bang. 'You cannot mean to do him such dishonour.'

Henry sat on his camp stool and looked up at Stanley, unperturbed by his stepfather's indignation. 'Richard *has* been dishonoured. He lost the battle.'

'But he was a king of England, Henry – '

Henry started up from the stool and thrust his face at Stanley. 'You will address me as Your Grace, Lord Stanley.'

There was a long moment of silence as both men held each other's gaze. Henry was determined to keep his nerve and willed himself not to blink.

'Your Grace,' Stanley said at last, lowering his eyes.

'Better.' Henry nodded and sat back down. 'And as for the tyrant, it is my command that he be stripped and tied to his horse for all to witness. The people must know how his wickedness was so great that it revealed itself in his body. The people must see the crookback and know him for what he was. Evil incarnate. The Devil's instrument.'

'I do not deny that Richard was evil – ' Stanley began carefully.

'Then you must have no quarrel as to the removal of his corpse.'

Stanley sighed, defeated. He shook his head. 'No, Your Grace. None.'

'Good.' Henry nodded, satisfied. 'England has a Tudor king now, Lord Stanley, and you and every other man in England must learn that things will be very different from now on.'

CHAPTER ONE

ELEVEN YEARS LATER

The dog lifted its head as the footsteps approached. He had been dozing in the porch, long experience fooling him into believing there would be no traffic at this time of night. The gates to the city had been closed, and respectable citizens were secure behind their front doors. A younger dog would have jumped up and alerted its owners by barking, but this dog was old and less inclined to be curious. His grey-flecked ears pricked and his nose twitched as he tried to pick up a scent over the stink of the unpaved street's detritus. The footsteps came nearer, and mindful of his duty at last, the dog rose stiffly to his feet and growled.

The growl halted the footsteps. A surprised laugh came out of the darkness, and a voice said softly, 'Well, boy. You with us still?'

The stranger came closer, an arm held out, the glove removed. The dog's dry nose pressed against the silvery pale hand and, despite its long absence, recognised the scent. His tongue slapped wetly at the appendage. The fingers edged beneath his grizzled chin and scratched, then moved around his jaw to tug gently at his soft, malleable ear.

'It is good to see you, boy. Rest you easy now. Go back to sleep.'

The dog was reluctant to lose the caress and pushed his face into the folds of the man's cloak as he stepped inside the porch and knocked on the door. A bolt was drawn back and the door opened. A rushlight cast a weak yellow glow over the face of the woman who appeared in the doorway.

'Who's there?' she called nervously.

'Bess, it's me.'

The woman lifted the rushlight higher, squinting into the dark. 'Thomas?'

'Aye,' Thomas Wolsey said. 'Will you let me in, sister, or must I bed down with old Growler here?'

Elizabeth Wolsey stepped back and let Thomas inside. Growler tried to follow, but she thrust him back, ignoring his whine, and shut the door upon him.

'Why did you not let us know you were arriving tonight?' Elizabeth scolded as she bolted the door and led Thomas into the parlour. 'I have made nothing ready for you. No bed, no supper – '

''Tis no matter.' Thomas slipped his leather bag from his shoulder and untied his cloak. 'I had thought of writing to say I was coming, but there seemed little point. I would have been but a mile behind the letter. I thought I would surprise you instead.'

'Well, you have certainly done that.' Elizabeth took his cloak and withdrew into the hallway to hang it up. She came back and looked him up and down, her light-brown eyes missing nothing. 'You're a little thinner than you used to be.'

Thomas smoothed his hand over his stomach. 'An Oxford scholar's life is a meagre one. We have our allotted meat and fish and are granted no more.'

'Oh, it must be such a hard life at your college.'

Thomas smiled at her scorn. 'I am grown used to it. And Mother always said I could do with losing a little weight. Where is she?'

Elizabeth's face fell. 'Upstairs with Father. She went up to him after we supped. She knows... we all know he will be gone soon.'

Thomas rubbed his forehead. 'Is he so very ill?'

She nodded. 'I think he has only been waiting for you to arrive. You should have come sooner, Thomas.'

'I am here now,' he said, knowing he failed to keep the irritation out of his voice. 'I should like to see him.'

'I'll take you up.'

Thomas followed Elizabeth into the hallway and up the stairs, the wooden treads creaking beneath their feet. The bedroom was at the top of the house, three flights up. They were both breathing heavily as they reached the top chamber, its sloping walls dressed with canvas hangings painted with green and white stripes.

'Mother,' Elizabeth said, keeping her voice low. 'Thomas is here.'

Joan Wolsey sat by the four-poster bed on a high-backed chair. She half rose as Thomas entered, then seemed to change her mind and sank back, holding her arms out for him instead. He crossed the small room in three strides and kissed her cheek, his eyes already on his father in the bed.

'Oh, Thomas, we were not expecting you – ' Joan began.

'I have already told him so, Mother,' Elizabeth cut her off sharply. 'Where is that stool?' She looked around the room, found the stool beneath a heap of blankets, and set it down behind Thomas.

'He's so thin,' Thomas said softly as he sat.

Joan sniffed and wiped her nose with her handkerchief. 'He lost his appetite a while ago and was only eating to keep his strength up. This last week or so, he has not been able to keep any food down, so... ' She shrugged, seeing there was no need to explain further.

'Can the physician do nothing?' Thomas asked.

'Your father is dying, Thomas,' his mother said wearily. 'There is nothing to be done.'

'The priest was here earlier to give him the last rites,' Elizabeth said.

'It will be soon.' Joan laid her cold hand on Thomas's arm. 'I am glad you managed to get here before he goes.'

Thomas's father stirred. 'Who's here?' he mumbled, opening his rheumy eyes.

Joan leant towards him. 'It's Thomas, Robert. He's come home to see you.'

Robert's eyes found Thomas. 'I want to talk to him.'

'Are you strong enough?' Joan asked worriedly.

'Yes, go.'

Joan rose without another word, and she and Elizabeth left the bedchamber, both casting glances back through the banisters as they descended the stairs. Thomas moved nearer the bed, wishing his father had not woken, wishing he had delayed his arrival even longer so he would not have to have this conversation, for he knew what his father would say.

Robert pushed himself up to a sitting position, the effort wearying him a great deal. He sank into his pillow with a grunt. 'You are not yet a priest, Tom, and 'tis past time you were. Do not look away, boy. You *will* be a priest.'

Thomas took a deep breath, annoyed as much by the 'boy' as his father's other words. 'And if I do not want to be a priest?'

'Why would you say such a thing? The priesthood is what you have been trained for, what you have been educated for. Well,' Robert demanded impatiently when Thomas again looked away, 'what else would you do?'

'I have not thought on it, Father. Take up the law, perhaps.'

'Be a lawyer!' Robert spat, wiping his mouth with his sleeve. 'Crooks, all of them.'

It had been a mistake to say the law; Thomas had known it as soon as he had spoken, but it was the first thing to spring to mind. Robert had a very poor opinion of the legal profession, for he had so often been caught on its wrong side. Thomas suspected he had been told of only a few of the allegations made against Robert for his business dealings. He knew his father had once been taken to court for keeping a bawdy house, an accusation not proven and one which Thomas did not consider likely, as well as being prosecuted for selling meat during Lent, which Thomas thought was probably justified.

'Why this doubt now?' Robert asked. 'You love God, do you not?'

'Of course I do,' Thomas replied without hesitation.

'Then why would you not want to serve him as a priest?'

Thomas could not say why, not to his father. He wouldn't understand.

'Nothing to say? No clever argument? Come, argue, debate with me. Is that not what clever fellows like you do up at Oxford?'

'You do not have the strength for such talk, Father, please.'

'Do not 'Father, please' me. You will be ordained, Tom,' Robert said, jabbing his finger at him. 'I would have you say masses for me.'

'But Father – '

'Do you want me to remain in Purgatory?' Robert croaked, and Thomas could hear the fear in his voice. Robert began to cough and bright red blood speckled the bed sheet.

There were rapid footsteps on the stairs. Thomas turned to see Joan hurrying into the chamber, Elizabeth close behind. Joan pushed Thomas out of the way, and he watched as his mother tended to his father, unable to take his eyes from them. Robert's coughing lessened but only, it seemed, because he had not the strength to continue. He fell back against the pillows, his eyes closed, his mouth flapping open. His breathing slowed, and his eyes remained shut.

Joan straightened, her chest heaving, and looked at her children. 'You may as well go,' she said sadly. 'There is nothing you can do.'

'We will stay, Mother,' Elizabeth declared, her voice crackly with emotion.

'You two go downstairs,' Joan said, her tone commanding. 'Thomas, you must be hungry after your journey. Bess, see your brother has something to eat.'

Thomas was only too glad to be given permission to leave the death chamber and touched Elizabeth's hand as an encouragement to move. She jerked at his touch but followed him down the stairs.

'Sit.' Elizabeth pointed to the bench by the long dining table. 'There is nothing hot. You will have to be content with cold meat.'

'That's fine,' Thomas said, pulling out the bench and sitting. He put his head in his hands and closed his eyes.

'What did you expect?'

He looked up, surprised. Elizabeth was staring at him.

She shrugged. 'You knew he was ill.'

17

'I… ' Thomas shook his head. 'I do not know what I expected.'

She grunted and put a plate of cold pork before him, gesturing for him to help himself to the round loaf of bread by his right hand. Two slices of the loaf had already been cut, and Thomas took one and began to butter. He had suddenly realised how hungry he was and guiltily wondered how he could have such an appetite when his father was dying in the room above him.

Elizabeth sat on the opposite bench. 'What did he say to you? Tell me,' she urged when he hesitated.

Thomas bit into the bread, savouring the taste of the salt and the creaminess of the butter, so much better than the butter served at Oxford. 'He told me I have to be a priest.'

'And?'

He swallowed. 'And I am not sure I want to be one.'

'Thomas!'

He laughed sourly and shook his head. 'I knew you would say that.'

'Well, of course I would. Why else were you sent to Oxford? Our parents sacrificed a great deal so you could go to Magdalen College. You owe them.'

'What do you mean I owe them?' Thomas snapped. 'It was my brains that sent me to Magdalen. It is I who has done all the work. I who have had to work so very hard – '

'Oh yes and do we not all know it? Mother never ceases to tell us.' Elizabeth's voice became high and mocking. 'My son Thomas, so clever, he got his degree when he was only fifteen. And now he has been made a master of the college at only three-and-twenty. It will not be long before he is president, I'll be bound.' She made a face as she cleared Thomas's plate away, not caring he had not yet finished. 'I do not understand you. Why not be a priest? Do you not have faith?'

'My faith is as strong as yours. It is not that which holds me back.'

'Then what does?'

He leant over and snatched up the jug of ale on the table, pouring himself a cup. 'My reason is mine own and is staying that way, sister.'

'I see.' Elizabeth nodded, her bottom lip thrust out. 'So, even though it be his dying wish, you will not do as Father asks?'

'Enough, Bess,' Thomas said loudly, then remembering his father in the room above, lowered his voice. 'I will do as my conscience guides me, and no man, not even Father, can ask more of me.'

Elizabeth opened her mouth to speak, but the door opened at that moment. Their brothers, Henry and Richard, entered.

'Thomas, 'tis good to see you,' Henry said, holding out his hand. Thomas, still smarting from Elizabeth's words, took it silently. Henry was very like their father, dark-haired and dark-eyed, but he had a kindlier nature. The youngest of the siblings, Richard, was amenable like their mother and was the best looking of all the Wolseys, though none could be said to be handsome. Richard sat on the bench beside him. He stank of the tavern, and Thomas guessed where his brothers had been. He wished he had been with them.

'How is Father?' Henry asked Elizabeth.

'Not at all well,' she said, folding a cloth with great determination. 'Thomas upset him.'

Henry looked from Elizabeth to Thomas, noted the tension between them, and decided not to question further. He moved to the window to look over an account ledger on his mother's desk.

'How is Oxford?' Richard asked, buttering the remaining slice of bread.

'Oxford is fine,' Thomas answered, adding with a candour that surprised him, 'I do not like to leave it.'

'But it has been so long since you were here,' Richard said, his tone betraying his hurt. 'If it were me, I would be pleased to come home.'

And now Richard resents me too. Thomas groaned as Richard turned away. He was doing a very good job of upsetting his family, it seemed.

There were footsteps on the stairs, and all eyes turned to Joan as she descended. From her dull expression, Thomas guessed what her news would be.

'Mother?' Elizabeth whispered, her voice breaking.

Joan nodded. 'He's gone.' Thomas thought he detected relief in her voice.

Elizabeth burst into tears and Joan stepped forward to take her daughter into her arms.

Henry went downstairs and came back a few minutes later carrying a large jug. 'Father's best wine.' He held it up to show Richard and Thomas, then gathered up clean cups from the sideboard. He poured the wine into them and handed one each to Richard and Thomas.

Henry raised his cup. 'To Father.'

Richard knocked his cup against Henry's, then held it up to Thomas.

Thomas felt strangely resentful towards his father. Why could Robert not have died before he arrived? It would have been so much easier. He could have expressed sorrow at being late, mouthed the usual sentiments about how good a man Robert had been and how he would do what he could for his family, then departed back to Oxford with a clear conscience. Now, he had to pretend to mourn a father he barely knew, a father who had rarely shown him any affection.

He obligingly banged his cup against those of his brothers. Some of the wine splashed onto his fingers, and the dark red drops looked like blood. 'To Father,' he growled and threw the wine down his throat, feeling it burn.

Thomas's head was throbbing. It had been a very long day, and he had drunk too much ale and eaten too little beef. But after the funeral there had been nothing to do but eat, drink and talk to people he hardly knew and cared nothing about. He missed Oxford, and he missed his studies. He felt his brain had stalled with nothing to occupy it.

'Is your head still hurting?' Elizabeth asked.

She looks tired, Thomas thought. Elizabeth had worked very hard the previous day to get the feast ready for their father's wake, and she had done it all alone, Joan and their brothers being preoccupied with the funeral and the family business. He could have helped her with the preparations, Thomas realised guiltily, but the truth was he had not given Elizabeth and her toils any thought at all. 'A little.'

'I'll make a lavender and marjoram potion for you to drink before bed. It should help.'

'You've done enough, Bess,' he said. ''Tis only a headache, it will pass. Do not worry.'

'If you say so. Oh, I wish he would go,' Elizabeth said, scowling as the last of their guests lingered in the hallway with their mother.

'Who is he?' Thomas looked the man up and down. He was one of the few people Thomas had not spoken with at the wake, for he had dogged Joan's footsteps and monopolised her company.

'William Patent. He exports our wool.'

'Was he a good friend to our father?'

'I would say he was more our mother's friend,' Elizabeth said, her tone heavy with meaning.

'You dislike him.'

'Not so, but 'tis not seemly for him to be so attentive. Look at him with Mother.'

Thomas saw what Elizabeth meant. William Patent had hold of Joan's hand and seemed determined not to relinquish it. Yet, to Thomas's eye, Joan did not seem to

22

mind. He wondered if he should intervene, but before he could reach a decision, it seemed William Patent had realised it was time to leave.

'I shall pray for you all this night,' Thomas heard Patent say as Joan opened the front door and a blast of cold air cut through the room. She bid him a farewell and Patent stepped out into the dark. Joan closed the door and heaved a sigh of relief.

'Come, Mother,' Elizabeth said. 'Henry and Richard are upstairs. Let us join them.'

They traipsed upstairs to where Henry and Richard were busy putting the furniture back in place. They had already restored the long table to the middle of the room and were placing the benches alongside when Joan, Elizabeth and Thomas entered.

'All gone?' Henry asked, using his foot to set the bench straight.

Joan nodded. 'Yes, all gone.'

Elizabeth plumped up an embroidered cushion and placed it in the bowl of the chair Joan used when working at her desk. 'Sit, Mother,' she instructed, and Joan obeyed.

'I know I should not say it, but I am glad this day is over,' Joan said, fingering the spectacles hanging off her writing slope. 'It will be a relief to return to work. I am so behind with the accounts.'

'Is that all you can think about, Mother?' Elizabeth scolded.

''Tis as well I do think about it, Bess. With you still unwed, you need someone to support you.'

Elizabeth coloured, and Thomas wondered why it was his sister was still a burden on her family. He knew their father would have made provision for a good dowry had any man offered himself as a husband. Elizabeth was not pretty, it was true; she was too plump to be called comely and her features too irregular to be called pleasant, but many men would overlook such failings if the dowry was ample and the family connection good. Perhaps there had been suitors, but Elizabeth had been disinclined to marry. Or perhaps, Thomas considered grimly, many men had been discouraged from wooing by her scolding tongue. He could not blame them.

Thomas sat on the bench and rubbed his aching forehead. He was about to say he would retire when Joan opened her slope and took out a parchment.

'Shall we do this now?' she asked him.

Thomas suddenly realised what the parchment was. 'Father's will?' he asked, pointing at it.

'You are his executor, Thomas.' She held it out to him. 'The family is all together, and I would rather get it over and done with. Bess, give this to Thomas.'

Elizabeth passed him the parchment and took a seat. They all watched as Thomas broke the seal, the old red wax splintering onto the table.

'You need not read out every word,' Joan said as he unfolded the paper, 'just the bequests.'

Thomas quickly scanned the writing and began to read aloud. 'To my eldest son, Thomas, I make provision of six marks to pay for the singing of masses for my soul, to be given over to him should he be ordained a priest within a twelvemonth of my death. If Thomas be not made a priest within this time, then whosoever prays for my soul shall receive the six marks.' He glanced at his mother and saw no sign of surprise in her expression. *She knows what Father said to me,* he thought with a touch of annoyance. He continued. 'Also to my eldest son, Thomas, goes my land held under freehold. All my other properties I give to my dearly beloved wife, Joan. To my wife, Joan, I also entrust the management of my business, to be helped by my sons Henry and Richard, until and unless they establish businesses of their own, and by my daughter Elizabeth, until such time as she be married.'

'All as expected,' Henry said, taking the parchment from Thomas and reading it for himself. 'No argument from anyone?'

'It does not give Thomas a role in the business,' Elizabeth said.

'Well, he doesn't need one,' Henry said carelessly. 'He is to be a priest.'

'Oh, but he has no intention of becoming a priest, Henry,' Elizabeth said with mock innocence.

'What?' Henry exclaimed. 'Thomas, is this true?'

'Is it?' Joan demanded.

Thomas's head was pounding. Why had he not retired to bed earlier?

'Thomas!' Joan's voice was shrill, not to be ignored.

'I am not sure, Mother,' he said.

'What are you not sure about?'

'That the priesthood is the vocation I want.'

Joan stared at him for a long moment. 'Bess, Henry, Richard, get you to bed. It is late, and we have to be up early tomorrow.'

'But Mother – ' Elizabeth began.

'Bed, Bess.' Elizabeth, Richard and Henry rose and made for the door. When they had gone, Joan said, 'Pour me some ale, Thomas.' He did so and handed her the cup. 'Now pull that bench over and talk to me.'

'I know you are disappointed, Mother.' He winced at the screech of the wooden bench against the floorboards as he pulled.

'I am confused. To be a priest is what you have studied for all these years. I thought – your father thought – it was what you wanted.'

'I thought I did too.'

'Then what has changed?'

'No one ever asked me if it was what I wanted when I was sent away.'

'You were a child of eleven. You were too young to be asked any such thing. We knew what was best for you.'

'And I am grateful for my education, Mother, but the choice of the priesthood was not mine. My tutor and Father decided I had a brain and that I was to be sent away to use it. But I believe that, because of my education, the priesthood is not the only path that I may take. Nor, in truth, am I sure I am suited to such a life.'

'It is a good life,' Joan protested.

'But if I am not called to the priesthood?'

She frowned at him. 'You do not love God?'

'Of course I love God, but I have had reason to wonder if I love Him enough to devote my life to Him.'

'There is no greater joy to be found than in serving God. As a priest, your person will be inviolable. You will have the respect of everyone who knows you. Heaven knows, this family has had little enough of that.'

It was the first word of reproach Thomas had heard from his mother towards his father. Thomas took hold of her hand. 'I understand how you feel. But it is my life.'

'But if not a priest?'

It was the same question his father had asked. 'A tutor, perhaps, or a lawyer. There are many opportunities for an educated man.' He smiled. 'Perhaps I shall come back to Ipswich and run the business.'

He was joking. The idea of becoming a butcher or wool merchant was appalling, but Joan evidently thought he was serious.

'Oh, you must not think of that, Thomas,' she said earnestly. 'Henry would never admit it, I am sure, but he has been looking forward to the day when he could take over.'

'Father left the business to you.'

'To a woman?' Joan laughed hollowly. 'That was just your father's foolishness.'

'Many widows take over their husband's business, and many run them better. I have seen it. *You* have seen it. Remember? You wrote to me of how Mistress Bassett was left the tannery by her husband and how she has prospered.'

'Mistress Bassett was ever eager to have a business

27

to run. I am not so. I would rather your father had legally left it to your brother. It will do Henry good to have a free hand.'

'You will need to keep an eye on him. He is young and does not have your good business sense.'

'I shall keep an eye.' She smiled indulgently. 'And you. Oh, Thomas, I do think you are foolish if you turn your back on the church. And, despite what you tell me, I do not think that a lack of calling is the reason you have this doubt. I want you to promise me that whatever it is holding you back from becoming a priest is worth it.' She grabbed his hands and tugged them to her heart. 'That *she* is worth it.'

CHAPTER TWO

Thomas could not help but smile as he passed beneath the city gate of Ipswich and headed out on the road back to Oxford. He was free, free to do as he liked, eat what he liked, go to bed when he liked, but most of all, free from his family.

It was only since leaving that he realised how much of a strain being back home had been. The closer his intended day of departure drew, the clingier Joan had become, and Thomas had felt as if he were suffocating. That morning as he had checked his bag, making sure he had packed everything, Joan had asked him to write to the dean of Magdalen College and ask for an extended leave of absence. Thomas had told her he could not because he knew the college masters would not tolerate his absence a day longer than they had granted.

It was a lie. Thomas had no doubt that if he had written, the dean would have given him leave to remain, but he did not want more time at home. He yearned to be back in Oxford. Oxford was his home, not Ipswich, and his fellow students and masters were his family. Joan had watched sorrowfully as he pushed the linen-wrapped bread and cheese she had insisted on giving him into his bag and headed for the door.

Thomas had said his farewells to Henry and Richard the evening before as they had an appointment with a wool merchant and had had to leave early. Elizabeth had presented her cheek for him to kiss, told him to have a safe journey, and had retreated to the kitchen where he heard her banging pots and ordering the kitchen maid around. Joan had followed him to the door and would have accompanied him to the city gates had he let her. He had kissed her, and she had held him tight. When he pulled away, Thomas saw that tears were likely. He had smiled and walked quickly away, waving to her over his shoulder.

It was a long journey back to Oxford. He had antici-pated having to walk most of the way, but upon reaching Colchester, had managed to get a seat on a coach that took him towards St Albans. On the third night, after a day of walking, he stopped at an inn and took off his shoes to find huge blisters on both heels. He tried padding his shoes with the linen from the bread and cheese he had eaten on the first day, but the cloth rubbed as much as his shoes. Fortune smiled on him again, however, when a merchant with a cartload of wine barrels for sale in Oxford invited Thomas to join him and so spared his sore feet. But as soon as he caught sight of Oxford's spires, Thomas said farewell to the merchant, suddenly wanting to enter the city alone.

Magdalen Bridge was ahead of him, the River Cherwell flowing serenely beneath its stones. Ducks glided across the water, making ripples behind them as they went. He leaned over the stone balustrade and watched them.

'Tom, is that you?'

Thomas turned, his face breaking into a grin at the sight of his friend's long thin face. 'It's me. How are you, Stephen?'

Stephen Alard took Thomas's hand and wrung it. 'Very well. How is your father?'

'Dead.'

'Oh,' Stephen said, embarrassed. 'Sorry to hear that. Are the rest of your family well?'

'They are, thank you.' Wanting to change the subject, Thomas asked, 'How have things been here?'

'Much the same. I am glad you are back. I have been deplorably lax in my studies. Needed my friend Thomas to keep me disciplined.' Stephen clapped Thomas on the shoulder. 'Come, then. Typical of you to arrive in time for dinner.'

They crossed the bridge, heading for Magdalen College. It was not the most impressive of Oxford's colleges, but to Thomas's eyes, it was the most pleasing. He did not even mind a part of the college being a building site – the college had started a bell-tower building project a few years earlier – because he loved to watch each course of stone laid down by the masons.

It fascinated him to see how the masons shaped each one, making something beautiful with only a hammer and chisel. To Thomas, stonemasonry was a marvellous skill, though not one highly rated by many of his fellows at the college. So many of the masters thought any labour not purely of the brain was a sign of baseness. No matter how often Thomas tried to convince them architecture was an art, a show of confidence in the future and a sign of wealth and prosperity, they would not alter their opinion. If ever he had the money, Thomas promised himself often, he would commission a stonemason to build him a fine house.

Thomas and Stephen entered the Great Hall of the college. Thomas gave his bag to one of the servants, asking him to keep it safe until dinner was over, then he and Stephen washed their hands in one of the water bowls provided. The long refectory tables were rather full, for dinner had only just begun, but Stephen saw their friend Hugh Sedley sitting near the rear of the hall, and they squeezed onto the bench opposite. Magdalen College was not noted for its fare, at least not on ordinary days, and there was only pottage on offer. But Thomas was hungry, and he tucked in.

'Glad to be back?' Hugh asked Thomas.

Thomas nodded through a mouthful of food.

'Did you tell him about Piers Gomfrey, Stephen?'

'Not yet,' Stephen protested. 'He's only just arrived.'

'What about Piers Gomfrey?' Thomas asked, looking from Hugh to Stephen.

Hugh dug his spoon into the pottage and took a large mouthful. 'Piers was nearly expelled.'

'What did he do?' Thomas asked, intrigued. He and Piers had shared many lectures over the years; Thomas knew him to be a lazy young man, content to do only just enough studying to ensure he scraped a pass in his examinations and nothing more.

'He tried to smuggle a girl into his room.' Hugh laughed. 'Would have managed it too if the porter's dog had not barked at her. Master Abery was all for having him expelled, but the dean said that as the girl had not actually got into the grounds, Piers had not broken any rules.'

'That's a fine distinction.' Thomas said.

Hugh nodded. 'The dean wrote to Piers's father, and he came here. You should have heard the shouting.'

'We think Piers got a whipping too,' Stephen added.

Hugh pointed his spoon at Thomas. 'So let that be a warning for you.'

Thomas coloured. 'What do you mean a warning for *me?*'

Hugh grinned at Stephen. 'Oh, look at him, blushing like a girl.' He gestured at their fellow diners. 'We all know you have impure thoughts about Alice Finch.'

'I do not,' Thomas protested, feeling his cheeks burn, wondering how on earth he had betrayed himself in regard to the eighteen-year-old daughter of Oxford's mayor.

'Have it your way.' Hugh held up his hands. 'But

just know you should think twice about smuggling her into your room.'

'Even if I wanted to,' Thomas whispered, leaning forward, 'she would not agree.'

'Oh, because she is not the kind of girl to enter a man's bedchamber alone, eh?'

'No, she most certainly is not.'

Hugh winked at Thomas, knowing he had teased his friend enough. 'Nothing like that trull Stephen here has his eye on.'

'Edith is no trull.' Stephen's voice was high and loud, and heads turned in their direction.

'Er, Stephen,' Hugh said, 'sweet Edith works in a brothel.'

'Cleaning,' Stephen insisted. 'Not doing what you think.'

'Of course not.' Hugh snorted a laugh, and Thomas joined in, knowing that Stephen was ever deluded when it came to girls. Only the previous term, Stephen had fallen for a girl who claimed to be nineteen but, it turned out, had only seen fourteen summers. Stephen had narrowly escaped a beating from the girl's outraged father.

'Yes, very funny, you two. Anyway, I must be off,' Stephen said haughtily, pulling the napkin from his shoulder and throwing it on the table. 'I have letters to write.'

Thomas and Hugh watched him go. 'The poor fool.' Hugh shook his head. 'Will he never learn?' He turned back to Thomas, and his face became serious. 'I assume that as you are back, your father is… '

'Dead? Yes, he is.'

'Thought so. My condolences. Did you have a chance to talk to him?'

'Not really. He only gave me a chance to listen.'

'So, you didn't tell him about your decision?'

'I mentioned it, but it was not something he wanted to hear.' Thomas sniffed and snatched up his cup of ale. He took a mouthful and gulped it down. 'His will stated that if I did not become a priest within twelve months, I would not receive six marks. He wanted me to say masses for his soul.'

'Six marks, eh? Hardly a fortune.'

'I can live without the money,' Thomas agreed sourly.

Hugh glanced down at his empty bowl. 'Still, it must be difficult for you.'

'Not really. His soul will be fine. We can pay a priest to say masses for him,' Thomas said, sounding as if he was trying to convince himself.

'Yes, of course you can.' Hugh took a deep breath, a signal he was ending that touchy subject. 'So, if your intentions are honourable, when are you going to ask for the lovely Alice's hand?'

'Soon,' Thomas said decidedly.

'And you think she will have you?'

'I can only hope she will,' Thomas said with a shrug. He frowned. 'I know my mother will be disappointed I am not to be a priest, but she will be cheered in my choice of a wife, will she not?' He looked at Hugh earnestly. 'My mother will not be sorry when she meets Alice?'

Hugh forced a smile. Alice was not, in his opinion, the sort of girl any mother would wish for her son. Alice was flighty. Hugh had seen the way she flirted with all the young men who were forward enough to seek conversation with her, and knew she did not keep her smiles only for Thomas.

~

'Lift your chin, Master Wolsey.'

Thomas obliged the barber, tilting his head back so the razor could be drawn over his throat. Thomas heard the rasp of his stubble against the blade and felt the tug on his skin. It felt good to be close shaved once again. Master Cotton really was the best barber he knew. His brothers' barber in Ipswich had been clumsy, nicking Thomas painfully over his jawbone on the three occasions he had used him. Thomas had decided he would let his beard grow and wait until he had returned to Oxford to be shaved by a far more competent barber.

Master Cotton drew a cloth over Thomas's face, wiping away the soap that was already tightening his skin. Thomas pointed to the bottle of rose water on the table, and the barber smiled and deftly applied the soothing perfumed water.

'Special occasion, is it, Master Wolsey?' Cotton asked as he tidied away his soiled equipment.

Thomas rubbed his hand over his jaw, feeling his newly smooth skin with pleasure. 'Because I have had you shave me?'

'No, my dear sir, but because of the rose water and your general demeanour.'

Thomas rose from the chair, eyeing Cotton sternly. 'There is nothing about my demeanour that is different from any other time you have shaved me.'

Cotton wagged his finger. 'Ah, there, I must disagree. There is a very definite air of intent about you this morning. I would venture a young lady is on your mind.'

Thomas's mouth pursed in annoyance. 'I think, Master Cotton, you misunderstand our relationship and begin to take liberties with me.'

'No need to be so abrupt,' Cotton teased. 'Come now, who is she?'

It was no good, Thomas thought. Master Cotton would not relent. 'The young lady is Mistress Finch, if you must know.'

Cotton frowned. 'The mayor's daughter?'

'The same. There now, you have learnt my secret. Be you content.'

But Cotton was still frowning. 'You are courting the young Mistress Finch?'

Thomas could not pretend such a definite description of his relationship with Alice, not even to a barber. 'I am privileged to visit her at home.'

'Oh, you and a dozen others.' Cotton laughed.

Thomas glared at him. 'Why do you say that?'

Alarmed by Thomas's vehemence, the smile fell from Cotton's face. 'No harm meant, Master Wolsey.'

'What did you mean?'

Cotton held his hands up, palms out. 'Only that I know of the young lady and know too she has many admirers.'

''Tis no sin to be admired, you fool,' Thomas said. He tended to his collar, making sure it was straight.

'No, indeed,' Cotton said with relief. He had been planning to ask Thomas to settle his account but decided against it, fearing another outburst. Instead, he smiled obsequiously as Thomas gave him a curt nod and left his shop.

He was angry, and Thomas did not want to be angry. It was the second time that week Alice Finch had been spoken of in a derogatory manner. He had half a mind not to call on Alice after all, concerned he would take his bad humour out on her, but then, he reasoned, if anyone could lighten his mood, it was the girl he loved.

The Finches lived only a little way from Magdalen College. Thomas had first spotted Alice when she had accompanied her father to the college to discuss the play the students wanted to present as part of the May Day celebrations the previous year.

Thomas remembered the day well. His lecture had just concluded, and he was ambling, deep in thought, through the Great Hall, not watching where he was going. Alice had been staring up at the roof, bored of waiting whilst her father talked with Richard Mayhew, the college president. Thomas had almost walked into her. Startled, he had looked up and upon her pretty face. For the first time in his life, he found himself unable to form a coherent sentence. He had managed to babble an apology, and Alice had giggled at his awkwardness. Her father had finished his discussion and called her away, and Thomas did not see her for more than a fortnight. When he did, at last, see her again one day in the street, he was smitten.

His life changed. Studying lost its appeal. He would offer to take messages to her father just for the chance of seeing her. He would go into shops he knew girls frequented in the hope he would meet her. Then he became braver, calling at their house when he had no reason at all to do so. To his delight, he found he was not refused admittance. Alice seemed to like his company.

Thomas found he could not concentrate on his studies anymore. He neglected to attend lectures or complete essays. The masters began to cast worried looks in his direction, but he did not care. The only thing he cared about was Alice.

Thomas reached the Finches' front door. Taking a deep breath, he knocked and prepared himself for Mark, their head servant.

Mark's permanently sullen expression became mingled with slight surprise as he opened the door and set eyes on Thomas. His bushy left eyebrow rose, almost meeting his hairline. 'Master Wolsey, well, well. You haven't graced us with your presence for weeks. Thought we'd seen the last of you.'

'Sorry to disappoint you, Mark,' Thomas said, struggling to keep his tone cordial. He'd just about had enough of barbers and servants getting above themselves. 'I left Oxford for a few weeks, that is all. Is Mistress Alice at home?'

'Aye, she's here.' Mark stepped back and opened the door wider to allow Thomas inside. 'She and the mistress are in the parlour.' He pointed to the door at the end of the corridor and, turning on his heel, disappeared through a door behind the staircase.

'Thank you very much for nothing, Mark,' Thomas muttered under his breath. It really was too much. Why on earth did Master Finch employ such a man? Mark was insubordinate and downright rude. Thomas would not have put up with him, no matter how cheap he came. And now, here Thomas was, expected to announce himself.

The door to the parlour was open just an inch. Thomas put his eye to the gap and saw Ellen Finch, the mayor's wife and Alice's mother. She was sitting by the window that looked onto the street, keeping her eye on all who passed by, Thomas did not doubt. She had probably seen him walking up the path.

'Come in, Master Wolsey,' Ellen confirmed a heartbeat later, even as Thomas raised his hand to knock. 'Do not linger in the doorway.'

This is a wonderful beginning, Thomas thought as

he fixed a smile on his face and pushed the door open. 'Good morning, Mistress Finch,' he said, bowing. He turned his head, his eyes drawn inexorably to the girl at the side window. 'And Mistress Alice.'

'We have not seen you for some time,' Ellen said, not giving Alice a chance to respond. She gestured at a chair that was a little too near her and a little too far from Alice for Thomas's liking. 'What have you been doing with yourself? Studying hard, I daresay.'

'No – that is, yes, a little, but I had to return to Ipswich for a few weeks. I did write to tell you so.' He glanced at Alice. 'You did receive my letter?'

'Did you, Alice?' Ellen asked sharply.

'Oh yes,' Alice said airily. 'I remember. You did tell me you would be away.'

'You did not tell me.' Ellen's thin lips pursed in annoyance. 'Why did you have to return to Ipswich, Master Wolsey?'

'My father was ill.'

'Oh, I see. And he is better, I hope?'

'He died, Mistress Finch.'

'Oh,' she said again, looking uncomfortable, and Thomas felt a little thrill of pleasure that he had managed to disturb her usually perfect composure. 'I am so sorry.'

'Thank you.' Thomas looked at Alice again, willing her to say something to him, something kind.

'Does that mean you will be leaving Oxford for good?' Ellen asked, drawing his attention back to her.

'You are the eldest son, I seem to remember you saying. Your father was a butcher, I believe.'

How was it possible to say a single word with so much contempt? Thomas felt his cheeks grow warm. 'Yes, but – '

'So, are you needed to – '

'No,' he interrupted emphatically. 'My father left the business to my mother, and she intends for my younger brothers to help her.'

'I see.' Ellen sniffed and turned to her daughter. 'Do you hear, Alice? Master Wolsey is to remain in Oxford.'

'Yes, I heard, Mother,' Alice said.

'Does that please you, Mistress Alice?' Thomas asked, desperate to know.

Alice looked at him then, her bright blue eyes wide and innocent. 'Of course it does,' she said sweetly. 'I have missed your visits these past weeks. Mother has too. Have you not, Mother?'

Ellen's lips tightened. Looking down her nose at Thomas, she breathed, 'Indeed.'

'You should not encourage him, Alice,' Ellen said, pressing her nose to the window to watch Thomas walk away down the street.

'*Did* I encourage him?' Alice tossed her embroidery away, bored with unpicking her mistakes. 'I barely said a word.'

'You said enough to give him hope. I saw his face

when you said you had missed his visits. He was over-joyed. I must say, I had not noticed you missing him at all. Not with that other young fellow calling all the time.'

Alice smiled. 'I thought to be kind in telling a little lie, Mother. You would not have me be cruel, would you?'

'I would have you not encouraging the son of a butcher to call on you.' Ellen snatched up her skirts and strode to examine her daughter's embroidery. She tutted at the mess Alice had made. 'I should really tell your father to forbid him to come to the house.'

'Why do you not?'

'Well,' Ellen sighed, 'your father thinks Master Wolsey may be somebody at the college one of these days.'

'What kind of somebody?'

Ellen's bony shoulders rose and fell. 'A master, maybe. Perhaps even higher.'

'Masters at Magdalen are all churchmen, are they not?'

'Yes. Why?'

'Then Master Wolsey cannot have me, can he?'

Ellen stared down at her daughter, surprised by the remark. 'He cannot marry you, no.'

'Then there is no need to worry about me encour-aging him.'

The frown lines on Ellen's brow deepened. 'Churchmen do sometimes ignore the rule of celibacy, Alice,' she said carefully.

Alice looked up at her mother, her eyes wide. She laughed and pressed her hand to her breast. 'Why, Mother! Do you think Master Wolsey means to make me his concubine?'

Ellen returned to her seat with a huff and began to unpick her daughter's embroidery. 'I do not know what Master Wolsey means to do. If he aspires to be a master at Magdalen, he cannot take a wife. And if he does not mean to be a master, then all I can think is that he will be a butcher like his father. Either way, he is no good suitor for you, and I would like you to discourage his attentions.' She looked up suddenly. 'You do not have feelings for him, do you?'

'Of course not,' Alice snapped, irritated by the suggestion. 'Do you imagine I could have feelings for Thomas Wolsey? He is fat and ugly, Mother. I could not bear to have him for a husband. Or as anything else, for that matter.'

'Well, I am very glad to hear it,' Ellen said. 'Though I do not think, in that case, it is a good idea to have him here. I shall speak to your father.'

'There is no need for that,' Alice said hurriedly. 'I can handle Master Wolsey well enough, and yes, I will be careful of my honour.'

Alice had no wish to forbid Thomas from visiting. She had spoken the truth to her mother; she had no intention of entering into any sort of liaison with Thomas Wolsey, but she did so like to be admired, even by one as ugly as he. The fat fellow had his uses, one of which she would never admit to her mother for fear of being called a wanton. The truth was that allowing Thomas Wolsey to call on her made Alice's other suitor jealous.

And when Roger Chase was jealous, he would bring Alice presents and make her promises of riches to come, and there was nothing Alice Finch liked to hear more than that one day she would be one of the richest women in Oxford.

CHAPTER THREE

Curiosity got the better of William Patent. Taking a quick glance over his shoulder to ensure he was unobserved, he bent over Joan's writing slope and studied the paper she had been working on before heading downstairs. The paper was a request from a new buyer to provide a quotation for wool. William was impressed at the quantity required. The Wolsey wool business must be doing well if Joan was able to fulfil such a large order.

William was glad for her. Joan deserved to do well. God knew she had had enough to put up with as wife to Robert Wolsey: all those court appearances on charges of illegality and immorality, having to endure the whispers and glances of her neighbours. It had been unfair of Robert, cruel even, to put his wife through such horrors. Not that Robert had been a terrible man, William reluctantly admitted, but he had never known what a treasure he had possessed in his wife.

I will not make the same mistake, William told himself, smiling at his own confidence. He had not even asked Joan to marry him yet, and here he was, deciding what kind of husband he would be to her. What if she said no? William did not think she would refuse him, but there was always the chance she might. He told himself not to think about that. If he did, he might lose his nerve, and this would become just another friendly visit like all the others he had been paying since Robert's death.

At first, his visits to the Wolseys had been made out of conscience, a family friend ensuring all was well. William had thought Joan and Elizabeth might struggle without Robert to tell them what they should do, but he had been wrong. Joan seemed to grow young in Robert's absence, happier, surer of herself. Elizabeth was just as sour as she had always been, and if there was any trouble in the family, it was between her and her mother. William had witnessed several petty squabbles between the women, Elizabeth always the provoker, and he believed she relished the conflict. William quickly realised any help he might offer, however well-meaning, would be rebuffed by Elizabeth as a suggestion of incompetence and had therefore resolved never to try.

When it became clear that the Wolsey women were not floundering without a man to command them, William's visits had become less of a duty and more of a pleasure. It had been a long time since his wife had died in childbirth, and he missed the company of women. He found it very pleasant to sit by a fire in a comfortable room that smelled of beeswax and lavender – to him, the scents of a well-kept home – to drink good wine and nibble on freshly baked cakes.

Joan enjoyed his company too. She invited him to call when he wished; there was no need, she said, to send his boy to see if a visit would be convenient. He took her at her word, even though Elizabeth took less than kindly to his impromptu visits. She would say she was too busy to sit and talk when Joan bid William come in and take some ale, looking pointedly at her mother as if she expected her to do the same. Either Joan did not understand her look or chose to ignore it, for she would simply say that Elizabeth need not stay, that she and William would be well enough without her.

William had been glad of Elizabeth's absence. With her out of the way, he and Joan's friendship had deepened into something more intimate until William found himself dismayed when the time came to leave. It had got to the point where he did not want to part from Joan, and he realised what he truly wanted: a wife.

William turned as he heard footsteps on the landing. The door opened and Joan came in carrying a tray. He hurried over and took the tray from her, setting it down on the table. On the tray was a freshly baked pork pie, a large triangle of cheese and two glasses of cider.

'That smells good,' he said, nodding at the pie.

'I know it is your favourite. Sit down,' she bid him, cutting a slice of the pork pie. She put it on a plate and pushed it towards him.

Get on with it, he told himself. *Ask her before Eliza-*

beth decides to come up or Joan starts talking about something else.

'Joan,' he began nervously, coughing to clear his throat, 'as much as I enjoy your cooking, it was not to eat that I came here today.'

'I know,' Joan said, not meeting his eye as she took a seat opposite. Her cheeks had gone the faintest hint of pink.

'You do?' William gulped.

She nodded. 'Ask your question, William.'

He took a deep breath. 'Joan Wolsey, will you marry me?'

She looked up at him, a smile tugging at the corners of her lips. 'Yes, William Patent, I will.'

He gave a cry of joy and grabbed her face, pulling her towards him and smacking his lips against hers noisily. The colour of her cheeks deepened, and she giggled like a young girl. But then her face fell.

'What is it?' William asked, worried he had been too importunate.

'I wonder… I wonder if I should ask the children first.'

'Ask them what?'

'Whether they agree to our marrying.'

'Why do we need them to agree?' William asked, a little annoyed. 'It is our decision, our choice.'

Joan reached across the table for his hand. 'I know, but I fear they may not like it so soon after their father's death.'

'My dear, it has been more than six months since Robert died.'

'Yes, still – '

'No, there is no 'still', Joan. You do not need your children's approval nor permission to wed me. Tell me, do you want to be my wife?'

'Oh yes, William.' Joan pulled his hand to her lips and kissed it. 'More than anything.'

'Good,' he said, smiling at her kiss. 'Yours is the only consent I need or ask for. You deserve to be happy, and I intend to make you so.' He glanced at the pie longingly. 'Now that is settled, shall we eat?'

'I knew this would happen.' Elizabeth threw salt on the kitchen table and began to scrub it into the wood far more vigorously than necessary. 'I could see what he was thinking. All those times he came around, pretending to care how we did.'

'It was kind of him,' Joan protested, watching her daughter move back and forth over the table.

'Oh yes, very kind,' Elizabeth retorted. 'Master Patent is no fool. He knows what a good business we have here.'

'What has the business to do with he and I getting wed?'

'Do not be foolish, Mother. Do you think he would have asked you if you were a pauper?'

'That is a horrible thing to say,' Joan stammered,

tears pricking her eyes. 'William has his own business. He does not need my money.'

Elizabeth grunted. 'So you think.'

'So I know. William loves me and I him.'

'Oh, of course you do not. You are too old to feel love.'

'We are not too old. No, I know why you are saying such cruel things to me,' Joan said, nodding. 'You are jealous. No man wants you, so you cannot conceive of anyone wanting me.'

Elizabeth cried out. Her face screwed up as though in pain and she flung the scrubbing brush at Joan. It hit Joan in the stomach and would have hurt had her stays not offered some protection. Mother and daughter stared at each other for the longest of moments, their chests heaving, both unable to quite believe what had just happened.

Elizabeth was the first to recover. She wiped her hands on her apron. 'Have you told my brothers yet?'

'No.' Joan wiped savagely at the tears falling from her eyes. 'William only asked me this morning.'

'Well, you should before you start making wedding plans.' Elizabeth turned to stir the contents of the pot bubbling over the fire. 'I do not think Thomas will approve of you marrying again. He may even forbid it.'

'Why should he? How can he?'

'He is head of the family now, and if he is not going to be a priest, he may decide to come home to run the business. If he does, he will not want William Patent sticking his nose in. And let us be honest for once, shall we? Thomas is your darling boy, is he not? If he says no, I daresay you will not disobey *him*.'

～

Thomas closed his chamber door, yawning. It had been another long day. He wished he could go straight to bed, but he had at least an hour's reading to do to be ready for Master Swan's lecture in the morning. His room was cold, and he dragged the blanket from his bed to wrap around his shoulders. He took a few steps to his small desk and noticed for the first time the letter that lay upon it. He took it up and recognised his mother's hand. He opened it with a sigh, wondering what his mother was bothering him about now.

My dear Thomas, I hope you are well. I have some news to tell you. I am to marry again. He is William Patent, you may remember him. We are planning to marry next month and hope you will be able to come home for the wedding. Please let me know. Your loving mother.

Thomas read the letter through twice. His mother was marrying again! He searched his memory for William Patent. Not the man they'd had trouble getting rid of after his father's funeral? Him?

Well, Thomas decided, it was up to her if she wanted to take another husband; he had no objection. But he would write to Henry and tell him to make sure the business was protected, that Patent could not legally get his hands on any part of it by marrying their mother.

Thomas was not going to have that. As for attending the wedding, that was out of the question. He had no time for such idle matters.

Thomas tossed his mother's letter onto the windowsill, pulled out a stool and opened his book. He would answer his mother's letter another day. There really was no rush.

CHAPTER FOUR

Thomas suddenly realised the other students were gathering up their books around him, and knew he had been daydreaming about Alice again. He closed his book and put the lid down on his ink pot, frowning at the large blob of ink he had allowed to drop upon his paper.

'Woken up at last, Wolsey,' the tutor, Master Norton, said with a smile. 'I am sorry I was not able to interest you.'

'Forgive me, Master,' Thomas said. 'I suppose I am tired today.' He glanced at the windows Norton insisted were never opened. 'And it is rather stuffy in here.'

'I cannot open the windows at this time of the year,' Norton said, pulling his fur-lined cloak tighter. 'My chest is too delicate. And do not use lack of cold air as an excuse for your inattention.'

Thomas dropped his gaze to the floor. 'My apologies again, Master.' He made to leave.

'Wait a moment, Wolsey,' Norton called before

Thomas got three yards. 'I would have a word with you, if you please.' He pointed to one of the stools near his desk, smiling comfortingly as Thomas returned, sensing his student's apprehension. 'It has been noticed amongst the masters that you are not as diligent as you were wont to be at your studies, and it has been wondered whether something is troubling you. We are aware your father's death was – '

'No, Master Norton.' Thomas shook his head, wanting to stop the master before he could speak further. Why could no one understand that his father's death had not unsettled him, it had freed him? And now, having to endure this prying into his private life was unbearable. Norton wasn't telling him anything he didn't already know. Thomas knew he was neglecting his studies. But it was embarrassing to be dressed down in this way and to know he had been the subject of disappointment amongst the masters. This was the first time he had been criticised for not working hard enough and it stung. 'The death of my father has nothing to do with this.'

'Then what is the reason? You do not want to say?' Norton enquired further when Thomas hesitated.

'I do not … ' Thomas made a hopeless gesture, unable to find the words to explain.

Norton sighed and shook his head. 'When I think of how you were when you first came to us, it pains me to see you so distracted. How old were you then?'

'Eleven.'

'Yes, so very young, but how hard you worked. The

Boy Bachelor. Was that not the nickname you were given?'

Thomas nodded. It was a nickname he had resented. The masters believed it had been bestowed out of admiration by his peers, but Thomas knew better. He had been called the Boy Bachelor because the other boys were jealous of his talent, and it had been their way of mocking him.

'And we all said,' Norton continued, 'all we masters, "this boy is destined to go far".'

Oh, please stop, just stop talking, this isn't helping, Thomas thought, hanging his head.

Norton leant forward and touched Thomas's arm. 'But you will not go far if you carry on as you have this last year.'

'I am working hard now,' Thomas insisted, jabbing his knee with his finger. 'The reason I am tired today, Master, is because I was up until two o'clock this morning working on an essay for Master Swan.'

'Good, good, I am glad to hear it.' Norton nodded. 'But working so late should not be necessary if you are working hard enough during the day.'

'I am not a child, sir,' Thomas retorted. 'I do not feel I should be spoken to as if I were a misbehaving schoolboy. It is up to me, surely, how hard I work?'

Norton had not expected such a rebuke. As a master, he was used to his pupils treating him with deference. He drew himself up, no longer prepared to be amiable. 'I do not know what has come over you, Wolsey,' he said, turning his back and pretending to search for a paper in the pile on his desk. 'I really cannot account for your rude manner.'

'Forgive me for my rudeness, Master,' Thomas said. 'I… I would tell you what troubles me, but I do not think you would understand.'

'Why, because I am too old?' Norton turned and raised an indignant eyebrow. 'I was once your age, young man. Every thought that has gone through your head, I can assure you, has at one time or another passed through mine.'

Thomas opened his mouth to speak, but he shut it again, no answer to make.

'I think I know your problem,' Norton said, his manner softening. 'As I say, I was young once. And though the body grows old, the mind and the heart often stay young. It is a woman causing you this anguish. Ah, I see from your face that I have hit it. So, a woman. Or should I say, a girl?'

'There is a young lady,' Thomas admitted. 'The truth is, Master, I am having second thoughts about the future you all believe is ahead for me.'

'You do not wish to be a master here, nor a priest?' Norton was aghast.

'I do not know,' Thomas said earnestly. 'I have been considering the law.'

'A lawyer!' Norton spluttered a laugh.

'As a lawyer, I could marry,' Thomas explained.

'You were not sent to Magdalen to become a lawyer,' Norton said, becoming serious again. 'Magdalen men are for God, not for the law.'

It was no use, Thomas realised. Norton thought the same as his father. Old men had decided when he was a child that he would be a priest, and there was nothing to be done.

'Your ordination is overdue,' Norton said. 'You should be a priest by now.'

'You have not listened to a word I have said,' Thomas cried.

'What have you said?' Norton asked brusquely. 'That you are not sure you want to be a master here or a priest. That your head has been filled with fancies because of some silly girl.'

'My love for Alice Finch is not a fancy,' Thomas burst out, forgetting in his anger that he had not wanted to mention her name. 'And she is not a silly girl.'

'Alice Finch? The mayor's daughter?' Norton's voice rose in his amazement. 'My word, Wolsey, you are aiming high there, and foolishly.'

'Why foolishly?' Thomas demanded.

Norton stared shrewdly at Thomas. 'Foolishly because I have met the young lady, and I can tell you she is a flighty thing. The poor fellow who marries her will be led a merry dance. You would do better to put Alice Finch quite out of your mind.'

Thomas's blood was boiling. Yet another ignorant fool telling him Alice was not worth his love. What did they all have against her? What had she ever done to make these churls talk of her so?

'May I go, Master Norton?' Thomas stood up to let

Norton know he was leaving whether he had permission or not.

Norton raised his finger. 'Wolsey, you will mark me. Women turn good men's minds to thoughts of the flesh, and when a man is young, such thoughts are all-consuming. But they fade, I promise you. As a man grows older, he realises there is more to his well-being than the press of flesh upon flesh. There is his faith and his love of God.'

'God will not keep my bed warm at night,' Thomas said before he could stop himself.

Norton's face flushed. 'Lust, Wolsey,' he spat. 'Lust was the cause of Man's downfall. All women are daughters of Eve. Remember that. They carry her sin in their very veins. Beware the daughters of Eve, Master Wolsey.'

Thomas forced his eyes away from the window, aware he had been staring out of it for almost ten minutes. There was nothing outside to warrant his attention, nothing but grey skies. *Concentrate, you numbskull,* he snarled at himself and fixed his gaze on his books.

There was no getting away from it; Master Norton's words had upset him, and he could not be sure why. To be sure, he had not liked the master speaking of Alice as a flighty thing, especially after it had been insinuated by others, but those words had bounced off him for the most part. He had not liked to be told he was being reckless to abandon the path chosen for him by far wiser men than he. He did not want to believe it was so, yet he could not but wonder if perhaps there was some truth in Norton's words. All the work he had done, the hours he had put in to gain his degree at fifteen years old – a prodigious, unheard-of accomplishment for any student in Oxford – was that all for nothing? And this idea he had of being a lawyer. Did he really care about the law, or had he just latched onto the only job he could think of that was a good fit for his skills and intellect? He wished he knew. He wished God would help him. He prayed nightly for guidance, and each night he went to sleep thinking he would be able to make a decision in the morning. But then he would visit Alice, and his mind would be turned topsy-turvy once more.

The only solace he found was in work. In his work, when he managed to apply himself and force Alice from his brain, he could lose himself. When he read his Bible, his mind became free from confusion. But he could not study the word of God nor work every minute of every day, and in those moments, his mind would wander back to Alice. He always came back to Alice.

He longed to see her. He had been told that his next lecture had been cancelled and had thought to use the free time to study, but to hell with it. He brushed his hair, cleaned his teeth and headed out of the college, making for the Finch house and hoping he would find Alice alone for once.

When he reached the Finch house and raised his hand to knock on the door, he hesitated. Mark would undoubtedly answer, and he was in no mood for his insolence. Thomas looked up at the sky. The day was bright and reasonably warm. It was just possible Alice would not be in the house at all but in the dairy or the drying room, possibly even in the garden, picking herbs to strew on the floor. It was worth taking a look to avoid alerting Mark, even if entering the Finch garden without permission was something of a liberty.

Thomas walked to the end of the row of houses and turned down the alley, turning again at the end to walk along the rear. The Finch garden was enclosed by tall stone walls, and he needed to open a wooden door to gain entry. Hoping the door was not locked, he tried the metal handle. With delight, he heard the bolt draw back, and the door swung inward with a slight creak.

The Finches kept a tidy garden. Thomas knew Ellen Finch was very proud of it, for much of the garden was her handiwork. One corner was for herbs, another for vegetables. The remainder was given over to beauty. Ellen Finch's pride and joy was the rose arbour, which was rather barren at this time of year. The only decoration was the brown stems and tendrils of the previous year's growth. Through a gap in the trellis, Thomas spotted the yellow cloth of a woman's skirts. He crept closer on tiptoe, just in case he was out of luck and it was Ellen Finch instead of the Alice he hoped for.

But then he heard a laugh, and his heart beat faster. It was the lovely, tinkling, coquettish laugh of Alice. It *was* she in the arbour. He was about to speak when he heard another laugh, low and masculine. Thomas edged closer, his eyes and ears straining to discover more. There came voices, just above whispers, and he couldn't make out what they were saying. They must be sitting close to one another to whisper so, he thought. And who but lovers whisper in a rose arbour? With a sense of dread, he took another step, then another, until he could see into the arbour and yet not be seen by its occupants.

Alice was sitting on the wooden bench, her yellow dress spread wide – spread, indeed, over the knees of a man. Thomas knew him; he was Roger Chase, the son of a goldsmith, an annoyingly handsome youth with fine prospects.

Thomas watched, his breath coming fast, as Roger leant towards Alice and pressed his lips to her neck. And she, she allowed him to do it! Alice had never allowed Thomas to so much as kiss her hand, and yet she allowed this callow youth to finger her skin. Thomas turned his face away, unable to watch. But then he heard the rustle of fabric, and his head turned back towards the arbour. He watched, feeling sick, as Roger lifted Alice's skirt and slipped his hand beneath, watched as Alice leant backwards to allow his hand easier access.

Thomas swallowed down the cry of anger and dismay that threatened to explode from his mouth. He stumbled away from the arbour, his hurried feet sending gravel shooting into the flower beds on either side. He did not care about the noise he made. All he knew was he had to get away from the garden and its dreadful sight.

As he ran back out onto the street, dodging side to side to avoid other pedestrians and carts, all he could think was that Master Norton had been right. All women had corruption running through their veins. They were impure and deceitful, the ruin of men. Well, Thomas was done with them. He would never think of Alice Finch with anything like love again.

~

Hugh Sedley was lying on his back on a stone bench in the college garden when he heard the gravel crunching beneath someone's feet. He opened one sleepy eye, turned his head in the footsteps' direction, and saw Thomas, his head down, shoulders hunched. Hugh raised himself to a sitting position and called out to his friend.

'What is that glare for?' he demanded as Thomas looked up at the greeting.

Thomas shook his head. 'Sorry.' He made to walk away.

Hugh lunged and grabbed his arm. 'Wait, what's wrong? You've got a face like thunder.'

Thomas tried to tug his arm away, but Hugh held on. Thomas, relenting, snarled, 'Women.'

'Ah,' Hugh said, beginning to understand. He pulled Thomas down onto the bench. 'Alice Finch?'

Thomas nodded. 'She's been deceiving me, Hugh. You were right about her. Everyone was right about her. Oh God, why did I not listen?'

'Because we are fools when it comes to women, my friend,' Hugh said, putting his arm around Thomas's shoulder. 'Do not blame yourself. Tell me what happened.'

'I thought I would surprise her,' Thomas said, 'so I called unexpectedly. I have told you about their servant, Mark. I did not want to encounter him, so I went straight into the garden. I saw her in the rose arbour with Roger Chase. Do you know him?'

Hugh screwed up his forehead. 'His father's the goldsmith, is he not? Well, she has good taste, I will give her that,' Hugh said, earning himself a filthy look from Thomas. 'I mean, she knows she is onto a good thing with him. He will be able to give her all the jewellery she wants, will he not?'

'Yesterday I would have struck you for saying such a thing, Hugh.'

'But today you are a better, wiser man. Be glad of it. Better to find out now than marry her and find out later she has made a cuckold of you.'

Thomas buried his face in his hands. 'It has all been such a waste.'

'Do not look at it as a waste. It has been an experience, that is all. And all experience is good. It helps you learn.'

'All I have learnt is that women are not to be trusted.'

'They have their uses.' Hugh patted Thomas's knee and winked. 'And in your present frame of mind, I recommend one of them as a remedy.'

Thomas looked at him with disgust. 'Are you suggesting what I think you are?'

Hugh grinned. 'I am. And why not? You will feel better, I promise you that.'

'Will I?'

Hugh put his hand to his chest solemnly. 'I stand as guarantor. Come, the coupling will be on me. Take me up on it, Tom. I do not make such offers every day of the week.'

Hugh felt sure Thomas would decline his kind offer, but to his surprise, his friend seemed to be considering his proposition. Maybe his heart really had been broken.

'Agreed,' Thomas said with a defiant nod.

'Really?'

'I said yes.'

Hugh rose. 'Then let us go now before you change your mind.'

'I will not change my mind,' Thomas said, standing up. 'Lead the way.'

Thomas had followed Hugh with such confidence, but now he was beginning to wonder whether visiting a brothel was such a good idea. He wanted to put Alice Finch completely out of his mind, but was burying himself in some other woman really the best way to achieve it? And yet, Hugh seemed convinced it would help.

It probably will help, Thomas told himself, *and it is*

only this one time. Once cannot hurt, can it? Every man must visit a whore at some time in their life. Like Hugh said, it will be an experience, and all experience is good. Still...

Thomas was glad it was not a true brothel Hugh took him to but rather a tavern where girls could be bought as extras. It was at the opposite side of town too, far from Magdalen College, so Thomas relaxed a little, knowing it was unlikely he would meet anyone who knew him. Hugh found them a table and ordered a jug of beer from the pot boy.

'What do we do?' Thomas asked, glancing uneasily around the room. 'Do we pay before – ?'

Hugh laughed. 'Don't worry, Tom, I'll take care of it. I said this would be on me.'

The boy brought over the jug of beer and two horn cups. 'Lucy's busy at the moment, Master Sedley,' the boy said, jerking his head at the ceiling. 'You'll have to wait awhile if you want her.'

'No, that's all right. Just send us any girls who are free. Unless' – Hugh raised his eyebrows at Thomas – 'you want something particular?'

Thomas flushed with embarrassment. He stared down at his hands and shook his head.

'Any two will do. I told you, relax,' he said when the boy had gone. 'There's no need to be embarrassed. 'Tis their business. There's nothing you can say or do that they haven't heard a hundred times before, and believe me, nothing shocks them.'

Thomas nodded but his cheeks still burned. He knew

there were some men who enjoyed perversions in their fornication; indeed, he had had an older friend at the college some years before who had boasted of the ways he had toyed with girls and the way girls had toyed with him, but Thomas had neither experienced it for himself nor heard of any sexual act that could be said to be out of the ordinary. A part of him wanted to question Hugh about what to do when he was alone with the girl – they would be alone, would they not? – but he was wary of exposing his ignorance in such matters. His fornication would be ordinary, he decided. Satisfying, hopefully, but ordinary.

Two women suddenly appeared at the table. Neither were particularly pretty, but what they looked like did not matter. It was what they had between their legs that was of consequence. The elder of the two was dark-haired, and greasy ragged tendrils stuck to her face. Her dress, like her companion's, was cut low, her small breasts pushed up and outward by a bodice that barely covered her nipples. Dark pink areolae peeked above the fabric. Her smile did not extend to her eyes, which were prematurely wrinkled. Thomas supposed the girl had seen too many years of whoring, of being used time and time again by men who cared not a jot for her, to smile with genuine pleasure. The younger girl was fresher than the other, less used. Her light-brown hair was tied back at her nape, and her skin glowed with life, not perspiration. Her features were plain but comely.

'Good even, sirs,' the elder said, pushing her hip towards them. 'What's your pleasure?'

'You two are the only pleasure we seek,' Hugh said, leaning back. He groped for the younger girl's hand and pulled her onto his lap.

The elder looked at Thomas. 'Haven't seen you here before,' she said, perching on his knees.

'My friend here wants taking in hand.' Hugh grinned at Thomas. 'Been disappointed in love, you see.'

'There's a shame,' the girl said. 'But don't worry, sir. I'll make you forget about her.'

'Nothing too exotic, mind,' Hugh said, seeing Thomas's startled expression. 'Just the ordinary will do.'

'Come with me, sir.'

The whore slid from his lap and held out her hand. Thomas slipped his into it. He knew his palm was sweaty, for she made a face at his touch. He followed her to the wooden stairs in the middle of the tavern and watched her backside sway as she mounted each step. He would have preferred the younger one, if truth be told, but he did not feel bold enough to argue with Hugh over who had which whore. This one would do for the purpose.

The room the whore led him to was small, barely large enough to house the narrow wooden bed set against the wall. In the far corner was a small trunk that served as a table, a bowl of water and a jug sitting on top. A dirty cloth hung over the edge of the trunk. The bedlinen was grey and ragged, the result of age and too hasty washing, the laundress not giving it enough time hanging over bushes to be bleached by the sun. The linen was likely in too great demand to allow for such leisure. How often did it get washed? he wondered as he drew near the bed. Beneath the wool blanket the grey sheet was stained, and he realised it had not been changed since the bed's last occupant had used it.

'Just the ordinary, then, sir?' the whore asked, keen to get down to business.

'Yes,' Thomas mumbled.

She stepped around him and lay on the bed. She hitched her skirts up over her hips, exposing her thighs and privates. Thomas had never seen a naked woman before, save for the various depictions of Eve painted onto church walls, and his mouth became suddenly dry even as his manhood stiffened.

The whore looked up at him enquiringly. 'Whenever you're ready, sir.'

Swallowing, Thomas nodded and began to unlace his hose. He wished she would look away. To his relief, her expression did not change as she looked upon him. She was not disgusted with his person, he was not abnormal in any way, and the knowledge filled him with a new surety of his ability. He climbed onto the bed and positioned himself over her. She moved her legs and hooked them over his hips, her heels pressing against the back of his thighs. Her hand found his manhood and guided him towards her entrance.

As he entered her, his brain stopped its workings. Sensation overwhelmed him and his body moved rhythmically, answering her thrusts with his own. It was pleasurable, as pleasurable as his friends had always said, and he closed his eyes until it was over.

It was over too soon. Panting, he opened his eyes and looked down on the whore beneath him. Her cheeks were a little rosier, he thought, but otherwise she looked the same, as if he had not just performed a magnificent feat. She looked bored, and an image of Alice suddenly appeared in his mind. She wouldn't have looked bored, he felt sure. She would have been smiling sweetly, her lips swollen with kisses and her blue eyes washed bright with tears of happiness.

Grimacing, he climbed off the bed and turned his back to the whore. His trembling fingers fumbled with the laces of his hose, and he had to tuck his wet, shrivelled member inside the cloth. He wiped his fingers on the tails of his shirt with disgust.

'How much?' he asked, keeping his back to her.

'You pay the mistress on your way out, sir.' He heard the bed creak as she moved, then the rustle of cloth as her skirts fell down to her ankles.

He half-turned to her, and her tired eyes looked up at him. He felt suddenly sorry for her. 'Thank you.'

She sighed and gave a wry if genuine smile. 'No need to thank me, sir. You get what you pay for.'

Thomas nodded and opened the door, hearing the creak of wood and the grunts of men from behind other doors on the landing. He had enjoyed his encounter for the few minutes it had lasted, but now he just wanted to leave. He hurried down the stairs. His eyes searched in vain for Hugh, then he realised that some of those grunts from upstairs must have been his.

A middle-aged woman with grey hair falling from beneath her cap stopped before him, carrying a tray of empty cups. 'All done, sir?'

'Yes,' he said, reaching for his cloak that had been put on a hook behind the woman.

'Just the ordinary, I was told by your friend,' she said, setting her tray on the bar. 'He's paid for you.'

'Do you know where my friend is?' Thomas asked.

'He's upstairs with Sally,' the woman said. 'He won't be long. You can wait over there.' She gestured to a stool by the fire. 'I'll bring you some more beer and a pie if you're hungry. Only tuppence.'

Thomas accepted the offer of food and drink. He had finished both by the time Hugh came down the stairs.

'Well?' Hugh asked, sinking into the chair opposite. 'Enjoy yourself?'

'Yes, thank you,' Thomas said irritably. 'Are you ready? Can we go?'

'Hold hard a moment, Tom. I could do with a cup of beer myself.'

'I have some in my chamber,' Thomas insisted, rising and putting on his cloak. 'Please, Hugh, I would much rather leave now.'

Reluctantly, Hugh agreed. They stepped out into the cold night air. Thomas closed his eyes and let the chill bite into his skin.

'Come now, how was it?' Hugh nudged Thomas in the ribs.

'It was… as expected.'

'Is that all you can say?'

'What do you want me to say?'

'Oh, I don't know. That you enjoyed it, that you want to do it again as soon as possible, that you've forgotten all about your Alice.'

'It was enjoyable, but I do not want to go there again. And no, it has not made me forget Alice. You reminding me of her does not help either.'

'You do not want to go again? You are not serious, surely?'

'I am perfectly serious. Such women have their uses, I know, and I thank you for today, but whores are not for me.'

'You'll change your mind,' Hugh said with assurance. 'You will get the urge again. 'Tis inevitable now you have tasted what you've been missing all these years.'

'I will try to fight that urge,' Thomas said decisively, almost as if to convince himself. 'I have come to the conclusion that women bring men low. I am sure the less I have to do with them, the better I will be.'

'You had best do what your father wanted and submit to the church, then. The way I see it, if you plan to deny yourself one of life's chief pleasures, you should at least get paid for it.'

'I suppose I shall,' Thomas murmured thoughtfully.

It had been more than two weeks since Thomas's visit to the brothel, and he had buried himself in his work, declining all Hugh's invitations to indulge their carnal desires again. He was done with that sort of thing, he told Hugh, it was not for him. Hugh grinned and wagged his finger, assuring Thomas he would come around, that he would feel desire for a woman again. Thomas knew Hugh spoke truth, but he was resolved; when he had the desire for a woman and acted upon it, it would be to satisfy a purely physical need, not an emotional one. Thomas was determined a woman would never break his heart again.

He had decided to take a short break from his studies and have a walk through the city. It was good to get beyond the college walls now and then. With nothing particular to do or anywhere to go, Thomas meandered through the streets, lost in his own thoughts.

'Master Wolsey!'

The words halted his steps at once, the voice both familiar and unwelcome. He turned to see Alice Finch staring at him, an uncertain smile upon her lips.

Alice crossed the street. She peered up into his face enquiringly. 'It has been such a long time since I have seen you. You have not been ill, I hope?'

Thomas fixed his gaze on a spot over her shoulder, determined not to meet her eye. 'No, I am in good health.'

'Oh, good, I am relieved to hear it. Why have you

not visited, then?' Alice asked, her expression faltering as she sensed something was wrong.

She thinks she still has power over me, Thomas realised with disgust. *Well, I'll show her.* 'I have no reason to visit, not anymore,' he said, fixing her with a hard stare.

Alice blinked, confused. 'What… what do you mean, you have no reason? Am I not reason enough to come calling?'

'You were,' Thomas admitted, 'until I realised you were not worth my trouble.'

'I – I – ' Alice gasped, taken aback by his words and the vehemence behind them. 'Why are you being so cruel to me?'

'Have you not been cruel to me?' Thomas growled. 'All those months you knew how I felt about you, letting me believe you felt something for me.'

'I promised you nothing,' Alice protested.

'True, you did not, but neither did you discourage me.'

'I thought we were friends – '

'Oh, we were never that.'

'Why this change in you?'

'Because I saw you with Roger Chase, allowing him such liberties.'

Alice swallowed. 'What liberties? I would never – '

'You cannot deny it. I saw you in the arbour with his hand beneath your skirts.'

Alice's face turned a deep shade of red. Her eyes

widened and her breath started to come fast. 'How dare you!' she gasped.

'How dare I say you are a wanton? I say you are one. Aye, the truth wounds, does it not, Mistress Alice?' he crowed, delighting in her anguish, not caring who heard. 'You know, I should thank you. My way had become clouded, and I had doubts about becoming a priest. Seeing you behave so shamelessly has set me right in my mind. So,' he bowed mockingly, 'I thank you, Mistress Finch. Good day to you.'

Thomas pushed past her, feeling her skirts brush against his legs, and did not look back. He left Alice Finch standing in the street with tears streaming down her cheeks and passers-by wondering what on earth the scholar of Magdalen had said to her.

CHAPTER FIVE

1498

John Squyer hurried through the streets of St Nicholas parish, almost skipping over the animal faeces and other debris to reach the Wolsey house. He had been so excited he had not even stopped to put on his cloak, though the late February morning was icy cold and the hand that clutched the letter was barren of a glove. By the time he reached the Wolsey front door, he had lost feeling in his toes. He stamped his feet, waiting impatiently for his knock to be answered.

'Mr Squyer,' Joan greeted him in surprise as the little man pushed past her, apologising for his hurried entrance but needing to feel the warmth of the interior. 'What do you do here?'

Squyer held up the letter. 'I have come to congratulate you, Mistress Patent.'

Elizabeth entered, drawn by the sound of voices. She had been boiling the family linen, and her face was red and damp. 'Congratulate us about what?'

'About your Thomas, of course,' Squyer said, looking from Joan to Elizabeth with a surprised look. 'Surely you have heard?'

Joan, who had been scalding her milk jugs when his knock came, wiped her hands on a cloth and gestured to Squyer to take a seat at the table. Elizabeth poured their guest a cup of ale and exchanged a glance with Joan. They had not heard from Thomas for a while. Thomas had written in October to say he had been made a fellow of Magdalen College and then, a month or so later, that he been appointed third bursar, but there had been nothing since. Elizabeth saw her mother was doing her best not to show her unhappiness that a mere family acquaintance had news of her son that she did not.

'Thomas has written to you?' Joan asked, her eyes fixed upon the letter in Squyer's hand.

'Thomas? Oh no, not Thomas.' Squyer shook his head. 'I have never received a letter from him. No, this is from Master Norton, a friend of mine at Magdalen. He writes to me often. In his last letter – '

'What of Thomas?' Elizabeth interrupted testily.

Squyer looked up at her, a little annoyed. 'I was coming to Thomas, my dear Mistress Elizabeth.' He cleared his throat importantly. 'Thomas is to be ordained on the tenth of March. He will be a priest. There, is that not good news?'

Joan clapped her hands together. 'Oh, Bess, do you hear? Thomas, a priest.'

'It has taken him long enough,' Elizabeth said, refusing to be pleased.

'Well, quite.' Squyer nodded. 'I did wonder if he ever intended to take his vows, and your late husband did too, I know.'

'It was Father's greatest wish that Thomas become a priest,' Elizabeth said.

'But I wonder why he has not written to tell us himself,' Joan said, frowning. She clutched at an idea. 'Unless his letter was lost.'

'Yes, perhaps,' Squyer agreed, draining his cup of ale. He smacked his lips. 'Well, I must be going, Mistress Patent. I just had to come and tell you how pleased I am for you. I always knew Thomas would go far.'

'Yes, you did. If it had not been for you, he would never have gone to Oxford, I expect. Thank you for coming around to tell us.'

'You do not really think Thomas's letter was lost, do you, Mother?' Elizabeth asked as Joan shut the door on Squyer. 'Thomas has not written to tell us his news, that is all.'

'Letters do get lost, Bess,' Joan said. 'And why would he not tell us? He told us of when he became a fellow and bursar.'

'They were just college appointments,' Elizabeth said dismissively, pouring herself a cup of the ale. 'Becoming a priest is different. There will be a ceremony.'

'And?' Joan asked, pushing the tendrils of hair that had escaped back beneath her cap.

Elizabeth sighed as if her mother were being stupid.

'And if there is a ceremony, there will be people to witness it. But Thomas does not want us to witness his ordination, does he?'

Joan shook her head. 'I do not know what you are talking about, Bess, really I do not.'

'Thomas does not want us embarrassing him in front of his friends, that is what I am talking about,' Elizabeth said, her voice hard and exasperated. 'He has as good as disowned us, Mother, surely you have realised that? He hardly ever writes, except when he has to out of duty to you. I daresay had Master Squyer not told us of his ordination, we would someday have received a letter from Thomas saying the ordination ceremony was done and that he was a priest, and that we should all be proud of him.'

'You are wrong,' Joan said, shaking her head, 'and it does you no good to speak of your brother so. His letter has been lost, as I say. Now, I shall write to Thomas to say we have heard of his good news from Master Squyer and that yes, we *are* all very proud of him.' She jerked her chin at Elizabeth as if daring her daughter to contradict her, but Elizabeth just stared at her with dull eyes, having nothing further to say.

Thomas closed his eyes and slowed his breathing. There was nothing to be anxious about, he told himself. Just another ceremony to be got through, that was all. He felt his heart stop its banging, settling back into its usual rhythm, and he opened his eyes. In just a few minutes, he would leave the priests' room and descend to the church.

He was more than a little disappointed with the church of St Peter. It was very small, and when he had arrived the day before, he had found himself wondering why a bigger church nearer to Oxford could not have been used for his ordination. He had not enjoyed the journey to Wiltshire either. It had been cold and uncomfortable in the hired coach, and to crown it all, his ordination would be performed by the bishop's suffragan rather than the bishop himself. The bishop, Thomas thought sourly, probably had better things to do.

Thomas wished his family had not come. They were downstairs in the church, he knew, sitting in one of the pews, no doubt grinning like imbeciles. He had received Joan's letter and read of her joy at his ordination with annoyance, cursing Master Squyer for interfering. His mother had had to find out and make a fuss about coming to the ceremony. He had tried to suggest that a woman of her advanced age should not be making long journeys in the coldest months of the year, but Joan would have none of it. And they were all there, his sister and brothers too, all to see him become a priest, the very thing he had told them he was unlikely to become. The knowledge of how foolish he had been still hurt.

Sacred music floated up from below. It was time. Thomas headed for the door and descended the stairs.

The small church was packed with locals. As Thomas walked along the aisle, his eyes scanned the congregation, recognising none of them until he caught sight of his family, their bright faces watching his every step. He looked away, not wanting to be distracted. He reached the altar, and the suffragan stepped forward, ready to question him. Would Thomas perform all the duties of the priesthood? Would he promise to respect and obey his superiors?

'Yes,' Thomas answered solemnly and lay on his front before the altar, feeling the cold of the stones seep into his body. There was a great shuffling behind him as all those watching knelt and began to pray, their whispered words a sibilant hiss. The suffragan put his hand upon Thomas's head and said a prayer.

Almost done, Thomas told himself, pushing himself up as the prayer ended, aware he managed the move with precious little dignity. He stood perfectly still as his new priestly vestments, the stole and chasuble, were put upon him, and held out his hands so they could be anointed with chrism oil. They were slick and greasy when the suffragan handed Thomas the chalice and paten that were now his to use whenever he performed the Eucharist.

As Thomas turned to face the congregation, his eyes involuntarily sought his mother. Even from a distance, he could see the tears streaking her cheeks, and he suddenly realised what this moment meant to her and he was ridiculously glad she had been present to see her dream realised. He knew he had been selfish to want to deprive her.

He felt the true weight of what he now was. He had

been too anxious about the ceremony to appreciate what his new status would mean, but now he was a true servant of God, the conduit between Him and the race he had created. He saw he had been wrong to resist becoming a priest for so long, wrong to have allowed himself to be diverted from his true calling by the bewitching eyes of a daughter of Eve. This felt right – the weight of the vestments, the chalice and paten in his hands.

It was so very clear to him now. To serve God was what he had been born for.

CHAPTER SIX

There was stone dust on the hem of his cloak and lime mortar on his shoes. He should have called the master mason to his office rather than go to see him, Thomas supposed, but he had wanted to see the building works close up. He could see the embryonic tower from his office window, and he had found the sight of it, growing course by course, endlessly fascinating. And now, as senior bursar, the building of it was in his hands. Figuratively speaking, of course.

How things had changed! In the past eight months, he had been ordained and become a man of God. At his college, he had been promoted from junior bursar, managing only the petty fiscal transactions of the college – paying washer women and brewers – to senior bursar, responsible for the college's income and management of all its properties.

Thomas had little time to teach students now. It had been his duty to teach as many pupils as possible when a mere fellow of the college, but he found it tiresome and frustrating; so few of his pupils had any brains to speak of. There were some who managed to show some intelligence, admittedly, but they were few and far between. But when these other, more important roles were given him, Thomas found to his delight that his teaching obligations had been almost cut in half.

In management and administration, Thomas found great satisfaction. When he had first been handed the account ledgers for the college, he had been shocked by the state they were in; columns of figures were incorrectly added up, blobs of ink obscured important details, and there were crossings out all over the pages. His first job had been to tidy and correct them, and he had set to the task with a will. And now Richard Mayhew, the president of the college, had handed over the entire bell tower construction project to his care.

Thomas knew something had gone badly wrong, for the project was more than four months behind schedule. He was determined to discover the reason for the delay and set things right.

One of the workmen crossed his path, looked askance at him and stopped. 'Who do you want to see?' he asked brusquely.

'Master Orchard, if he is about,' Thomas replied, shielding his eyes against the sun.

'Aye, he's over in the lodge.' The man jerked his head to indicate around the corner.

Sidestepping debris, Thomas made his way to the masons' lodge. He heard the lodge before he saw it, for the almost musical tap of hammer on chisel drew him in. The masons' lodge was merely a raised wooden platform with upright poles to support the roof. Inside were benches with blocks of stone upon them, the wooden floor covered in chippings and dust. Three masons were each working on a stone block, seemingly oblivious to anything beyond them. Thomas had to call twice before one of them noticed him.

'I am looking for Master Orchard,' Thomas called.

'I am William Orchard.' The mason at the far side of the lodge came forward. He was a short thickset man with blue eyes and dark brown hair that looked grey, so covered was it with stone dust. 'Can I help you?'

'Indeed, you can.' Thomas held out his hand, and Orchard put his own into it. Thomas's hand came away covered in white dust. 'I am Thomas Wolsey, senior bursar. I have been appointed to oversee the construction of the tower.'

'I see.' Orchard looked Thomas up and down, unimpressed.

'I would like to know how the work is progressing. It is behind schedule, I understand.'

'That's not my fault,' Orchard said at once. 'The winter frost meant the lime mortar would not set properly, and then I lost two of my men. I haven't been able to replace them yet. And,' he continued as Thomas opened his mouth to speak, 'I cannot buy any more timber for another two months, I was told, because all the money allotted for the timber has been spent elsewhere.'

'A very succinct account, Master Orchard, thank you.' Thomas drew a deep breath. 'It seems to me that the main problem is the lack of funds. Do you agree?'

Orchard nodded. 'I could order the timber and hire more men, but the money is not there to be had, Master Wolsey. I only wish it was.'

Thomas rubbed his chin as he did a quick mental calculation. His eyes flicked over the half-cut stones, the lime mortar in tubs, and the wooden scaffolding and reckoned it would take almost ten years to complete at the present work rate. 'Too long,' he murmured to himself, 'far too long.' To Orchard, he said, 'Well, thank you, Master Orchard. I do not want to take up any more of your time.'

'So, we are to carry on?' Orchard called after Thomas.

'Oh yes,' Thomas called back over his shoulder. 'Carry on. And in the meantime, I shall see what can be done about the funding.'

'But I have already asked the dean if he could increase the allowance. He said it was impossible.'

'Yes, Master Orchard.' Thomas grinned. '*He* would.'

Thomas entered the Great Hall and headed for the high table at the far end. As he strode past the long refectory tables, his eyes scanned the occupants of the high table, noting the presence of Swan and Norton at one end,

Arnott badgering Richard Mayhew on the far side, and an empty chair on the other. *Excellent*, Thomas thought, *room for me*.

Thomas pulled out the empty chair and sat down. He helped himself from the platters laid out before him, taking two large slices of roast beef and tearing them to make slivers. 'Master Mayhew, may I speak with you?' Thomas asked, smiling an apology at Arnott for interrupting.

'Of course, Thomas,' Mayhew said a little too enthusiastically. The president was obviously glad to be able to turn his back on Arnott.

'I inspected the building works at the bell tower yesterday,' Thomas began, 'and I found that the work is woefully behind in its execution. The master mason told me the work would be further along had the money allotted been forthcoming.'

'I daresay it would be.' Mayhew nodded, chewing painfully on his beef.

'Can the money not be found?'

'Tell me where,' Mayhew said. 'All the monies for this year are allocated. And you are not the only master asking for funds, you know. I had Goodryke only last evening asking me to find the money for the purchase of a book he has been offered. He says it is special, but I know not. I had to tell him no, so he is none too happy with me at the moment.'

'I think I can find the money,' Thomas said quietly.

Mayhew looked at him in surprise. 'Where?'

Thomas kept his voice low. 'By taking it away from somewhere else. But I would need your permission.'

Mayhew shifted closer and matched his voice to Thomas's. 'I do not see how I can authorise that. There would be an uproar from the masters whose projects you took it from.'

'Only if they were told,' Thomas countered. 'What I mean is,' he hurried to explain at Mayhew's shocked expression, 'I will take a little from several places so no one project suffers. Each will just take a little longer to complete, 'tis all. The missing amounts will not be noticed.'

Mayhew tapped his fingers on the table, considering. 'No,' he said after a minute. 'I cannot approve such an action. Not because it is not a good idea, Thomas, but because I cannot justify taking from others to fund the tower. Remember, I have had to say no to Goodryke over his book. It will look like favouritism if I were to allow you to scoop up funds in this way.'

'Goodryke wants a new book,' Thomas snapped. 'There are hundreds of books in the college library. His new book would simply be one more amongst many. The tower is special. It will give the college prestige. What would you rather, Master Mayhew? A beautiful tower adorning our college or a debris-strewn patch of ground where the tower should be? You put me in charge of the building project. I like to think you did that because you knew I would get things moving, but I cannot do that if my hands are tied over funding. You appointed me to come up with a solution to the problem.

This is my solution. I implore you, let me have the money.'

Mayhew grimaced and sighed. 'Well, when you put it like that... very well, Thomas, do what you think necessary. But for goodness' sake, keep what you are doing to yourself. I do not want to have all the masters haranguing me about it.'

'I will, Master Mayhew, thank you,' Thomas said. He added another slice of beef to his plate, grinning. That had been a great deal easier than he had thought it would be.

CHAPTER SEVEN

Thomas wiped the sweat from his neck with his hand-kerchief, ducking to step through the doorway in the college gate. It was the hottest summer he could remember, and he half wished he didn't have to wear the heavy robes of a master and could strip down to his shirt like a common labourer. But that would never have done, not for someone of his standing. Instead, he consoled himself with the promise of a cooling cup of beer and a bowl of strawberries taken in the shade of the yew tree outside his office.

'Master Wolsey!'

Thomas turned to see the college porter hurrying to catch up with him. 'What is it, Baines?'

'Message from Master Mayhew,' Baines panted, resting his hands on his knees. 'You are to go straight to his office the moment you return.'

'Do you know why?' Thomas asked with dismay,

the image of his beer and strawberries rapidly fading. 'Is something wrong?'

Baines shook his head. 'I don't think so. He has people with him. High-ups.'

'Who?'

'Couldn't say, Master Wolsey.' Baines shrugged. 'Four of them, there were. Three boys and a lord.'

And me sweating like a pig, Thomas thought with irritation, thanking Baines and hurrying into the college. He washed his hands in the bowl of water kept on one of the cupboards in the Great Hall and hurried up the stairs to Mayhew's office. Stopping to catch his breath, he knocked on the door.

'Come,' Mayhew instructed.

Thomas opened the door, and his eyes immediately fell upon the president's four visitors. There was no doubting they were nobles, for their clothes were of the best quality, and they each had an air of confidence that only good breeding could bestow. The eldest, the young men's father judging by the striking resemblance between them, was seated by Mayhew's desk, the three sons ranged behind him.

'My lord,' Mayhew said to the father, 'this is Master Wolsey, of whom I spoke. Master Wolsey, this is Lord Thomas Grey and his sons.'

Thomas bowed, wondering what was going on. He had heard of Thomas Grey, knew him to be the marquess of Dorset, son of the former queen, Elizabeth Woodville, and a staunch ally of King Edward IV. There had been rumours that Grey had supported Lambert Simnel, the pretender to Henry Tudor's throne, but the rumours had never been proven, and Grey had demonstrated his loyalty to Tudor by ably putting down an uprising in Cornwall in the king's name. Thomas Grey was now in his fifties, plump and ruddy faced, but Thomas saw the man he had once been in the faces of his sons and thought Grey must have once been very handsome, no doubt an inheritance from his famously beautiful mother.

'My sons will be studying here, Master Wolsey,' Lord Grey said, gesturing at the three young men. 'Master Mayhew tells me you are one of the best masters here, so I want you to have the care of my boys.'

Thomas was delighted to be described as one of the best masters Magdalen had to offer, even as he realised he was being given extra teaching duties. 'It would be an honour, my lord,' he said. 'If I may say, it is not often a college is graced with the sons of such nobility as your family.'

'Yes, I know,' Grey said, making no attempt at modesty. 'Many of my friends believe there is no sense in educating sons, that sons are only good for fighting, drinking to excess and losing money at cards, but I am not of that mind. It is a new world we are in, Master Wolsey, and fighting and drinking are no longer enough. A man must know about history and foreign languages and more if he is to take his place in the world.'

'I could not agree more, my lord,' Thomas said. 'Education is always valuable. I believe it places us closer to God, helping us use the gift of intelligence He gave us.'

Grey's eyes narrowed as he stared at Thomas. 'I had not considered that before. I can see Master Mayhew was wise to recommend you. A good choice, Master Mayhew.'

Mayhew bowed his head in thanks.

'Well, that's arranged, then.' Grey slapped his knees and rose. He turned to his sons. 'Remember well what I have told you. Attend your studies, respect the masters and say your prayers daily. I have asked Master Mayhew to furnish me with regular reports of your progress so I will know if you be not behaving as I expect my sons to behave. Do not let me down.'

The young men bent their heads to receive their father's blessing, and Mayhew took the opportunity of Grey's turned back to glance meaningfully at Thomas. His look communicated clearly that this was an important moment for the college to have such august pupils in their care and Thomas was not to ruin it.

Mayhew need not have worried. Here was a chance, finally, to impress someone outside of the college. Thomas had no intention of ruining the opportunity.

Thomas leant as far as he could out of his office window, craning his neck to get a better view of the bell tower. The construction was really coming along. It was twice as high as it had been when he took the project over, and it now looked like the beginnings of a tower rather than the hole in the ground it had been. He thought back to how William Orchard said it was impossible to find the money to fund it properly. Well, Thomas had made the impossible happen, and he was proud of himself for it.

There was a knock on the door, and Thomas ducked back into the room. 'Come in,' he called, sitting back at his desk, where a pile of paperwork awaited him. 'My lord Leonard,' he said, rising again as he saw who had come in.

Leonard Grey, the youngest of the Dorset sons, flapped his hand at Thomas. 'Please sit, Master Wolsey. And Leonard will do, you know.'

'If you will forgive me, my lord, I do not think it will do. I am sure your father would not appreciate such familiarity.'

'As you please, Master Wolsey.' Leonard shrugged. He held up a sheaf of papers. 'I have brought our essays as you asked.'

'Thank you. Put them there, will you?' Thomas indicated a smaller pile of papers at the far edge of his desk. He expected Leonard to leave and was surprised to see the young man hovering. 'Was there something else, my lord?'

'No, not really. I just – my brothers, they have gone out to… ' Leonard shook his head. 'Somewhere.'

Thomas understood. Leonard's brothers, Thomas and Anthony, had gone to their favourite tavern, an excursion not strictly allowed by college rules, but a rule which students often broke. Most of the masters turned a blind eye, understanding that young men needed to enjoy themselves on occasion, but there were others who enforced the rules rigidly, and many a student had been dismissed for drinking and whoring.

'You did not want to go with them to the tavern?' Thomas asked, his mouth curling up in amusement.

'No.' Leonard smiled shyly at Thomas's understanding. 'I find it a little... ' He shrugged, and Thomas mentally filled in the unspoken word: overwhelming. He sensed young Leonard felt himself not quite ready for the strong atmosphere of the tavern nor the pleasures on offer.

'We shall be leaving Oxford at Christmas, did you know?' Leonard asked. 'I do not think we will be coming back.'

'Oh, that is a great shame, my lord.'

'I think so too,' Leonard said, 'but Father wants us to go to court with him next year. He has written to Master Mayhew to suggest we take a master with us when we leave at the end of the Michaelmas term, so we can complete our studies.'

Thomas leant forward. This was news to him. 'Did he ask for anyone in particular?'

'I could not say.' Leonard shook his head. 'It is for Master Mayhew to decide. I do hope he picks you, Master Wolsey. I would like for you to accompany us home.'

'And I would be very pleased to do so,' Thomas said, trying not to let his excitement show. How could he best phrase a request to be chosen without sounding desperate? The chance to leave Oxford and be in the home of a noble for even a short while was too good to be missed.

'I do not think Master Mayhew has decided yet who it will be,' Leonard said. 'I expect he has too much on his mind, what with everything that is being said. I am sorry for him.'

Thomas only belatedly realised what Leonard had said, and the young man's words confused him greatly. 'Why should you feel sorry for him, my lord?'

'Why? Because of – ' Leonard's eyebrows rose. 'Oh, Master Wolsey, have you not heard?'

'No, I have not heard.'

Leonard looked worried. 'Then I should not have spoken. Forgive me, I should go.'

'Stay, my lord.' Thomas got to his feet and held out his hand to prevent Leonard from leaving. 'I would be most grateful if you would tell me what is being said about Master Mayhew.'

Reluctantly, Leonard sat down on the stool by Thomas's desk. He kept his eyes cast downward. 'It is being said that Master Mayhew is corrupt.'

'Corrupt? In what way?'

'You must understand that I do not know all the details, I merely speak of what I have heard, Master Wolsey.'

'Yes, yes.' Thomas waved impatiently. Would Leonard never get to the point? 'Go on.'

'Well, it is being said Master Mayhew has misappropriated college funds. That he has deliberately lied about bequests made to the college, that the amounts were less than they truly were and that he kept the rest. Also, that he has involved other colleges in his corrupt deeds. Something to do with Morton College, I think, and a water mill.'

Thomas was horrified. 'Why have I not heard any of this?'

Leonard looked embarrassed. 'It is known you are a friend of the president, Master Wolsey.'

Thomas felt sick. 'Are there rumours about me?'

'Oh no, hardly anything,' Leonard said, turning his face away.

'Please, my lord, tell me. I need to know.'

Leonard looked towards the window. 'That.'

Thomas followed his gaze. 'The tower? What about the tower?'

'It is wondered how you managed to increase the funding for the tower. Apparently, everyone knew the money had all but dried up.'

Thomas's jaw tightened. Now he understood all the broken-off conversations he had witnessed, the coolness from fellow masters with whom he had believed himself to have been on good terms. And now he understood too the increasingly drawn look on Mayhew's face of late. Why had Mayhew not confided in him?

'Thank you, my lord, for your honesty,' Thomas said, picking up his pen and dipping it into the ink pot to signify the conversation was over. He heard

Leonard close his office door. He dropped his pen onto his papers and stared out the window at the tower.

~

Thomas knocked on the door, not waiting for an invitation to enter. Mayhew was sitting by his small fire, staring into the feeble flames. He started as Thomas said his name, having neither heard his knock nor seen him enter.

'I have just heard.' Thomas closed the door quietly. 'Why did you not tell me?'

Mayhew's mouth puckered, and he turned his face away. 'I was embarrassed, if you must know. To have such things said of me. I cannot bear it.'

Thomas drew up a stool opposite and sat down. 'Where have these rumours come from?'

'Master Swan, I think.'

'Ah, well, he has never been a friend to you.' Thomas looked at the fire, wondering whether he ought to add a log to revive it.

'Thank you,' Mayhew said.

Thomas glanced up. 'For what?'

'For not asking if the rumours were true.'

Thomas gestured as if it had never occurred to him that Mayhew could be corrupt. In truth, Thomas did not care if the rumours were true. As far as he was concerned, if Mayhew had misappropriated funds, that was his business.

'Are you doing anything to deny what is being said?'

'How can I?' Mayhew threw up his hands. 'No one has accused me to my face. It is all whispered. I cannot refute the accusations because none have officially been made.' Mayhew sighed. 'I suspect they will be coming after you too. I am afraid it has got out how you funded the tower.'

Thomas straightened. 'There is nothing there I cannot justify.'

'Ah, perhaps you have not heard all.' Mayhew smirked sourly. 'It is being said you dipped your hand in the college's privy purse.'

'Wh – ?' The indignant exclamation died on Thomas's lips. He stared at Mayhew, his mouth open.

Mayhew nodded in understanding. 'Never mind. I daresay it will blow over. You are young. You have time to live rumours down.'

Thomas was furious. He could not deny he had been clever with the funding for the tower, but he had never stooped to petty theft. The accusation drove all other thoughts from his mind for a time, and the two men sat in silence, staring into the fire. As Thomas's fury cooled, he recollected what he had wanted to speak to Mayhew about.

'Leonard Grey tells me the marquess would like a tutor to go to Bradgate Park with his sons after the Michaelmas term.'

Mayhew drew his cloak tighter about him. 'Yes, he did write to me of that.'

'May I – '

'I am thinking of sending Master Norton.'

Thomas gave a snort of exasperation 'Norton! Forgive me, Master Mayhew, but I do not understand your thinking. I am the obvious choice for such an appointment. The marquess put his sons' care in my hands. Leonard has already told me he would like the master to be me.'

'As much as I respect our young charges, Thomas, it is I who decides where my tutors go,' Mayhew said testily. 'And I say that Master Norton will be a better choice.'

Thomas was struggling to keep his temper under control. 'This presents a great opportunity. I am sure you realise that.'

'There will be other opportunities. The truth is I need you here to support me at this time.'

'I think you overestimate the support I can give you.'

'Not at all. I think you underestimate your influence in the college.'

Thomas gritted his teeth. 'If, as you say, they – whoever they are – will be coming for me too, then my support for you will be tainted. I can do you no good. Indeed, I may even do you harm were I to stay.'

'I need you here,' Mayhew snapped, banging his hand on the pommel of his chair. 'I will brook no argument from you, Thomas. Good day.'

Thomas had come to a decision. It was unfair of Mayhew to hamper his chances with the marquess of Dorset simply because he needed Thomas to support him through a crisis. Thomas was prepared to shout anyone down who said Mayhew was corrupt, but he wasn't prepared to scupper his own chance of getting on in the world. Thomas could not help but think that being appointed by the marquess to continue teaching his sons at the family home would lead to something – he had no idea what, but something. Ever since his ordination, it had been on his mind that his ambitions might take him outside Magdalen's walls. An Oxford life was too confining. It had served its purpose – Thomas had received a superb education; he had become a priest; he had status and some little money. Now it was time to move on. And if he couldn't count on Mayhew's help, he would have to make his own fortune.

He rose early and made his way to the student accommodation within the college. Some of the poorer students slept in dormitories, but those with wealth had private rooms. The Greys had two rooms to themselves, and it was to these Thomas went. It pricked at his pride to have to go begging in this way, but he had no choice. He knocked on the door.

'Master Wolsey,' Anthony, bleary-eyed, said in surprise. 'It is early.'

'Forgive the hour, my lord. I wondered if I could have a word?'

Anthony stepped back and gestured for Thomas to enter.

'What can we do for you, Master Wolsey?' Thomas Grey, the eldest of the brothers, asked as he propped himself up in bed. He looked as perplexed as Anthony and Leonard to see their tutor in their bedchamber at such an early hour.

Thomas cleared his throat. 'I understand your studies are to continue at your home when you return at Christmas and that your father has asked for a master to accompany you. Master Mayhew has suggested Master Norton. But I am here to ask that you recommend me to your father.'

'Indeed,' Anthony said, 'we would rather you came home with us, but Master Mayhew said you could not be spared.'

'If I may say so, my lord,' Thomas said, shifting his feet uneasily, 'that is Master Mayhew's opinion, but it is not mine. I would consider it an honour to be your tutor at Bradgate Park.'

The boys looked at one another. Thomas licked his lips, impatient for their answer.

'I shall write to my father this morning, Master Wolsey, if that is what you wish,' Thomas Grey said.

'I would appreciate that a great deal.' Thomas nodded gratefully.

'But he may not act upon it,' Anthony warned. 'He may think more of Master Mayhew's opinion than our desire.'

'I understand, my lord,' Thomas said. 'I would just like your father to know that I am more than willing to take up the position. Well, I should go. Forgive the intrusion, I beg you.'

Thomas hurried from the room, not stopping until he was back in his own chamber. He fell down on his bed and took a deep breath. He had betrayed Master Mayhew and had uncovered his desperation to three young men who had, he believed, regarded him with some respect. He hoped he had not debased himself for nothing.

'So, you have got your way after all.' Mayhew stepped out from the doorway into the stable yard. 'Going behind my back, getting the sons to do your dirty work with the marquess.'

'It was not a question of it being my way, Master Mayhew,' Thomas said, trying to keep his voice even.

'What was it a question of, then?'

'Of not missing opportunities,' Thomas said, returning to tie his bag to his saddle on the waiting horse.

'And what of me?' Mayhew asked, moving around to stroke the horse's chin.

'You will weather this storm, I know it.'

'Whilst you escape the odium and set yourself up in a noble's household.'

'Have I not earned this chance?' Thomas burst out resentfully.

'And have I not earned some loyalty?' Mayhew shot

back. 'I have looked after you ever since you came to us as a boy. I saw your talent and I nurtured it. I have helped you to rise within the college, and now you abandon me.'

Thomas stepped up to Mayhew and took a deep breath. 'I know I owe you a great deal, Master Mayhew, and I do thank you for it. But I do not owe you my life.'

Mayhew stared back at Thomas, opening and shutting his mouth like a fish. The Grey boys came noisily into the stable yard, saw Mayhew and Thomas, and quietened. Mayhew looked them over, looked back at Thomas, then walked back into the college. *He did not even say goodbye,* Thomas realised.

'Is all well, Master Wolsey?' Leonard asked, looking after the president.

'Yes, all is well, my lord,' Thomas said insistently, wanting to prevent any further enquiries. 'We should be on our way if we are to get to the inn before nightfall. Come.'

The boys mounted their horses, and their small party set out, crossing the bridge over the River Cherwell and heading out of Oxford. As they passed beyond the city gates, Thomas looked over his shoulder at the place that had been his home for the past fourteen years. He felt a small twinge of sadness at leaving it, even if it was only for a short whilst. Then he set his face forward and nudged his horse's sides.

CHAPTER EIGHT

The Grey boys were good company. Thomas and Anthony Grey, free of the confines of the college and the censorious stares of the masters, laughed and joked for much of the journey. Thomas came to realise Leonard was habitually quiet, it was not just his manner in lectures and tutorials. His brothers, though not at all unkind to him, overwhelmed their younger sibling somewhat.

They stopped at an inn overnight, the two older brothers sharing one bed, Thomas and Leonard another. As a master, Thomas had had the luxury of both a room and a bed to himself for years, and Leonard's fidgeting ensured Thomas had a troubled, unrestful sleep that night. He was yawning when they reached Bradgate Park.

'There it is,' Leonard said, pulling his horse along-side Thomas. 'That's home.'

Thomas squinted into the distance, wondering what

on earth Leonard was pointing at. Surely not that small manor house? Where was the home fit for a marquess that Thomas had been anticipating?

'That is Bradgate Park?' Thomas asked, perplexed.

Leonard waved his arm wide. 'The land is Bradgate Park, and Father has decided to call the house that when it is built. At the moment, the whole family is squeezed into Groby Manor.' He pointed at the manor house Thomas had spotted.

'It is not what I was expecting,' Thomas admitted.

'You were expecting something very grand, I think,' Leonard said with a grin. 'Sorry to disappoint you, Master Wolsey.'

'No, not at all,' Thomas hurried to say. 'The manor looks very fine indeed.'

'It is fine, though as I say, with all the family there, it is very cramped. The house Father has planned will be five times the size of Groby when it is finished. You see?' Leonard pointed to the centre of the large field. 'He has already started. He has had men levelling the ground, ready for the house to be plotted. And when spring comes, he will have the foundations laid.'

Thomas made a mental note to ask the marquess if he could take a look at the plans for the intended Bradgate Park. He would be fascinated to see what Lord Grey was hoping to create. And yet, Leonard was correct. There was a small part of him that was indeed disappointed. Back at Magdalen, he had imagined a large house, gardens, stables, perhaps a chase for hunting; instead, he had a crowded manor house. *Oh well,* he told himself, *make the best of it.*

'Race you,' Anthony shouted to Leonard. Leonard dug his heels into his horse's sides and galloped away, trying to catch up with his brothers.

Thomas dusted himself down of the clods of earth Leonard's horse had kicked up at him. Not being the most natural of horsemen and having found riding a horse for days on end very trying indeed, he followed at a much gentler pace, not willing to risk his neck in a gallop.

It had been a wonderful Christmas. Thomas learnt that the land around Groby Manor was prime hunting ground, and there was venison caught in the park by the marquess and his sons, beef, capons, and various other delicacies, so that each night, he would retire to the small room at the top of the house set aside for him with a very full stomach. His teaching duties had been pleasing too, not arduous, enjoyable even. Thomas had been concerned that once home the boys would not attend to their lessons, but the marquess had proved a stickler for discipline, and the lads were more attentive than ever.

It was towards the end of Thomas's appointment when the marquess summoned him to his private chamber. Worried he had done something wrong, Thomas entered apprehensively, ready to apologise profusely if required.

'Come in.' Lord Grey waved him over to the window where he sat in a wooden chair stuffed with cushions. Thomas was offered a small bare wooden stool.

Grey was looking out of the window. Thomas heard the shouts and laughter of the Grey children, all eight of them, as they played in the snow. He had been watching them from his own window minutes earlier, and, though he was not usually fond of winter weather, he had hankered after joining them in a snowball fight.

'The boys have improved greatly under your tute-lage, Master Wolsey,' Lord Grey said, keeping his eye on the children. 'And yet,' he drew his gaze to Thomas, 'despite your talent, I sense teaching is not your true vocation. Am I correct?'

Thomas hesitated. He felt he had to be very careful in his answer. To confirm that his heart was not in teaching may make him appear to have been the wrong choice for this sojourn at Bradgate Park. 'I enjoy teaching when I have intelligent pupils, as your sons are, my lord.'

Lord Grey inclined his head to acknowledge the compliment.

'But yes, you are correct,' Thomas continued. 'I feel my future lies outside the confines of a university.'

'You are a priest, are you not?' Grey asked.

'I am, my lord.'

'But you have no parish?'

'No, my lord,' Thomas said carefully, wondering where the marquess was going with this line of enquiry. 'My duties at Magdalen have occupied all my time. I have not considered pastoral work.'

'But it is something you intend to do if, as you say, you feel you should leave Oxford?'

Thomas opened his mouth but did not speak. He did not know how to answer this question. Yes, he wanted to leave Oxford and move on to better things, but he had not seriously considered becoming a parish priest. Was that really what he wanted? Was that all that was on offer outside of Oxford?

'I expect you're wondering why I'm asking you this,' Grey said. He punched one of the cushions to plump it up. 'The truth is I need a priest, or at least a rector for the time being. You see, I have a parish lying vacant down in Lymington in Somerset.' He looked at Thomas as if he expected him to know where Somerset was. Thomas had only a vague idea. 'It is only a small place – tiny, really. They call it a village, but it is more of a hamlet. But still, the rectory has stood empty for some time now, and I am being badgered to fill it. I have been at a loss as to who to give it to, and then I met you.'

Thomas licked his lips. A position in the marquess's gift was not to be sniffed at. Very well, it was only small – Grey himself did not seem to think it would promise much – but it was something, and Thomas would have the marquess as a patron. He knew other priests who would kill for such an opportunity. Well, maybe not *kill*…

'And you would recommend me for the post?' Thomas asked.

'Recommend?' Grey laughed loudly. 'No, by God, I don't need to recommend anyone. If I say you shall have it, Master Wolsey, you shall have it.'

Thomas smiled, embarrassed by his naivety. 'It does sound like just the living I am looking for, my lord. It is very good of you to think of me.'

'Not at all. The truth is you will be doing me a favour, Master Wolsey. I would like the rectory filled as soon as possible, if only to get the damned villagers off my back. Good, that's decided, then. I shall have my secretary make the arrangements. He will write to you when all is ready. You will be returning to Magdalen, I think?'

'I will, my lord,' Thomas said, wondering what he would be returning to. Would he be welcomed back, his name having been cleared of all suspicion of wrongdoing, or would he be viewed askance, the subject of whispered conversations and suspicion? What did it matter? He would not be there long. Thank God he had followed his instinct, disregarded Mayhew and asked for Lord Grey to take him on as temporary private tutor. If he had not, he shuddered to think where his career would be heading.

'I shall tell him to write to you there. Well, till then, Master Wolsey.'

Thomas realised he was dismissed and rose. He

bowed his head. 'I thank you most respectfully, my lord, for this opportunity you have given me and for the great kindness you have shown me over this Christmas season.'

Thomas left the room with a spring in his step. Things were certainly looking up for him.

Thomas set his bag down on his bed, its thump echoing the feeling in his stomach. He was back at Magdalen, and the past month with the Greys already seemed a very distant memory. He had enjoyed being part of a nobleman's household. It had been a freedom he had never known. Ever since he had arrived at Magdalen College all those years ago, his life had been bound by rules. There had been rules about what he could eat and drink, when he could talk and when be silent, when he could leave the college grounds and by what hour he must return.

There had been expectations of him at Bradgate Park too, of course. He was there to work, after all, but there had been plenty of leisure time. He had even dared to ask the marquess about his building plans for the park and had spent several happy hours examining the architect's drawings and the small-scale model of the finished house.

'So, you are back.'

Thomas turned to see Richard Mayhew standing in his doorway. Mayhew looked tired. His cheeks had hollowed, and there were dark circles beneath his eyes. He stared around the small room with a lacklustre curiosity.

'Good afternoon, Master Mayhew,' Thomas said. There was a long pause. 'How are you?'

Mayhew raised his eyebrows as if surprised by the enquiry. 'I am… as you see me.' He shrugged.

'How has it been?'

'Well… ' Mayhew laughed bitterly. 'It has not been easy, Thomas. But I suppose you knew that it would be so.'

'Master – ' Thomas protested wearily.

Mayhew continued as if Thomas had not spoken. 'And I understand this is a fleeting visit. You will not be with us long.'

How the devil had Mayhew found out about his new job? 'That is so.' Thomas nodded. 'The marquess has appointed me to a living in Somerset.'

'You must have impressed him over Christmas.'

'I believe I did,' Thomas replied, refusing to be cowed by Mayhew's mockery.

'So, when will you be leaving us?'

'Soon, I hope,' Thomas said, intending to wound a little. 'The marquess is eager for the living to be filled quickly.'

'Fortunate for you, then. You escape the opprobrium.'

Thomas turned back to his bag and began unpacking. 'I have done nothing wrong in my management of the college's finances, and my actions will bear any scrutiny. I am not escaping anything; I am trying to advance my career.'

'Aye, and the rest of us can go to hell,' Mayhew said with sudden vehemence.

'Oh, you exaggerate your situation,' Thomas cried. 'This whole matter of your maladministration will blow over, I am certain of it, and the college will realise how fortunate they have been to have you.'

Mayhew shook his head. 'I wish I had your faith in our fellow man, Thomas. But I wish you good fortune in your new position. I hope it delivers all you desire.' He looked Thomas up and down with loathing in his eyes. 'And I am sure it will, if you have your way.'

Mayhew left, leaving the door open, and Thomas heard him shuffling away along the corridor. He pulled out his clean shirts, laundered for him at Bradgate, his hose and his Bible, meaning to put them where they belonged, but in his anger, he threw them at the wall instead. Damn Mayhew and his spite. He had not abandoned Mayhew to his fate, whatever the president thought and tried to pretend.

Thomas strode to the wall and snatched his shirts up from the floor. And so what if it was the end of Mayhew's career? Thomas shook the shirts out and folded them neatly. Mayhew was an old man with a long and distinguished career behind him. If he had come to a rocky path, it was his misfortune, nothing to do with Thomas.

Thomas looked out of his window and saw Mayhew crossing the courtyard. Masters Norton and Swan were coming from the opposite direction, deep in conversation. When they saw Mayhew, they abruptly altered their course, giving him a wide berth.

'Bastards,' Thomas muttered. Despite his anger at Mayhew, he felt a twinge of sympathy for the old man. He thought for a moment, then knelt by his bed and pressed his palms together. He prayed for Mayhew, that his problems would soon be over and that their friendship could be restored.

But his most fervent plea to God was that his deliverance from Magdalen College would come sooner rather than later.

CHAPTER NINE

The letter from the marquess's secretary had arrived. Thomas was to take up the position of vicar of St Mary's church on the fourteenth of February.

The secretary was very thorough in his instructions. He estimated it would take Thomas about a week to journey from Oxford to Lymington if he travelled at a reasonable rate. There were several inns along his suggested route that would provide accommodation, and he enclosed a list for perusal. There was a lodging attached to the church where Thomas would reside – he would need to bring his own bed linen – and a servant, should Thomas wish to employ one, could undoubtedly be found in the village. Thomas was to write to the secretary to confirm his arrival. Any complaints or otherwise should also be directed to him, though, the secretary had been quick to add, he did not expect Thomas would have any complaints to make.

So, it was on the evening of the sixth of February

that Thomas made his goodbyes to his friends and colleagues at Magdalen College. He went to bed before everyone else and rose early the next morning to begin his journey into Somerset.

~

Thomas could have arrived at Lymington the previous evening, but he hadn't wanted his first sight of St Mary's to be in the semi-darkness, its grey stone facade steeped in shadow. He had waited until the following morning to cover the distance from the last inn on the secretary's list to Lymington to see his new church in the full glory of the morning sun.

Except it did not have a glory. St Mary's was a truly unexceptional church. It had been built in the thirteenth century, and for a church that was almost two hundred years old, was in good repair. But to Thomas's critical eye, it was out of proportion. The tower to the west was too large, giving the rest of the building a squat appearance. It was prettily situated, though, surrounded by cedars that must have been planted as long ago as when the Romans occupied Britain. Thomas suppressed a sigh. He should have known from the way the marquess had spoken of the church that it would be nothing much. *But it is all mine,* Thomas reminded himself and started towards the front porch.

He drew the large iron key sent to him by the secretary out of his bag and fitted it into the church door keyhole. There was a loud clunk, and he heard the bolt turn.

The interior was as unremarkable as the outside. There was a dark timber roof, pews made of the same dark wood and burnished by the backsides of villagers, and a stone font with an ornate wooden lid just inside the door. The stone walls were painted with scenes from the Bible – the expulsion of Adam and Eve from Eden, the flood and the ark, the fiery pit of hell and the shining gates of heaven. Thomas walked up the short aisle towards the altar and knelt before the large cross framed by the stained-glass window to pray. He heard footsteps on the tiles behind him and turned to look over his shoulder.

A man with shaggy blond hair holding a rake was staring at him. 'Who are you?' he asked, his West Country accent rich and smooth.

'Thomas Wolsey,' Thomas replied, getting to his feet. 'Your new rector.'

The man's mouth made an *O*, and he tugged his jerkin straight. 'Is that right? I'm Samuel Bell, sexton.' He brandished the rake. 'Been clearing the long grass away from the graves at the back.'

'I am pleased to meet you,' Thomas said.

''Tis good to have a priest here again,' Bell said. 'I don't know how we've managed without one for so long.'

Thomas nodded politely. 'I believe there is a lodging for me nearby.'

'Aye, just out that door there.' Bell pointed through

an archway to a small door in the corner of the church. 'Past the yew tree. I cannot say what state you'll find it in, though. I daresay it will need to be cleaned.'

'Shall I be able to find someone in the village to do for me? I understand Lymington is close by.'

'Aye, 'tis close.' Bell nodded. 'I can arrange a woman to look after you, if you like. The last rector had me do that.'

'That is very kind of you. Yes, as soon as you can.'

Bell pointed at the bag Thomas had deposited on one of the pews. 'Do you want me to take that for you? I can put it in your lodging.'

'Thank you. I have bed linen in there; I was told I would need it.'

Bell picked up Thomas's bag and lifted it onto his shoulder, his fingers stroking the leather in admiration.

'I think I will take a walk into the village,' Thomas said. 'I could do with something to eat and drink.'

'Well, there's only one tavern. You'll find it easy enough, and you'll have a warm welcome, I warrant.' Bell grinned a wide gummy grin. 'Everyone will be very glad to see you, Master Wolsey.'

The village of Lymington was indeed close by – not far beyond the churchyard, in fact. Thomas saw at once what the marquess had meant by it being more of a hamlet than a village. From his entrance at one end of the main street, he could see its exit at the far end. In

Oxford and other large towns, streets were narrow and crowded, the houses having to stretch upwards to find the sunlight. Here, the houses seemed to sprawl. In the spaces between the houses, wheat, barley and grass grew. Thomas concluded it was the unambitious who lived in Lymington, those who found a town such as Ilchester just a few miles away unappealing, too bustling, too noisy. Lymington, he suspected, was a nothing place on the Somerset map.

He was stared at as he walked along the street, and he found the observations not unpleasing. He was going to be the most important person in this village. In Oxford, he had been one master amongst many; here in Lymington, he was *the* priest, the one person every villager needed in their lives. He would have respect, and he would have status.

Thomas soon found the tavern Bell had spoken of. When he produced his purse to pay for his food, he was told by the tapster to put his purse away, his money was no good there. Then the tapster's wife bustled over, kissed his hand and thanked God for his arrival.

Lymington may not be much to look at, he thought as the villagers stepped forward to meet him, *but this will be a stepping stone to greater things. I will make sure of it.*

CHAPTER TEN

Thomas had too little to do, that was the trouble. Aside from the routine duties of a parish priest – baptisms, weddings, funerals – there was the preaching and performing of services, but not a great deal else. There were few people in Lymington to talk to who were on the same intellectual level as Thomas or as well educated, and he found he missed intelligent conversation more than anything.

Starved of society – Samuel Bell, who was often around the church, was a poor companion – Thomas would often walk into the village just to find someone to talk to, even if the conversation was only about the price of wheat or wool. He was striding along the path behind the church when he heard a noise from the normally quiet village. He quickened his pace, intrigued by the idea that something was actually happening.

It was market day, but many of the stalls were unattended, their owners having formed a ragged circle in the middle of the street. Thomas pushed his way through.

Thomas had come to know every inhabitant of Lymington, it being such a small place, and he recognised at once the object of everyone's attention. Peter Dimmock was a young boy whom Thomas had had to clip around the ear a few times for talking during services. He had a saucy way about him that Thomas secretly found quite amusing. But when he saw who was also in the centre of the circle, he suspected that this time, Peter had gone too far.

Sir Amyas Paulet was Lymington's local gentleman, the only titled personage in the vicinity, and he took his honour very seriously. When Sir Amyas came to St Mary's to worship, he would wait until all the villagers had trooped in just so he could make an entrance, his nose in the air, and stride past to take his privileged seat at the front as they stood to attention in the pews. He had even presumed to tell Thomas what to preach about; sometimes Thomas had agreed with the subject matter and framed his sermon to suit, but other times he had not. On those occasions when Thomas had delivered the sermon *he* wanted to give, he had seen Sir Amyas's mouth pucker and the knight snort in a show of dissatisfaction.

Sir Amyas had a firm hold of Peter. Peter was doing his best to get away. The noise that had attracted Thomas was the villagers shouting at Sir Amyas to let the boy go. Thomas knew Sir Amyas was unpopular in the village, and he had a feeling the matter could turn very ugly if he did not intervene, especially with two of the knight's burly servants standing close by.

'Sir Amyas,' he called loudly, wanting to be heard over the crowd's shouts. The cries and chatter quietened immediately. 'Let the boy go.'

The knight turned his fiercest stare on Thomas. 'You would do well to mind your own business, Master Wolsey.'

'This is my business. Young Peter there is my parishioner.' Thomas took a step nearer. 'How has the boy offended?'

'He has insulted me.' Sir Amyas took an even tighter grip on the struggling boy.

'Did he, indeed? What did he say?'

Sir Amyas tutted. 'I will not repeat his insult in this company.'

This remark roused the crowd to find its voice again, and Thomas held out his hands in an attempt at pacification. 'Well, whatever Peter said, Sir Amyas, I am sure he is very sorry for it and will apologise.'

'I won't,' Peter declared and kicked at Sir Amyas, catching the knight about his ankles and earning himself a severe blow to the head. The crowd surged forward, the only things holding them back their inbred subservience and the reverence they held for a man of the cloth.

'Peter!' Thomas warned, glaring at the boy. 'Sir Amyas, I think this spectacle has gone far enough. I insist you release him.' He hadn't meant to, but Thomas had let menace creep into his voice. His words had been a challenge, not a plea.

Sir Amyas's mouth twisted, and his eyes blazed. 'Get back to your church, priest,' he snarled, 'and do not try to command your betters.'

If he had hoped to make Thomas quail, he was to be disappointed. Sir Amyas's words had jabbed at Thomas's mounting irritation and turned it into anger. Thomas grabbed Peter, dragging him from the knight's grasp. Peter fell down, grazing his knees, and Thomas pulled him to his feet.

Sir Amyas was astonished. 'How dare you!' He reached for the boy. Peter jerked away and ran to his mother, who quickly bundled him up in her skirts and whisked him away out of danger. 'You come back here, boy!' Sir Amyas yelled after the retreating pair.

'Do not waste your breath, Sir Amyas,' Thomas said, straightening his surplice and trying to calm his temper. He was very aware of the watching villagers and had no desire to be their entertainment. 'Maybe now everyone can get on with their business.' He clapped his hands and made to shoo the crowd away.

But Sir Amyas was not ready to let the matter drop. He thrust his face at Thomas. 'How dare you interfere, and how dare you talk to me this way in front of all these peasants?'

'How dare you speak to *me* like this?' Thomas countered. 'I am a man of the church, and you will show me respect, Sir Amyas.'

'Show respect!' Sir Amyas spat, daubing Thomas's chin with spittle. 'To a butcher's son?'

Thomas had no idea how Sir Amyas had discovered his antecedence. All he knew was that the knight's words made his blood surge through his veins. Without thinking, Thomas grabbed Sir Amyas's cloak, ready to kick him in the stomach or groin, whichever his knee found first.

But the look of surprise and incredulity on the knight's face made Thomas hesitate, that and the two burly servants stepping forward, ready to lay hold of him. He calmed down at once, his anger giving way to reason. Thomas might be a churchman, but Sir Amyas was a knight of the realm. He no doubt had powerful friends, and perhaps one of them was Thomas's noble patron, the marquess. Whatever he thought of the man, it would not be wise to make an enemy of Sir Amyas. Thomas unclenched the hand that held the knight's cloak and mumbled an apology.

'An apology will make me neither forget nor forgive your insolence, butcher's son,' Sir Amyas assured him fiercely. He clicked his fingers at his two servants. 'Take hold of this impudent fellow and put him in the stocks.'

The two men looked at Thomas, their gaze raking up and down his surplice, lingering on his cross. They looked at each other, then at their master.

'What are you waiting for?' Sir Amyas demanded.

The elder of the two spoke. 'Master Wolsey is a priest, my lord.'

'I know what he is, damn you,' Sir Amyas said

through gritted teeth. 'Take hold of him this minute or I will have you put in the stocks as well.'

The two men hesitated for the smallest of moments, then started towards Thomas. Thomas's heart banged in his chest. Was he actually going to be manhandled and bundled into the village stocks, a spectacle for all to see?

But he was saved from that particular humiliation. A voice from the crowd called out, 'You touch our priest and there will be hell to pay, knight or no knight.'

The cry was taken up by the rest of the crowd, some less enthusiastic than others, but it was clear Thomas had the villagers on his side.

Sir Amyas turned his glare on as many individuals as he could, then clicked his fingers at his men again, pointing at Thomas for them to carry on. But they appeared to be unwilling to do his bidding and shuffled their feet. Realising that he himself could not drag Thomas to the stocks, Sir Amyas pushed his way through the crowd and quickly made his way out of the village.

Thomas felt his breath coming fast and shallow. What a fool he had been to oppose Sir Amyas so publicly. Had he not interfered, Peter would have got a thrashing, which Thomas had no doubt he deserved, and the whole affair would have soon been over.

His desire for company quite reversed, Thomas pressed his hand to the cross dangling against his stomach, nodded a tight thank you to his supporters and hurried back to his church, wondering how best to make a full apology to the pompous knight he had so offended.

~

'So, how are you finding Lymington?'

Thomas smiled at the questioner. He was standing in the hall of Groby Manor, his backside warmed by the huge fire that blazed in the hearth, a cup of good Burgundy wine in his hand and his stomach full of venison and marchpane. When the invitation from the marquess had arrived for him to spend Christmas with the Grey family, Thomas had kissed the red wax seal on the letter and thanked God for his deliverance.

'Very quiet, my lord,' he replied to Leonard Grey with a smile, sensible he should not appear in any way ungrateful or disappointed with the marquess's appointment.

'Really?' Leonard narrowed his eyes and grinned. 'I heard differently.'

Thomas's smile faltered. 'Heard what, my lord?'

'Oh, something about a quarrel with Sir Amyas Paulet.'

Thomas's breath caught in his throat. Damnation, the Greys had heard about that bloody mess. He had hoped the incident would not get beyond Lymington, but he realised now that had been foolish. He had intended to apologise to Sir Amyas at the next church service, but Sir Amyas had not come. He had not come to the next service, nor the next, and soon Thomas heard that Sir Amyas was worshipping at a church in Ilchester, loudly refusing to have anything to do with the insolent priest of St Mary's. And so the opportunity for an apology passed, and the affair became something Thomas thought of only with cringing regret, when he thought of it at all.

'Oh, that.' Thomas half laughed, hoping to play the matter down. 'A lot of fuss over nothing.'

'Sir Amyas did not seem to think so,' an older, deeper voice said.

Thomas winced and looked up to see the marquess drawing near. 'Your Grace,' he greeted him.

'Sir Amyas wrote to me about what happened,' Grey said, stepping into the spot Thomas had obligingly vacated. 'He wrote to me. You did not.'

Thomas swallowed, feeling awkward. 'I did not think it worthy of your attention, Your Grace. I beg your pardon if I did wrong by not notifying you.'

'It would have been wise to do so, Master Wolsey, if only that it would have allowed me to reply appropriately. I know Sir Amyas. I know him to be a pompous man, but he is a knight of the realm, and he should have been shown due respect.'

Thomas opened his mouth to speak, but the marquess held up his hand.

'Yes, I know you should have been shown due respect as a man of the cloth, and Sir Amyas was very wrong to order you stocked. I am glad his servants saw the folly of such an act and declined to obey, though he told me they were punished for their disobedience. Well, such is the man.'

'I know I should not have opposed him, Your Grace,' Thomas hastened to say. 'I was going to apologise to him in person, but the opportunity never arose. Perhaps I should have tried harder.'

'Yes, you should, but it is done now.' The marquess belched quietly, and his face creased in pain. Leonard touched his arm in enquiry as his father pressed his hand to his chest. The marquess shook his head. 'Cursed heartburn.' He paused a moment, then looked back at Thomas. 'Just remember my words for the future, Master Wolsey.'

'I will, Your Grace,' Thomas assured him, bowing his head as the marquess walked away. 'I am sorry to have offended your father,' Thomas said to Leonard.

'Oh, do not fret so, Master Wolsey. My father paid Sir Amyas lip service only. He has no fondness for him. You are here, are you not? You would not have been invited had you truly offended my father. Be of good cheer. I feel for you having to deal with such a man as Paulet. It must have been a humiliating situation to find yourself in, the threat of the stocks.'

'It was, my lord,' Thomas assured him.

'And bearing that in mind,' Leonard said, 'you should go and talk to people.' He gestured at the guests scattered around the room. 'There are other churchmen here, and if I have learnt anything, it is the value of influential acquaintances.'

He smiled at Thomas and walked away. Leonard had

become quite the young lord in the past year, in manner and outlook as well as in name. And, Thomas acknowledged, he was right. To be able to call men of influence friends had served Thomas well, and such was the way of the whole world. He looked around the room and spotted an old man in a furred cloak at the end of the long table, eyeing the fire jealously. Thomas headed for him and introduced himself.

'Henry Deane,' the old man said in reply, holding out his hand.

Thomas took it. 'You are the bishop of Salisbury, I think.'

'You know of me?' Deane asked, turning his rheumy eyes on Thomas in surprise and not a little pleasure.

'Of course. It is a very great honour to meet you, Your Grace.'

'One of the marquess's finds, are you?'

Thomas was not sure he liked being described as a find. 'The marquess was kind enough to offer me a position earlier this year. I am at St Mary's in Lymington. In Somerset,' he added at Deane's perplexed expression.

'Ah, Somerset. I have never been there. Nice place, is it?'

'Very charming,' Thomas said, 'if a little dull.'

'Well, we all have to start somewhere, you know.'

'I understand that, Your Grace. Of course, I am very grateful to Lord Grey for all he has done for me.'

Deane's mouth curled up on one side, almost making him look as if he was winking. 'But you would like to move on, eh?'

Dear God, was he so transparent? 'One day. If I could be of more use elsewhere.' Thomas swallowed and ploughed on. 'You see, there is so very little for me to do there. I like activity. I like to be useful.'

'And the spiritual needs of villagers does nothing for your soul?' Deane smiled knowingly. 'I understand, Master Wolsey, I do. But you know, there is no need for you to tend to your flock all by yourself. In fact, there is no real need for you to do any of the work, not if you can afford not to.'

Thomas leant closer, intrigued. 'Forgive me, Your Grace, but what do you mean?'

'Why, you can hire a curate to do everything for you. Oh, 'tis common practice,' Deane said, waving his hand at Thomas's astonished face. 'You pay them – I think the going rate is about five pounds per annum – they are grateful for the position, and you are free to come and go as you please.'

'And the church allows this?'

'It does. In truth, the church cares not who is preaching and performing its ceremonies as long as someone is. Well, that's my advice, Master Wolsey. Find yourself a poor curate. Now, you must excuse me. I am frozen to the bone.' Deane hurried over to the fire before Thomas could say another word.

Another Christmas spent with the Greys was over, and Thomas returned with regret to Lymington. He had done his best to introduce himself to as many of the marquess's guests as possible, hoping to make a favourable impression, then he had left, thanking Lord Grey for his continued good graces. Their parting had worried Thomas a little, for the marquess seemed not entirely well. The heartburn Thomas had witnessed continued to plague the marquess over the Christmas season; Leonard told Thomas he had stopped riding out to hunt and spent much of his time in his chamber, wrapped up in a blanket by the fire. Leonard tried to make light of it, but Thomas could not help but think the marquess was suffering from more than a common winter chill.

On the journey back to Lymington in a coach Leonard had arranged for him, Thomas worried what would happen to him if the marquess were to die. Would his position as rector of St Mary's be safe? He doubted the younger Thomas Grey, who would inherit the Dorset title, would throw him out of the living, but would he have any concern for Master Wolsey's future? Thomas thought it unlikely. The young man would be too busy making a name for himself at court. Thomas's biggest fear was that he would simply be left at St Mary's, a youngish priest growing old in the village that the rest of the world had forgot.

Stiff from the cold, Thomas climbed down from the coach and hurried to his lodging at the rear of St Mary's. His housekeeper had not had notice of his coming, and so he had to make his own fire. It took him some time to produce a flame, his hands so cold they trembled as they struck the flint against the tinder. The only food was that he had brought with him, so his supper was a cold pork pie and a loaf of bread without any butter. It was a meagre meal compared to the abundance of the Grey table so recently enjoyed, but it would have to do. He would walk into the village early in the morning and let the villagers know he had returned.

Thomas pulled his chair closer to the fire, hoping the logs were dry and that it would soon be blazing. He stared into the flickering flames, thinking he would have to do something about his career. He could not bear to be in this backwater for another year. He rose and dragged over a small table to his chair, then picked up the ink pot and quill pen from his desk by the window. He lit a rushlight and took a few sheets of paper from the shelf where he kept his books.

Resuming his seat, he dipped his pen into the ink pot and began to write. He wrote first to Hugh Sedley, still in Oxford and doing well as a schoolmaster, telling him of his recent holiday in Leicestershire and casually mentioning he had been there at the invitation of the marquess of Dorset. Hugh had a great many acquaintances in Oxford and was a great gossip; Thomas knew it would get around that Master Wolsey, former senior bursar of Magdalen, enjoyed the favour of one of England's greatest peers. Such information could only help his reputation, he reasoned.

That letter written, Thomas drew another sheet of paper towards him and wrote 'His Grace, the Bishop of Salisbury' at the top. Thomas thought it a good idea to write to Henry Deane merely to say how happy he had been to make the bishop's acquaintance. That and nothing more. Thomas considered it best to remind the bishop he existed rather than reiterate his ambition to move up in the church. He did not want to seem too forward.

Thomas looked up, pausing a moment to think, and saw four letters propped up on the mantel. Pushing the table away, he took them down. He recognised the spiky handwriting of Hugh on the topmost letter; the second was from his mother; the third was from a new acquaintance, a merchant in Ilchester; and the fourth was in a hand he did not know. He sat back down and opened the fourth letter first.

It was from an acquaintance of Hugh's, and from the language the writer used, Thomas knew it was from an individual who wanted something from him, for he had written similar letters himself. He read on. The writer had a nephew who had been ordained the year before but had yet to establish himself in a living. With his finances growing desperate, the nephew wondered if Thomas could put in a good word for him in his church circles in the hope of finding a parish to serve in. Even the smallest of livings would be acceptable, the writer assured Thomas.

Thomas laughed out loud. Had this letter arrived before he left for Bradgate Park, he would have written back, assuring the writer that he would mention the nephew to his superiors in the church, and that would have been the end of it. But the letter had arrived most propitiously. Since his conversation with Henry Deane, Thomas had decided he would look for a curate to take his place at St Mary's, whatever the cost. And now he did not even have to search for such a man; here was one very conveniently available. Fortune was certainly smiling on him.

He drew the last sheet of paper towards him and started to pen a reply to the hopeful writer. Yes, of course, he was eager to help a fellow churchman when and wherever he could. In fact, as luck would have it, he was in need of a curate at his church in Lymington. If the nephew was certain that a pittance for a salary was acceptable, then Thomas would be pleased to welcome him to take up the post as soon as convenient.

Thomas put his pen and ink pot to one side, wiped his inky fingers on a cloth and tucked into his pork pie and bread supper with rather more pleasure than he had anticipated.

Thomas pressed his nose to his parlour window. There was a young man walking up the path to his lodging. *He looks like a boy*, Thomas thought, taking in his rosy cheeks and energetic gait, his eyes that roamed every-where. So, this was George Golding, the good fortune that was going to relieve Thomas of so much tiresome duty in Lymington.

George knocked. 'Master Wolsey?' he asked

brightly as Thomas answered the door. 'Good day. I am
– '

'George Golding,' Thomas finished for him, extending his hand. 'Welcome. Come in.'

Thomas led him through to the parlour and bade him sit, pouring him out a cup of ale. The young man would be thirsty after his journey. After a few pleasantries, Thomas got down to business.

'You understand what you are here to do?'

George swallowed a mouthful of ale and nodded. 'Yes, I am to perform the services.'

'Not the Sunday ones. Those I shall do – for the time being, at least. You shall perform the weekday services.'

'I understand.'

Do you really? Thomas wondered. Young George Golding was to become the resident priest of St Mary's in all but name, and for that privilege, Thomas was going to pay him a fraction of the salary he himself received from the church. Part of him cringed at the unfairness of the arrangement, but then he looked at George's eager face; the young man seemed happy enough. Perhaps George regarded this chaplaincy as the first step in his career. Maybe he aspired to be the priest of a big church in a large town one day and he would give the same opportunity to another young man. In any case, Thomas was resolved not to let pity change his mind. He was already looking forward to being free of Lymington.

'I do not know if your uncle told you all. It is likely

I will not be around much of the time. There will come a time when you will be here on your own.'

'My uncle did explain, and I understand, of course,' George assured him, eyeing the bread and cheese on the table. 'You must be very busy with the marquess of Dorset as your patron. I expect he has you travelling here and there all the time.'

Thomas pushed the food towards him. How he would have loved to lie and say it was true, that he was as good as the marquess's personal priest. 'Not quite all the time,' he said instead.

The church bells were ringing, the wedding was over. Thomas looked up from his letter as the wedding party exited the church, George smiling on all the guests.

George had slipped into his duties at St Mary with impressive ease. Thomas even had reason to believe that the Lymington villagers preferred George to him. Bell let it slip one day after George had stood in for Thomas for a Sunday service that the villagers, despite liking having such an educated man as their spiritual shepherd, had always found Thomas rather aloof whereas George was all warmth. Thomas did not mind; in fact, he felt their partiality for George was all to the good.

He let his gaze drop back down to the letter he had been reading. It was a reply to one he had written to the marquess four days earlier. Along with the usual assurances of his enduring gratitude, Thomas had taken the liberty to enquire after his patron's health. He had sent the letter and promptly forgotten about it, his attention being taken up with affairs at Magdalen he was being consulted on. As Thomas had predicted, Richard Mayhew had weathered the storm of his alleged corruption and renewed his friendship with Thomas, all enmity seemingly forgotten. Thomas, for his part, had been pleased to pretend that nothing amiss had gone on between them.

The reply he had received from Bradgate that morning had been a surprise, not least because it came not from the marquess's secretary, but from Leonard Grey.

Master Wolsey, Leonard wrote, *I thought I would write and tell you of the news myself rather than leave it to my father's secretary. It is with a heavy heart that I must tell you my father died only hours before your letter reached us. You know he was feeling unwell over Christmas, so mayhap this news will come as no surprise, though I know you will feel the loss of so great a man as much as we do ourselves. My best regards, Leonard Grey*

Leonard gives me too much credit, Thomas thought, refolding the letter and running his fingers over the edges. He didn't feel sorrowful; he was thinking, thinking hard about what the death of the marquess meant for him. Would it hamper his chances of leaving Lymington, or was it an opportunity to do so? The obligation to remain was gone, he reasoned. To seek a new position now would not be a sign of ingratitude to the late Thomas Grey.

He glanced down at Leonard's letter and realised he should write a reply. He pulled a sheet of paper towards him and dipped his quill in the pot. He wrote the usual words of condolence – as a priest, they came easily – and some of them were genuine, for he knew how much Leonard had loved his father. He finished the letter and sealed it. As the red wax dripped onto the paper Thomas was already thinking of what he would do next. He took off his signet ring and pressed it into the hot red wax, then set the letter to one side. He took another sheet of paper, dipped his quill in the ink pot once again and began to write.

My most dear Bishop Deane.

CHAPTER ELEVEN

1501

Thomas's shoulder bumped against the side of the coach as its front wheel sunk into a pothole and lurched to the left. His oomph of pain made the other passengers glance in his direction. He smiled at them as he rubbed the flesh around his shoulder bone, glad this journey was almost over.

Thomas and George had been at dinner when a reply from Henry Deane arrived at St Mary's. Bell had brought the letter in, glancing wistfully at the food, and handed it to Thomas. Normally, Thomas would have left it till later, but when he saw the seal, he had snatched it from Bell's hand.

'Good news, is it?' George had asked.

Thomas laughed loudly. 'Very good news, my dear George. This' – he brandished the letter – 'is from the archbishop of Canterbury.'

George's eyes widened in awe. 'You know the archbishop?'

'I met him at Lord Grey's when he was bishop of Salisbury. His appointment to Canterbury is recent. I had no idea when I wrote to him that he had been promoted.'

'You have friends in high places, Master Wolsey.' George helped himself to another almond cake.

''Tis the only way to get on in this world, George, remember that.'

'I will, Master Wolsey. And are you getting on?'

'The archbishop has been kind enough to appoint me his chaplain.'

'You're leaving Lymington?' George cried.

'I will be,' Thomas confirmed happily. 'And you will have this place all to yourself.'

Thomas saw the nervous swallow, and yet there had been a flicker of excitement in George's eyes. *So, he is ambitious after all,* Thomas thought, pleased for the young man.

And so, he had given his last sermon in St Mary's, said goodbye to George, promising he would be keeping an eye on him, however distant, and mounted the coach that would take him to his new post in the famous city of Canterbury.

Thomas looked out of his window as the yellow stone tower of Canterbury Cathedral came into view. The sheer perfection of the edifice, with its highly deco-rated stone and spires reaching almost to heaven, made his breath catch in his throat.

'Your first time, is it?'

Thomas turned his head to look back into the coach.

An old man sitting opposite, his grey beard buried beneath a woollen cloak held tight across his chest with gnarled fingers, was looking at him with milky blue eyes.

'Yes,' Thomas said. 'First time.'

''Tis quite a sight, is it not?' the old man asked proudly.

'It is very beautiful. I had not thought I would see anything as lovely as Oxford, but this…' He pointed out the window.

'Scholar, are you? Coming from Oxford?'

'I was.' Thomas let his own cloak fall away to reveal his surplice and cross beneath. 'Priest now.'

The man smiled. 'There are plenty of priests in Canterbury. You are visiting or coming to stay?'

'To stay,' Thomas said, realising their conversation had attracted the attention of all the passengers and relishing the opportunity to tell more of himself. 'I am appointed to be the archbishop's new chaplain.'

The looks of admiration from his fellow travellers was immensely satisfying, but there was no time to elaborate. The coach passed beneath the city gates, and the passengers began to check their belongings, ready to climb down from the coach.

Thomas waited for his old interlocutor to leave the coach first, then stepped down onto ground freshly sown with horse manure. He checked his shoes to see if he had managed to avoid stepping in the dung. Confident he had, he held out his arms to take his small chest that had been stacked behind the coach on a shelf. He tucked it under his arm and took a few steps towards what looked like the main thoroughfare.

In the letter confirming his appointment, Thomas had been told to present himself at the Old Palace upon his arrival in Canterbury. He knew the building was attached to the cathedral, so he headed for the great church, certain he would find the way easily enough. With each step the chest under his arm felt ten times heavier. Just as he reached the large wooden gate of the walls that bounded the cathedral, the chest slipped and banged on the ground.

'What's that noise?' a voice, male yet quite high, called from inside the gate. A moment later, a head appeared in the aperture.

'I dropped my trunk,' Thomas said, bending to retrieve it.

'Haven't damaged the gate, have you?' The man peered down to examine it.

'I don't think so.' Thomas hefted the trunk back under his arm. He sighed. 'Are you the porter?'

'Aye, that's right.' the man said, straightening and looking Thomas up and down. 'Can I help you?'

'My name is Thomas Wolsey.' Thomas waited, then when no response came, continued, 'The new chaplain.'

'Oh, I see.' The porter waved him through.

'You did know I was coming?'

'Aye, I was told. I didn't know there was going to be two of you, though.' He banged the door shut.

'Forgive me, two of us?' Thomas asked.

'Aye. I took the other one through an hour or so ago. You had best let me take that.' He pointed at the trunk.

Thomas passed it to him, for the moment speechless. He had not been told that he would be sharing the chaplaincy with another. What else had he not been told?

The porter chuckled as he led Thomas along the path. 'Thought you were the only one, did you? Never you mind. Canterbury is a big city, and the archbishop, well, he does his best, but he's old and can only do so much. There will be plenty of work for both of you.'

The Old Palace was one of the grandest buildings Thomas had ever seen. It was old, built centuries before and made of flint and ashlar. It was big, three storeys high, and sprawled over a large area. His nose told him they were passing the stable yard; the earthy smell of hot flesh and manure hung in the air, and his eyes wandered over the low building. There had to be room for at least twenty horses. Even Groby Manor had not had so many.

The porter led him through a side door in the Old Palace. 'You are to go through there,' he said, pointing to the end of the hallway. 'That will take you into the hall. A secretary will take care of you. I will take this up to your room.'

'Thank you,' Thomas said, but the porter was already climbing the stairs. Thomas walked along the passageway and came out into the hall as the porter said he would. A man was sitting at a table at one side of the hall, and he looked up as Thomas entered. Thomas introduced himself and said he had an appointment with the archbishop.

'Ah yes, Master Wolsey.' The secretary stood. 'If you will follow me.'

Thomas followed the secretary to a door just outside the hall.

'Your Grace, Master Wolsey is here.'

Thomas recognised Henry Deane at once. The old man was sitting in a high-backed chair, a blanket covering his lap. Thomas went to him and sank to his knee. Deane held out his hand for Thomas to kiss his ring.

''Tis very good to see you again, Master Wolsey,' Deane said, gesturing to a stool near his feet. 'I had not thought to do so quite so soon.'

'Indeed, no. When we met at the Greys, you were the bishop of Salisbury, and now you have been translated to Canterbury. I thought you had moved far beyond my orbit, Your Grace.'

'You took my advice, I think,' Deane said. 'You employed your own chaplain.'

'Ah yes, I did. I was so very grateful for your advice, Your Grace.'

'Yes, well, I am always ready to be of aid to men who actually listen to me,' Deane said with a little laugh. 'Old men are too ready to be dismissed by younger.'

'I do not know how you can say so, Your Grace,' Thomas assured him, 'when the king has given you such responsibility as Canterbury.'

Deane's face crumpled. 'He has given me some responsibility.' He reached for his cup and took a small sip. 'I expect you are not aware that the post of archbishop of Canterbury usually comes with the lord chancellorship of England. In my case, that is not so. I am Keeper of the Great Seal only.'

Thomas opened his mouth to reply but could not think of an answer that would satisfy. Why had the king not entrusted Deane with the Lord Chancellorship? He quickly glanced over the old man and wondered if age was the problem. Was Henry Deane simply too old to be of any use? Had the king been kind, wanting to spare Deane the burden of office? *Oh God*, Thomas mentally prayed, *please do not let Deane die before I have had a chance to show what I can do.*

Deane suddenly looked over Thomas's shoulder, and Thomas turned to see what he was looking at. A man, tall and thin, had entered wearing the surplice and cross of a priest. This, Thomas reasoned, was his companion chaplain.

'Ah, Master Wolsey, this is Master Gregory Trevot. He is my other chaplain recently appointed. You will be working very closely together.'

Gregory Trevot came up to Thomas, his hand held out. 'Very good to meet you, Master Wolsey.'

'And you, Master Trevot,' Thomas replied, shaking his hand. He took in his fellow chaplain, gauging his potential as a rival. Younger than him, certainly, but malleable, Thomas thought. He did not have the look of

145

a particularly hard worker. Well, that was somewhere Thomas could outshine him.

'Sit you down, Master Trevot,' Deane said, looking around for another stool. 'Or would you both mind if I called you Gregory and Thomas? All this "Master this" and "Master that" gets on my nerves.'

'By all means, call me Gregory, Your Grace,' Trevot said, finding a stool and carrying it over to sit beside Thomas.

Thomas nodded his agreement.

'Good,' Deane said with satisfaction. 'Now I will explain your duties.' He took a deep breath. 'Canterbury is responsible for sixteen of England's dioceses. As you can imagine, that makes for a great deal of work, much of it mundane and tedious.' He nodded at their hands in their laps. 'Your fingers will be worn down to stumps and permanently stained with ink before you have been six months here, I warrant. You enjoy administration?'

Thomas was quick to answer first. 'I do, Your Grace.'

Gregory shrugged.

'Fortunate for you. And in addition to all the routine matters, you two will need to arrange our removal to London by the end of next month.'

'We are going to London?' Gregory asked, his eyes wide in surprise and wonder.

'Indeed, we are,' Deane said, amused by his enthusiasm. 'We will reside at Lambeth Palace. Ironically, you might say, it is the proper seat for the archbishop of Canterbury. You have never been to London?'

Gregory shook his head. 'No, Your Grace.'

'You must have been, Thomas,' Deane said.

'Once only, Your Grace,' Thomas said. 'And only for one day.'

'What did you think of it?'

'Busy, noisy.' He thought for a moment and added, 'Exhilarating.'

'Yes, young men like London.' Deane nodded. 'Of course, an old man like me… ' He waggled his head as if he need say no more. 'Gregory, you show Thomas here where your office is. You will find plenty of paperwork already to do, so you may as well get on with it.' Deane yawned. 'I shall have my nap, and we shall meet again this evening for supper. Off you both go and get to work.'

Thomas turned his fur collar up to his ears and huddled deeper into his cloak. It was damnably cold on the Thames, and the oarsmen were spraying river water over him and Gregory every time they pulled up their oars. It was all very well for Deane, protected by the barge's canopy from the breeze and blanketed from the cold, but Thomas and Gregory were very exposed at the stern.

'How much farther is the palace, Thomas?' Gregory asked, his teeth chattering.

'Not far, I think,' Thomas said, his gaze on the riverbank. 'You forget, Gregory, London is almost as new to me as it is to you.'

'Aye, but you do not show it,' Gregory said enviously. 'You could have been born in London. I am a country bumpkin in comparison.'

'You will have to learn to look as if you belong here,' Thomas said unsympathetically. 'We will be in daily contact with the court and dealing with all sorts of courtiers. They will not appreciate clumsy manners.'

'We will be talking with nobles?' Gregory's eyebrows disappeared into his fringe.

Thomas rubbed his hands together to warm them. 'On occasion.'

'And that pleases you.' Gregory shook his head in admiration. 'You cannot wait, can you, to mix with the nobility?'

Thomas turned his face away, unhappy at being so easily read. His eyes focused on the riverbank and was pleased to be able to say, 'We are here.' He turned his fur collar down and wiggled his toes to coax some feeling back into them.

'We're here, Your Grace,' Gregory shouted over the heads of the oarsmen, making Thomas cringe. What had he just been telling Gregory about manners?

The barge pulled up at the landing stage, knocking gently against the other boats tied to the upright poles. Thomas got to his feet, holding out his arms to steady himself as the barge wobbled from side to side. He stepped carefully between the oarsmen, heading for Deane, who was attempting to fold up his blanket.

'Let me, Your Grace.' Thomas took the blanket from him and folded it deftly, laying it on the seat beside Deane. He held out his hand and Deane took it. It took quite a bit of effort to help Deane to his feet; the old man had become stiff from sitting for so long, and Thomas heard his bones crack as he straightened. 'A warm fire and a comfortable chair for you, I think.'

'I can but dream,' Deane said wistfully as Thomas more pushed than helped him onto the platform.

'Both should be waiting for you if my instructions have been followed,' Thomas said as he climbed up onto the stage after him.

'Ah, Thomas.' Deane turned to him, smiling. 'If only all those who served me were as assiduous as you. Is Gregory following?'

'Here, Your Grace,' Gregory called, running to catch up.

'I will have a sleep first,' Deane said to them both. 'Then, when I have rested, we must begin work on the infanta's coming.'

'Did you say the infanta, Your Grace?' Thomas asked.

'The Spanish infanta, yes,' Deane said as they passed a row of tall elms and beneath a stone gateway. 'I received a letter from the king last week.'

'Was that the letter you did not allow us to open?' Gregory asked with a wink at Thomas.

'Oh, far too important a letter to be read first by a chaplain, my dear Gregory,' Deane said. He stopped to look up at the red-brick facade of the palace. 'Fine building, is it not?'

'Very fine,' Thomas replied impatiently, barely noticing. 'But the letter, Your Grace?'

'Oh, the letter. Yes, Prince Arthur is to marry the Spanish infanta. Katherine, I think her name is. The negotiations have all been settled, and the girl is on her way here. I believe she is scheduled to arrive next week, and the king has asked that she lodge here at Lambeth Palace for a few days. So, you see, my boys, we are going to be very busy. Ah well, there's no rest for the wicked.'

Thomas stared up at the grey sky. The infanta would find England quite an unpleasant change from her native land, he thought. From what he had heard of Spain, it was a land of blazing sun and scorching heat. *The poor thing will need to get used to English weather*, he mused.

His gaze returned to the river, to the landing stage where he had ordered a page to act as a lookout. He hoped the breeze would keep any rain off, for if not, he would have to order straw to be laid on the mud to keep the infanta's shoes clean. Should he do it anyway, he wondered, just to be on the safe side? And what about the canopy he had ordered made? Should he have that erected too, even though he had his doubts whether the cloth would stop any rain?

Deciding it was too late to worry about the canopy now, Thomas turned from the window and descended the narrow staircase to the Great Hall. He had left Gregory to cope alone with their guests, and he had seen his friend's pleading expression as he had walked away. Thomas had mouthed to him that he would not be long, and Gregory had accepted this nervously. Thomas understood his anxiety. Their visitors were amongst the noblest in the land, and Gregory was worried he would commit a grievous error, disgracing not only himself but the archbishop. The thought had occurred to Thomas too.

When he entered the Great Hall, Gregory was standing by the large fireplace, watching with amusement he tried to hide as a ten-year-old boy drew the sword from the duke of Buckingham's scabbard and held the pointed end to the duke's chest. The boy was obviously playing, but the duke's face told of his displeasure at being used as a target, and Thomas could tell he was itching to snatch the sword from the boy's hand.

But he dared not, for the ten-year-old boy was Prince Henry, and not even a duke could tell a prince what he could and could not do.

'Any sight of them yet, Thomas?' Deane asked from his seat by the fire.

'Not yet, Your Grace, but my boy is watchful. He will let us know.'

'My chaplain, Thomas Wolsey,' Deane muttered an introduction to the duke, and Thomas bowed. The duke

151

looked him up and down with something like distaste before being distracted by the young Henry.

'My lord,' the young boy squeaked, holding up the sword, 'may I have this?'

His patience spent, the duke held out his hand for his sword. 'It is too big for you, my prince. Perhaps in a few years' time.'

Henry's bottom lip jutted out in a pout, but he handed the sword over. He ran to the window. 'I cannot see the river from here. Archbishop, let us wait by the river steps.'

Deane shook his head. 'My lord, the royal barge could be awhile yet, perhaps even an hour or more.'

'So?' Henry whined.

'The day is too cold to wait outside,' Deane said.

'I do not mind the cold.'

'No, my lord, because you are young. If you were as old as I, you would not wish to venture outside before it is necessary.'

Henry gave an exaggerated sigh, expressing clearly what he thought of old people. Deane looked appealingly at Thomas.

Thomas nodded and took a step towards the prince. 'Can I get you anything to eat, my lord? There are cakes here.' He gestured towards the corner of the room where a small octagonal table stood with a large plate of cakes upon it.

'Cakes?' the boy asked eagerly.

'Indeed.' Thomas watched with amusement as

Henry scampered over to the table, grabbed a cake and crammed it into his mouth.

'I wonder if the infanta likes cakes,' Henry said, crumbs clinging to his lips.

'I expect she does, my lord,' Thomas replied. 'Are you looking forward to meeting her?'

Henry shrugged and grabbed another cake. Believing he had done enough to distract the boy from insisting the archbishop venture outside, Thomas moved to stand beside Gregory.

'He's a miserable bugger,' Gregory said out of the corner of his mouth as they watched the duke and Deane talk.

'He's a duke,' Thomas murmured.

'Quite. What has he got to be miserable about?'

'Not being king, I expect.'

Thomas knew that the duke of Buckingham with his Plantagenet blood had a claim to the throne, and it was rumoured he had a great desire to sit on it. Buckingham certainly had an air of arrogance about him, and Thomas found it very easy to believe he had ambitions for the throne. But he was out of luck. King Henry had produced the heirs so necessary to a king, and unless Buckingham was willing to fight for the crown, it would go to Prince Arthur by divine right of inheritance.

For almost ten minutes, Buckingham paced the Great Hall impatiently, clearly not relishing this job he had been given by the king. Deane watched him from his chair, and Thomas could tell the archbishop had no idea how to converse with the duke, no idea what topic of conversation would interest him. It was a relief for all concerned when the boy Thomas had posted at the landing stage hurried into the hall and declared he had seen the royal barge.

'At last,' Buckingham said. Without waiting, he stormed out of the hall.

Prince Henry started to run after him, then halted and looked around for Deane, unsure whether he was expected to wait. 'Go on, my lord.' Deane waved at him. 'No need to wait for me.'

Glad to be relieved of any duty, Henry ran out as Thomas helped Deane to his feet. Gregory proffered his arm for the old man to lean on, knowing Thomas was as anxious as the prince to get to the landing stage.

'Is everything ready, Thomas?' Deane asked, his face creasing as the cold wind hit them.

'Everything, Your Grace,' Thomas assured him as he glanced up at the sky, glad the rain had held off.

'The rooms – '

'All the rooms have been cleaned, aired and furnished, Your Grace. The kitchens have brought in all the provisions they need and have planned some Spanish recipes.'

'Oh, good, that should make the infanta feel at home,' Deane said.

'I thought so, Your Grace.'

'You have done well, Thomas,' Deane said as they neared the landing stage. The duke and Prince Henry were standing near the edge, the prince jumping from one foot to the other in his excitement. 'I know how hard you have worked. It has not gone unnoticed, I assure you.'

'Thank you, Your Grace.' Thomas bowed his gratitude, catching sight of Gregory's knowing smile out of the corner of his eye.

The royal barge drew up alongside the landing stage and was tied off. In their green and white Tudor livery, the oarsmen set their oars on end. A figure, small, hunched and dressed all in black, stepped out from the canopy. This was the Spanish ambassador, de Puebla. A veiled woman, also small, followed him, and another woman in black, followed her. The veiled woman, Thomas reasoned, must be Katherine, and the tall woman was her duenna, Dona Elvira.

Buckingham bent down to give Katherine his hand, and she slipped her gloved fingers into his as he helped her over the gunwale and onto the platform. The ambassador introduced the duke who looked bewildered by the sound of the Spanish tongue, but Thomas did not hear Katherine's reply.

Without waiting for an introduction, young Henry stepped forward and bowed low. In his high boyish voice, he declared who he was and how delighted he was to meet his future sister-in-law, then waited, grinning, as the ambassador translated his words. Thomas heard a giggle from behind the veil and knew that the boy had worked his not inconsiderable charm on the infanta.

It was then Deane's turn. Katherine raised his outstretched hand to the place where her lips were

155

behind the veil and kissed his ring. Deane, making an effort to stand unaided, gestured towards the palace, and the party passed by Thomas and Gregory.

'Is she going to remove the veil, do you think?' Gregory asked as they followed a discreet distance behind.

'I believe it is Spanish custom for the bride not to reveal herself before the wedding.'

'I wonder why that is a custom,' Gregory said. 'Do you think it is so as not to frighten the groom beforehand if the bride is ugly?'

Thomas shushed him angrily. 'Keep your voice down, you fool.'

'All right, all right,' Gregory said, a little put out. 'What are we to do once we get inside? Do we serve them all?'

'It will depend on whether the infanta intends to be sociable or not, I suppose. She may go straight to her rooms. But we must be on hand, so no disappearing. I want you where I can see you.'

'Why yes, my lord,' Gregory said sarcastically. 'Of course. Anything you say, my lord.'

Thomas ignored him. He liked Gregory, but he wasn't going to let friendship get in the way of his making a good impression. Gregory would do as he was told whether he liked it or not.

The king had summoned Deane to Greenwich. Before

Gregory could offer, Thomas had told Deane it would please him to accompany the archbishop. He had not yet had the chance to visit court, and he was dying to see what it was like. Deane had taken Gregory to court soon after they had arrived at Lambeth, and Gregory had told Thomas of the people, the lavish decorations and gardens with something rather like awe. Thomas knew Gregory was easily impressed but even so. He had to see it for himself.

Going to Greenwich meant crossing the river, and Deane made a fuss in the barge, moaning there were not enough blankets and that he was chilled to the bone. Thomas absently murmured words of consolation to the old man, his mind on other matters.

'Now, Thomas,' Deane said when he had finally given up complaining, 'this will be your first visit to court. It is important you behave.'

'When have I ever not behaved, Your Grace?' Thomas asked indignantly.

'Now, now, no need for that tone. I told Gregory the same thing. I will not have you embarrassing me. I know you have worked hard these past weeks, but that will be of no interest to the king. He will not notice you, you can be assured of that, and it is right and fitting he does not. You are, after all, my servant. As far as the king is concerned, I have made all the arrangements for the infanta, and that is how it will stay. You understand?'

Thomas understood well enough. Deane was to take all the credit for Thomas's hard work. 'I understand,

Your Grace,' Thomas said, swallowing down his resentment.

They arrived at Greenwich Palace and were ushered into the presence chamber. Early though it was, the room was already crowded. With so many people in one place, it reminded Thomas of the Great Hall at Magdalen College during the dinner hour. Except these people were not eating nor were they sat at tables. There were no chairs or stools in the presence chamber, only window seats. If a person waited in the presence chamber, they were forced to stand. Despite the discomfort, Thomas knew that many, if not all, were prepared to wait all day just for the chance of an audience with the king or even one of his ministers.

'See if you can get me a seat there.' Deane pointed to the nearest window seat, which was currently occupied.

Thomas hastened over to the man, who looked up with surprise and irritation as Thomas begged the use of his seat. The man was inclined to refuse, thinking it was Thomas who wanted it, but he rose hastily when Thomas pointed to Deane, who was looking up at the ceiling, pretending not to notice what Thomas was about.

The seat made vacant, Thomas waved the archbishop over. Deane sat down with a grateful sigh. 'I do not know how long we will have to wait,' he said, looking over the company they kept in the chamber.

Thomas thought it unlikely it would be long, the king having summoned them, and said so to Deane.

Deane closed his eyes and shook his head. 'You are not used to court, Thomas. A summons need not mean the matter is urgent.'

And so it proved. Perhaps an hour passed before a page came out of a door in the corner of the presence chamber and scanned the room. Seeing the archbishop, the young man hurried over to the window seat and told Deane the king would see him now. Thomas helped Deane rise and followed close on his heels as they exited the chamber and entered a wide corridor. A door at the far end had guards on either side. The page lifted the latch and pushed open the door. 'The archbishop of Canterbury,' he announced.

Standing behind Deane and unable to see farther than the back of his head, Thomas nevertheless bowed. He heard a voice tell Deane to take a seat, and as Deane moved to sit at the table, Thomas could see two men already there. One was clad in church garb, his heavy cross banging now and then against the wood of the table, and Thomas guessed this was Bishop Fox, one of the king's closest advisors. The bishop had a very grim visage; his long-nosed, triangular face ended in a deep chin, and the wrinkles below his cheeks and between his eyes were etched deep.

The other man could only be King Henry, his chin-length, dark brown hair streaked with grey and his face scored with worry lines. Had this thin-faced, weary-eyed man really produced the bonny creature that was Prince Henry? It was hard to believe.

King Henry looked up suddenly, and Thomas

quickly averted his gaze. It was against protocol to stare at a king, so he kept his gaze on the floor.

Bishop Fox spoke. 'Archbishop Deane, good day to you. We are sorry if you have been kept waiting, but there was much business to get through. Now, the marriage of Prince Arthur and the Spanish infanta is nigh upon us. The king would like your assurance that every possible arrangement has been made.'

Deane settled his gnarled hands on the tabletop. 'I can give Your Grace that assurance. The infanta's processional route from Baynard's Castle to St Paul's has been established and your personal bodyguard informed. The bishop of London and I have rehearsed the wedding ceremony with the couple's proxies, and both parties have been informed of what they must do and say. The Spanish ambassador has been most helpful in communicating our expectations to the infanta.' Deane paused, his brow creasing. The moment of silence lengthened.

'Is there a problem, archbishop?' the king asked.

'Er, no, Your Grace, I – ' Deane half-turned in his seat and looked up at Thomas. 'What else?' he snapped.

Thomas bent and whispered in his ear. 'The wedding feast, Your Grace.'

'Speak up, man,' Deane snarled, and Thomas straightened and repeated his words loudly. 'Yes, yes, the wedding feast,' Deane said.

King Henry stared at the archbishop for a long critical moment, then looked up at Thomas. 'What of the feast, Master… ?'

'Thomas Wolsey, Your Grace,' Thomas said quickly. He glanced at Deane, knowing he was disobeying his master's instructions, but it was not his fault the king had spoken to him. He could not refuse to answer, could he? 'The kitchens at Lambeth Palace were informed a month ago of the dishes that were to be prepared, and I confirmed yesterday that all meats and other provisions have been ordered and will be delivered the day before the wedding. Musicians have been hired to play a selection of both English and Spanish tunes, and extra stabling has been made available for those of Your Grace's guests who have no homes of their own in London.' He was aware that this all came out in a rush, so nervous was he.

'Yes, yes, I recall the details now,' Deane said, waving at Thomas to be silent. 'You see, Your Grace, all will be ready.'

'I am grateful for your assurances, archbishop,' the king said, his eyes moving from Deane to Thomas. 'I am confident the wedding is in good hands.' This was said with a last glance at Thomas.

'Thank you, Your Grace,' Deane said. The interview was over and Deane rose. He scowled at Thomas as he turned. Thomas did his best to look apologetic, but he knew his expression lacked sincerity.

The king had noticed him, and on his first visit to court too. Thomas hoped Deane would either forgive him for his interjection or forget it, and that this visit to court would not turn out to be his last.

CHAPTER TWELVE

Thomas carried his candle to the window and looked down onto the path below. It was late, the sky outside the window as black as pitch. The path itself was illuminated by braziers that burned fiercely, their flames whipped this way and that by the November wind. Thomas had insisted on them, despite Deane baulking at the extra expense, stating they were necessary to provide security for their expected guests.

There had been a cooling of affection between Deane and Thomas since their visit to Greenwich, a cooling that irked rather than upset Thomas. It had not been his fault Deane's memory had failed him in the presence of the king. It had not been his fault the king had looked to him to supply the information he required. Had he not been so good at his job, Thomas was sure the old man would have dismissed him the moment they got back to Lambeth Palace. As it was, he felt that perhaps his days as Deane's chaplain were numbered,

Dona Elvira's nostrils flared, but fortunately, she [made] no further comment.

Thomas glanced at Katherine. 'Would the infanta [like] for some wine to warm her before she retires?'

De Puebla answered for her. 'I believe we could all [do] with some, Master Wolsey.'

'Then please follow me.' Thomas led them through [the] hall to a much smaller room, a cosy parlour used by [the] archbishop, in which a fire still burned. Wine and [glas]ses waited on a table by the fire, and Thomas busied [hi]mself bringing an extra chair near to the small blaze.

Katherine sank into the archbishop's chair with a [ru]stle of silk, holding out her petite slippered feet to the [fi]re. Dona Elvira took the stool beside her, passing her [th]e wine Thomas held out for them both. He poured [a]nother cup and passed it to de Puebla, who had taken a [s]tool a little way away. De Puebla jerked his head at the [s]tool beside him and Thomas sat down.

'What a day,' de Puebla sighed. 'First mass, then an [a]udience with the king and queen, then dinner, then a [m]asque, then more food, another entertainment, mass.' He blew out a puff of air. 'I am too old for all this.'

Thomas smiled at the ambassador's self-deprecation, knowing that de Puebla rather enjoyed court life. 'Did the infanta enjoy herself?'

'She has been magnificent.' De Puebla smiled proudly at Katherine, who was gazing into the fire as if in a trance. 'She has proven herself a true daughter of Ferdinand and Isabella. I shall write to them of how well she

that the archbishop was just waiting for the wedding to be over and then Thomas would go. He would have to tread carefully.

Thomas had no desire to be on bad terms with Deane, and he had done what he could to repair the damage their visit to Greenwich had caused. He had been attentive to Deane's health, persuading the old man he need not wait up for the infanta and her retinue to arrive to greet them. It being so late, Thomas had told Deane that their guests would almost certainly retire immediately upon their arrival, and Deane's absence could easily be explained away by Thomas telling the infanta he needed his rest to be ready for the ceremony on the morrow. Eager for his bed, Deane had agreed and headed for the staircase to his chamber, pausing only to remind Thomas to make his apologies to the infanta.

Thomas wished the Spanish party would make haste and arrive. He was tired too. There had been so much to do, so many things to arrange. Over the past month, Thomas had had to be not only a priest and a chaplain, but a tailor, baker, butcher, ostler, chandler, musician, master of revels and a hundred other jobs that had no definite name. He was proud of what he had thus far achieved, but he knew that if anything were to go wrong on the morrow, whether it be with the procession, ceremony or the feast, Deane would not hesitate to point the finger of blame at him. It was a great deal of responsibility to carry.

He yawned, his breath misting up the window. The candlelight made a mirror of one pane, and he caught his reflection in the glass. His left eyelid was drooping rather far over his eye and twitching every now and then, the result of his extreme tiredness. He knew that with sleep the lid would retract a little, but he also knew the droop had increased in the last year, becoming more of a disfigurement. There was nothing he could do about it but wish it were not so. He carried the candle back to his desk and set it down, intent on resuming the paperwork that awaited him as he would not be able to go to bed just yet.

Ten minutes or more passed before Thomas heard the crunch of gravel. Hurrying once more to the window, he spied a coach coming up the drive.

'Thank God for that,' he muttered and weaved around his desk, pinching his surplice so as not to fall as he ran down the stairs. He reached the front door and yanked it open, the chill air blasting him.

The coach pulled up, the horses snorting steam. Thomas waited in the doorway as a coachman jumped down from his seat and opened the coach door. The Spanish ambassador, de Puebla, appeared first, and he reached back into the coach to take the hand of the infanta.

She stepped down from the coach. Thomas had heard that de Puebla had convinced the infanta it would be politic to assume English customs rather than continue with Spanish ones. The veil that had shielded her from view on her first visit had gone, and Thomas was able to look upon the infanta's pretty face.

For pretty it was, he thought. He had expected a

dark-skinned, dark-eyed, long-faced gi was none such. She was plump of face, tifully pinched pink from the cold, he bright. Thomas glimpsed her hair beneat it seemed to be fair, almost honey-colou with a grimace that the ever-present Don the coach a moment later, and she was hi of a Spanish woman. He gestured them door, eager not to detain them in the cold ni

'Good evening, Your Excellency, Your Elvira,' Thomas said as he slid the bolt o door into place once they were all inside. have had a good day.'

'A very tiring one,' de Puebla said, r hands to warm them.

'My lady is extremely tired, señor,' Do said. 'She must rest.'

'Of course, my lady. Your chamber is ready.

'Where is the archbishop?' de Puebla asked.

'He was reluctantly forced to retire earl Excellency,' Thomas said sorrowfully, leading th farther into the hall. 'He needs all his strength ceremony tomorrow.'

Dona Elvira tutted. 'He should have been h greet us.'

'He wished me to convey his apologies,' Th said, hoping the duenna would not make a fuss. If i back to Deane that the Spanish had complained a his absence, it would be yet another black mark aga Thomas's name in Deane's book.

has behaved, and they will be very pleased. And King Henry and Queen Elizabeth! How they smiled upon her, the queen especially. Do you know, Master Wolsey, the queen called me over and said that a more perfect creature could not have been found for the prince. And do you know what I did? I told the queen that she was right.'

Thomas laughed with de Puebla and took a sip of wine. 'And were they able to converse? I think Queen Elizabeth has no Spanish and the infanta no English.'

'True, but the infanta has a little French, and your queen speaks French very well. The king, of course, spent a great deal of time in France during his youth, and so they managed well enough.' He sighed. 'The infanta will have to learn English, of course. But she is a quick learner and will do so.'

'What of the prince?'

'Prince Henry?' De Puebla grinned. 'Oh, he was here, there, everywhere – '

It was odd how the young Henry seemed to overshadow his brother. 'No, I meant Prince Arthur.'

'Oh, they spoke Latin together. I heard the king ask him what he thought of his bride, and Prince Arthur said he was delighted with her.'

'And Prince Henry?'

De Puebla evidently liked the boy, for his face broke into a grin again. 'He is a little rascal. He chatters over his parents and laughs at his brother. He tells the musicians what to play and how to play, and pulls the ladies into dancing with him, though he be but little.' He laughed. 'I do not think the young prince will make a very good priest.'

Thomas knew Prince Henry was destined for the church. As the second son of the king and queen, there really was no other path for him. His brother was to marry and hopefully produce an heir. 'I will contradict you there, if I may, Your Excellency,' Thomas said, considering. 'I do not believe that a bonny and blithe disposition means a lack of fitness for a priest. All men love God in their own way, and it may be Prince Henry's way to love Him cheerfully.'

'To love God, yes, I agree, but to become celibate and contemplative?' De Puebla shrugged. 'Many men would find such a life difficult.'

Thomas hid his smile from the ambassador. What a pure idea he had of a man of God. Celibacy amongst the priesthood was demanded by the church in theory, but it was often ignored in practice. Thomas knew for a fact that Gregory had an arrangement with one of the laundresses in Lambeth Palace, and Thomas had himself indulged once or twice since coming to London. It was possible to be far more discreet in London than in Canterbury, and he had seen no reason to abstain for mere propriety's sake. Thomas would be the first to swear he loved God, but he loved to live his life as well.

'We may find that the church curbs Prince Henry's exuberance,' Thomas said, thinking it would be a shame if it did.

De Puebla nodded, then looked over to Katherine. Her eyes had closed, and her chin nudged her breast.

Dona Elvira had finished her wine and was staring into the fire, unaware. De Puebla called softly to Dona Elvira, who started. Recollecting herself, she looked to her mistress. She nudged Katherine awake, and Thomas heard them exchange words in Spanish. Dona Elvira helped Katherine to her feet and looked at Thomas expectantly. Without another word, he led his Spanish guests to their rooms for the night.

Deane padded out from his bedchamber to the landing, his long dressing gown swishing over the rush matting, and leant over the banister. 'Thomas. Where the devil are you?'

'Here, Your Grace,' Thomas answered, running out from the kitchen to the base of the stairs. 'What is it?'

'My feet have swollen,' Deane barked. 'I cannot get my shoes on. Where are my other shoes, the larger ones?'

'They are in the kitchen. I'll fetch them.'

'What are they doing in the kitchen?'

'Being cleaned. I thought you might be wanting them.'

'How did you – ' Deane began, but Thomas had already darted away. Deane shook his head and returned to his bedchamber.

Gregory had been listening at the kitchen doorway. 'Become a fortune teller now, have you?'

Thomas clicked his fingers at the boy cleaning the

archbishop's shoes. 'Take those up to His Grace,' he told him. He turned to Gregory. 'I saw his feet were swollen last night. I need not be a fortune teller to work out that he would want his larger shoes.'

'You do not miss a thing, do you, Thomas?'

'I have told you before, we must pay attention to the details if we do not want the larger events to go awry.'

'So says the man hoping to be important one day.'

'Must you mock me?' Thomas sighed.

'You deserve to be mocked.' Gregory leant over the kitchen table and snatched an apple from a bowl. 'When you work this hard, you show me up. I have to get my own back somehow.'

'Well, one of has to do some work,' Thomas said, taking the apple from his friend's hand and putting it back into the bowl. 'Be ready to leave in half an hour for the cathedral.'

'Why so early?' Gregory whined as he followed Thomas into the hall.

'So we get there before the procession starts. The streets will be packed, and we will never be able to get through. If we leave later, the infanta will be at St Paul's before the archbishop which would not be good. God's teeth, why are you following me about?'

Gregory shrugged. 'I have nothing else to do.'

'You could help, you know.'

'What and steal all your glory?'

'What glory? None of this today will be credited to me. Unless it all goes wrong, of course, and then His Grace will say it was all my doing.'

Gregory patted Thomas's arm. 'Nothing will go wrong. 'Tis not possible, not after all the work you have put in. And I think you are wrong.'

'About what?'

Gregory grinned. 'Why do you think the king did not appoint Deane to be lord chancellor? 'Tis because the king knows Deane is not able. King Henry knew he had to give him something for all his loyalty over the years, so he gave him Canterbury, but why do you think Deane has had to keep reporting to Bishop Fox about the arrangements for this wedding? Because the king and Fox know Deane too well. King Henry will know that we' – he pointed a finger at his chest and then at Thomas – 'have done all the work. And I know that *you* have done all the work. If anyone is going to get credit for something he did not do, my friend, trust me, it will be me.'

It was so frustrating. After all the organising, after all the long and late hours, after all the hard work, Thomas was not even allowed to watch the wedding take place. Instead, he and Gregory had to wait in a back room at St Paul's whilst the wedding ceremony was performed. Gregory did not care; he put his feet up on a stool and made himself comfortable.

Thomas had left the door open so he could hear the ceremony, even if he could not witness it. He knew there were nineteen other churchmen standing with

Deane at the altar, all there to assist with the ceremony, each one with a specific role to play. His biggest concern was something he had no control over and could not predict, and that was the archbishop himself. It worried him that the old man might forget the order of the ceremony or stumble over his words. These were not catastrophic faults, Thomas acknowledged, but such mistakes would mar the day all the same.

But Thomas could hear Deane from his back room, the church's admirable acoustics amplifying the old man's weak voice, and Deane had neither stumbled nor forgotten his words. From what Thomas could tell, the ceremony had passed off without a single hitch. Prince Arthur and Katherine had become man and wife, and now they and the entire congregation were making their way out of St Paul's to greet the crowds that lined the London streets to cheer them.

At last, Deane shuffled into the back room and held out his arms so Thomas and Gregory could remove his ceremonial robes.

'How was it?' Thomas could not help asking as he lifted the stole from Deane's shoulders.

'It went very well, thank you,' Deane said.

'There were no problems?'

'None.'

'Were the king and queen pleased?'

'I believe they were.'

'They did not say?'

Deane tutted. 'There was no opportunity. But they

that the archbishop was just waiting for the wedding to be over and then Thomas would go. He would have to tread carefully.

Thomas had no desire to be on bad terms with Deane, and he had done what he could to repair the damage their visit to Greenwich had caused. He had been attentive to Deane's health, persuading the old man he need not wait up for the infanta and her retinue to arrive to greet them. It being so late, Thomas had told Deane that their guests would almost certainly retire immediately upon their arrival, and Deane's absence could easily be explained away by Thomas telling the infanta he needed his rest to be ready for the ceremony on the morrow. Eager for his bed, Deane had agreed and headed for the staircase to his chamber, pausing only to remind Thomas to make his apologies to the infanta.

Thomas wished the Spanish party would make haste and arrive. He was tired too. There had been so much to do, so many things to arrange. Over the past month, Thomas had had to be not only a priest and a chaplain, but a tailor, baker, butcher, ostler, chandler, musician, master of revels and a hundred other jobs that had no definite name. He was proud of what he had thus far achieved, but he knew that if anything were to go wrong on the morrow, whether it be with the procession, ceremony or the feast, Deane would not hesitate to point the finger of blame at him. It was a great deal of responsibility to carry.

He yawned, his breath misting up the window. The candlelight made a mirror of one pane, and he caught his reflection in the glass. His left eyelid was drooping rather far over his eye and twitching every now and then, the result of his extreme tiredness. He knew that with sleep the lid would retract a little, but he also knew the droop had increased in the last year, becoming more of a disfigurement. There was nothing he could do about it but wish it were not so. He carried the candle back to his desk and set it down, intent on resuming the paperwork that awaited him as he would not be able to go to bed just yet.

Ten minutes or more passed before Thomas heard the crunch of gravel. Hurrying once more to the window, he spied a coach coming up the drive.

'Thank God for that,' he muttered and weaved around his desk, pinching his surplice so as not to fall as he ran down the stairs. He reached the front door and yanked it open, the chill air blasting him.

The coach pulled up, the horses snorting steam. Thomas waited in the doorway as a coachman jumped down from his seat and opened the coach door. The Spanish ambassador, de Puebla, appeared first, and he reached back into the coach to take the hand of the infanta.

She stepped down from the coach. Thomas had heard that de Puebla had convinced the infanta it would be politic to assume English customs rather than continue with Spanish ones. The veil that had shielded her from view on her first visit had gone, and Thomas was able to look upon the infanta's pretty face.

For pretty it was, he thought. He had expected a

dark-skinned, dark-eyed, long-faced girl, but Katherine was none such. She was plump of face, her cheeks beautifully pinched pink from the cold, her eyes blue and bright. Thomas glimpsed her hair beneath her hood, and it seemed to be fair, almost honey-coloured. He noticed with a grimace that the ever-present Dona Elvira exited the coach a moment later, and she was his exact image of a Spanish woman. He gestured them towards the door, eager not to detain them in the cold night air.

'Good evening, Your Excellency, Your Grace, Dona Elvira,' Thomas said as he slid the bolt of the palace door into place once they were all inside. 'I trust you have had a good day.'

'A very tiring one,' de Puebla said, rubbing his hands to warm them.

'My lady is extremely tired, señor,' Dona Elvira said. 'She must rest.'

'Of course, my lady. Your chamber is ready.'

'Where is the archbishop?' de Puebla asked.

'He was reluctantly forced to retire early, Your Excellency,' Thomas said sorrowfully, leading the party farther into the hall. 'He needs all his strength for the ceremony tomorrow.'

Dona Elvira tutted. 'He should have been here to greet us.'

'He wished me to convey his apologies,' Thomas said, hoping the duenna would not make a fuss. If it got back to Deane that the Spanish had complained about his absence, it would be yet another black mark against Thomas's name in Deane's book.

Dona Elvira's nostrils flared, but fortunately, she made no further comment.

Thomas glanced at Katherine. 'Would the infanta care for some wine to warm her before she retires?'

De Puebla answered for her. 'I believe we could all do with some, Master Wolsey.'

'Then please follow me.' Thomas led them through the hall to a much smaller room, a cosy parlour used by the archbishop, in which a fire still burned. Wine and glasses waited on a table by the fire, and Thomas busied himself bringing an extra chair near to the small blaze.

Katherine sank into the archbishop's chair with a rustle of silk, holding out her petite slippered feet to the fire. Dona Elvira took the stool beside her, passing her the wine Thomas held out for them both. He poured another cup and passed it to de Puebla, who had taken a stool a little way away. De Puebla jerked his head at the stool beside him and Thomas sat down.

'What a day,' de Puebla sighed. 'First mass, then an audience with the king and queen, then dinner, then a masque, then more food, another entertainment, mass.' He blew out a puff of air. 'I am too old for all this.'

Thomas smiled at the ambassador's self-deprecation, knowing that de Puebla rather enjoyed court life. 'Did the infanta enjoy herself?'

'She has been magnificent.' De Puebla smiled proudly at Katherine, who was gazing into the fire as if in a trance. 'She has proven herself a true daughter of Ferdinand and Isabella. I shall write to them of how well she has behaved, and they will be very pleased. And King Henry and Queen Elizabeth! How they smiled upon her, the queen especially. Do you know, Master Wolsey, the queen called me over and said that a more perfect creature could not have been found for the prince. And do you know what I did? I told the queen that she was right.'

Thomas laughed with de Puebla and took a sip of wine. 'And were they able to converse? I think Queen Elizabeth has no Spanish and the infanta no English.'

'True, but the infanta has a little French, and your queen speaks French very well. The king, of course, spent a great deal of time in France during his youth, and so they managed well enough.' He sighed. 'The infanta will have to learn English, of course. But she is a quick learner and will do so.'

'What of the prince?'

'Prince Henry?' De Puebla grinned. 'Oh, he was here, there, everywhere – '

It was odd how the young Henry seemed to overshadow his brother. 'No, I meant Prince Arthur.'

'Oh, they spoke Latin together. I heard the king ask him what he thought of his bride, and Prince Arthur said he was delighted with her.'

'And Prince Henry?'

De Puebla evidently liked the boy, for his face broke into a grin again. 'He is a little rascal. He chatters over his parents and laughs at his brother. He tells the musicians what to play and how to play, and pulls the ladies into dancing with him, though he be but little.' He laughed. 'I do not think the young prince will make a very good priest.'

Thomas knew Prince Henry was destined for the church. As the second son of the king and queen, there really was no other path for him. His brother was to marry and hopefully produce an heir. 'I will contradict you there, if I may, Your Excellency,' Thomas said, considering. 'I do not believe that a bonny and blithe disposition means a lack of fitness for a priest. All men love God in their own way, and it may be Prince Henry's way to love Him cheerfully.'

'To love God, yes, I agree, but to become celibate and contemplative?' De Puebla shrugged. 'Many men would find such a life difficult.'

Thomas hid his smile from the ambassador. What a pure idea he had of a man of God. Celibacy amongst the priesthood was demanded by the church in theory, but it was often ignored in practice. Thomas knew for a fact that Gregory had an arrangement with one of the laundresses in Lambeth Palace, and Thomas had himself indulged once or twice since coming to London. It was possible to be far more discreet in London than in Canterbury, and he had seen no reason to abstain for mere propriety's sake. Thomas would be the first to swear he loved God, but he loved to live his life as well.

'We may find that the church curbs Prince Henry's exuberance,' Thomas said, thinking it would be a shame if it did.

De Puebla nodded, then looked over to Katherine. Her eyes had closed, and her chin nudged her breast.

Dona Elvira had finished her wine and was staring into the fire, unaware. De Puebla called softly to Dona Elvira, who started. Recollecting herself, she looked to her mistress. She nudged Katherine awake, and Thomas heard them exchange words in Spanish. Dona Elvira helped Katherine to her feet and looked at Thomas expectantly. Without another word, he led his Spanish guests to their rooms for the night.

~

Deane padded out from his bedchamber to the landing, his long dressing gown swishing over the rush matting, and leant over the banister. 'Thomas. Where the devil are you?'

'Here, Your Grace,' Thomas answered, running out from the kitchen to the base of the stairs. 'What is it?'

'My feet have swollen,' Deane barked. 'I cannot get my shoes on. Where are my other shoes, the larger ones?'

'They are in the kitchen. I'll fetch them.'

'What are they doing in the kitchen?'

'Being cleaned. I thought you might be wanting them.'

'How did you – ' Deane began, but Thomas had already darted away. Deane shook his head and returned to his bedchamber.

Gregory had been listening at the kitchen doorway. 'Become a fortune teller now, have you?'

Thomas clicked his fingers at the boy cleaning the

archbishop's shoes. 'Take those up to His Grace,' he told him. He turned to Gregory. 'I saw his feet were swollen last night. I need not be a fortune teller to work out that he would want his larger shoes.'

'You do not miss a thing, do you, Thomas?'

'I have told you before, we must pay attention to the details if we do not want the larger events to go awry.'

'So says the man hoping to be important one day.'

'Must you mock me?' Thomas sighed.

'You deserve to be mocked.' Gregory leant over the kitchen table and snatched an apple from a bowl. 'When you work this hard, you show me up. I have to get my own back somehow.'

'Well, one of has to do some work,' Thomas said, taking the apple from his friend's hand and putting it back into the bowl. 'Be ready to leave in half an hour for the cathedral.'

'Why so early?' Gregory whined as he followed Thomas into the hall.

'So we get there before the procession starts. The streets will be packed, and we will never be able to get through. If we leave later, the infanta will be at St Paul's before the archbishop which would not be good. God's teeth, why are you following me about?'

Gregory shrugged. 'I have nothing else to do.'

'You could help, you know.'

'What and steal all your glory?'

'What glory? None of this today will be credited to me. Unless it all goes wrong, of course, and then His Grace will say it was all my doing.'

Gregory patted Thomas's arm. 'Nothing will go wrong. 'Tis not possible, not after all the work you have put in. And I think you are wrong.'

'About what?'

Gregory grinned. 'Why do you think the king did not appoint Deane to be lord chancellor? 'Tis because the king knows Deane is not able. King Henry knew he had to give him something for all his loyalty over the years, so he gave him Canterbury, but why do you think Deane has had to keep reporting to Bishop Fox about the arrangements for this wedding? Because the king and Fox know Deane too well. King Henry will know that we' – he pointed a finger at his chest and then at Thomas – 'have done all the work. And I know that *you* have done all the work. If anyone is going to get credit for something he did not do, my friend, trust me, it will be me.'

It was so frustrating. After all the organising, after all the long and late hours, after all the hard work, Thomas was not even allowed to watch the wedding take place. Instead, he and Gregory had to wait in a back room at St Paul's whilst the wedding ceremony was performed. Gregory did not care; he put his feet up on a stool and made himself comfortable.

Thomas had left the door open so he could hear the ceremony, even if he could not witness it. He knew there were nineteen other churchmen standing with

Deane at the altar, all there to assist with the ceremony, each one with a specific role to play. His biggest concern was something he had no control over and could not predict, and that was the archbishop himself. It worried him that the old man might forget the order of the ceremony or stumble over his words. These were not catastrophic faults, Thomas acknowledged, but such mistakes would mar the day all the same.

But Thomas could hear Deane from his back room, the church's admirable acoustics amplifying the old man's weak voice, and Deane had neither stumbled nor forgotten his words. From what Thomas could tell, the ceremony had passed off without a single hitch. Prince Arthur and Katherine had become man and wife, and now they and the entire congregation were making their way out of St Paul's to greet the crowds that lined the London streets to cheer them.

At last, Deane shuffled into the back room and held out his arms so Thomas and Gregory could remove his ceremonial robes.

'How was it?' Thomas could not help asking as he lifted the stole from Deane's shoulders.

'It went very well, thank you,' Deane said.

'There were no problems?'

'None.'

'Were the king and queen pleased?'

'I believe they were.'

'They did not say?'

Deane tutted. 'There was no opportunity. But they

were smiling, Thomas, so I assume they were pleased. Does that satisfy you?'

Thomas bent his head. 'Forgive me, Your Grace. I… I just wanted to be sure I had not let you down.'

His words mollified Deane and his expression softened. 'I know who I have to thank for today. If I have been ungracious, I am sorry. This has all been a great responsibility for someone of my age, you must understand.'

'I do, Your Grace, I do,' Thomas said. 'Will you want a short rest before we go to the feast?'

Deane shook his head. 'I have excused myself from the feast, Thomas. I am too tired.'

Thomas's face fell. 'We are not going?'

'No, we are not.' Deane patted Thomas's arm. 'I am sure you will have other opportunities to shine, Thomas. But not today. Not today.'

Thomas moved to put away the robes in silence, too angry to trust himself to speak.

Gregory came up to him. 'Rotten luck, Tom,' he whispered, glancing over his shoulder at Deane, who had collapsed into a chair.

'I swear he is determined to thwart me,' Thomas hissed, banging down the lid on the chest in which he had put away the robes.

'That's not true. He is tired, just look at him.'

'Aye, well, maybe 'tis time to look for another position with a younger man.'

'You do not mean that.'

'Oh, do I not?'

'Very well.' Gregory nodded, seeing clearly Thomas's anger. 'But consider this. A younger man will have ambitions of his own. Such a man is unlikely to help you achieve yours, do you not think?'

Thomas opened his mouth to reply, but upon realising Gregory was right, he shut it again. His resentment had got the better of him, and he had been stupid. If he stopped to think, he would realise that Deane's old age might actually be an advantage. Deane would be out of the world soon, then who knew where Thomas might end up? Thomas nodded at Gregory, acknowledging the rightness of his words.

'Have some patience, Thomas,' Gregory said, his hand on his shoulder. 'Your time will come.'

CHAPTER THIRTEEN

Henry Tudor wanted to be a peacemaker. All his adult life and much of his childhood, in one way or another, had been spent relentlessly fighting for the English throne. Now he had won it, he was done with war. But making peace rather than war did not meet with the favour of every English noble at court. Martial warfare was in the English blood; it was what the peers of the realm trained for from an early age, so they would be ready to fight for their king and country if and when the need arose. But Henry was adamant. England would have peace, and he would use his children to ensure it.

Henry had already begun with the marriage of Prince Arthur to Katherine. That marriage had been the last item in the Treaty of Medina del Campo, a treaty between England and Spain which agreed a mutual political stance towards France and the reduction of tariffs on imports and exports.

Now there was Scotland to deal with.

Scotland had been England's enemy for centuries and was a constant threat, not having the security of the English Channel to separate the two countries as it did England from her Continental enemies. But King James IV of Scotland seemed to want peace too. In 1497, James and Henry had signed the Treaty of Ayton, with James supporting Henry rather than the pretender to the throne, Perkin Warbeck. Now Henry was keen to take their amity further. His idea was to have a Treaty of Perpetual Peace with Scotland to put an end to the centuries of strife, most especially to the frequent bloody conflicts on the English-Scottish border, and to establish an efficient and friendly means of administering the border between the two countries. Like the Medina del Campo treaty, this treaty was to be sealed with a marriage. King James IV was unwed and in need of a wife. King Henry's eldest daughter, Margaret, had just turned twelve years old and was ripe for marriage.

Henry knew what he wanted from such a treaty. He told his ministers and churchmen that it was up to them to see that he got it.

Deane had tried hard not to complain, but Thomas could tell by his expression as he helped the old man off his horse that the journey from England into Scotland had been more than tiresome and inconvenient, it had been painful too. Days and days of riding had jolted their bodies until they felt like they were mere bags of bones.

The cold, wet weather hadn't helped. Despite their leather cloaks and gloves, he and Deane were soaked to the skin, their noses red and their lips chapped and broken. Thomas himself yearned for a blazing fire, warming wine and hot food, so he did not doubt that the old archbishop yearned for them even more.

The Scots sent to welcome them at the border were more friendly than he had been led to expect. At first he had trouble understanding their words; their accents were so strong, it could hardly be said they were speaking English at all. Deane made a face, shaking his head, annoyed that they were unintelligible to him, and Thomas feared the old man would say something offensive. Stepping forward, he asked them to speak more slowly so their feeble English ears could understand. The Scots looked with amusement at one another and slowed their speech to the speed of an idiot's understanding, and Thomas quickly learnt the cadence of the Scottish tongue.

Rooms, not sumptuous but comfortable enough, had been prepared for them in the palace of Holyrood. Thomas was relieved to see that a fire did indeed blaze heartily in the stone fireplace and that platters of food – bread, venison, cheese – awaited them on a table nearby. Thomas thanked the Scots heartily, then politely asked them to leave so Deane could change into dry clothing.

'I hope this treaty is worth all the effort,' Deane said, falling into a chair and stretching out his legs for Thomas to remove his boots. Thomas sank to his knees, hearing his bones crack, and tugged first one boot, then the other, free. 'The Scots are forever changing their minds, saying they agree, then saying they do not.'

'Not this time.' Thomas took the boots to the fireside to dry out. 'I believe the Scots want to end the strife with England as much as we.'

'I told King Henry the Scots cannot be tamed.' Deane noticed the jug of wine on a table at his elbow and helped himself. He tested the red liquid gingerly, decided the wine was passable, and took a mouthful. 'They are an uncivilised people. Always have been, always will be. We may as well try to civilise a pack of wolves.'

'And yet you told the king that you will do all you can to bring about this treaty, Your Grace.'

'Of course, I did. 'Tis my duty, Thomas. Much rests on the work we do here, not least the happiness of two people.'

'I did not think happiness was looked for in royal marriages.' Thomas moved to the table beneath the window and began selecting morsels for the archbishop's plate.

'If happiness can be achieved, we should hope for it.' Deane took the plate Thomas offered and put it on his lap. 'Now, I shall need you to make a list of all the Scots I shall be sitting down with to negotiate this treaty. Who I need concern myself with most and who are merely making up the numbers, that sort of thing.'

'How am I to determine that, Your Grace?'

Deane smiled impishly. 'By supping with our counterparts this night. I am too weary to be sociable. I want nothing but my own company and a soft mattress.' He cast an eye at the bed a few feet away. 'I can manage the former, at least. Go, get some food and wine in your belly and conversation in your mouth. And do not pretend you would rather stay with me. I know you will enjoy the task I have set you.'

'You know me too well, Your Grace,' Thomas said.

'That I do. Good night, Thomas.'

'Good night, Your Grace. Sleep well.'

Thomas closed Deane's door and went to examine the room he had been given opposite. It was small and rather spartan, just a low, narrow bed and a rickety table, but Thomas hadn't expected more; he was, after all, a mere servant. He unpacked his leather bag, laying his nightshirt upon his pillow and slipping his Bible beneath it, then he left the room, heading for the spiral staircase at the end of the corridor. As he descended the narrow stone stairs, taking each step carefully, he heard voices coming from the bottom.

'Where the devil have they put us?' a gruff voice snarled.

Thomas turned the corner of the stair and almost walked into the speaker.

'Oh, you're here, are you?' Thomas Howard, Earl of Surrey, looked down his long nose at Thomas and stepped back to avoid a collision. 'Deane up there, is he?'

179

'He is, my lord,' Thomas said. 'I believe your rooms are up that staircase.' He pointed towards the other end of the corridor.

'Well, why did they say here, for God's sake?' Howard cried, gesturing at the staircase Thomas had just come down. 'Typical bloody Scots. Well, I might as well see Deane first.'

Thomas quickly blocked his way. 'Archbishop Deane has retired for the night, I'm afraid, my lord.'

'But I want to speak with him about tomorrow,' Howard blustered. 'I want us to work out what we are going to say.'

'I fear the archbishop is not up to such conversation tonight. However, if you have any particular concern, you can tell me, and I will ensure the archbishop is told of it in the morning.'

Howard looked Thomas up and down contemptuously. 'You? You say I should tell *you?*'

Thomas bit back the retort he was tempted to make, knowing that if he offended the earl, his career prospects would be doomed. 'I do have the archbishop's complete confidence, my lord,' he said smoothly.

Howard's top lip curled in a sneer. 'You do not have mine. I will speak to Deane myself in the morning.'

'As you wish, my lord.'

Howard gave him another filthy look. 'Well, are we to be fed tonight or must we shift for ourselves in this godforsaken place?'

'I believe food will be awaiting you in your room, my lord,' Thomas said.

With a grunt of displeasure, Howard stormed off down the corridor, his servant scurrying after him. Thomas watched him until he disappeared from sight. Howard was not the first noble to show his contempt for a man of Thomas's class, nor would he be the last. Admittedly, not every noble was as rude as the earl of Surrey, but many were. Thomas was trying to teach himself to become used to it.

With a resigned sigh, Thomas made his way to the Great Hall to seek his supper and gain as much information as he could to aid his master on the morrow.

~

'And so we are agreed.' Deane looked around the table, meeting every man's eye in quick succession. 'The treaty can be signed.'

Howard began to bang the table with the flat of his hand. The others quickly joined him in the applause until the room was ringing with the sound of bony flesh upon wood.

Thomas, from his standing position behind Deane, watched the men at the table with something rather like pity. They probably thought they had negotiated this treaty, these noblemen and high churchmen, when really it was their aides and servants who had made it all possible. Thomas knew the information he had garnered that first night, innocent though it might have seemed at the time, had been invaluable to Deane in his preliminary conversations with his Scottish counterparts. And it had been Thomas's conversations over supper and during church services with the Scottish aides that had let Deane and Howard know what the Scottish were prepared to concede and what they were not that had smoothed the negotiations.

But it really didn't matter who had achieved what; King Henry was going to get what he wanted and the Treaty of Perpetual Peace was going to be ratified, signed and ultimately sealed by the wedding of King James IV to Margaret Tudor.

As the great men around the table rose and mingled, shaking hands and laughing, Thomas began packing up the archbishop's papers, lingering over the draft of the treaty that Deane had been reading from. It was an ambitious treaty, Thomas thought. Perpetuity was a long time, and he thought it unlikely that England and Scotland would be able to stop their quarrelling for ten years, let alone forever. Still, the intention to do so was worth celebrating. Wars were expensive affairs and damaged a country's economy for long after the swords had stopped clashing and the cannon had stopped booming. Any piece of paper that offered a peaceful alternative had been worth pursuing, in his opinion. Thomas rolled the draft up and slipped it into a leather roll, securing the lid with a buckle.

Deane would want to leave as soon as possible, Thomas knew. In truth, he did too. He had enjoyed the whole process of the treaty negotiations. It had been fascinating to watch Deane and Howard examine clauses, discuss their merits and drawbacks, refuse to accept some and insist on others, but it would be very pleasant to return to London and the comfort of Lambeth Palace.

Thomas had discovered that he liked comfort. Scotland was an austere land, not suited to soft men of the south such as he and Deane. He was eager to return to London and to be back in the heart of power.

CHAPTER FOURTEEN

LUDLOW CASTLE - 1502

Katherine wiped her nose with her handkerchief for the third time in as many minutes. It hurt when she wiped it, for the skin was red and raw. She had thought England cold and wet, but Wales, she had discovered, was ten times worse. She sniffed to try to dislodge some of the mucus in her nose, but it was no good; she could not breathe through it.

Oh, when would this end? She had caught this cold in February and still suffered all these weeks later. Katherine could not remember having ever felt so ill in her life. She had been forced to keep to her bed for almost a sennight, Dona Elvira hovering and fussing over her, trying to persuade her to eat. But everything Katherine had put in her mouth had tasted of dust and she had no appetite. Dona Elvira tutted and shook her head, telling her charge she had lost weight and adding with some sort of grim satisfaction that England would be the death of Katherine.

Katherine had not succumbed to her duenna's blandishments or recriminations. She knew well that Dona Elvira had no liking for England. It had been a very unpleasant day for her duenna when she was told Katherine was to be sent there. Dona Elvira had considered resigning from her post, she had admitted to Katherine one particularly cold day, but she could not bear to leave her darling, and so she suffered. If she had hoped to rouse Katherine's sympathy, she was disappointed. Katherine had become rather weary of Dona Elvira since her marriage and almost wished she had a different duenna to keep her company.

Dona Elvira did not know how fortunate she was to have a choice. Katherine had had none. She had not been permitted to choose her husband nor where she would live. And this had been her fate. To be wed to a young man – a boy, really – and sent to live in this cold, wet country, far from her beloved parents and home. But Katherine knew this was what she had been born to do. She knew her duty and would carry it out as best she could.

Arthur had succumbed to the same cold. Whether he had caught it from her or she from him, it did not matter. Poor Arthur had it far worse than she. Her cold lingered with a blocked nose, sore throat and bones that ached. Arthur had all of these and a dry, wracking cough that sounded as if his lungs were being shredded. When he coughed, he brought up an ugly green sputum that he tried to hide in his handkerchief. The last time she had caught him doing this, she had seen that the green slime was tinged with red.

She had tried to talk to his doctors to find out what her husband's symptoms betokened, but they merely smiled and nodded knowingly without telling her anything. She doubted their competency and wished she had a Spanish doctor to tend to Arthur. Spanish doctors seemed far more advanced in their learning than these English quacks.

And then they suggested the cause of Arthur's continued ill health was her. She had stared at them open-mouthed, wondering what on earth they could mean. Sexual exertion, the doctors explained, had weakened Arthur's health.

Katherine had run out of the room when she heard this, her cheeks burning with shame. How could they say such a thing? And to know it was not true, could not be true, was worse. But she would die before she confessed the truth, that since their marriage, Arthur had done nothing more than kiss her mouth and hold her hand. All those nights lying in bed together side by side, and Katherine was as good a maid as the day she was born.

The shame of it had silenced her, even before Dona Elvira, who knew everything about her. If Katherine had told her of her continued virginity, Dona Elvira would have raised her thin dark eyebrows, pursed her lips and sneered. She would have derided Arthur as a boy, called him a pathetic English eunuch, not fit to be joined with a daughter of Spain.

It would hurt Katherine to hear her husband spoken of so demeaningly. Arthur may not be a perfect specimen of masculinity, but he had been kind and gentle with her, had treated her with respect. Her fate might have been very different. She might have been wed to a prince or noble who fit Dona Elvira's ideal of manhood and used her every night, taking no care to be gentle, not minding whether she enjoyed their intimacies or not, his only desire to produce an heir. Katherine was grateful Arthur was the man he was.

She had also kept her virginity to herself because she knew Dona Elvira would write to her parents and tell them. And then there would be letters from her parents to the king and queen, Arthur would be interrogated as to why he had not performed his duty, and she would be accused of not being comely enough to attract him. Katherine was sure she could not bear such a humiliation. Far better for everyone to believe she and Arthur were man and wife in deed as well as words.

Katherine took out her handkerchief again and blew into it. Nothing happened. She pinched her nostrils, willing the mucus to run just so she could breathe through her nose instead of her mouth and spare her sore throat for a moment or two. Her gaze drifted towards Arthur in their bed. She had insisted on staying in the room with him, though she knew the doctors and Dona Elvira would have preferred her absence. She had a feeling, so very strong, that Arthur was going to die, and it terrified her. The doctors might pretend their potions and their bleeding would work a miracle and bring the prince back from the edge of death, but Katherine knew her husband was going to die.

And what would happen to her then? Would she be sent back to Spain, a worthless asset now she was the widow of an English prince? How much value would she have on the marriage market now? Her virginity presumed lost, she had not even proven herself to be fertile. Was her fate to be married off to a minor English noble or sent to a nunnery? An inconvenience that needed to be got quickly out of the way?

Her head was aching, and she leant back against her chair, her eyes closing. *Just five minutes,* she told herself, *just five minutes' sleep.*

When she opened her eyes again, they immediately fell upon her husband. It took her a moment to realise his chest was not rising or falling. He was perfectly still. Katherine stretched out a hand and put her fingertips to Arthur's cheek. She jerked them away. Arthur's skin was cool. Soon it would be cold. Her husband had died whilst she was asleep.

'Dona Elvira,' Katherine called loudly. 'Dona Elvira!'

Her duenna came running. 'What is it?' she asked, pushing past her mistress to lean over the bed and examine Arthur.

'He's dead,' Katherine's voice trembled as Dona Elvira picked up Arthur's hand, held it for a long moment, then let it drop back onto the bed.

'Yes, he is.' Dona Elvira straightened. She turned to

Katherine. 'Be strong, princess. Do not cry. Do not let these English see you cry.'

'My husband is dead,' Katherine said, her eyes starting to fill.

Dona Elvira grabbed her chin and jerked her face up. 'Remember who you are. You are the daughter of Ferdinand and Isabella of Spain. You do not weep for a dead English boy.'

Katherine stared at her and said nothing. But neither did she weep.

Deane had sent Thomas to court to deliver a message to Bishop Fox; there was a small amount of money owing to the archbishop from the privy purse, and he wanted it back.

Thomas handed the archbishop's note to Bishop Fox and waited patiently whilst he read. He kept his eyes from Sir Thomas Lovell, who was also present, but let them scan the paper-littered table Lovell, Fox and a secretary sat at. The detritus of administration was a familiar sight to Thomas, and to his eyes, an attractive one. As he stood waiting, his mind mused on what those papers might contain: letters from foreign ambassadors, the latest stage in a political negotiation, legal matters to be settled, people to be put in their place. What he would give to have just a glance at them.

Fox passed Deane's message to his secretary. 'Write

"Agreed" on it,' he told him, watching as the secretary did so. 'Give it back.' He jerked his head at Thomas.

The secretary sealed the letter and held it out to Thomas. Thomas felt the bishop's eyes upon him as he put it away in his leather folder.

'How is life at Lambeth Palace, Master Wolsey?' Fox asked.

'Oh, the same as it always is, Your Grace,' Thomas replied pleasantly. 'Things rarely change.'

'Getting bored, are you?' Lovell asked with a grin.

Thomas hesitated a moment too long.

'There, you see, bishop?' Lovell pointed and laughed. 'He is bored.'

Fox shared an amused glance with Lovell. 'Could do with a fellow like you here, really,' he said to Thomas, looking disconsolately over the papers. One of the papers slid from the table onto the floor. Thomas bent and retrieved it, handing it to the secretary. 'Who's that from?' Fox frowned as the secretary put it back on a pile of other letters.

Thomas had recognised the seal and answered for him, eager to show off. 'I believe it is Sir Richard Poole, Your Grace, chamberlain to the Prince of Wales.'

'Give it here.'

Thomas saw the bishop's expression change from one of mild interest to shock as he read Poole's letter. 'Your Grace?' he asked.

'The prince is dead,' Fox said in a hushed voice, passing the letter to Thomas. 'You read it to me. I could not take it all in.'

Thomas, surprised but pleased to have become part of this matter, quickly scanned the text. 'He died from a short illness, Your Grace, having contracted a severe chill to his chest earlier in the year which the doctors were unable to remedy.'

'God rest his soul,' Fox murmured. 'Is there a letter to the king and queen from Poole?'

The secretary quickly sorted through the pile in front of him. 'No, Your Grace. That appears to be the only one from him.'

'Then it is up to the council to convey this terrible news to them.'

'How will they take it, do you think?' Lovell's face was ashen.

'The queen will be distraught. The king... ' Fox shrugged. 'I cannot tell.'

'Solace will be required, all the same,' Lovell said.

'Indeed,' Fox said heavily. He glanced at Thomas. 'Master Wolsey, I believe you had better accompany me to tell the king and queen. As a priest, you will be able to administer to them.'

'Of course, Your Grace.' Thomas nodded. 'Though I did not know Prince Arthur, I understand he was the best of young men. And I feel for the princess. I was acquainted with her upon her arrival in England, and she struck me as being a very lovely creature.'

'A very lovely creature! Is that proper language for a man of the cloth?' Lovell asked.

'I can appreciate beauty and grace, my lord, though I be a man of the cloth.'

'Appreciate it from afar, do you, Master Wolsey, or close up?' Lovell asked with a wink.

'I appreciate God's work from wherever I am, my lord,' Thomas returned with an unshakeable smile. 'I was a man before I was a priest.'

'Really, Master Wolsey, you intrigue me. What saucy misdemeanours did you commit in your youth?'

'This is not the time for such talk, Sir Thomas.' Fox got to his feet. 'Master Wolsey, come with me. We must deliver this news to the king and queen at once.'

The king and queen were together in their private chamber. Fox checked his clothing was in good order, ran a glance over Thomas to confirm the same about him, and bid the guard open the door.

Queen Elizabeth was sitting in the window seat, her eyes bent on the needlework in her lap. King Henry was sitting at a small table at the next window, a pen, as usual, between his fingers, papers before him. They both looked up as Fox and Thomas entered.

It is incredible, Thomas thought, *how we can pick up so easily on another's mood*. Neither he nor Fox had spoken, yet both Elizabeth and Henry sensed they brought bad news. Thomas saw Elizabeth's throat tighten as she looked at them, saw her fingers curl up tightly, the skin over her knuckles whitening. Henry's eyes were wary.

'Your Grace,' Fox began, 'we have this day received a letter from Sir Richard Poole in Wales.'

Elizabeth started up from the window seat. 'Is it the prince?'

'It is, Your Grace,' Fox said. 'I am sorry to say that the prince is… ' His voice trailed away, the usually loquacious bishop for once unable to speak.

Henry too had risen from his seat. 'Dead?' he asked flatly.

'Yes, Your Grace,' Fox said.

A cry escaped from Elizabeth. Her hand flew to her mouth. Her legs gave way, and she fell back onto the window seat. Henry hurried to her and took her hand in his. Cradling her head between his neck and shoulder, he kissed her forehead tenderly.

'How?' he croaked over his shoulder.

'An illness, Your Grace,' Fox said quietly. 'Both the princess and the prince caught a severe cold in February. The princess herself was very ill but recovered. The prince, alas, declined.'

Elizabeth suddenly gave a low, wrenching sob and slumped against Henry, all queenly dignity gone. Henry held her tight. When he next spoke, Thomas heard the tremble in his voice that told of his own sorrow.

'We must pray for our son, bishop.'

'Indeed, Your Grace. I should return to the council chamber to answer Sir Richard's letter, but I have Master Wolsey here with me. He is a priest.'

Henry turned glistening eyes on Thomas. 'I do not

think my wife will be able to walk to the chapel. We will pray here, Master Wolsey.'

Assured his suggestion of Thomas had been accepted, Fox nodded at Thomas. Bowing, he left the room.

When the queen's sobs had subsided a little, Henry asked, 'Shall we pray now, Elizabeth?'

The queen nodded and took the handkerchief Henry offered, wiping her eyes. Henry stood, still holding her hand, and helped her to rise. She was unsteady and looked at Thomas with red, puffy eyes. He hoped the smile he gave her expressed his sympathy. What did one say to a grieving mother, and that mother, the queen?

The king and queen moved to the table at the other side of the room that held a large gold cross. Henry held her hand whilst Elizabeth lowered herself to her knees, then he did the same.

Taking his cue, Thomas moved towards them and began speaking the words he hoped would provide solace.

More than an hour had passed when Thomas returned to the council chamber. He felt exhausted. The king and queen's grief had been very tiring. Fox and Lovell were waiting.

'How are they?' Fox asked as soon as Thomas entered.

'I was able to provide some consolation,' he said, 'though the queen has taken it very hard.'

'A terrible thing for the king and queen,' Lovell said.

'I should think any parent would grieve so,' Thomas retorted unthinkingly.

'It's hardly the same if a baker or cobbler loses a child,' Fox snapped at the rebuke. 'To such parents, the death of a child is almost a relief; it means one less mouth to feed. But for a monarch to lose his heir... 'tis not just a tragedy for the king and queen, but for the country. Oh, do not look at me like that, Master Wolsey. You know I speak the truth. Children are a burden. Be thankful you will never know this for yourself. And we should also be thankful the king has another son.'

'Have the children been told yet?' Thomas asked.

'I despatched a messenger to Eltham as soon as I left you. Changes will have to be made, of course. Prince Henry has been very much left to his own devices. He has had only the company of women.' Fox's lips curled up in a grimace.

'Prince Henry was destined for the church,' Thomas said. 'To find he is suddenly heir to the throne may be something of a shock to the boy.'

'And it may not, Master Wolsey,' Fox said testily. 'Prince Henry is a rather boisterous young lad. I have often wondered whether he has the right character to be a son of the church.'

'Perhaps God wondered too,' Thomas mused.

'Perhaps He did, and this is what He has chosen for England. You have done well, Master Wolsey.'

'Thank you, Your Grace. I am only glad to have been on hand to help.'

'Yes, I bet you were,' Thomas heard Lovell mutter as he closed the council door behind him.

~

Elizabeth took off her dressing gown and laid it with great deliberation over the chest at the end of the bed. She had dismissed her maids early, their chatter and solicitous enquiries wearying her, forcing her to be polite.

They hadn't pressed her to let them stay, for the king was with her. Henry often was with her these days. He had not said so, but she knew it was because he did not like sleeping alone anymore. She didn't mind, not really, although she had grown used to having a bed all to herself. It was not Henry's presence that disturbed her; it was his mood.

Henry had never been a happy man. His life had been too hard for him to ever relax and be happy. Elizabeth hadn't understood that when they had first married. All she knew was that she was being married to a man she had never met, who had been the cause of her uncle's death, to make England secure after decades of trouble. She had resented being used in that way back then, but she had been young and indulged all her short life, and that had led her to think she could do as she liked. It had been a shock to discover she had no choice in her future. Elizabeth had been told she would marry Henry Tudor, and that had been that.

And those first months of marriage had been so very difficult. But then her first child had been born, and she had finally understood her purpose in life. That child, her boy Arthur, had bound her to Henry in a way she would never have believed possible. Together, Henry and she had made that lovely boy, and she had loved Henry for the gift, just as Henry had loved her for giving him an heir. It had all been so perfect, and in the end, so simple.

Elizabeth pulled back the covers on her side of the bed, taking care not to disturb Henry. She climbed into the bed and slid her feet down the sheet, feeling the chill of the cloth against her own cold flesh. She wriggled her toes in the vain hope it would warm them up. In the past, she would have rubbed her feet against Henry's calves and laughed as he laughed and bid her stop. If she did that now, she knew there would be no laughter. She pulled the covers up to her chin and lay her head on the pillow, her eyes fixing on the canopy above.

She heard a sniff beside her. *Say goodnight and go to sleep*, she told herself. *Don't look at him. He will stop soon.* But Henry sniffed again, and she impulsively turned her head towards him.

'Do not weep.'

'I cannot help it.'

'He's with God now, Henry.'

'He should be here with us.'

'I know. I wish it too.'

'My heir, Elizabeth.' Henry turned over onto to face her. 'What was it all for? All those years waiting to be king, having to fight for it?'

'We have Henry,' Elizabeth said. 'He will make a good king.'

'Will he?' Henry asked doubtfully.

'Of course he will. He's your son, how could he not? And we are young enough to have more.' She said this quietly, not wanting to say it, as if considering a potential replacement could hurt Arthur, but she knew Henry needed to hear it. He needed reassurance his life had not been for nothing.

'I am not young.' He smiled ruefully. 'But then, I do not think I was ever young.'

'No,' she agreed with a smile, 'but you are not old to me.' She leant towards him and kissed him, a deep kiss of the kind they had not shared for years. There was meaning behind it; Elizabeth hoped Henry understood her.

Henry did. His hand slid beneath the curve of her waist and pulled her close. He kissed her again, gently pushing her onto her back, his hands pulling up her nightgown so he could caress the flesh of her thigh.

God, give me another child, she prayed as she put her arms around him.

CHAPTER FIFTEEN

TOWER OF LONDON, 1503

Henry's eyes were aching. The smoke from the guttering candles was making them feel gritty and scratchy. He longed to lie down and close them, to go to sleep, to forget about everything for just a few hours. But he would not. He would not leave his wife to die alone.

The door opened, and Henry turned his head. It was the archbishop's chaplain, the Wolsey fellow, and he felt suddenly sick. He knew why Wolsey had come, sent by Fox to give his wife the last rites – proof, if it was needed, that there was no hope for Elizabeth.

The king was glad Fox had sent for Wolsey and not come himself. Bishop Fox was an excellent minister but of an unsympathetic disposition, even at the best of times. Such a trait was useful in a chief minister but not what a man wanted in his priest. This day, this day when his beloved wife was dying, Henry needed a priest who would understand what he was losing – or, at least, if he didn't understand, would say all the right words that would offer comfort. Fox, Henry suspected, would be just as likely to give his wife the last rites then whip out the latest state paper for his attention.

Henry accepted the chaplain's bow with a closing of his reddened eyes, then turned them back to Elizabeth in the bed. Her face was coated in perspiration, her breath coming shallow and fitfully. Henry thanked God the pain in her privates had ceased. It had been agony to watch; what it must have been like for Elizabeth to bear, he did not like to think. And for what had Elizabeth endured such pain? To give him another child that had not lived for more than a few hours. He cursed himself for his lasciviousness. He should have realised that Elizabeth was too old to bear children. He should have spared her the ordeal.

Henry was glad his mother was not present. She would have insisted on standing beside the bed like a statue, hard-faced and silent, or else been on her knees praying for Elizabeth's soul. There would have been little sympathy from her. He knew his mother had never truly cared for Elizabeth.

He was frightened. Again. He couldn't really remember a time when he hadn't always felt afraid. Those days in Brittany, when he had been convinced he would be king one day, had been dreadful, always wondering if a stranger was indeed just an unfamiliar face or a would-be assassin sent by Edward IV or one of his diabolical brothers to kill him. Then, when he had become king, knowing that all those at his court had once served the Plantagenets and had done so, for the most part, faithfully. Never knowing where his nobles' true allegiance lay had been a source of constant worry for him.

He had been scared of Elizabeth too, a little. Not that she threatened him, of course, but because he knew he would never know whether she had married him simply out of duty or whether she had truly believed he had a right to be king, and that, as such, she should be his consort. He had not expected love from Elizabeth, but he had come to love her, and he had never known whether she had felt the same about him. And yet, when they had had their first child, he had felt Elizabeth grow warmer towards him. Then came more children, and suddenly, they were no longer two houses, Tudor and York; they were a family. Henry had begun to feel safe with Elizabeth by his side. How would he cope without her?

Henry watched the chaplain administer the last rites. *Go*, he mentally begged as he listened to his wife's ragged breathing, *go and be safe. Here's no place for you anymore. Be at peace.*

A few moments later, Elizabeth's breathing slowed. He grabbed her hand and squeezed it, hoping she would squeeze it back, regretting his earlier thoughts. But she did not. Elizabeth's hand was lifeless in his, and he knew she was gone from him.

Henry looked up. The chaplain glanced at Henry, then leant over the bed and put his chubby hand beneath the queen's mouth. He held it there for a long moment, then straightened.

'Your Grace,' he said quietly, 'it grieves me to say the queen is dead.' He tactfully stepped away from the bed into the shadows, giving Henry a little privacy.

Henry bent his head and closed his eyes, his lips mouthing a silent prayer. Then he rose, his joints and back creaking from their long hours of immobility. He bent over Elizabeth, his tears flowing freely to bedew her pale cheeks, and kissed her lips. He winced as they did not press against his.

'God bless you, my love,' he whispered.

Fox had instructed Thomas to remain at court. He had been impressed with the chaplain's handling of the queen's death and the king's need for sympathy and had written to tell Deane he thought Master Wolsey might be useful again. Deane had made a half-hearted protestation, but it changed nothing. For the moment, at least, Thomas was staying at court.

For his part, Thomas was thrilled, and he made sure he stayed near the king's chambers should he be called for. So, it was he that Fox spoke to when he came hurrying along the corridor.

'How long has he been in there?' the bishop demanded, pointing at the closed door of the king's chamber.

'Near two days, Your Grace,' Thomas promptly replied.

'Has he eaten or slept?'

'I could not say. The king has admitted no one. He said he wished to be alone.'

Fox snorted in irritation. 'He cannot be left alone, Master Wolsey. We must do something.'

'I do not know what we can do, Your Grace. It is natural the king would want to grieve for the queen.'

'It is unmanly grief,' Fox chided. 'A king does not have the luxury of time to grieve. His children have arrived at court and there are matters to be dealt with.' He indicated the stuffed folder he was carrying. He groaned suddenly. 'Oh and now look who is coming.' Fox fixed a smile on his face as Lady Margaret Beaufort approached. 'My lady.'

'What is going on?' Lady Margaret demanded, looking from Fox to the door, to Thomas, then back to Fox.

'The king has been in his room for two days, my lady,' Fox said. 'He is refusing to come out.'

'What nonsense! Move out of the way.' Margaret stepped up to the door and banged on it loudly. 'Henry. Let me in.'

'I wish to be alone, Mother,' Henry called. 'Please go away.'

'Henry, this foolishness must stop. Mooning over Elizabeth is not going to bring her back.'

They all listened intently and heard what sounded like a sob.

Margaret rolled her eyes. 'Is there another key?' she demanded of Fox. Fox looked to Thomas, eyebrows raised in enquiry.

'I believe not, my lady,' Thomas said, wondering how he was supposed to know if there was more than one key but erring on the side of caution. 'And as the king wishes to be left alone, perhaps it would be best to do as he commands?'

Margaret stared at Thomas, her dark eyes showing her outrage. 'Who is this man?' She demanded of Fox.

'Who, this?' Fox pointed to Thomas. 'Oh, this is Archbishop Deane's chaplain.'

Margaret's eyes narrowed at Thomas. 'Then why is he here and not at Lambeth Palace?'

'He proved useful when Prince Arthur died, my lady. The king seemed to value his ministrations, and so when the queen died, I sent Master Wolsey to him to provide comfort.'

'I do not like him,' Margaret said, and Thomas felt her gaze linger on his droopy eye. 'He is an impertinent fellow.'

Thomas dropped his gaze to the floor, determined not to show any emotion. It was infuriating the way Fox and Lady Margaret were talking about him as if he were not standing before them, and he was powerless to rebuke them.

'The king has a liking for him,' Fox said apologetically.

'You are the proper person to minister to my son, bishop. Not some jackanapes chaplain from Lambeth.'

Margaret glared at the door as if she wanted to kick it down. 'Get the king to come out of there,' she snarled at Fox. 'I do not care how you do it, but do it.' She turned and left, her heels ringing on the flagstones.

'Yes, my lady.' Fox bowed to Lady Margaret's retreating figure. When he was convinced she was out of earshot, he turned on Thomas. 'What do you think you were doing, speaking like that to Lady Margaret?'

'I just thought – ' Thomas began.

'Remember your place, Master Wolsey.' He made to push Thomas away from the door. 'I'll get him out.'

'Your Grace.' The urgency in Thomas's voice made Fox pause. Even as he spoke, Thomas wondered what he was doing persisting in this manner. 'Perhaps you would allow me to talk to the king? I am sure you are much busier than I and cannot spare the time it may take.'

Fox frowned at Thomas, seemingly unsure whether he was being facetious or merely overly helpful. 'Very well.' He grunted. 'But I want him out by this afternoon, or I will come back and drag him out of there.' He pulled his stole straight and strode down the corridor.

Thomas watched him go with relief. He knocked gently on the door and moved his mouth close to the wood. 'Your Grace, it is Master Wolsey. Would you kindly open the door?'

'I do not want to see anyone.'

'Your Grace, please allow me to do my duty and help you.'

'You cannot help me.'

'Allow me to try, Your Grace, I beg you.'

Thomas waited, expecting another refusal or command to leave him alone. Instead, there was silence. He was just about to speak again when he heard a key in the lock. Surprised and pleased, he took a step back and waited.

The door creaked as it opened, only a few inches. Henry's face appeared in the gap. He looked terrible. Always looking older than his years, Henry's cheekbones now stood out sharply. He had lost weight over the last few weeks, and lack of sleep had worsened the effects. His eyes were bloodshot, the skin beneath them purple.

'Is it just you?' Henry asked, his eyes searching the corridor warily.

'Just me, Your Grace. May I come in?'

Henry opened the door wider. Thomas stepped through and closed it behind him. 'It saddens me to see you so low, Your Grace, if I may say so.'

'I am saddened to have come to this pass, Master Wolsey. I would not have wished it so.'

'Have you prayed, Your Grace?'

Henry gestured at his knees. His hose were bagged and soiled with dust. 'Constantly, but no consolation have I yet found.'

'You will allow me to help you?'

Henry shrugged and walked away towards the window. 'You can try.'

Thomas wondered how to begin. If praying had not helped the king, what would?

'You loved the queen, Your Grace?'

'I did.'

'And the queen loved you?'

Henry laughed bitterly. 'I do not know. She said she did. But tell me, Master Wolsey, can one man ever know the secrets of another person's heart?'

Thomas shook his head. 'The heart is a secret to us all. Only God knows.'

'I could have been kinder to her in the beginning. When I first became king, I treated her roughly.'

'It was a difficult time for you.'

'It was. My mother told me I should not to give in to Elizabeth's whims – that was what she called them – so that was what I did.'

'Perhaps you made up for that initial unkindness, Your Grace? You had many years together and begot many children, though it has pleased God to take some of your children from you. I believe your children, and indeed you, made the queen happy.'

Henry looked up at him hopefully. 'You think so?'

Thomas smiled. 'I do, Your Grace. And you must console yourself with your children. If you wish to see your lady wife still, look for her in the faces of your son and daughters. You will see the queen there, I promise you.'

The thought seemed to please Henry. His grim expression lightened, and his lips widened in the faintest of smiles. 'Yes, I think you are right. My little Mary, she especially resembles her mother.'

'And children are perhaps the best consolation any

man can have when his wife is taken by God,' Thomas continued, wondering where this knowledge came from. 'They are, after all, a man's legacy to this world. His way of living forever.'

Henry nodded. 'Yes, you are right.'

'Would you like to see your children, Your Grace? I understand they have arrived in the palace this very morning and are most desirous of seeing their father. If you would but tidy yourself, perhaps eat something to sustain you, they await your pleasure.'

Henry ran his fingers through his thin hair, considering. After a moment, he nodded. 'Yes, yes, I will do that. Thank you, Master Wolsey. Send my grooms to me. I wish to be washed and shaved.'

'Certainly, Your Grace.' Thomas bowed and headed for the door.

'Master Wolsey,' Henry called.

He halted and turned back. 'Yes, Your Grace?'

'Should my children need consolation for the loss of their mother, I would like you to deliver it.'

'Spiritual consolation, Your Grace?'

'Any kind of consolation,' Henry said. 'I believe you are better suited to it than either Bishop Fox or my mother.'

Thomas bowed. 'I shall make your children my utmost priority.'

～

Feeling very pleased with himself, Thomas told the

king's gentlemen who were waiting, bored, in the antechamber that they could go in to him and get him bathed and dressed, ready to be seen at court.

He had not missed the sneering looks cast in his direction as the gentlemen walked past him. He understood those looks. They were the disdainful glances of men envious of Thomas's ability to manage the king where they had failed. Thomas ignored them. He had been thanked by the king, and for a man of Thomas's background, a king's gratitude was worth more than the good opinions of a few nobles.

Thomas made his way to the presence chamber, eager to see the king when he made his entrance. Word had got around that the king was going to appear, for the chamber was filling up quickly. Little groups had formed, men and women talking animatedly in hushed tones. Thomas looked around the large chamber, his frequent visits to court making him able to put names to all the faces he saw there.

He saw the king's children. There was Mary, the king's little darling, holding her nurse's hand and looking around with excited, wide blue eyes. Recollecting the king's words, Thomas squinted to detect any resemblance to the late queen in her features. He struggled to find any, but he supposed the king saw his daughter with very different eyes. Margaret was standing on her sister's other side, her big blue eyes watching everyone. It was her marriage to King James that Thomas had helped seal in Scotland. As he looked at her, he thought she was too young to be sent to that cold, dreary country in a few months' time. She looked so fragile. And then there was Henry, taller and carrying a little less weight than when Thomas had seen him last, the puppy fat having fallen away. The boy, not unnaturally, seemed a little subdued, and Thomas thought that was a shame. Henry's exuberance was one of the most attractive things about him.

The king had asked Thomas to be kind to his children. Wanting to waste no time, Thomas made his way through the crowd towards them. He saw Lady Margaret standing not far off and studiously avoided looking at her. He did not want another confrontation or to suffer her interference again.

'Good day to you, my lord, my ladies.' Thomas bowed and smiled, he hoped kindly, upon the children. 'I am Master Thomas Wolsey, chaplain to the archbishop of Canterbury. Your father the king wished for me to attend you.'

Mary smiled prettily at him, and Margaret curtsied. Henry stared.

'I remember you,' he said, his young face looking very adult as he searched his memory.

'You honour me, Prince Henry.' Thomas inclined his head. 'I was present at Lambeth Palace when you welcomed the Spanish infanta to London.'

'Yes, I remember your eye.'

Thomas's smile slipped a little. Was his droopy eye such a disfigurement that people used it as a tool to remember him by? 'Allow me to express my sorrow at the loss of your dear mother. If you should need me for anything, please send for me.'

From the corner of his eyes, Thomas could see Lady Margaret edging towards him and the children, and he decided he had done enough for the moment. He bowed to the children and removed himself to the side of the room, out of Lady Margaret Beaufort's way.

The king came out of his chamber, faced his court and accepted their condolences. He greeted his children but did not seem to know what to say to them, so he kissed their cheeks and sent them back to their nurse whilst he retired to the council chamber with Fox and Lovell. Fox indicated that Thomas was not needed, so he meandered around the chamber, engaging in conversation with those who appeared amenable and keeping out of the way of any who did not.

He had left the chamber to piss in a pot in the corridor when he heard a sniffling. He followed the sound down the corridor, stopping when he came to a window embrasure. Prince Henry was curled up in the corner, his head on his knees.

'Prince Henry?'

The young Henry started. His face was red and streaked with tears. 'Leave me alone.'

But Thomas was determined to stay. 'I cannot leave you alone in so sorry a state, my lord.'

'I command you to leave me,' Henry said loudly.

Unperturbed, Thomas shook his head and sat down next to the boy on the window seat. 'Your father commanded me to attend to his children. Let me help you.'

'I do not need a priest,' Henry said defiantly.

'Maybe you need a friend,' Thomas suggested.

This seemed to catch the young boy off guard. He stopped sniffing and stared at Thomas in surprise. 'Grandmother says people of royal birth do not have friends, only allies.'

'If you will permit me to say so, my lord, every person needs friends, whether they are of royal birth or no. I admit that members of a royal family need to be careful about who they call friends, but that does not mean they cannot have them. I would like to be your friend, if you would like it too.'

Henry lowered his head but looked Thomas over from beneath his lashes. They were long lashes, more like a girl's, and very fair. Thomas waited, knowing the boy was wondering whether to trust this forward, lowborn man in priest's raiment who professed to be a friend.

'Is my father well, Master Wolsey? Without my mother, I mean?' Henry asked.

'Your father misses your mother greatly and he has been very sad, but you must not worry about him. He has many people about him who will see to his welfare.'

Henry wiped his nose on his sleeve. Thomas took out his own clean handkerchief and handed it to the boy.

Henry took it with a grateful smile. 'Thank you.' He

blew his nose noisily. 'Grandmother says I must not weep. She says it is a weakness to be sad for my mother. She says she will beat me if she sees me cry. She says I should be like my sister Mary, for she does not cry. But my sister does not understand. Mary thinks Mother has gone away for a whilst and that she will come back to Eltham and visit us.' His voice cracked. 'She's so silly.' He began crying again.

So, this was why he was hiding, Thomas realised, so that his hard-faced and hard-hearted grandmother would not see him grieve for the mother he had loved. Thomas looked around the window edge and saw that the nearest people were at the other end of the corridor. There would be no witnesses. He shuffled nearer to the boy and tentatively put his arm around Henry's small shoulders, squeezing and tugging him a little closer. He felt the boy resist, then lean against him, burying his face into Thomas's chest.

Thomas did not speak, he merely allowed Henry to cry. He felt it was the kindest act he could perform.

I may as well move to court, I am here so often, Thomas thought as he followed the page to the council chamber at Whitehall on another mission for Deane.

Deane was going to court less and less, preferring to stay at Lambeth Palace with its particular comforts, his old age and frail body his excuse for his dereliction. Thomas did not mind; indeed, he was pleased to be the archbishop's proxy, but he minded the constant travelling, especially if the court was at Windsor, which necessitated a lengthy boat journey, the water never being his preferred means of travel.

It was true Deane was not fit for travel at present. Thomas was, in truth, a little concerned. The old man had barely been able to sit up in bed this past week. When Thomas had told him of the queen's death, Deane had believed it was his duty to present himself to the king, but he could not swing his legs out of bed without pain and had given up the attempt, telling Thomas to convey his apologies and condolences instead.

Thomas arrived at the council chamber. It was empty save for the clerk who looked up at Thomas's entrance and raised his eyebrows in bored enquiry. Thomas passed him the paper from the archbishop, related details he knew Deane had forgotten to include in his message, and duty done, bid the clerk good day. Thomas considered remaining at court for dinner, but it was a good hour away and with Deane incapacitated, there was more work than ever piling up at Lambeth. He made his way out of the palace.

Carts were arriving when he reached the courtyard, laden high with trunks and other household goods. Thomas saw a bed broken in two being unloaded, carried by puffing, red-faced men who were to take it to its destination and reassemble it. There was another man carrying a bow and quiver of arrows.

Curiosity roused, Thomas paused to watch. At the sound of hooves, he looked towards the gateway to see

Prince Henry canter into the courtyard on his horse. A stable boy took hold of the reins and the prince dismounted, his expression almost grim. Thomas cast a quick look around the stable yard. There were only servants around, no nobles to interfere. He strode up to the boy and bowed. 'Good morning, my lord.'

'Master Wolsey, good day,' Prince Henry greeted him. 'Are you here to take me to my father?'

'No, my lord, I was actually just leaving the palace. I did not know you were coming to court. But if that is your wish, I will accompany you to the king.'

Henry opened his mouth to accept, Thomas was sure, but then the boy's gaze shifted sharply, and his mouth closed. Thomas turned and saw Lady Margaret a few feet away. *Perfect*, he thought sourly as he bowed to her. 'My lady.'

'You did not know of my grandson's coming to court, Master Wolsey, because you did not need to know,' she said, not even looking at Thomas. 'And *I* shall take my grandson to the king. You can be on your way. Come, Henry.' She held out her hand, flicking her fingers impatiently.

Henry gave Thomas a look that managed to combine an apology with a farewell as he hurried after his formidable grandmother.

'It appears the king's mother does not care for you, Master Wolsey,' a voice said.

Thomas turned to the speaker, smiling. Lord Darcy was frequently at court due to his administrative work, and Thomas and he had crossed paths often. Thomas liked Darcy very much. He was that rare courtier, one who actually worked hard for his position, and Darcy found himself buffeted from one post to another, one country to another in the king's service. Whatever was needed, the short, dark-haired, blue-eyed lord seemed to achieve, not spectacularly, but quietly, rarely looking for reward and often signally failing to receive any. If Darcy had one fault, in Thomas's opinion, it was his reluctance to demand more from his masters.

'Indeed, my lord, it seems she does not. I wish I knew why.'

Darcy squinted at him. 'You do not know?'

'I do not. Do you?'

'I can guess. An Oxford man you may be, Thomas, but your father, you'll forgive me, was a butcher, a mere merchant. And yet, here you are.' Darcy gestured at the palace, 'visiting court, essential to all church business, instrumental in treaty negotiations and I know not what else. The king has favoured you, and it looks as if the prince does too. All of that is reason enough for the king's mother to despise you.'

Thomas's jaw tightened. 'She dislikes me for something I cannot help.'

'That you are lowborn is not your fault, admittedly, but how dare you rise above your station?'

'Her mind is still in the last century, my lord. But that is well. Lady Margaret will not live forever. I can wait.'

'Careful, Master Wolsey.' Darcy moved closer, his

levity gone, his voice serious. 'You must not speak so freely here. Remember, walls have ears at court.'

Thomas took a deep breath. 'Yes, thank you for reminding me, my lord. Tell me, as you seem to know everything, why is the prince here?'

'Rumour has it the king has brought Prince Henry to stay for good. He's the Prince of Wales now, and 'tis thought the king wants the boy where he can keep an eye on him. And of course, the prince needs to be trained for the day he will become king. At Eltham, Prince Henry had none but women for company. I never thought that was good for the boy. A boy needs men about him.' Darcy looked Thomas up and down. 'Where are you off to?'

'Back to Lambeth,' Thomas said. 'I cannot leave the archbishop for too long.'

'Aye, I heard he is ill. Is it serious?'

'I think it might be,' Thomas said sadly. 'He has been in bed for more than a week now.'

'I will pray for him,' Darcy said. 'Fare you well, Master Wolsey. I daresay we shall meet again soon.'

'Good day, my lord.' Thomas bowed and headed out of the stable yard.

Thomas finished adding up the column of figures. He had added them up twice, just to be sure he had been right the first time. Calculation confirmed, he added a tick to the total sum with satisfaction. His personal finances were looking very healthy. The salary from his first living, St Mary's in Lymington, had been joined by several others over the years following his receipt of a special dispensation from the Pope allowing him to hold several benefices at once. He had few expenses at present, having little to spend his money on, so the coins in his strongbox seemed to be breeding.

Thomas leant back and raised his arms over his head, groaning with pleasure as his muscles stretched and his bones cracked. He pushed himself up from his chair, needing to move after the long hours of inactivity at his desk. The church bells rang the eleventh hour, and he realised he had finished just in time for his turn with the archbishop.

Deane was very ill. It seemed the event he had planned for so long, his death, was finally upon him. Ever since Thomas had joined Deane as his chaplain, it had been the archbishop's chief joy to plan his funeral. Thomas knew the details by heart, for Deane had had him draft his various plans, every change he made, every addition of pomp he wanted. Thomas and Gregory had laughed at the old man's plan, finding it strange that anyone could take comfort in such an occupation, but Deane wanted his funeral to be exactly as he would wish it, and he did not trust anyone else to plan it correctly.

Thomas left his room and stepped quietly along the corridor to the archbishop's bedchamber. He lifted the latch and peeped inside, not wishing to wake the archbishop if he was sleeping. Gregory, sitting by Deane's bedside, twisted in his chair and jerked his head for Thomas to enter.

Thomas moved to stand at the foot of the bed and looked down on Deane. The old man looked shrivelled, bundled up beneath sheets and blankets. 'How has he been?'

'The same,' Gregory said. 'He said he wasn't hungry, just had a little wine. Most of the time he's been asleep.'

'At least he is not in any pain. You can go to bed now. I'll sit with him until morning.'

Gregory stood, arching his back. 'You look tired yourself. I can come back in a few hours. I only need a little sleep.'

'It is my office as much as it is yours. You have done your duty. Let me do mine.'

'Very well. But do call me if he worsens. I want to be here.'

'Of course. Get you to bed.'

Thomas sat in Gregory's chair, hearing the latch drop behind him as Gregory closed the door. Gregory was right, he was tired, but Thomas knew from experience that he could manage with very little sleep, and a slight deprivation at this time would do him no harm. He owed it to Deane to watch over him.

His eyes strayed to the bedside table where Deane's Bible lay. Thinking it would help him stay awake, Thomas slid it off the table and onto his lap, letting it fall open at a random page. He began to read.

His eyes had started to close when Deane suddenly

snorted and started awake. Thomas closed the Bible and put it back on the table. Leaning forward, he touched the old man's hand gently. 'Your Grace?'

'Thomas?' Deane croaked, blinking his milky eyes. 'Is that you?'

Thomas bent over the bed so Deane could see him more clearly. 'Yes, it's me.'

Deane seemed reassured and closed his eyes. 'Not long now.'

'Do not speak so, Your Grace,' he scolded.

Deane smiled weakly. 'You are very gentle with me, Thomas, but I know I will meet my maker soon. The knowledge cheers me. I am not afraid.'

'That is because you have no need to be. You have lived a most godly life.'

'I have tried to.' Deane opened his eyes. 'And I mean to do what I can for you, Thomas. I know I have not always been grateful for your work, but I do know what I owe you.'

Thomas suddenly felt a lump in his throat. 'It was my honour to serve you as best I could.'

'I have written to Sir Richard Nanfan,' Deane said, speaking even as his eyes closed.

It was a name Thomas knew well. Sir Richard Nanfan was the deputy lieutenant of Calais. There had been almost daily correspondence between Calais and Lambeth Palace, most of it handled by Thomas. Thomas was curious how he had come to miss the letter Deane was speaking of.

'I had Gregory write it so it would be a surprise for

you.' Deane managed a smile at his stratagem, looking like a little boy. 'I have asked Sir Richard to give you a post when I am gone and he has agreed.'

'A post in Calais?' Thomas asked.

But Deane had fallen asleep, and Thomas did not receive an answer. He sank back into his chair, knowing he should be grateful. Deane had thought of him even as he lay dying and had secured his immediate future. But to leave London… Calais seemed so far away.

Think of the advantages, he told himself as he watched Deane's eyelids flutter. Calais was the only English territory in the whole of France, and as such, was vitally important to England. It served as a gateway between France and England and was constantly trafficked with merchants, diplomats and other travellers. There would be many in Calais who would need not only spiritual guidance and consolation from a priest but the talents of an expert administrator.

Less than an hour later, Thomas rushed to Gregory's room and shook him awake. Deane's breathing had become slow and shallow, and Thomas knew the old man had little time left. Clad only in his nightshirt, Gregory followed after Thomas, and the two chaplains knelt either side of the bed, each holding one of Deane's hands, and prayed as the old archbishop breathed his last.

CHAPTER SIXTEEN

The boat was going up and down, up and down, and Thomas prayed it would stop. He had never endured a sea journey before, and he was sure he would never do so again if he could help it. From the moment he had stepped aboard the ship that would take him to Calais, he had not had a minute when he did not feel sick. He had spent most of the journey hanging over the side of the ship, spewing his breakfast into the water roiling beneath him.

When the ship dropped anchor in Calais harbour, Thomas was told to climb down a rope ladder to a small boat that would take him ashore. The short journey from the ship to the shore was almost as unpleasant as the sea voyage had been, and it was with very unsteady legs that Thomas stepped onto the port's jetty.

'Rough trip?'

Thomas could only manage a grimace at the man who helped him from the boat. He knew he must look dreadful; he did not need this idiot making fun of him. He pushed past the man and took firm hold of an upright wooden post, leaning his entire body weight against it. With his eyes closed, he waited for the ground to become solid beneath him, then said a prayer to God, thanking Him for getting him to Calais safely.

'Excuse me, are you Thomas Wolsey?'

Thomas pulled his eyelids apart to look at the speaker. It was a young pageboy dressed in the livery he knew belonged to the deputy lieutenant. 'Yes.'

'I have been sent to fetch you, sir.'

Thomas nodded with his eyes closed, then pushed himself upright with an effort. 'My trunk is still on board the ship.'

'It will be sent on,' the page assured him. 'If you will follow me, sir.'

The page walked away up the jetty. Thomas started after him at a much slower pace, noticing that the page slowed down so as not to go too far ahead.

Thomas began to feel better. The ground beneath his feet was reassuringly firm, and his stomach settled. The air was fresh, even though it was full of the smell of humans and animals, the cargoes of spices and all the other goods being loaded and unloaded.

Calais was even busier than he had expected it to be. He counted the languages he heard as he walked along the dockside: English, French, Flemish, German, Spanish, and those were just the ones he recognised. Everywhere was movement, whether it was people heading towards the dock or moving away from it, and every one of those people was in a hurry, it seemed. Heads down, hands holding bags onto shoulders lest they be knocked away, determination in every step. And if it wasn't people, it was animals, either being loaded onto ships for transportation or coming off them, their hooves filthy with the excrement they had been forced to stand in, trailing it along the cobbled streets.

Thomas and the page reached the city gates. Thomas raised his gaze to the inscription carved in the archway: 'When shall the Frenchman Calais win? When iron and lead like cork will swim'. *Calais may have a French name and be in France*, Thomas thought, *but its Englishness is loud and defiant*.

The residence of the deputy lieutenant was not far, the pageboy told him, and soon Thomas found himself standing outside a set of stone gates wide enough for a large cart to pass comfortably through. The page banged on the wooden doors, and a square hatch set at eye height opened a moment later. A face peered out.

'It's me, Master Pickett,' the page said. 'I've got him.'

The hatch slammed shut and Thomas heard a bar lift on the other side. The left-hand door was pulled open about a foot, and the page slipped through, gesturing to Thomas to follow. Thomas did, nodding at Master Pickett as he shut the door behind him. Then it was on to the residence, which was large if unappealing, its dull grey stone facade lacking any decorative flair or artistry.

'I am to take you to your room, Master Wolsey,' the

page said as he led him inside. 'Sir Richard will dine in an hour, and you are to join him then.'

The page led him up a staircase and along a narrow corridor, stopping at a door at the end. He pushed it open. 'This is you,' he said, pointing Thomas in.

The room was inviting, larger than the room Thomas had had at Lambeth. There was a small fireplace and a comfortable-looking bed with elaborately carved posts and heavy red hangings.

'Can I get you anything, Master Wolsey?' the page asked.

Thomas's stomach was still a little unsettled, and he shook his head. 'I am not needed for an hour, you say?'

'An hour,' the page confirmed.

'Then I shall rest until dinner.'

'Very well, sir.' The page stepped out and closed the door behind him.

'Well, you're here,' Thomas said aloud to himself, sinking onto the bed and feeling the mattress give agreeably. 'But please God, do not let this place be the end of my career.'

The page came to get Thomas. The short nap Thomas intended had turned into a deep sleep, and it took a few shakes of his shoulder for the page to get Thomas to wake up. Thomas felt groggy and grumpy, the usual result of his sleeping in the afternoon, which was why he tried to avoid it. As the page led him back along the corridor and down the stairs, all Thomas could think of was getting a drink; his throat was parched and his head heavy.

They reached a large room towards the back of the stairs and the page announced Thomas. A voice said, 'Come forward, Master Wolsey,' and Thomas angled his body past the page to step farther into the room.

Another old man, was Thomas's first thought. Sir Richard Nanfan was thin and scrawny. His skin was unhealthily grey, save for a large blob of a liver spot that marked his left cheek. He looked unaccustomed to cheerfulness. He did not smile as Thomas neared.

'So, you are the fellow who so impressed Deane,' he said, looking Thomas up and down.

Thomas guessed he was thinking he did not look very impressive. He knew he had put on a little weight since he had been with the archbishop, the dinners at Lambeth Palace being so very generous, and he knew from the way his vision was sometimes impaired that his left eyelid still drooped. 'The late archbishop was kind enough to acknowledge my meagre talents.'

Nanfan winced as if in pain. 'Oh, no false modesty, please. I hope Deane was not exaggerating, else I would not have you here. Are you good or are you not?'

'I am very good, Sir Richard,' Thomas said after the smallest moment's hesitation.

'That is better.' Nanfan clapped his hands. To Thomas's surprise, his face broke into a smile. 'Now, sit you down.' He kicked a stool towards Thomas. 'Take some wine. Tell me about yourself.'

'Well,' Thomas said, staring down at the flagstones. He was surprised by Nanfan's informal manner, so different from Deane's. Thomas rather liked it. 'I served His Grace the archbishop for almost three years as chaplain, sometimes in Canterbury, but mostly in London.'

'At court?'

'On many occasions.' Thomas nodded. 'I helped arrange the marriage of Prince Arthur and the Spanish infanta, and that needed a great deal of liaising with the king's council. And as Deane became more infirm, he would despatch me to act in his stead.'

Nanfan chuckled. 'Now, when you say you helped arrange the marriage, what you really mean is you organised the whole bloody thing, do you not? Come, I knew Henry Deane of old. Speak truth.'

'His Grace was kind enough to entrust most of the arrangements to my care,' Thomas said.

'I see you are loyal, Master Wolsey.' Nanfan nodded approvingly. 'And rightly so. You may have thought Deane a silly old fool, and lazy too. Yes, I can see you did. But he was a deal cleverer than people thought. And what if he did take it easy? He worked hard in his youth. He deserved to rest in his twilight years. But I tell you, he would not have done so had he not known he could trust those about him. He was a good judge of character.'

Thomas acknowledged the implied compliment with a smile.

'You probably think I am like Deane,' Nanfan said,

looking at Thomas over the rim of his cup. 'An old man.'

'I would never think so, Sir Richard,' Thomas lied at once.

Sir Richard ignored him. 'I *am* an old man. I have worked hard all my life and want to have an easy time now, I will not deny it. And that is what I mean to do, Master Wolsey. It is a busy life here in Calais, too busy for an old man like me to enjoy. Were I your age, it would be a different matter.'

'I think I understand you, Sir Richard,' Thomas said. 'You mean to allow me to take on many of the responsibilities of Calais.'

'You are quick, are you not?' Nanfan laughed. 'Yes, I do. What do you think of that?'

Thomas swallowed and looked his new master straight in the eye. 'I think it would be an honour, sir.'

'That,' Nanfan leant forward and gave a light slap to Thomas's knee, 'is the correct answer.' They both laughed. 'I expect you were disappointed when Deane said you were coming here.'

Thomas shrugged.

'Very well, do not say so. But I can imagine, and I imagine you were thinking that by coming out to Calais, to this small port town, part of England yet not part of it, you would be forgotten by everyone that mattered. Am I right?'

'You may be, Sir Richard,' Thomas admitted reluctantly.

'Well, you were wrong. Tell me, when you got off the boat and stepped onshore, what did you think?'

'I thought I would never feel well again.'

'Not a natural sailor, then. Ha ha.'

Thomas grinned. 'I thought Calais was very busy, Sir Richard.'

'It is busy here, every day. Every day that harbour out there is full of ships, the docks full of people. It feels like the whole world passes through this town and, in a sense, it does. What does that mean for us? I shall tell you. It means we are busy. Unforgivably busy. And no two days are the same, I promise you. One day, Master Wolsey, you will be dealing with complaints from merchants about too expensive toll charges, the next you are entertaining ambassadors and stealing private papers intended for the king's eyes only. You will not be bored, Master Wolsey, whatever else you might be.'

'I am very pleased to hear it.'

Nanfan nodded, his eyes narrowing. 'Deane told me you were ambitious. Never fear, you will make your mark here.'

'I always meant to do my duty, Sir Richard,' Thomas said, concerned Nanfan had thought he would be lax.

'I never thought otherwise.' Nanfan held up his hands to forestall any further protestations. 'You seem to me a man of honesty and diligence, as well as having the makings of a true politician. Time will pass quickly.' He winked. 'You will do well here in Calais, Master Wolsey.'

CHAPTER SEVENTEEN

1507

Someone was hovering near the doorway; Henry could see him out of the corner of his eye. He did wish people would not hover. It made him uneasy. He half expected one of these shadow-huggers to pounce and stick a dagger between his shoulder blades. 'What is it?' he called irritably.

At Henry's elbow, Fox hadn't noticed the presence of another person. He frowned, following Henry's gaze. Recognising the intruder, he clicked his fingers and gestured for the secretary to draw near.

'I have an urgent message for Your Grace,' the secretary said, unhappy at being snapped at. He showed Fox the letter in his hand and Fox held out his own for it.

'From Calais,' Fox said, raising an eyebrow at the impression in the wax seal.

'Read it,' Henry ordered peremptorily.

Fox broke the seal and unfolded the letter. It

crackled noisily. 'Sir Richard Nanfan has died, Your Grace,' Fox said, nodding, the news unexpected. 'This letter is from his chaplain, Master Wolsey.'

Henry reached for the letter to read for himself. 'Have we prepared for this, Fox? Do we have someone lined up for the post? Calais is too important to leave without a deputy.'

'Yes, Your Highness. I did have knowledge that Sir Richard was not in the best of health and had considered his replacement. I had thought of Sir Edward Poynings for the post. I believe he will accept.'

'Make haste in writing to him.'

'Of course, but if I may say so, there is no real need for haste. Master Wolsey – you remember him, Your Grace – is very capable and will manage matters well enough until Poynings is installed. I understand Sir Richard left much of the deputy lieutenant's job in Master Wolsey's hands. Barely had to lift a finger.' Fox's tone was decidedly disparaging.

Henry's eyes narrowed. He didn't like to know that any of his servants did not earn the money he paid them. 'I do remember Master Wolsey. How long has he been in Calais?'

'Since the death of Archbishop Deane, I believe, so that is, what, five years? Oh,' he breathed.

'What is it?'

'Now I remember,' Fox said, tapping the letter. 'I had a letter from Sir Richard in his own hand a month ago. Very badly written, the writing hard to read, I recall. I did wonder why he had written it and not his secretary. In it, he recommended Master Wolsey to me. Said he would make an excellent royal chaplain should the opportunity arise. He must have realised he was dying, poor man, and wanted to do something for his chaplain.'

'Master Wolsey must have been very dear to him,' Henry mused. 'And he was of great comfort to me and my children when my dear wife died. Yes, I think Sir Richard was right. Master Wolsey would be useful to have at court. As soon as Poynings is installed in Calais, have Master Wolsey come to court as my royal chaplain. See to it, Fox.'

Fox made a note, content he had made it seem as if Master Wolsey coming to court was the king's idea.

Thomas closed his eyes, waiting until the giddiness had passed before opening them again.

It was the second time that morning he had had a bout of giddiness. He knew he should still be in bed, that he had risen too soon after his illness, but he could not stay in bed. There was simply too much to do. Since Sir Richard's death, all the work at the port of Calais had been on Thomas's shoulders. He could not complain; it was his own fault. From his arrival at the English port all those years ago, he had gradually and deliberately acquired more jobs and, consequently, more power. All those men he worked with had been content to let him take on the responsibility, so was it any wonder they all sat back now and left him to get on with it?

Thomas had been up since five that morning. He had attended a very early mass, then made straight for his desk with only a cup of beer to sustain him until dinner. It was not only the business of the port that claimed him. Sir Richard had named Thomas executor of his will, and there was a great deal of correspondence from his relatives and creditors, all asking for their due portion of Nanfan's estate. And so, there were bills to examine, letters to read and answer, and all of them were seemingly urgent and requiring the personal touch. Thomas did not trust his secretary to deal with them; Bartholomew had a habit of lining his own purse with the funds intended for the coffers of the deputy lieutenant. Thomas had been aware of this from the start, had seen the sneaky business his secretary carried out on an almost daily basis, and had chosen to ignore it. Petty pilfering was a common if unappealing aspect of the job and, in truth, he did not begrudge the man the few extra pennies if it made his own life a little easier and caused no great detriment to the money chests of the deputy lieutenant. Thomas would not play the hypocrite and stop the practice, for he had done the same thing when he continued to pocket the salary of St Mary's along with all the other benefices he had acquired over the years.

Thomas dined at his desk, asking the steward to add a spoonful of honey to his cup of ale to soothe his sore throat. The relatives' letters were answered one by one, and the creditors were paid at least a portion of what was owing to them to keep them quiet for a while. He knew they would be back, clamouring for the remainder, and did not blame them. Unlike the nobility, who seemed to have a reluctance to pay any bills, he understood how important a steady flow of money was to traders and merchants.

When the church bells rang the fifth hour, Thomas laid down his quill, wiped his fingers free of ink and yawned. Just a nap, he told himself, rising from his desk and making his way to his bedchamber. Just an hour or two, no more. He passed his secretary on the way out and told Bartholomew that if he had not returned by seven, he was to wake him.

Thomas lay down on his bed and fell asleep almost immediately. The church bells ringing the quarter hour of six woke him, and he rose, stretched his arms over his head and headed back down to his office.

There was a letter on his desk that had not been there before. He turned it over, and his eyebrows rose when he saw the impression in the wax seal. It was the seal used by Bishop Fox.

Thomas grabbed his letter knife and slid it gently under the fold of paper, sawing gently at the hard red wax. With the lightest of pressure, the wax came away from the paper clean and unbroken. He unfolded the paper and read.

Most beloved Master Wolsey,

The king is most grateful for your continued good

administration of the business in the port of Calais. He has this day appointed Sir Edward Poynings as deputy lieutenant of the Port of Calais, and he will be arriving within one week to take up his post. We trust you will remain in place until he has arrived and has settled in. Once that is accomplished, the king is desirous of your leaving Calais to take up a position as royal chaplain at court. You should know that this appointment is offered to you on the recommendation of Sir Richard Nanfan, who conveyed his good opinion of you to the king shortly before he died.

Further instructions will be forwarded in due course.

Bishop Fox

Thomas read the letter three times, his throat tightening with each word. Sir Richard had recommended him to the king and not said a word to Thomas. Oh, that good old man. Thomas felt his eyes water and tried to blink away the tears that threatened. He refolded the letter and placed it carefully in his desk drawer, a very special treasure.

He rose from his desk and strode through the residence to the chapel. There, he fell on his knees and said a prayer to God, thanking him for his deliverance and saying a prayer for his good late master, Sir Richard Nanfan.

~

'Bess! Bess!' Joan's voice ran throughout the house.

Elizabeth wiped her bloodied hands on her apron with a sigh. What did her mother want now?

'I cannot come, Mother,' she called. 'I am cutting up the meat.'

Joan came breathless into the kitchen, strands of grey hair escaping her cap. Her cheeks were flushed, Elizabeth noted, and thought unkindly that her mother had been abed with her stepfather. But no, she was waving a piece of paper at her.

'Thomas has written, Elizabeth,' Joan said breathlessly.

'Oh yes?' Elizabeth returned to her work. She could not conjure up any excitement at the arrival of a letter from Thomas. She saw so little of him, heard from him so infrequently, that her love for him was buried deep. He had written when he was appointed to Calais, and she had enjoyed the faint note of disappointment she had sensed in his words. Since that letter, the Wolseys had had nothing from Thomas. He had no news to give nor inclination to receive any, Elizabeth had said one night after supper when Joan had been sighing over the deficit. Now it seemed Thomas had something about himself to impart that he thought worthy of their knowledge. Well, good for him.

'He's coming back to England,' Joan declared.

'Why?'

'The man he served in Calais has died, and the king – hark, Elizabeth, the king! – has asked Thomas to be his chaplain.'

This was news that could not be swept aside, not even by Elizabeth. 'You cannot mean it!'

'It is true. Here, read for yourself.'

Elizabeth wiped her hands and took the letter. 'Oh my,' she breathed upon reaching the end.

'My Thomas,' Joan said, hugging herself. 'Just think, Bess. Thomas will talk with the king of England.' She clasped her hands in front of her heart, her mind filled with images of Thomas and King Henry head to head, their breaths mingling as they discussed kingly affairs almost as equals.

'And will the favoured priest come to visit us?' Elizabeth asked, handing back the letter as her awe diminished.

Her sarcasm punctured Joan's joy. 'Why must you be so bitter towards Thomas? He is your brother. We must take pride in his success.'

'Oh, Mother, Thomas has more than enough pride for all of us.'

Joan stared at her daughter for a long moment, wondering how she could convince Elizabeth this was a joyous day for the whole family. The moment lengthened, and Elizabeth returned to her work.

Joan looked down at the letter and winced as she saw the red stain Elizabeth's fingers had left. The letter had been soiled – the bloodstain would always be there. Joan quietly refolded the paper and ran her thumb over the broken seal. She turned away from Elizabeth and shuffled quietly away, her resentment at her daughter growing with each step.

She was proud of Thomas, she was. She wanted to write and tell him so, but she did not know where to send a letter. Thomas had written that he would be leaving Calais on the fifteenth, and it was now the eighteenth. He would be on his way to London, but he had not said where he was heading. A small part of her still hearing Elizabeth's words, Joan wondered if this had been a deliberate omission. Was he perhaps worried she would turn up at a palace and embarrass him?

Joan returned to her writing slope; the account ledgers, as always, were waiting for her. She took down a locked iron chest from the shelf and found the key on her garter that fit. Inside were a number of important papers – property deeds, licences, her will – and to these she added Thomas's latest letter. With a sigh, she closed and locked the small chest and sat down at her slope, determined to put to the back of her mind her son's most recent success. For the time being, at least.

He felt like celebrating. Calais, with all its stink, with all its bustle, would soon be a memory. He was going to be back in England and serving the king.

But how did a churchman celebrate? There were not rules exactly, but expectations of such men. They should be sober at all times; how else could they be considered trustworthy and able to intercede with the Almighty? And besides, getting drunk was not quite in Thomas's line. He appreciated fine wine, when he had been allowed to partake of Sir Richard's substantial cellar, and ale was a necessity of life, not an indulgence. A fine dinner, then? But he had always eaten well at Sir Richard's table, so there was nothing really celebratory about that either. He knew what he really wanted to do, but did he dare do it?

Thomas had to inspect a cargo coming off one of the English ships moored in the port, and he headed down to the harbour in the late afternoon as the daylight was beginning to fade. He realised he should have brought a boy with him to carry a torch to guide him back to the residence when the business was done. As it was, he would have to make his way back in the dark, and the thought did not please him. Calais could be a dangerous place, especially at night, for a lone traveller. He tried to hurry the business along, but the buyer of the cargo was not a man to be rushed, and so the hour passed and the sun disappeared. It had gone entirely by the time Thomas's business was concluded, and he made his way along streets lit only by the moon.

The streets were full of noise. Thomas knew his churchman's garb would offer him a substantial measure of protection and found himself minding the lack of a torch because he could not see where he was putting his feet. He had already sunk into something soft, and the smell that had wafted up suggested it was manure. *Some celebration this is*, he thought sourly as he scraped his shoe against a stone. Someone brushed by him and knocked him off balance, and he put out a hand to steady himself. As he did so, a door opened, and a great noise of laughter wafted over him. He looked inside what was one of Calais's many taverns and decided he would not return to the residence just yet but treat himself to a drink and a pie and some robust, if earthy, conversation. If eyebrows were raised at his entrance, he could always claim to be meeting someone on business. If the person did not turn up, that was not his fault.

No eyebrows were raised, and Thomas soon realised that this tavern, as all taverns in Calais, was used to receiving all sorts of people; clergymen were the least unusual. He sat down at a table by the fire and ordered a jug of ale and a pie and cheese. Men came and sat with him, and Thomas passed a companionable hour or so in their company. But when the watchmen called out the hour, he knew he really should be making a move. He rose with a contented sigh.

'Not going so soon, Master Wolsey?' a female voice asked him.

He stared at the woman, his mind recognising the face but not able to place her name. 'It is time I was on my way, Mistress... '

'Parker,' she supplied with a smile.

'Parker, yes, of course.'

'I was just leaving too,' she said. 'Perhaps we could walk together?'

They exited the tavern. Thomas felt Mistress Parker swing her skirts against him, and then, when they had reached a street less busy than the others, her hand curve around his arm. 'For safety,' she said when his expression enquired.

'When do you leave Calais?' he asked by way of conversation.

'In the morning around eleven.'

'And where do you go to?'

'Flanders. My husband went on ahead.'

'And left you here alone?'

'Oh, he knows I can look after myself. And I have a boy to keep me company. Not that he is much company, of course.'

'No?'

'He's so young, barely fifteen. Has not a word to say for himself of any account.'

'And no other company?'

'Only that I find on the road. I would have liked to have talked with you this evening, Master Wolsey.'

'And I you, Mistress Parker,' Thomas assured her not entirely wholeheartedly, for he suspected the lady was flirting with him and he was unsure how to behave. 'Would that you had come into the tavern sooner.'

'Aye.' She paused. 'We have not entirely lost our chance, though, you know. You could join me in my lodging.'

She was flirting with him, and more, Thomas thought, his heart beating faster. He swallowed, his mouth suddenly dry. 'Would that not look odd, Mistress Parker?'

'There's none to see but the landlord, and I know him of old. He turns a blind eye.'

'Still… '

'But if that is all that bothers you, there's a back

entrance, goes right up to my chamber. No one need see.'

Thomas hesitated. It was what he had wanted but dared not pay for, not in Calais where there were eyes everywhere. But Mistress Parker was no whore, just a woman in need of a little company. Better yet, she would be gone on the morrow, her business taking her away.

'Mistress Parker,' he said, bending low to speak in her ear, 'I would like that very much.'

CHAPTER EIGHTEEN

Thomas's hands were sweating. He stroked them over his surplice, then felt his palms with his fingertips. Dry, for the moment, at least. He wished someone would talk to him, distract him from his thoughts, but those others in the chamber merely looked at him askance. Not unpleasantly, merely curiously.

Thomas had dressed with great care that morning. His best surplice had been washed and kept in a trunk so it had not become soiled with dirt or dust nor his own sweat. He had ordered his boy to shave him, warning him to concentrate fully on the blade. The last thing he wanted was to be presented to the king with bloody nicks all over his face. His shoes had been polished with sheep fat to make them shine, and he hoped they didn't smell.

He saw a page in the Tudor livery of green and white threading his way through the crowd towards Thomas. He straightened, immediately alert.

'Master Wolsey?' the page asked, and Thomas nodded. 'You are to come with me, sir.' The page turned and began back the way he had come. Thomas followed hard on his heels. He knew the palace, knew where he was being taken – the king's privy chamber. The doors creaked as the page opened them. Thomas took a deep breath before stepping inside.

Four men sat at the long oak table in the middle of the room. They all looked up at his entrance.

'Ah, Master Wolsey,' Bishop Fox said, 'welcome back to court.'

Henry looked Thomas up and down, his flinty eyes missing nothing. 'It is good to see you again, Master Wolsey.'

'Your Grace honours me,' Thomas said. 'I would like to thank you for this appointment.'

Henry's thin lips jerked a brief smile of acknowledgement. 'I like to have able men about me. I need men who can get things done without complaint.'

'I can do that, Your Grace,' Thomas assured him.

Henry nodded. 'You understand your duties?'

'The duties of a chaplain, Your Grace?'

'The duties of a *royal* chaplain, Master Wolsey. There is more to the appointment than administering to the spiritual needs of your king.' Henry gestured at the papers that littered the table. 'There is an endless flood of paperwork to be attended to.'

'It will be my privilege to deal with it, Your Grace,' Thomas said and meant it. *What a challenge*, he thought, eyeing the table. To read all the papers sent to the king and put them – and by that virtue, the entire country – in order.

～

Fox had dismissed Thomas but told him to wait in the corridor. Thomas paced up and down outside the council chamber, his mind racing with his new situation, and wondering what the bishop wanted to say to him.

The door opened and Fox appeared. He saw Thomas and said, 'Come to my room.' He strode away down the corridor, Thomas hurrying after him. When they reached Fox's room, Thomas was pointed to a stool. He sat down as Fox closed the door and took a seat at his desk.

'I thought it would be wise to talk in private, Master Wolsey,' he said. 'I need you to understand your role here at court.'

'The king explained what was required, Your Grace. I thoroughly understand what I am to do,' Thomas assured him.

'Understand thoroughly, do you?' Fox grunted. 'Master Wolsey, you have been an ordinary chaplain, not a royal chaplain. There is a very great difference.'

'Of course.' Thomas shook his head, annoyed at himself for speaking before Fox had explained. 'Please, do continue.'

'Your official duty is to be a chaplain to the king,' Fox said. 'Your unofficial duty is to serve the church.'

'Are the two not entwined, Your Grace?'

'We would like to think so, Master Wolsey, but alas, that is not the case.' Fox sighed. 'The church is under attack. Our authority is being eroded. You may not have noticed it, the process has been so gradual, but it is happening, I assure you. The simple truth is that the church no longer commands the respect in this country it once did.'

Thomas thought back to his time in Lymington, to the incident with Sir Amyas Paulet. Fox was right. Where had been the respect for Thomas's office then?

'This lack of respect troubles me and my fellow clergy greatly,' Fox continued. 'The king is a lover of the church, but there are others at court who are not, and they sometimes have his ear. We must do all we can to ensure the king is not swayed by these evil-talkers. We must make ourselves the people the king turns to when he wants advice, and we must be very careful that the church's interests are continually represented here at court.'

Thomas understood. He was to do his job as royal chaplain – perform mass, offer spiritual guidance – but he was also to be an ambassador for the church and further the interests of Rome.

Certain he had made himself clear, Fox had dismissed him, leaving Thomas to make his way to the royal chapel where he reasoned most of his time at court would be spent. It was not large, he noted, but then he reasoned a chapel did not need to be, no, not even a royal chapel. A chapel had only one function: to act as a place in which God could be worshipped, and this one fulfilled that function admirably, Thomas thought, as he genuflected before the large golden cross on the altar. This was where he would perform his duty to the king. There, to the side, the small room where all the apparatus of the church was stored – silverware and gold cups, ceremonial robes – and for which he, among the other royal chaplains, would be responsible.

'And where am I to sleep?' he wondered aloud.

A head poked around the door of the small anteroom. 'Who's there?'

'Oh,' Thomas said, 'I thought I was alone. I am Thomas Wolsey, the new chaplain.'

The man came out of the room. He wore the familiar uniform of the chaplain. 'You're the new man,' he said and held out his hand. 'I'm John. Pleased to meet you.'

'And you. Have you been a royal chaplain long?'

'Aye, coming up for six years now,' John said. 'It's not a bad post, but we're always busy. There, you have been warned.'

'I like to work,' Thomas said.

John smiled. 'Just as well. Now, you wanted to know where you'll sleep. I'll show you.'

Thomas gestured for John to lead the way. He led him out of the chapel and along several corridors towards the rear of the palace.

'Here you are,' John said, opening a door and standing back to allow Thomas to pass.

Thomas stepped inside the small room. There was a bed, not large but big enough to sleep two, up against the far wall, a table beneath the window with a chest thrust between its legs. A comb and a small pair of scissors lay on the table. 'Are you sure? This room appears to be already occupied.'

John laughed. 'Aye, Lord Darcy sleeps here. You are to share.'

Thomas stared at him. 'To share?'

''Tis obvious you've not been in the king's service before. You see, we all share, Master Wolsey,' John said. 'This may be a palace, but there are very many people living here and only a few rooms to go around.'

'But I am to share with a lord? Why not with you or one of the other chaplains? Surely, that would be more appropriate.'

John shrugged. 'This is how it is. Fear not. You will find Lord Darcy amenable.'

'I know Lord Darcy,' Thomas nodded. 'He is a friend, of sorts.'

'All the better, then. I'll leave you to settle in and give instructions for your trunk to be brought up.' He left, closing the door behind him.

Thomas cursed himself. Another blunder. That made two before he had been a royal chaplain twenty-four hours. He realised he had been spoilt having beds and bedchambers to himself these past years. He had grown used to spreading out at night and keeping his chamber in a state that pleased him, not having to worry about another.

Well, Thomas, you shall have to get unused to it. You're a servant of the king now and that means some hardship.

CHAPTER NINETEEN

Thomas turned his collar up and pressed it close to his neck. It did not help. The rain still battered his skin and ran down to wet his undershirt beneath the cloak. What with the rain and the hours of riding, Thomas was feeling thoroughly fed up.

When Bishop Fox had called him into his office and told him he had an important mission for him, Thomas had been thrilled. A mission for Fox! But then Fox had gestured for Thomas to sit and began to explain what he needed. At the mention of Scotland, Thomas's heart sank a little. The last time he had been to Scotland, five years or more ago with Archbishop Deane, he had not been enamoured of the country nor the people. They had not been unfriendly, exactly, just less than welcoming, and the accommodation had been spartan to say the least.

Thomas cheered up a little when Fox explained his objective. King James had been trying very hard to make Scotland a force to be reckoned with. Since his marriage to Margaret Tudor, the king had built a navy and opened gunpowder factories to show that Scotland could defend herself, or more worryingly, attack others. He had also, it was said, made great efforts to make his court more like his rival's – in other words, more impressive – and he had mostly succeeded. King Henry could put on a good show when he wanted; for all his reputed miserliness, the Tudor king did not mind spending money when it would make a good impression, and so his court often staged plays and masques, and held dances and jousts that entertained and impressed foreign visitors. King James was keen to emulate this and had filled his court with beautiful women, as well as respected poets and other names.

Despite his marriage to an English princess, King James had never repudiated the relationship Scotland had with France, and had even sent his own cousin, the Earl of Arran, to renew the terms of the Auld Alliance. Such an alliance meant Scots travelling to France, and this was the problem for James. For his Scottish subjects to reach France and return safely, they either had to go by ship around England's coasts or by road through her. If by sea, then bad weather could force ships to take refuge in English coastal towns, where there would be no guarantee of safety. If the Scots went by road through England, they would need guarantees of safe conduct, which James knew very well were unlikely to be granted because the English did not want the Scots strengthening their relationship with France. On their way back to Scotland, the earl of Arran and his companion, Hamilton, had been arrested in Kent as illegal aliens and taken to King Henry's court, although officially they were called honoured guests.

King James sent letters objecting to their detainment. Henry was not keen to make an international incident out of the matter, but at the same time, he could not be seen to concede his prizes without a fight. And then the council had received reports that there were Scots tramping all over England, in disguise and without passports. If true, Henry asked his council, what were they doing? Henry's greatest fear was that they were spies on their way to report to their old allies, the French, about what the English were up to. What was England to do? Henry himself had no doubt. James needed to know Henry was aware of the Scottish spies that travelled through England without permission. It could not go on. The matter needed delicate handling, Fox told Henry, so he had suggested that Henry's new chaplain be sent to Scotland.

At least Thomas had good company on the journey for Lord Darcy was with him. Thomas had at first supposed Fox had sent Darcy to accompany him because Thomas was of low birth and therefore unfit to be the sole envoy to a king, but this turned out not to be the case. Once they were on the road, Darcy explained he had other business in the north of England and that he had told Fox he would welcome a companion. Fox had suggested he and Thomas travel together. For his part, Darcy was glad to be able to call on Thomas's assistance, and Thomas was gratified that Fox did trust him to deal with the king after all.

'I am wet through,' Darcy moaned, plucking at his sodden hose.

He rode by Thomas's side, and Thomas had at last come to understand how one man could be a better rider than another. Darcy sat the horse with ease, as if it was not the most uncomfortable position imaginable, as if the rubbing of his testicles was not exquisitely painful. Darcy had not complained once about the ride, only the weather and the uncleanliness of the beds they had occupied on their journey at various roadside taverns.

'Should not be long now,' Thomas said. 'I think that is the castle there.' He pointed towards the crest of the hill.

Darcy squinted into the distance. 'That's it, is it? Thanks be to God for that.'

They rode in silence towards the castle. The rain was subsiding now, and with every yard taken, Thomas could feel his weary bones yearning to dismount and walk on solid ground again. They reached the castle gates, and Darcy had to show his letter with the king's seal to gain entrance.

'Is there no one here to receive us?' Darcy muttered as they dismounted.

It certainly seemed not. Thomas and Darcy were resigned to holding their horses steady. 'This looks like someone,' Thomas said after more than five minutes of waiting, jerking his chin at a middle-aged man hurrying towards them, buttoning his coat.

'Good day, sirs,' the man said breathlessly. 'What business have you here?'

'King Henry of England's business,' Darcy replied tartly, passing his reins to a stable boy who had suddenly appeared. 'We are here to see King James about an important matter.'

'I see,' the man said. 'Well, you had best follow me. I shall take you to the steward.'

Darcy rolled his eyes at Thomas, a look that Thomas understood very well. Darcy had no love for the Scots, and his expression said he had expected nothing less than this poor welcome. He and Thomas followed after the man, stepping over horse dung and scowling at the barking of a mangy dog tied up near the door to the castle.

The man stepped inside the door and ducked his head into an inner doorway. Thomas heard only the words of the Gaelic language and understood none of them. A moment later, the steward emerged, wearing a supercilious expression and a fine tunic bearing the king's badge.

'May I see your paper from King Henry, my lord?' he asked Darcy, holding his hand out in expectation.

Darcy delved into his doublet and extracted a paper, passing it to the steward.

'That all seems in order,' the steward said, handing it back to Darcy. 'I will inform the king's ministers that you have arrived. Regrettably, Lord Darcy, no arrangements have been made to lodge you at the castle.'

'No lodgings?' Darcy cried indignantly.

'I fear not. The castle is filled to capacity at present. So many important visitors. There is simply no room for you.'

The implication was clear. King James reserved his castle for those visitors he showed favour to, and that did not include English envoys.

'That is not good enough,' Darcy said. 'As emissaries of King Henry, we demand lodgings. It is the custom.'

'It cannot be helped,' the steward said unapologetically, and Thomas saw that Darcy was about to start shouting. He thought it would not be wise.

'I am sure adequate accommodation can be found in the town,' Thomas said to Darcy, his eyes conveying a warning.

Darcy opened his mouth to protest but understood the warning and nodded grumpily. 'I suppose so. Though I shall make a complaint when this is all done,' he murmured to Thomas as the steward led them to the presence chamber.

When they reached the chamber, Thomas looked around in astonishment. It was common for the public chambers of a palace to be busy, but this one was positively bursting. He strained his ears to listen and heard snatches of several tongues. There were certainly Frenchmen here, as he had suspected, but he thought he heard Dutch too, though he was not as familiar with the language or the accent. He sought out the presence chamber steward, gave their names and their business with the king, and registered the suspicious look the steward gave him. Using his privilege as a man of the cloth, he acquired two of the few stools the chamber offered to sit upon. He and Darcy sat and waited.

And waited. It seemed the king was in no hurry to see King Henry's envoys.

They had to wait four hours or more, Thomas reckoned. Four hours before the steward called out their names and beckoned them forward. Thomas stood and surreptitiously stretched, wincing as his muscles complained. He and Darcy made their way through the crowd, Thomas inwardly cursing that movement had made him conscious of his bladder. He willed away the need to urinate; there was no time for such matters.

'Lord Darcy, Master Wolsey.' King James's greeting was careless, his disinterest obvious. He almost lounged in his upholstered chair, his long legs stretched out before him, the toes of his boots tapping together in a silent rhythm. 'What message does my brother of England have for me?'

'King Henry offers greetings to Your Grace and hopes you and his daughter Queen Margaret are in the best of health.'

James smiled and waved Thomas on.

Thomas cleared his throat. 'King Henry wishes to express his perturbation at the number of Scotsmen travelling without passports through his realm and is concerned about their intentions.'

'Their intentions?' James asked.

'It may be that they are travelling through England as the safest means of reaching France, Your Grace.'

'And why should my subjects not travel to France, Master Wolsey?'

Thomas smiled uneasily. 'Because, Your Grace, it is not known what mischief they hope to cause once there.'

'Mischief! Ha.' James slapped his thigh in merriment and clicked his fingers at a servant to bring him wine.

'Your Grace, if I may,' Thomas continued as James drank, 'the Treaty of Perpetual Peace, signed some years ago by yourself and sealed by marriage to King Henry's daughter, is being undermined by these activities. Scotland's Auld Alliance with France was supposed to be made null by the treaty, yet it is King Henry's belief that the alliance is flourishing.'

'I believe it is my business who I choose as friends, Master Wolsey,' James said, licking his thick lips made wet by the wine. 'And yet I will do my father-in-law the courtesy of obliging him with an answer. I make no treaty with the French. If Scots are travelling through England, then it is without my knowledge or my consent.'

Thomas wiped his top lip with one chubby finger. He remembered Bishop Fox's words before he left London. *Do not be too obsequious with the king. He is but a Scot and a liar. Press him if you have to. You have the king's permission to be unpleasant.*

As long as I don't end up in a prison cell, Thomas thought ruefully.

'Your cousin, the Earl of Arran, and his brother,

Patrick Hamilton, were apprehended in Kent after leaving France. King Henry keeps them, Your Grace, in comfortable accommodation, and they have been very happy to be pleasant with the king. King Henry knows they were sent to France on your orders to renegotiate the terms of the Auld Alliance.'

James started from his chair and took three steps towards Thomas. 'This is outrageous. How dare you deliver such a message to me!'

'I act on the king's authority,' Thomas said, feeling his skin prickle with sweat. He was on dangerous ground; he felt it buckling beneath his feet. 'He insists you stop sending men to France, that you stop sending men into England without passports, and that you end all negotiations with France.'

'He insists, does he?' James sneered and drew his hand back.

Thomas thought for one terrifying instant that James was going to strike him. He resolved to take the blow, not step back and cower. But the blow never came. James's arm quivered for a moment, then dropped to his side. 'Well, you can go back to King Henry and tell him he's not in a position to insist upon anything with me. And moreover, you tell him to release Arran and Hamilton. Go back to London, Master Wolsey, and tell your king that.'

Darcy had wanted to take it easy on their return journey,

their journey to Scotland having been so busy, but Thomas wanted no delay. He was eager to get back to court and deliver his news, however insignificant his news might be.

And so, as soon as they arrived at the palace, Thomas had made himself presentable, changing his dirty clothes for clean ones and washing and shaving. He left Darcy collapsed on the bed in the chamber they shared and headed for the privy council chamber.

It was empty at that early hour, save for the pages who were making it ready for the council, banking up the logs in the fireplace and ensuring there were jugs full of wine and cups to drink from on the table. They looked up in surprise, normally having the place to themselves at such an hour, but they returned to their work when they saw it was Thomas. They were used to him being up and working when they were. Not long after, Bishop Fox arrived.

'Master Wolsey, you are back.'

'Yes, Your Grace, I arrived late last night.'

'Successful?'

'Not entirely,' Thomas said, waiting for Fox to sit before doing the same.

'Why not?' Fox demanded.

Before Thomas could answer, the door opened, and the king entered with Sir Thomas Lovell. Fox and Thomas rose and bowed.

'Good morning, Your Grace,' Fox purred.

'Good morning, bishop,' Henry said, taking his seat

at the head of the table. 'And Master Wolsey, I see you are returned. Tell me, how was King James?'

'Uncooperative, Your Grace,' Thomas replied.

Henry smiled wryly. 'As we expected. Did we not, bishop?'

'Indeed, Your Grace.'

'King James claims to have no knowledge of any Scotsmen travelling through England without papers of safe conduct,' Thomas said, a little surprised by the king's reaction.

Fox snorted a brittle laugh.

'The truth is,' Thomas said, 'that there are far more Englishmen in Scotland who have no permission to be there than there are Scots in England. And I suspect King James knows this.'

'He'd be a poor king if he did not,' Henry said.

'My point being that our argument does not hold much water, Your Grace,' Thomas said, determined to make his point. 'King James has more to complain of than we.'

'Whose side are you on, priest?' Lovell demanded unpleasantly.

'I am on King Henry's side, my lord,' Thomas said evenly. 'I believe the king prefers to have facts, not fiction.'

'Now, look here – ' Lovell began.

'Master Wolsey is right,' Henry interrupted, waving a finger at Lovell to silence him. 'But it was worth a try all the same. Did King James have anything else to say, Master Wolsey?'

'King James insists Arran and Hamilton are released immediately.'

Henry shared a sideways glance with Fox. 'In that we cannot oblige him. The earl and his accomplice will remain our guests. Did you make any progress with regards to the Scottish relationship with the French? Did you make it clear I will not tolerate a renewal of the Auld Alliance?'

'I did, Your Grace,' Thomas said, 'but I fear that my words had little effect. If I might make a suggestion?'

Henry nodded for him to go ahead.

'Perhaps a meeting between you and King James would yield better results. I feel sure that if you were to meet face to face, you would be able to reach an amicable resolution to this dispute. Not least because your daughter would undoubtedly do all she could to bring about amity between you two.'

'And where would this meeting take place, Master Wolsey?' Fox asked.

'Wherever is most convenient for both parties, my lord,' Thomas suggested. 'Perhaps halfway between here and Scotland. York might be acceptable.'

'I do not see that a meeting would achieve anything,' Lovell muttered. 'How many times have we had to treat with the Scots? And how often have we come away with pretty words and no deeds? They are all talk, Your Grace.'

Henry pondered for a moment. 'I think you are right,' he said to Lovell. 'A meeting would not be of any benefit, but I thank you for the thought, Master Wolsey, and for your endeavours in Scotland. But enough of King James. What other business?'

The talk moved on to other affairs, and Thomas fell silent, speaking only when spoken to and keeping his answers concise. He could not help but feel a little disappointed. He knew there was little that could not be aided by a personal touch. People found it much more difficult to say no when they were in the same room as their adversary. And often, if people did not talk, a situation would worsen and come to blows; if that situation was between two countries, that could mean war. Thomas knew war was costly and wasteful and best avoided if possible. Thomas would always prefer to engage in diplomacy over martial might. It was so much more civilised.

CHAPTER TWENTY

'Your Grace should consider marrying once again.' Lovell glanced across at Fox. They had discussed this topic before sitting down at the council table and knew it was risky.

It had been five years since the queen had died, too long for the king of England to be a widower. No one had thought Henry VII an uxorious husband and yet his grief for Elizabeth had proved just how much he had loved her.

Henry's mouth pursed. 'Yes, I suppose I should. Do you have anyone in mind, Lovell?'

With a suppressed sigh of relief, Lovell pulled out a piece of paper he had hidden in his leather folder. 'There is the queen of Naples, although I do not think she would please Your Grace greatly. She does not possess much land or wealth, and from what we can ascertain, she is not likely to inherit any either. Also, her personal appearance is, shall we say, somewhat lacking.'

'Lovell,' Fox grimaced, 'the king does not want to know that.'

'The king does want to know,' Henry said. 'In what way lacking, my lord?'

'Our ambassadors report her breasts are on the small side, Your Grace.' Lovell looked away to hide his smile.

'I see,' Henry said, unamused. 'Who else?'

'Margaret of Angoulême and Margaret of Savoy.'

'Margaret of Savoy is the lady I favour, Your Grace,' Fox said. 'She has been regent in the Netherlands and is the daughter of the Holy Roman Emperor and sister of the archduke of Flanders. You may remember, Your Grace, when the archduke visited your court, he promised his sister in marriage to you two years ago. He even stated the dowry. Three-hundred thousand gold crowns.'

Henry's eyes gleamed at the sum named. 'And the lady's own inclination?'

'Well,' Fox drew the word out, 'Margaret is a widow twice over and has expressed a desire to remain unmarried.'

'But she will do as her brother commands,' Lovell put in.

'She is known to be wilful,' countered Fox.

'What does that matter?' Lovell exploded.

'Gentlemen.' Henry patted the air. 'We can make enquiries, can we not?'

'We can, Your Grace,' Fox agreed. 'We can send a suitable emissary to Flanders to discuss the proposition with Emperor Maximilian. The question is who? It must be a man of sense, a man who can adapt to changing situations, who we can rely on not to cause offence.'

The three men contemplated this question in silence for a long moment. Then Henry spoke. 'My chaplain, Master Wolsey.'

Fox nodded, unsurprised at the suggestion. 'Indeed, Your Grace. Master Wolsey could go, if you could spare him from his duties in your chapel.'

'I could spare him, bishop. Can you?' Henry asked with an amused smile, knowing full well how busy the bishop kept Thomas, using him as his unofficial secretary.

'Of course, Your Grace,' Fox said quickly, a little embarrassed.

'Is he up to it?' Lovell questioned. 'I know he is a clever fellow, but he is only a priest.'

'Oh, I think Master Wolsey has proven himself to be an able emissary,' Henry said. 'He has spoken with King James and managed to keep his temper. That is a miracle in itself. He has a persuasive tongue, by all accounts, and does not mind hard work. Yes, we will send Master Wolsey to Flanders and he must be quick about it. No dawdling on the journey. Whether or not Margaret is to be my wife, I want to know about it sooner rather than later so I can make other plans.'

Thomas had been told to present himself in the privy chamber. He had snatched up his Bible as he rushed out of his chamber in case the king wanted to pray with him. But he need not have bothered. When Thomas arrived in the privy chamber, the king was waiting with Fox and Lovell.

'Master Wolsey,' Henry greeted him, 'you appear a little out of breath. You are well, I trust?'

'Very well, Your Grace,' Thomas said, swallowing down a belch. 'I hurried here, 'tis all.'

Henry nodded approvingly. 'Good. You need to be in good health. We intend to send you on an embassy to Flanders.'

'To meet with the Emperor Maximilian regarding Margaret of Savoy?' Thomas asked at once.

Lovell laughed. 'I told you, my lord, this fellow does not miss a trick. I swear he knows more about what we intend than we do.'

'You must not dawdle,' Henry said, ignoring Lovell. 'I need to know how serious Margaret is about this matter.'

'Margaret is known for her fickleness,' Fox explained to Thomas. 'And we do not have time to indulge a woman famous for procrastination. Do you understand, Master Wolsey?'

'Fully,' Thomas nodded, his mind already working on his travel arrangements.

'Good.' Fox nodded, pulled out a paper from the pile before him and held it out to Thomas. 'Your instructions. They tell you what you may concede and your limits.'

'The fellow doesn't need those,' Lovell protested. 'He knows what he's about.'

'I have experience of chaplains, Sir Thomas,' Fox replied patiently. 'It is best to give them full instructions. It saves time and misunderstandings.'

Thomas bit his lip. As much as he respected Fox, there were times when the old man was a condescending little shit. He took the paper with a smile and took his leave.

Thomas had done very well. He had set out from the palace at Richmond within an hour of receiving his instructions. He despatched messengers at once to arrange a series of post horses to be made available to him at Rochester, Sittingbourne, Faversham, Canterbury, and all the way to Dover. Another messenger would secure passage on a ship out of Dover and to Calais. In Calais, he would beg a bed of Sir Edward Poynings for one night before making his way very early the next morning to the Netherlands and the court of Emperor Maximilian. So careful had been his preparations and so swift his travel, that he arrived at the emperor's court within three full days of leaving England, waking the porter to give him entrance and rousing a steward to give him a bed for the night.

The emperor had been very welcoming, his chief minister, the bishop of Gurk, less so. The bishop had looked on Thomas disdainfully, affronted by his eagerness to have an answer for King Henry as to whether Maximilian would agree to the marriage. Gurk was all for delaying, but Maximilian had waved him quiet and confirmed that yes, King Henry could marry Margaret of Savoy with his blessing if, he held up a finger, Margaret herself agreed. The agreement was set down on paper.

It was enough for Thomas. He thanked the emperor and was on his way back to England before the sun had reached its zenith. It was not until he had reached Richmond once again that he allowed himself to take a breath, and when he did at seven o'clock, exhaustion struck and he fell down on the bed he shared with Darcy fully dressed, not waking until eight the following morning. It was the soundest sleep he had had for years.

Thomas made his way to the chapel, knowing the king would be at mass. He waited at the chapel's entrance, smoothing down his surplice and bouncing on his toes in his eagerness. The mass concluded, and courtiers as well as the king headed for the door.

'Master Wolsey, what do you here?' Henry demanded, his eyes looking tired. 'You should be on your way to the Emperor Maximilian. What do you mean by delaying my important business?'

Henry's aggression was disconcerting. 'Your Grace,' Thomas stammered, 'I have already been to Flanders. I returned late last night.'

'You have been to Flanders?' Henry scowled. 'And come back again?'

'I have, Your Grace.'

'Impossible,' Fox declared. 'It has been but six days. Too short a time to make such a journey. Speak truth, Master Wolsey.'

'I do so, my lord,' Thomas insisted, a little outraged by Fox's tone. 'I have been to Flanders, I have met with the emperor, and I have his reply here.' He showed Henry and Fox the sealed paper Gurk had given him that contained Maximilian's agreement.

Lovell, standing at Henry's side, looked at the paper, looked at Thomas, and laughed out loud. 'Well, I would never have thought it possible. Did you sprout wings and fly to Flanders, Master Wolsey?'

'I was instructed to make haste, Sir Thomas,' Thomas said.

'My most beloved Master Wolsey,' Henry said, smiling at last. 'You must forgive my lord bishop and myself for ever doubting you. We are so used to indolence at court that we suspect it in everyone. Tell me, what is the emperor's reply?'

'He is agreeable to your proposal of marriage and to the dowry, Your Grace,' Thomas said with relief. 'All that is wanting is the lady's agreement.'

Fox harrumphed. 'Well, that is good news. We can proceed – '

'If you will forgive me, my lord,' Thomas interrupted him, 'I think we should not place too much faith in the Emperor Maximilian's assurances.'

'In your opinion,' Fox glowered.

'In my opinion, my lord,' Thomas confirmed.

'And your opinion is worth a great deal, Master Wolsey,' Henry said, glaring at Fox. 'Never mind. If I do not marry, it is no great matter to me. Take your ease, Master Wolsey, for this day I believe you have earned it.'

CHAPTER TWENTY-ONE

1509

It was late, and the summons from the king had got Thomas out of bed. He had retired early, having been troubled with an upset stomach for most of the day – the result, he suspected, of a slice of pork on the turn. He remembered he had thought it tasted a little peculiar, but he had been hungry and had wolfed down the dinner, regardless. He had paid the price, for that day all he had wanted to do was crawl into his bed, pull up the covers and sleep the day away.

But then a page had knocked on his door and told him the king wanted a mass said. It was his own fault; he always made himself available for the king. The other chaplains would groan and make a fuss and were more than happy when Thomas volunteered to oblige the king on his early morning or late night desires to praise God. But on this night, Thomas wished he could say no and leave it to another.

He went slowly to the king's chamber, ready to

make a dash to the nearest close stool or piss pot should his bowels demand it. He yawned as he passed the guards on the outer chamber door, who simply nodded him through.

No one bothered Thomas as he crossed the antechamber to the king's privy chamber door. It was partly ajar when he reached it. He was about to enter when he heard the voice of Lady Margaret. He hesitated, his hand hovering above the handle, and listened.

'You are not well, you need rest, Henry,' he heard Margaret say. 'You've already heard mass twice today. You do not need to hear it another time.'

'That is strangely ironic coming from you, Mother,' Henry's voice was weary but amused.

'I thank God every moment of every day for you and our family, but there is a limit to what the body can endure. You need your rest. You are looking so very tired.'

'I do not sleep well, you know that. Ever since Elizabeth died – '

'Do not go on about her,' Margaret snapped, and Thomas could imagine the look on her face very easily. 'It is not as if you shared a bed every night and cannot sleep alone.'

'It was knowing I could share a bed with her if I wanted to, Mother. Now I do not have that consolation.'

'You should have married again.'

'I told you, the marriage negotiations with Margaret of Savoy fell through, and in truth, I was not sorry. I did not wish to marry again.'

There was silence for a long moment, and Thomas heard the pace of soft-soled footsteps – Margaret's, no doubt. Should he enter now, he wondered? Before he could make a decision, Margaret was speaking again.

'And I suppose it is Master Wolsey you have sent for?'

'It is.'

'Why must it be him? Why could you not send for Fox or one of the other chaplains?'

'I do not understand what it is you have against Master Wolsey.'

'That man!' she growled. 'And now you have made him your almoner, in charge of all your private money. Why you favour him so greatly, I do not know.'

'He is one of my best servants, and you find fault with him for no other reason than he has an unfortunate cast in his eye.'

'It is a deformity, Henry. It is God's way of showing us those creatures who are corrupted by the devil.'

'There is nothing devilish about Master Wolsey. He will be here soon. If you do not wish to meet him, I suggest you retire.'

It was his cue. Thomas coughed and pushed the door open.

'You wish to hear mass, Your Grace,' he said, directing his attention to Henry and ignoring Margaret.

'I am sorry to get you out of your bed, Master Wolsey,' Henry said, 'but my soul is in need of consolation this night, and I know you will not begrudge me for disturbing you.'

'Indeed not, Your Grace. It is my pleasure and my duty.' Thomas looked directly at Margaret. It was a wilful stare – a challenge, even.

She stared straight back at him, and without another word, pinched her skirts between her fingers and strode out of the room.

It was a victory of sorts. Thomas returned his gaze to the king and smiled gently. 'Shall we begin, Your Grace?'

~

'Will it be enough?'

Thomas glanced at Henry's hands. His clenched knuckles had turned the skin white, and the veins stood up, knotted and blue against the skin. The king was in earnest; he truly wanted to know if all the money he had given away of late would be enough to secure him a place in heaven.

'Your Grace has been most generous. I am sure God will welcome you when the time comes which I trust will not be for some time yet.'

Henry scowled. 'You are not a fool, Master Wolsey. You know I am not long for this world. But that is not what bothers me.'

'What does, Your Grace?'

'I believe I was right to take the throne,' Henry said. 'Richard Plantagenet was a tyrant. My victory over him brought an end to decades of civil strife. I married Elizabeth of York to secure my throne.' He broke off, his eyes closing at the memory. 'But I grew to love her. And then to lose our first born. Was it a judgement, do you think?'

'No, Your Grace, I do not,' Thomas said with certainty. 'Many parents lose their children. It is the way of the world. And if there is solace to be found, Your Grace, you must find it in knowing that the queen and the prince have been reunited in heaven, as we will all be reunited with those we have lost.'

Henry bit his bottom lip hard, unconvinced. Thomas was moved to speak further.

'Your Grace, you saw fit to make me your almoner, to oversee all your contributions to the church and other institutions and individuals in need of financial aid. As such, I have seen the good you have done. You have given so much money and begun so many building projects on behalf of the church. All this is known to God, and He will be pleased by your great generosity.'

Henry closed his eyes at Thomas's words and nodded. Thomas had satisfied him that he would be welcomed by God into His kingdom.

Thomas rolled his shoulders to relieve his aching muscles. He was sure he wasn't the only one feeling uncomfortable. All this time standing, waiting for the king to die… the backs of his legs were cramping, and he was so hungry he felt sure his stomach would grumble soon. He had not had time to break his fast that morning, and no one in the room dared suggest leaving to eat because the king might die in the very next minute. He might die the next day. No one knew.

The room was very warm, packed with people who had come to witness the king's demise. Only the king's mother had the luxury of a seat. Margaret sat by the king's bedside, her hands in her lap, her dry eyes fixed on her son as he lay quite still in the bed.

Fox had summoned her from Eltham as soon as it had become clear the king was dying, and she had hurried lest she miss his last moments. She asked Fox if Henry had asked for her and was disappointed to learn he had not. She had taken a look around the room, noted who was present, her lip curling as her beady eyes landed on Thomas, and taken the seat offered. She had not moved since, despite Fox begging her to take some ease.

Thomas's glance shifted to the boy who stood behind Margaret. *Young man,* Thomas corrected himself, *a boy no longer.* Young Henry Tudor had certainly sprung up in the last few months and was now close on six feet tall, a giant at court. Thomas thought Prince Henry must take after his grandfather, for Edward IV had been very tall too. Henry certainly resembled the portrait of Edward that hung in the late queen's privy closet at Sheen. But he was a boy still in many ways. The king's regime for his heir had been harsh, and the boy had not fared well under it. *At least when the king dies, he will be free,* Thomas thought.

That is, if his grandmother does not take over completely.

Suddenly, Margaret leant forward, her hand clutching her son's forearm. All eyes were on the king.

'He's stopped breathing,' Margaret cried and looked up to Fox.

Fox frowned and came around the other side of the bed. Leaning over, he put his hand beneath the king's nose and kept it there. No one spoke. He straightened.

'Bishop?' Margaret pleaded.

Fox folded his hands on his belly. 'The king is dead, my lady.'

Thomas watched Margaret. He saw her throat tighten and her jaw clench, and he knew she was trying not to cry. He had no liking for the woman, but he could not help but feel sorry for her loss. Henry had been her only child. She had been but thirteen when she had given birth to him, no more than a child herself. The birth must have damaged her in some way, for despite her four husbands, she had never again been fruitful. All her love and ambition had been channelled into Henry. It had been her determination and her unwavering belief in God's will that had truly put Henry on the English throne; Bosworth Field had been a mere finale to her battles.

But Lady Margaret Beaufort was accustomed to holding her emotions in check, and Thomas continued to watch as she struggled to pull herself together. She turned to her grandson and reached for his hand. He jumped as her fingers touched his, for Henry had been staring at his dead father.

Margaret lifted her grandson's hand and put her dry, cracked lips to the knuckles. 'Long live the king,' she said, and it was then she broke down and buried her face in her hands.

Thomas kept his eyes on Henry. Henry's breath was coming hard and fast, his face, normally quite rosy, almost girl-like, was very pale. He looked at his grandmother, and Thomas could read the indecision in his face. He knew Henry was wondering whether or not to comfort her. He evidently decided against it because he looked up and met Fox's eye.

'Bishop Fox, I would like to be alone with my father for a moment.'

This seemed to surprise Fox. 'Of course, Your Grace,' he said after a moment. 'We will leave you.'

The room began to clear, and Thomas joined the queue to exit. He looked back and saw that Margaret had not moved.

'Master Wolsey,' Henry called, and Thomas turned back.

'Your Grace?'

'Would you escort my grandmother to her chamber?'

Margaret looked up, her eyes streaming. 'You want *me* to leave?'

In answer, Henry stepped away from the bed and looked down at the floor. Margaret stared at him, her tears stopping. When she realised her grandson was in earnest, she rose, using one hand on the back of the chair to steady herself. The look she cast at Thomas was one of fury.

It must be killing her, Thomas thought, *to be dismissed by her grandson and put in the care of one she despises so.*

He extended an arm towards her. She drew herself up, wiping her face with her handkerchief and strode past him. Thomas, the last in the room save Henry, took hold of the door handle. With one last look at the young man, he pulled it shut behind him.

He wondered what Henry was doing. Praying, perhaps, or just contemplating his new situation? Margaret was halfway down the corridor. Thomas hurried to catch up with her, ignoring the people who lined the corridors and spoke quietly between themselves.

'I do not need you, Master Wolsey,' Margaret said without looking at him.

'The king specifically asked me to – '

Margaret halted and turned on Thomas. 'How easily you say "the king" and mean my grandson.'

'I cannot say "the prince" any longer, my lady. He is the king now.'

'After all my son gave you and did for you, you can speak so. Is there no shred of feeling beneath that church gown?'

'I grieve for your loss, my lady. King Henry was a great king, and England shall mourn him. If you really do not require my assistance, I shall, of course, leave you as you wish.' He bowed and backed away from her.

You old bitch, he thought as she walked away. *I hope your grandson shows you he's not the walkover you're hoping for.*

~

Thomas pinched his surplice between his fingers and thumb and curved his way around the other bodies to reach a spot in the middle.

It had been a busy few days since the king had died. Soon after his death, before the skin started to droop, a plaster cast had been taken of the king's face so work could begin on his funeral effigy. Thomas had been appointed to oversee that strange task. He had been curious to see how it was done, feeling only fascination as the plasterer drew his palette knife over the slackening skin and bony nose. But when the plasterer was done and the king's body needed to be washed clean, Thomas felt a small stab of revulsion.

It was the first time he had been so close to death, his previous experience having been solely to do with officiating, and he discovered he did not particularly care for the handling of a corpse. He knew there was nothing to be afraid of in a dead body, but still, he did not like the feel of the cold skin. He breathed a sigh of relief when the winding cloth was passed over Henry's face. Henry's body had been placed temporarily in the chapel, and it was the chaplains' job to say continual prayers for his soul. Thomas had been excused from this, Fox needing his help with the funeral arrangements.

And now Thomas was part of the night-time procession conveying the dead king to his last resting place, various other members of the church on every side. He had made sure he had put his oldest shoes on. They were well worn, scuffed and shabby, but they were his most comfortable pair and he was sure no one would be looking at his shoes. It was a long walk to St Paul's, and Thomas did not want blisters on his heels making the journey feel even longer.

The procession began and the pace was slow, the air busy with the sound of shuffling feet. It was a solemn event and at the beginning, everyone seemed to respect it. But as the minutes wore on and turned into an hour, Thomas soon started to hear the susurration of chatter as the mourners grew bored and began to talk amongst themselves. Thomas felt something brush his elbow and looked around. Thomas Grey, marquess of Dorset, was walking alongside him. *How he has grown up since I saw him last*, Thomas mused.

'I saw you from where I was and thought I would have a word,' Grey explained quietly with a smile. ''Tis a long walk in which to be silent.'

'How are you, my lord?' Thomas asked.

'Oh, well enough. And you? You look hale and hearty, Master Wolsey.'

'I am, I thank you.'

'Worried a little, perhaps?'

'Why should I be worried?'

Grey shrugged. 'We all are, are we not? We do not know what to expect from the new king. Will we be in favour or out of favour?'

'In truth, my lord, I have been so busy these last few days, I have not had time to think about it.'

'You should,' Grey warned. 'I know you are probably secure, but it does not do to be complacent about these things.'

'I thank you for the advice, my lord,' Thomas said sincerely.

Grey prattled on, but Thomas was no longer paying much attention. Was Grey right? Should he be worried he would be out of favour with the new king? Thomas had been kind to him when Henry was a young boy and needed comfort over the loss of his beloved mother. Would that go unremembered? It was true Thomas had allies at court, men such as Fox, Lovell and even Archbishop Warham, all of whom had made themselves necessary to the previous king and would no doubt do the same to the new one. But there were others, nobles who bore him a great dislike, perceiving him as an upstart, a parvenu, and who would do all they could to block his advancement.

Before Thomas realised it, the procession had reached St Paul's. It was there that Henry VII's body would rest for the night before making the journey to Westminster Abbey on the morrow. The mourners fell deathly quiet again as the king's effigy was removed from the coffin. Thomas saw the orb wobble in the effigy's left hand. His heart stopped beating when he thought it might fall, but it remained secure and Thomas relaxed. Four knights were needed to keep vigil over the coffin whilst it lay in the church, but everyone else was dismissed for the night. Many of the mourners had houses in London, and they hurried to reach them. Those that had come up from their country houses to attend the funeral had had to find lodgings in the city for the night, and many of them had appealed to the council for help in finding suitable accommodation. Thomas had had a hand in that too and knew there were several men who only had to travel a little way to find the houses that would give them a bed for the night. For himself, he had a bed awaiting him at the bishop of London's residence courtesy of Fox, who had requested it on his behalf.

Thomas bade Grey good night and made his way there, his mind working hard to discover what he could do to ensure he would still have a job after the funeral.

Thomas tramped along the corridor to his bedchamber. He was tired and glad the three-day funeral of Henry VII was over. He opened the chamber door and was started.

'Darcy! I thought you were still in the city.'

Darcy threw Thomas a sour look. 'I have been given orders to decamp,' he snarled, stuffing a shirt into a large holdall.

Thomas deposited his own bag on the bed. 'You're leaving?'

'Not because I wish to, but because I have been told I must.' He slumped down on the bed. 'I am no longer Vice Chamberlain of the Household. Sir Henry Marney has been given that position.'

Thomas's heart sank. Was it really happening so soon? And to someone so close to him? 'You cannot have displeased the king, surely?'

'I think not.' Darcy shook his head. 'It is just the way of things, you know. I suspect the new king has been heeding the advice of his grandmother.'

'Lady Margaret?'

'Aye. Marney is a creature of hers, and I suppose she is looking after him.'

'I am sorry.'

Darcy smiled ruefully at him. 'Thank you for that. But I have heard a rumour. Perhaps I should not say.'

'Speak if you know something about me,' Thomas said, feeling suddenly sick. 'I would know it.'

'I have heard that you are to lose the post of almoner. Lady Margaret wants to give it to one of her followers.'

Thomas sank down on the bed, deflated. 'I am to lose my post. I cannot believe it. I have not offended the king.'

'You have offended the king's grandmother, Thomas. I told you this might happen.'

'Am I still royal chaplain?'

'I have heard nothing to the contrary,' Darcy said.

'So, you will still be at court at least, not sent away like me. Oh well, my wife will be pleased to have me home.' He laughed. 'Who am I fooling? She will be annoyed not to have the place to herself anymore.'

'I am sure she will not.'

With a sigh, Darcy slapped his thighs and got up from the bed. 'If you do lose the chaplaincy, do not worry. You have talents and abilities to spare. You will find another position soon enough. There are plenty of nobles who would have you.'

'But there is only one king,' Thomas snapped. 'For myself, I wish no other master.'

CHAPTER TWENTY-TWO

'My father wanted me to marry Katherine.' Henry slammed his hand down on the council table, making the ink pots jump. He glanced at the men seated around it. 'We need to reinforce our alliance with Spain and...' he took a deep breath, 'I must have an heir.'

Fox said hesitantly, 'Katherine is your late brother's wife, Your Grace.'

'I know who she is,' Henry snapped. 'But she was never his wife, not in that sense. My brother never knew Katherine.'

'A dispensation would need to be sought from the Pope, however,' Fox said, twiddling his quill pen between his fingers. 'Although, I believe that would be forthcoming.'

'As does my grandmother,' Henry said. 'Are there any here who would oppose my marriage to Katherine?'

The counsellors looked at one another, each waiting for one of them to answer. Eventually, Warham spoke.

'We only have Katherine's word that her marriage with your brother was never consummated,' he said. 'I do not say the lady lies, but...' He gestured, palms up. 'There is doubt. You may remember, Your Highness, you yourself expressed concern on this matter when the idea of your marrying Katherine was put forward by the late king.'

'I was but fourteen then, archbishop,' Henry said testily. 'I knew not of what I spoke.'

'If you will forgive me, Your Grace; your concern showed great wisdom. Think on Leviticus. Such a marriage would be an unclean thing, and sin would manifest in your being childless. Is it worth the risk?'

'Leviticus is contradicted by Deuteronomy, Your Grace,' Fox said before Henry could comment. 'In Deuteronomy, it is quite clear that should a brother die without issue, the surviving brother should take his widow to wife.'

'There is too much confusion surrounding this matter,' Warham persisted.

'There is much to be gained from a marriage with Katherine,' Fox said. 'Her dowry is already in our possession, and our ties with Spain need to be strengthened. Once agreed, the wedding can take place almost immediately, whereas if the king must woo half the families of Europe to find a suitable bride, we could be talking a year or more before a marriage takes place.'

'And I must have an heir,' Henry said, leaning forward and appealing to Warham. 'My father was very clear about that. I will not go against his dying wish, archbishop. Your concerns are noted.'

'But disregarded,' Warham said, sinking into his chair. 'I understand.'

Fox glanced with irritation at Warham, then turned his gaze to Henry and nodded, content that Warham was silenced.

'Good,' Henry said. 'Then, my lord bishop, send for the Spanish ambassador so the proposal can be broached with Spain. I want to be married to Katherine as soon as may be.'

'I think,' Fox said, nibbling on his fingernail, 'that we should view this new regime as an opportunity.'

Thomas set down the cup of wine the bishop had bid him pour. The bishop acknowledged it with a nod, and Thomas retreated to the end of the table, ready to listen.

Sir Thomas Lovell, leaning back lazily in his chair, frowned. 'What do you mean, bishop?'

'An opportunity to rid ourselves of those members of this court who are undesirable.'

Lovell grinned. 'Can we do that, do you think? Just get rid of our fellows? Will not our new king have something to say about that?'

'Our new king is two months shy of his majority,' Fox reminded him, 'and is untrained in the ways of the court. He will be grateful for our advice, I am sure.'

'The king, maybe, but what of Lady Margaret? She will not be swept aside, that I can tell you.'

'Perhaps you are right, Lovell,' Fox conceded. He looked up the table to Thomas. 'What do you think, Master Wolsey?'

Thomas licked his lips. 'I would be able to give you my opinion were I to know whom you had in mind, Your Grace.'

'I know who you are thinking of,' Lovell said, resting his arms on the table. 'Empson and Dudley.'

Thomas's stomach lurched. He knew of Richard Empson and Edmund Dudley, having first seen them huddled together conspiratorially at a joust he had attended soon after being made a royal chaplain. He had been watching the joust from one of the temporary wooden stands put up, his court bedfellow Darcy by his side. Darcy had noticed Thomas watching the two men.

'They are the king's maggots,' Darcy said, his face screwing up in distaste. 'The one on the left is Richard Empson, the other Edmund Dudley. Empson is a nobody, a commoner, but Dudley, well, he has a little breeding, but I would not willingly shake his hand. They are the king's tax collectors.'

'Someone has to collect taxes,' Thomas had pointed out.

'Aye, someone does, but it is how they go about it that is so despicable. They are ruthless. And what is worse, they operate with the king's full authority. The king has instructed them to find out every bad law ever made and wring every penny that can legally be wrung out of people. And they enjoy it too. You should hear Empson bragging about how he got so much coin out of this farmer or that.'

'But the king favours them?'

'He values them for what they do for him, but he does not favour them. Best to avoid them, my friend. They won't do you any good and may do you harm in the long run.'

Thomas had heeded his friend's advice and kept out of Empson's and Dudley's way, but he could not help noticing how similar their positions were to his. They had done the king's bidding, as had Thomas, and yet here were Fox and Lovell talking of getting rid of them for being such good servants. Was Thomas likely to be any safer in this new court?

'On what grounds could they be dismissed, my lord?' Thomas asked Lovell.

'On the grounds that they are upstarts,' Lovell laughed.

'We may need reason stronger than that,' Fox said, his mouth curving in amusement.

'Do you think so?' Lovell asked. 'As I see it, most of the men on the council would be glad to see the back of both of them.'

Fox shrugged one shoulder. 'Even so.'

'Well, if you're looking for a better reason,' Lovell said, 'then say it is because of their rapacious natures in extorting money from the English people.'

'If I may, Sir Thomas,' Thomas said, drawing the attention of both men, 'it is my understanding that both

Masters Empson and Dudley were working on the late king's orders. That it was, in fact, the late king's express command they seek out old laws, long forgotten, and prosecute those who broke them, whether unwittingly or no. They pursued those who avoided paying their taxes.'

'Whose side are you on, Master Wolsey?' Lovell demanded angrily.

Thomas held out his hands. 'I merely play the role of devil's advocate, Sir Thomas. Their defence will surely be that they were obeying the orders of their king.'

'Be that as it may, they will have little support in the council,' Fox said. 'No, I do not think we will have any difficulty there. I think the only question we have is how to approach the king about it. Any thoughts on that, Master Wolsey?'

Thomas's heart was fluttering. He knew he had to be careful. His superiors seemed determined to be rid of the hated tax collectors; they were not asking for his agreement, merely his opinion on how it should be handled. He was conscious that the removal of two good servants might make a dangerous precedent, but he needed allies in the council if his own position was to be secure. And he also had to ask himself what King Henry wanted most.

'Our new king has a pleasant disposition,' he said carefully, 'and I think he would like to loved by the people. Perhaps he would like to mark his accession with an event the people would like. If he were to announce the dismissal of two men the people hate as much as they hate Empson and Dudley, that would be a popular declaration, I imagine.'

Thomas had the satisfaction of having both Fox and Lovell grinning at his ingenuity. There was no chance of him being out of a job, he told himself. He was too damn useful.

CHAPTER TWENTY-THREE

Thomas was in the royal chapel preparing for mass. The new king had surprised the chaplains by ordering the service to be performed more than an hour before its usual time, so now Thomas was hurrying to get ready. His hurry was made worse by the presence of the king and his grandmother in the chapel with him, impatiently waiting for him to begin. He was glad that neither of them paid him any attention.

'Your friends are very loud, Henry,' Margaret said, smoothing her skirts over her bony knees from her seat in one of the pews.

Thomas watched the king out of the corner of his eye. 'Are they, Grandmother?' Henry sighed, and Thomas turned away to hide his smile.

Henry had gathered ten or more of his closest friends about him, boys he had known since childhood, and they were a rowdy lot. Far too noisy for an old woman such as Lady Margaret to bear with equanimity.

'Yes, they are, and you can take that sulky tone out of your voice. I say they are too loud. You should not have them at court if they do not know how to behave. You must send them away.'

'I will not,' Henry said quietly. 'They are my friends, and I want them here. I will not be surrounded by old men.'

'Nor old women, I suppose,' Margaret said stiffly, tightening her arms beneath her bosom and pursing her mouth.

'You will not wish to be always at court, Grandmother,' Henry said. 'Though you are, of course, always welcome,' he added quickly.

'That is good to know, Henry,' Margaret said sarcastically. 'You have made your own mind up about marrying Katherine –'

'I thought you agreed to it.'

'I agreed that the Pope would give you a dispensation to marry, not that you should.'

'It was what Father wanted.'

'So you say. I do not think it is wise to marry your brother's widow, but that is only my opinion. I know you are determined. I would like to think my advice about other matters is to be heeded, however.'

Thomas could have sworn he heard Henry groan. 'Of course, Grandmother. I –'

'Then you will hear me on the choice of your clergymen.'

Thomas held his breath and strained his ears.

'Your father made some unfortunate appointments in

that regard. He promoted lowborn men to important posts who are quite unworthy of such positions.'

She means me, Thomas thought, *the old cow.*

'That man, there.'

Thomas could not help himself; he looked around to find Margaret gesturing towards him.

'That man, I believe, is the son of a common butcher. To think he should have been allowed to perform the mass before the king of England and manage his charitable affairs!'

Thomas knew his face was bright red. He could feel it, could feel the blood burning in his cheeks, the blood rushing in his ears. *Speak*, he urged himself, *say something, defend yourself. You've already lost the post of almoner. You'll be out of your chaplaincy as well if she has her way.* But no words came. He could think of nothing to say.

'Commoners at court!' Margaret snorted. 'I do not know what your father was thinking in appointing them. The Plantagenets never did so. Only nobles for them, and they were right. You will not do the same as your father, Henry. You will have men worthy to be your churchmen.'

Thomas held his breath, waiting for Henry's answer, but it did not come. Unable to delay any long, Thomas, his hands shaking with anger as well as nerves, moved to the altar. 'Shall we begin, Your Grace?'

CHAPTER TWENTY-FOUR

It had been cold in the chapel and Thomas returned to his office, rubbing his hands and wondering if he should send down to the kitchens for some bread and cheese. His fellow chaplain, John, passed him as he entered the chaplains' office.

'A letter has come for you, Thomas. I left it on your desk.'

Thomas thanked him and moved to look. On top of his normal correspondence lay the newly arrived letter. He recognised Elizabeth's writing with a sigh, wondering what his sister was bothering him about now. He sat down and reached for it, cracking open the red seal.

My brother Thomas, I hope you are well. I and our brothers are well, but I am sorry to say that Mother is not.

Mother suffered greatly in the winter with a cold that settled on her chest. We sent for the apothecary and he gave her ointments to rub in, but they do not seem to have done any good. She has been asking for you, and though I have told her you could not possibly leave your important work, she keeps on. It would be a kindness if you could come home and visit her.

Elizabeth.

Bess never gives up, he thought. *She takes every opportunity to twist the knife.* She did not understand how precarious his position at court truly was. What a time for his mother to become ill!

But there was no remedy. He could not stay and let his mother die, if indeed she was so very ill, without seeing her once more. He would have to risk leaving court and return to Ipswich. All he could do was hope, and pray, that he would have a position to return to.

Elizabeth was sweeping the front step of the house when he arrived. As she gave a last vigorous sweep of her broom, she looked up and caught sight of him coming towards her. She smiled at him, but to Thomas's eyes, the smile was one of weariness rather than welcome.

'So, you've come,' she said as he halted in front of her.

'Did you think I would not?'

Elizabeth shrugged. 'Come in, then.'

Thomas hung up his cloak and bag on the wooden pegs in the hall. The scent of lavender and rosemary filled his nostrils along with the smell of boiling meat. It made his mouth water.

'There's an hour till supper,' Elizabeth said as if reading his mind. She thrust a cup of ale into his hand.

Thomas drank it down, then followed her into the parlour. 'Is Mother in bed?'

Elizabeth nodded. 'She gets up when she feels able to, which is not often. The smoke from the fire makes her cough, so she prefers to stay upstairs. Do you want to see her now?'

He nodded, then held out his hand as Elizabeth made to rise. 'You stay here. No need to trouble your-self.' He left Elizabeth at the bottom of the stairs and went up to his mother's bedroom.

'How do you, Mother?' he said softly as he sank onto the stool by the bed. He took hold of her thin, bony hand and Joan opened her eyes.

'Thomas,' she breathed, reaching up to stroke his face. 'Bess said she had written to you, but I wasn't sure you could manage to get away.'

'There was never any question of my not coming home once I knew you were unwell,' Thomas lied.

Joan pushed herself up and Thomas plumped her pillow. His heart had lifted a little when he saw her. He had half expected to see his mother close to the grave, and though she did not look to be in the best of health, it was true, she looked only a little under the weather. And after all, she was how old now? In her sixties at least. No one could expect her to look plump and rosy cheeked.

'How are you, my dear?' she asked, and Thomas saw her gaze move to his left eye.

His fingers went impulsively to the drooping eyelid. 'I am fine, Mother,' he assured her. 'How are things with you?'

'Oh, 'tis only this blasted cold that bothers me. I cannot seem to shake it off. It will pass, I am sure.'

'The business is doing well?'

'Yes, yes, all is good there.' She grabbed his hands and pulled them onto her lap. 'I want to hear about you. What have you been doing at court?'

Thomas told her about the late king's death and the accession of the young Henry, but he kept to himself his concerns for his position and his future at court. He did not talk long with his mother, for he could see their conversation wearied her. Indeed, Joan had fallen asleep before he had left the room.

Thomas's presence seemed to rally Joan. Perhaps anxious Thomas would hurry away, she rose from her sickbed and spent most days before the parlour fire, watching Elizabeth and too often criticising her daughter as she went about her daily work whilst ensuring Thomas had all he could possibly want. Her mother's attitude irked Elizabeth, but Joan either did not notice or was ignoring her. William Patent always hurried from the house on business, but Henry and Richard called every day to see their mother and were neither pleased nor otherwise to see Thomas being treated like the prodigal son. Unlike Elizabeth, they now had their own families, and it made no difference to them if their mother chose to make a pet out of Thomas.

The days turned into a week, then another, and Joan seemed to continue to improve. News came to Ipswich of first King Henry's marriage to Katherine, then the splendour of his coronation, events which Thomas was dismayed to realise had not required his presence.

Thomas felt low, lower than he had ever felt before, and not even his mother's cloying attention could pull him out of his despondency. A steady stream of letters flowed between Ipswich and the court, Thomas writing almost every day to his friends and allies to glean information. John had replied that many of their acquaintance simply did not know what the new king was going to do with them, and all the royal chaplains were as anxious as he. It was Lady Margaret, John wrote, who kept everyone on tenterhooks. The new king, though seemingly his own man in so many ways, had proven unable to deny his grandmother, and still gave an ear to her advice on who he chose to serve him.

And remember, Thomas, John concluded in his most recent letter, *the Lady Margaret has no liking for you.*

Thomas knew it, and cursed the Lady Margaret. And then another letter came, this one from Sir Thomas Lovell, and its contents quickened Thomas's heart.

He could feel Elizabeth's anger coming off her in waves. Thomas ordered himself to bear it and buckled his bag.

'You will write soon, I hope?' she asked. 'Mother frets so when you do not.'

'Yes, I will write. Satisfied?'

'Not really, but it will have to do, I suppose.'

Thomas kicked the wall and turned to her. 'What is it I have done to earn your dislike, Elizabeth? Tell me. I want to know.'

She stared him straight in the eye. 'I do not dislike you.'

'Really? Yet every time I return, I get... ' He gestured with both hands at her. 'This.'

'And what is *this?*'

'Well, if it is not dislike, then I cannot say.'

Elizabeth closed her eyes for a long moment, then sank into the nearest chair, rubbing her temple. 'It is as if we do not exist to you,' she said. 'I remember when you left for Oxford. A fat little boy of eleven years, too clever for the local grammar school. "Thomas must have every opportunity," that was what Master Squyer said. I heard him, I was listening on the stairs. So, off you went, and all I heard for years from Mother and Father was how well you were doing, how proud you made them.' She smiled at him bitterly. 'They never once said that about me. But what was I? Only a girl. Worth nothing. A wife in waiting, that is what they thought. Only no one wanted to marry me, so I became an unpaid servant here.'

'You are more than that – '

'Let me speak,' she said, her tone desperate. 'We are your family, Thomas. We are not nothing.'

'I know that.'

'Then why do you treat us the way you do? We hardly hear from you, and when we do, your letters are all about you. I cannot remember the last time you asked how we are, how Henry and Richard are faring with their businesses. Every word you write that concerns us is what you were taught to write at school. "I trust you are well, you have my best wishes." And yet, despite all that, Mother still worships you. You are her God, Thomas, do you know that?'

'That is blasphemy, Bess,' Thomas said through gritted teeth.

'Oh, so there is a true priest beneath the skin,' she said, laughing hollowly. 'I have always wondered whether your prayers and piety have been only for show.'

'You want to know why I treat you the way I do?' Thomas suddenly burst out. 'This is why, Bess, this is why. You mock me, you treat me with disdain – '

'Only because you do the same to us.'

'Do you know, at court, no one does so. At court, I am respected, I am valued. Here, I am just someone you can bait and turn your shrewish tongue upon.'

Elizabeth opened her mouth to protest, found no words and shut it again.

His words had been harsh, true, but harsh, and he

was about to make his sister cry. He turned away so he would not have to see.

'Now, Mother seems better, and I am needed at court,' he lied, tying on his cloak. 'I have said goodbye to her. Would you say farewell to Henry and Richard for me, please?'

Elizabeth didn't answer, but he didn't hear her crying either. He wanted to turn around to see, but he didn't dare. 'Goodbye, Bess,' he said, yanking the door open and hurrying out before anything more could be said.

CHAPTER TWENTY-FIVE

1509

Henry couldn't bear to watch his grandmother die.

Margaret had asked her friend, Bishop Fisher, to send for her grandson, and Henry had dutifully come and sat by her bedside. He had listened as she croaked out advice on how he should rule, biting down the words he wanted to say, that he had had enough of being told what to do. He had turned eighteen only the day before. No longer was he in his minority. He was a man. More, he was a king. Henry would do as he pleased.

Margaret had fallen silent at last. Her eyes had closed, and Henry avoided Fisher's disapproving stare as he rose from the stool and left his grandmother's chamber. He waved away those who waited outside, eager for his attention, and went to his own chamber. He lay back on his bed, hearing the low murmurs of his gentlemen talking in the antechamber beyond.

Henry tried to imagine what life would be like without his grandmother. She had been a part of his life for so long, always there, always influencing him, her training present in everything he did. He loved her, but he didn't need her, not anymore. He was king; he was a husband and, God willing, he would soon be a father. And what was more, he wasn't a fool. He would be able to determine what was in England's best interests and identify the people who could serve him best. And despite what his grandmother thought, he did not choose people to serve him simply because he liked them. She had complained about his gentlemen, about Brandon and Compton and the others, simply because they liked to have fun, liked to drink and feast and tilt and dance. What was wrong with that? Just because his father had liked none of those things.

Well, he was not his father. He was Henry; he was himself. And he was loved for it. He had seen as much during his coronation. His subjects had lined the streets of London and cheered him, jubilant he was their king. Where was the sorrow for his father? Nowhere to be seen, that was where.

Henry heard raised voices from the antechamber; someone had entered. He lifted his head from the pillow and saw Katherine coming towards him.

'Henry?' Katherine eased herself onto the bed beside him and laid her small hand on his muscular thigh. 'Your grandmother?'

'Alive, but only just.'

'I am so sorry, my love.'

Henry grunted and stared up at the tester.

'Should you not be with her?' Katherine asked.

'She has Fisher. He can give her more consolation than I can.'

'You will miss her when she is gone,' Katherine said, rubbing her hand around the firm flesh and squeezing.

Henry's eyes closed. 'Yes, I will.'

'She has helped you so much with affairs of state. It will be difficult for you without her.'

Henry's eyes snapped open. 'I am not a boy.'

'No, of course you are not,' Katherine said soothingly, alarmed by his outburst. 'But these men about you. How will you know who you can trust?'

'I know who,' Henry said. 'I can trust Bishop Fox, though I do not care for the man.'

'He is sly,' Katherine agreed.

'But he served my father well, and he knows when he is well off. And I have those I know and can trust as well as my grandmother. When she is gone, there will be changes made.'

'Henry, be careful.'

Henry laughed at his wife's solemn expression. He threw his arms around her waist and pulled the giggling Katherine down onto his chest, his grandmother banished from his thoughts.

'Is she dead?' Thomas asked Fox the moment he entered his office.

Fox looked at him coolly. 'Rather abrupt of you, Master Wolsey.'

Thomas closed his eyes and sighed. 'Yes, forgive me, Your Grace. But… is she?'

Fox moved around Thomas to sit at his desk before answering. 'Yes. Lady Margaret died late last night. Bishop Fisher was with her at the end. The poor man is very upset. They were very close, you know.'

'Her death must be a blow to him.'

'But not to you.'

'Your Grace?' Thomas asked innocently.

Come now, Master Wolsey. You forget I know you, I know how you think.'

Thomas took a seat at the desk. He felt his hands shaking. 'What am I thinking, Your Grace?'

'That your fortunes may be improving with the death of the king's grandmother. As indeed they may.'

'You think so?'

'Lady Margaret did not like you,' Fox said. 'I expect she had her reasons. But her reasons are not the king's, and *he* likes you. I think you may hope to regain your position as almoner when the post becomes vacant.'

'Is that likely?' Thomas asked eagerly.

Fox's face became hard. 'The present incumbent is an old man and not well. I think it likely he will be dead before the year is out. But you would do better to curtail your ambition, Master Wolsey. It is not becoming.'

'Everyone at court is ambitious.'

'Courtiers are ambitious,' Fox corrected, 'not

churchmen. It is unseemly for us to seek riches and favour.'

'To seek them? Or be seen to seek them?' Thomas had grown angry at Fox's manner.

The corner of Fox's mouth curled upwards. 'To be seen to seek them, Master Wolsey, as well you know. And you have done very well for yourself so far. How many benefices do you currently hold?'

'Three or four,' Thomas answered a little sulkily.

'More like five or six. I imagine that little money chest you have tucked away in your room is groaning with coin. And yet it is not enough, is it?'

''Tis an uncertain world, Your Grace,' Thomas said, his mouth set defiantly. 'As I have found out these last few months. It is not a world in which I would like to be without means.'

'You are letting your anger show, Master Wolsey,' Fox wagged a finger at him. 'Do not think I am reprimanding you for your ambitions. I understand them. I have had them myself. I would not have held the position I have for these past twenty-odd years if I had not. So, as a long campaigner' – he smiled to himself – 'let me offer you a word of advice. Do not be so obvious in your ambition that you engender the disrespect of your betters.'

'My betters?'

'The nobles of this land.'

'And they are better because… ?' Thomas waved his hand in the air, frowning.

Fox's head tilted to one side. 'Now, Master Wolsey,

be very careful. There is an order to this world. It separates us from the beasts.' He leant forward on the desk, speaking confidentially. 'You and I are from the same world. Both lowborn, both had fortune thrust upon us early and received excellent Oxford educations, becoming acquainted with people of a higher class than ourselves. Years spent working hard to prove we are capable. And yes, being rewarded for it by men who understand that lowborn men do have their uses.' He smiled. 'I thank God daily for the Tudors. No other kings would have raised us so high, Master Wolsey.'

'I do not consider it a sin to want to better myself, Your Grace,' Thomas said. 'Lady Margaret did consider it a sin, and that is why she disliked me. But now, she is gone, and the king has no one left to tell him what he can and cannot do. No, not even you, Your Grace, though I admit he would be wise to take your advice. Now, as I see it, I do not pretend to have nobility. I do not attempt to fabricate a noble history for my family. I know what I am. I know what I am good at. No noble would begrudge me aiming for what I am due.'

Fox sucked in air and leant back in his chair. 'Are you really so naïve? Or is it arrogance that makes you speak so? Believe me, Master Wolsey, our English nobles are capable of despising anyone lower than themselves who thinks they deserve better. And be assured, they can hold a grudge for a very long time.'

～

'Come with me.' Bishop Fox flicked his fingers at Thomas and turned briskly away.

Thomas closed the book he had been reading and tossed it onto the table beside him. With raised eyebrows to John, he hurried after the bishop.

'What is this about, Your Grace?' Thomas asked breathlessly.

'I'm taking you to the king,' Fox said airily.

They were already at the door to the privy chamber. Fox took a deep breath and looked at Thomas. 'Be grateful, but not overly familiar. The king invites familiarity and we must guard ourselves against it. It will do us no good in the long run.'

Grateful for what? Thomas wondered as Fox opened the door.

The king was writing as they entered, and Thomas saw the parallel lines that indicated a sheet of staves. Working on a new composition, Thomas thought, knowing how Henry loved music.

'Your Grace,' Bishop Fox said, bowing, 'I have brought Master Wolsey as you asked.'

Henry laid down his quill. 'Ah, Master Wolsey. You have been away, I think. I have not seen you at mass these past weeks.'

'I have been away, Your Grace,' Thomas said, touched the king had noticed his absence. 'My mother was ill and I returned home to see her.'

'I see. She is well now?'

'She is better, Your Grace. But she is of advancing years and... ' His voice broke off as he felt a lump rising

310

in his throat. He swallowed it back down, embarrassed and discomfited.

Henry seemed to understand. His voice became kind. 'Death is all around us, is it not, Master Wolsey? I myself have lost much. My brother, my mother, my father and now my grandmother.'

'It is the way of the world, Your Grace,' Fox said, rocking on the balls of his feet. Thomas knew the bishop was growing bored and perhaps embarrassed by such sentimental chatter. 'You wanted to see Master Wolsey, you remember.'

'Indeed, I did.' Henry nodded. 'Master Wolsey, I am appointing you to the privy council.'

Thomas stared at Henry for a moment, forgetting protocol. He had not expected this when Fox had flicked his fingers at him. He had thought he was needed to take notes or worse, be reprimanded for some misdeed. Henry had already made him almoner once more. He had not hoped for more, not so soon. 'Thank you, Your Grace. But I thought the Lady – '

Henry stopped him 'I was very sorry of the way my grandmother spoke of you. She could be very…'

Rude, Thomas wanted to say as Henry searched for an appropriate adjective.

'She was used to saying what she pleased,' Henry continued, the memory of his grandmother making him smile. 'I owed her a great deal, so when she said I should do such-and-such, sometimes I listened. But she was not always right. And' – he smiled shyly – 'I remember when people have been kind to me.'

Thomas remembered that day when he had put his arm around a grieving young prince and offered a shoulder to cry upon. It had been an instinctive act, not done in the hope of reward, and yet, all these years later, that small act of kindness had stayed in the memory of a king. Thomas, at last, had his reward.

'I understand you have no house of your own,' Henry continued. 'I would like to remedy that. Empson, that foul man who languishes in the Tower until I decide what to do with him, had a place at St Bride's called La Maison Curiale. Perhaps you know it. No, well, Fox here tells me it is a goodly house, ample for a churchman such as yourself. It is yours.'

Thomas's mouth fell open. He did not know what to say. To be gifted a fine house as well as being made a privy counsellor!

'Your Grace is most generous,' he said, wondering if this meant Empson was not likely to leave the Tower.

Henry grinned, enjoying the compliment. He nodded at Fox, and Thomas saw Fox bow and did the same. They departed.

'Dare I ask, Your Grace,' Thomas began as they stepped into the corridor, 'if I have you also to thank for my advancement and this gift?'

'I may have spoken for you, yes,' Fox conceded. 'And I expect you to remember that, should an occasion arise when I need you to speak for me.'

'I cannot imagine you ever needing my help, Your Grace.'

'We all of us need one another at some point, Master

Wolsey. Remember that, if you remember nothing else. The king is showing you favour, but remember to whom you owe your loyalty.'

'I owe it to you, Your Grace.'

'To me, and to the church. Fortunately, the king, with his early training in theology, is already on our side, but things can change. We need to remind the king of what the church is, how vital it is that it remains strong.'

'I believe that, Your Grace,' Thomas assured him. 'I have no wish to see the church diminished.'

'I am very glad to hear you say so. You know we have our enemies at court.'

'I do, Your Grace. I will be vigilant.'

'I am sure you will.' Fox nodded and left him.

Thomas stared after him, a smile working its way onto his face. What a magnificent day! No longer a mere royal chaplain but a royal almoner, privy counsellor and a man of property at last.

CHAPTER TWENTY-SIX

1510

Elizabeth was tired. Her eyes had closed many times over the past few hours, and she had had to force herself to open them. It wasn't fair, she kept telling herself, that she had to bear the brunt of this. Where was her stepfather? Oh, that's right. The other side of the city, tending to his business. Where were her brothers? Doing the same a few streets away. Men, they could always escape the horrid things. Not women. They had to keep the fire going, ensure everyone had food in their bellies, wash the soiled linen and sit by the bedside as a family member died.

Elizabeth loved her mother, but there was a part of her, a part of her that would have to confess later when it was all over, that wanted her mother to go. Looking after her had become a burden, just another chore on top of all the other things she had to do every day, day after day. And did her mother feel better for it? No, not that Elizabeth could tell. She just lay in bed, not eating,

314

getting thinner, hardly ever waking, unable to speak more than a word at a time. What was the point of living like that?

Elizabeth's chin touched her chest, and she jerked upright. She blinked, her eyes drawn to the window which showed darkness beyond. She had been asleep, and for a while too, she realised, for it had been light when last she looked. She looked to her mother, suddenly fearful, and gasped. Something was different. She rose and bent over her mother, her eyes searching the lined face frantically for signs of life.

There were none.

Elizabeth let out a sob, her tears splashing down onto her mother's cold cheeks. 'No, I did not mean it. I did not mean it! Come back, Mother, please. Please come back.'

'You should have written to me sooner.' Thomas drew his wooden spoon through the pottage Elizabeth had set before him, watching the thick stew ripple and turn.

Elizabeth wiped her hands on her apron. 'What, and disturb you in all your new important affairs? Surely a privy counsellor cannot spare the time to think of family?'

Thomas took a deep breath. Now was not the time to start a quarrel. 'She was my mother, Bess. I had a right to be told.'

'You were told.' Elizabeth slammed a jug down on the table. 'I wrote, did I not?'

'And I had a right to be present at her funeral.'

'I told you when it would be.'

'Told me when it was too late for me to get here in time.'

'Well, we could not leave her unburied until you managed to tear yourself away from the king.'

Thomas opened his mouth to retort, but Henry, coming into the room, quickly stepped between him and Elizabeth, his hands held high and patting the air.

'Mother would not want us to argue,' Henry said. 'Can we not all try to get along?'

'I will do my best,' Thomas muttered, taking a spoonful of pottage and curling his lips at the bland taste. He was used to eating much better at court. He looked up at his brother. 'Did she suffer much in the end?'

Henry shook his head. 'It was peaceful. She died in her sleep. Bess was with her.'

Elizabeth sniffed, making Thomas glance her way. Elizabeth's eyes were red and veins were standing out on her neck as she tried not to cry.

'And what of her husband?' Thomas asked uncomfortably, looking back at Henry. 'Where is he?'

'About his business in town. He will be back later.'

'I will order a mass for Mother this evening,' Thomas said.

Henry sat down and held out an empty bowl for Elizabeth to fill with pottage. 'You are dining with Edith and myself tomorrow evening, Thomas. We have some guests down from Huntingdonshire we would like you to meet.'

Thomas stifled his groan. 'Who?'

'Peter Larke and his granddaughter. Mother had a great deal of business with him and they corresponded often. You should see Edith bustling around trying to get all the provisions in. She's as nervous as a cat about putting on a good dinner.'

'I am sure it will be delicious. Will it not, Bess?'

'Oh no,' Henry said, 'Bess is not coming, just you. Our stepfather needs her here. Poor fellow is quite undone by Mother's death.'

Elizabeth rose from the table and moved to the fire, her face turned away from her brothers. But Thomas was not fooled. He knew Henry's words had stung her. Not for Elizabeth the pleasure of a little company and eating a dinner for once not cooked by herself. No, she had to stay at home and continue to look after her stepfather because *he* was grieving. *Poor Bess,* Thomas thought, though he could not help being glad that there would be one night on this visit home when he could escape her ever-constant disapproval.

The Larkes turned out to be very jolly dining companions. His stomach rumbling, Thomas had walked to Henry's house just a few streets away, picking his way over debris and trying to avoid getting his shoes dirty.

He was greeted by Henry, his red cheeks evidence he had already been generous with the wine.

'Ah, Thomas, there you are. Come and meet Master Larke.' Henry took hold of Thomas's arm and guided him towards the table.

Peter Larke was a plump man with a balding pate and double chin. Thomas felt an immediate liking for him as Larke's hands clasped his in a vigorous shake.

'I have heard a great deal about you, Master Wolsey,' Larke said.

'Good or bad?' Thomas asked, taking the seat Henry pointed him to.

'Oh, all good, all good,' Larke assured him. 'Your brother is very proud of your achievements.'

'Is he?' Thomas cried, turning his surprised gaze on Henry, who smiled shyly as he poured Thomas a drink.

'Henry has much to be proud of, by all accounts. You are a privy counsellor and royal almoner, are you not?'

'I am. The king has been most gracious,' Thomas said, swelling a little with pride.

'Thomas is in daily attendance on the king,' Henry said, pouring out more wine. 'He has the king's ear and works with the Lord Privy Seal. Let me put it this way, Master Larke, there is not much happening at court that my brother is unaware of. Is that not true, Thomas?'

'Much passes through my hands,' Thomas admitted proudly, his gaze suddenly drawn to the end of the table, at the person talking to Henry's wife, Edith.

Larke saw him looking and turned on the bench. 'Joan,' he called. 'Come over here.'

Thomas had thought her to be young when she had been in shadow, but as Joan rose from her stool and came near, he saw that she was in her late twenties. She dipped a curtsy.

'Master Wolsey, this is my granddaughter, Joan,' Larke said. 'Joan, this is Master Wolsey, Henry's brother of whom we have heard so much.'

'Good evening, Master Wolsey,' Joan said as he rose to greet her. Her voice was low and smooth, not shrill like Elizabeth's, and very pleasant to Thomas's ears. 'As my grandfather says, we have heard so much about you, I feel I know you already.'

'Then you have me at a disadvantage,' Thomas said and wondered where this new gallantry had sprung from. As he had towards her grandfather, he felt a great liking for Joan. She was not pretty, it was true, but her face, like her voice, was pleasant in an unassuming sort of way and her eyes were bright and inviting. 'Will you not sit by me here?'

Joan glanced at her grandfather, and he nodded his agreement, shifting up on the bench to accommodate her. She smiled at Thomas, and they soon fell into easy conversation as the rest of the company talked around them. By the time the dinner was served, Thomas had discovered Joan's father owned an inn in Thetford and that her grandfather had twice been made mayor of that town. Her face shone as she spoke of her family, and Thomas envied the genuine affection that seemed to exist between them. Joan, he found, was easy to talk to. He felt none of the awkwardness he usually experienced around women and soon relaxed in her company.

When the time came for Joan and her grandfather to retire to their lodgings, Thomas found himself bidding her good night with regret the evening was over. She seemed to feel it too, for her hand remained in his far longer than was necessary. But the door shut upon them at last, and Thomas returned to the table to drink one last cup of wine.

'Well, Thomas?' Edith raised an eyebrow, her expression amused and expectant.

'Well, what?' Thomas asked innocently.

'You liked Mistress Joan Larke, did you not?' Edith asked.

Thomas nodded. 'She and her grandfather make for very enjoyable company.'

'She is not married, nor does she have a sweetheart,' Edith said, gathering up the dirty plates from the table.

'What good is such news to Thomas?' Henry asked. 'He cannot marry her.'

'I do not speak of marriage,' Edith said. 'Oh, come,' she said into the silence that followed, 'let us not be hypocrites, Henry. We know of many churchmen who keep women as mistresses.'

'It is not allowed,' Henry said, a little scandalised by his wife's honesty.

'It happens, Henry, we know it does,' Edith insisted. 'Our own priest, here in this parish, has at least three mistresses to my knowledge.'

'It is a sin in the eyes of the church, Edith.'

'Better a man have a mistress than use whores.' Edith shrugged. 'And if you ask me, 'tis not natural for a man to be chaste. No one expects a churchman to be so.'

'Our sister does,' Henry declared, winking at Thomas.

'No one with any sense,' Edith said. She looked at Thomas. 'Peter liked you, and you are well connected and prosperous. Joan liked you, I could tell, and she has no prospect of marrying, despite her good fortune in her family.'

'Has no one offered for her?' Thomas asked, surprised. With a mayor for a grandfather and a successful businessman for a father, he would have thought Joan would have many men wishing to wed her.

'I think there were suitors some years ago,' Edith said carefully, 'but Joan did not care for them, and her father is not a man to force her to marry if she does not want to. A kind man, is Joan's father.'

'Edith may be right about this, you know. You should think on the matter,' Henry said, taking a seat with Thomas by the fire. 'You could give Mistress Larke a very comfortable life. As long as you do not mean to discard her, that is. I warn you, she is not a woman to be cast aside when you have done.'

'I would not do that to her,' Thomas vowed and meant it. Joan was too sweet a creature to be unkind to. 'Do you think she would have me? She may be outraged at the suggestion.'

'Oh, I think she may be persuaded,' Henry said. 'Indeed, I have met her often, here and in Thetford, and I have never seen her so animated in company before. She liked you greatly, Thomas, though what she sees in a plump ugly fellow like you is beyond me.' He laughed as Thomas punched him lightly on the arm. 'In all seriousness, though, you will want for company if you do not have a woman to take to your bed. A woman soothes a man, is a helpmeet. Woo her, Thomas. Visit her tomorrow and play the part of a suitor. I am sure she will soon tell you if your attentions are unwanted.'

Joan smiled and leant towards him, her lips gently puckered. Thomas pressed his lips to hers and closed his eyes.

'There,' she said as she pulled away.

Thomas opened his eyes. She was smiling, laughing at him, and he did not mind.

'Are you sure?'

'Thomas,' she cooed, drawing a finger gently down his cheek. 'I am sure.'

'Your family – '

Joan laughed. 'Oh, you goose. They all said I should.'

Thomas gulped. 'They did?'

'Of course. They will be glad to be rid of me.' She drew her hand away and tucked a strand of black hair back beneath her headdress. 'I am eight and twenty,

Thomas, unmarried, and no other man has looked at me twice for years. I am no beauty. No,' she shushed him with two fingers on his lips, 'I know I am not. I have met many men who I could consider as husbands if I wanted, but not one of them made me feel as you do.'

'I am no great lover, Joan,' Thomas said, embarrassed.

'I do not need you to be. I myself am not passionate, and besides, that is not what I mean. You make me feel safe. I know you will not beat me.'

'But do you understand all, Joan? I will not be able to publicly acknowledge you. When people come to my house, you will have to stay out of the way. When we have children, they will be bastards.'

'But you will do what you can for them?'

'Of course I will, but I will have you know what you are entering into if you become my mistress. I will not lie to you.'

'There are benefits to be had for me and mine if I become your mistress. You should know my family will expect you to be generous.'

'What do they want?' Thomas asked, not at all put out by her admission. He knew that for all their mutual attraction, this was a transaction like any other business deal. He did not expect to be allowed to take Joan as his mistress without giving something in return to her family.

'My brothers are both churchmen. You are well placed to help advance them, if the opportunity arises.'

'And I will do so whenever I can. You have my word. Your family will be as my family.'

'Then I am content,' Joan said. 'Where will my new home be?'

'I have a house in London now, a gift from the king. It is near the Palace of Bridewell. We will live there when it is ready.'

Joan smiled, then became serious, her eyes wary. 'There is something you should know, Thomas. My grandfather does not want me to tell you, but I will have no secrets from you, of that I am resolved.'

'Tell me,' Thomas urged, worried by her manner.

She hesitated a moment, biting her lip. Then she took a deep breath. 'I am not a maid, Thomas.' She stared at him, watching for his reaction.

Thomas was a little taken aback. He had expected Joan, with her avowed disinterest of other men, to be a virgin.

'When? Who?' he blustered.

'When I was very young, a girl of no more than fourteen. The loss of my maidenhead was not my choice.'

'You were ravished?'

She nodded, a flush creeping up her neck. 'He was a customer at the tavern, he was very drunk. He came upon me as I was washing the cups in the back and took me. I tried to fight him off, but he was strong and determined. Father came in and found us. I was so ashamed.'

'It was not your fault.'

'Father beat the man, very nearly killed him. He

would have done, I think, had not my brothers fetched Grandfather. Grandfather had him put in the pillory and branded a thief.' Joan laughed hollowly. 'Mother said he stole my maidenhead, but Father would not have my shame bruited abroad, and so he was merely a thief. My ravisher died in the pillory. Someone, I do not know who, threw a stone at his head. I was glad, God forgive me.'

'My poor Joan,' Thomas breathed.

'Have you changed your mind?' Joan asked, and Thomas could see tears in her eyes. 'I would understand if you have.'

'Not at all,' Thomas said. 'We will never mention it again. I will speak to your grandfather and settle the matter this afternoon. I return to London tomorrow, and as soon as I can, I will send for you.'

'You promise?'

'I promise,' he said, drawing her towards him.

There was no time for Thomas to dwell on the new arrangement he had made whilst in Ipswich. As soon as he arrived back at court, there was work to be done.

As well as the bequests the king was in the process of making to various monasteries and churches around the country, there was the routine administrative work of the privy council to sort through. Many of the papers merely needed his eye run over them before handing them over to the council secretaries, but some required greater attention. Thomas settled at his desk, knowing he had hours of reading to get through before he could retire to his bed.

He had been at work for many of those hours when his private secretary announced that the marquess of Dorset was asking to see him. Thomas told his secretary to show the marquess in and rose with a smile as Thomas Grey entered.

'Good evening, Master Wolsey,' he said, flapping the gloves he held idly against his other hand.

'Good evening, my lord. Forgive me, I had no idea you were at court, else I would have paid my respects.'

Grey waved the gloves dismissively. 'No need for that. I know you have been away.' He glanced down at the desk. 'And already hard at it, I see. You were ever industrious.'

Thomas begged Grey to take a chair, waiting until his guest was seated before resuming his seat. 'Are you visiting court?'

'No, no, I am come to stay. The king asked for me,' he explained as if a request from a king was an irksome thing. 'He said he wants his friends about him, so here I am. Though I am not quite sure I qualify as a friend, if truth be told.'

Thomas smiled. 'I believe the king enjoys having men his own age around him. He finds it dull with so many aged counsellors at court.'

Grey nodded. 'Do you count yourself amongst the old men, Master Wolsey?'

'I would like to think not,' Thomas said, bridling a

little at the suggestion. 'May I enquire after your family? They are well?'

'Yes, all well,' Grey said with a sigh. 'You should see home now, Master Wolsey. Bradgate Park is coming along splendidly.'

'I am glad. I remember viewing the plans when I was first invited to stay at Groby Manor with you.'

'Oh yes, all those years ago.' Grey's expression became wistful. 'In a way, I am sorry to be called away. I would have liked to oversee the construction, but… '

'One cannot say no to a king,' Thomas finished.

'Indeed, one cannot. Still, I hope the king has more in mind for me than merely playing cards and dice and chasing the odd stag. One can have enough of those, you know.'

Thomas did not know. He rarely had time to play at cards or dice and had never hunted stags. He preferred it that way. The life of the idle rich had no appeal for him. He would much rather be working. 'I predict your company will be greatly appreciated,' he said. 'Especially as the queen will soon enter her confinement.'

'Yes, he will want diversion then, to stop him worrying. I pray the child is a boy.'

'As do we all,' Thomas said, 'and we should also pray the queen comes through her trial safely.'

'Well, yes, of course,' Grey hastened to agree, and Thomas understood that the young man had not given a thought to Katherine and what she must endure to give the king a healthy child.

After half an hour of pleasant conversation, Thomas

all the while casting yearning looks at his paperwork, Grey said he would leave so Thomas could get on with his work, inviting Thomas to dine with him on the morrow. Thomas thanked him and said he would be delighted. As soon as Grey was out of the door, he picked up his pen and got straight back to work as though he had not been interrupted.

~

Thomas pushed open the door of La Maison Curiale and peered inside. The sight that greeted his eyes pleased him more than he could say. Dust sheets covered the stone floor of the hall, a wooden ladder stood by the wall, a bucket of lime wash with a boar bristle brush sticking out on its top. At its base, a workman was tying his shoe. He looked up as Thomas entered.

'Can I help you, sir?'

'I am Master Wolsey,' Thomas said. 'The owner of this house,' he added when the man continued to stare.

The man immediately swept the cap from his head. 'Forgive me, sir. I did not know you.'

Thomas waved him silent. He didn't blame the man for not knowing him; he had hardly set foot in the house. He moved deeper into the hall, staring up at the ceiling, examining every corner. 'The work is coming along well, it seems.'

'Aye, sir, it is,' the man said. 'The house is almost done.'

By this, Thomas knew the man meant all traces of

Richard Empson had been expunged. The house itself had been in very good order when Thomas acquired it. His first inspection of the property, a hurried and excited dash from court to see exactly what kind of house the king had given him, had been an hour of pure delight. He had never before owned anything as substantial as a house. Thomas had money and quite a bit of it, but gold coins hoarded in a chest meant little; they needed to be spent. Thomas had been at a loss as to how to spend his coins until he had become a man of property.

Property, land – they were the only assets that mattered, he had come to realise. That was how the nobility had prospered and survived. The only advantage they had over the common man was their antecedence. A noble name could not be bought, but property and land could. What had Fox said about the Tudors? That they valued new men. The Tudors did not care about family names or a lineage that could be traced back to the Conquest. All the Tudors cared about was whether these new men could get the jobs they asked for done. If the answer was yes, the Tudors did not care how high these new men rose.

Thomas wandered through his house, making mental notes of how he would furnish this new property of his. He would be bringing Joan here when it was ready, and she would probably want to have a say in how it was decorated. Whatever she chose, it would be the best his money could buy, Thomas decided.

The bleeding had stopped. There had not been so much of it, really. Her baby had slipped away from her so easily, it had been so small. A girl, they told her. She had almost had a baby daughter.

Almost.

Katherine had thought it would be so easy. Marry a prince, become a queen, have a child, secure the dynasty. After all those years of waiting, of wondering what was to become of her, she had been rewarded for her determination. Henry had whisked her away from her solitude and poverty and made her his queen. He loved her; Katherine knew he loved her. She felt it in the way he touched her, in the way he spoke of her to others, in the way he confided in her. Henry loved her, had trusted her to give him a child, and she had failed him.

Henry had been wonderful. She had not been able to stop crying when they took her baby away, hastily wrapped up in a white towel, her women trying to hide the smears of blood. Henry had come in, his normally pink face pale, his eyes puffy. He needed her, she had realised, and she had to put aside her own grief and be a comfort to him. She had held her arms out to him and he had rushed to her, burying his face against her breast and sobbing. Her ladies had shuffled out of the room, leaving the grieving parents alone.

When they had no tears left, Katherine had brushed back Henry's hair where it clung to his cheeks and laid featherlight kisses all over his face. 'We will have more children,' she had whispered, though it hurt her to say so, as if the little girl lost was nothing more than a worn-out pair of shoes that could be easily replaced. Henry had nodded and said, 'Yes, yes, we will have more.' Then, exhausted by crying, he had fallen asleep, his head on her shoulder, as if he were the child and she the mother.

Yes, the bleeding had stopped from between her legs, but it had not stopped in Katherine's heart. Her baby gone, her husband disappointed; she had to make amends and become pregnant again soon. She resented the necessity, for she had discovered the pleasures of the marriage bed only recently, had enjoyed their couplings for their own sake. Now those couplings would no longer be for love; they would have a purpose.

The fairy tale was over.

Joan was arriving. Thomas had arranged for her to reach La Maison Curiale in the early evening when the skies had darkened and her coming would pass unnoticed by the gatekeepers.

Thomas stood by his office window as the barge he had sent to fetch her from Tilbury moored alongside the river steps. He wanted to rush out and meet her, help her from the boat, but it would be unseemly, and he would have to explain his actions to his secretary who was reading aloud a letter from the governor of Calais. As far as the household was concerned, Joan Larke was a friend of the Wolsey family who was to be employed as a servant, albeit one whose exact role was undefined.

He squinted as a figure was helped out of the boat, but the torches flickered too greatly for Thomas to make her out clearly. He had given instructions Joan was to be shown to her suite of rooms upon her arrival, and for her to take food if she so desired. He would have to wait to see her for perhaps another hour or two, but it could not be helped.

His secretary coughed, a polite reminder he was still waiting, pen poised. Thomas resumed his seat at his desk and began dictating his reply to the governor.

Joan's heart was beating fast. She had not expected a house quite as grand as this. She had known Thomas was wealthy, but this was more than she could have hoped for. This great house was to be her new home, she its unofficial mistress. Over the past few weeks there had been moments of doubt, wondering whether she had made the right choice. *Well, Joan Larke,* she told herself, *wonder no more. No Norfolk merchant would ever have been able to give you this.*

Thomas sent word he would be with her before midnight unless she was weary from her journey and wanted to retire, in which case he would see her in the morning at mass. Joan was too excited to be tired and sent a reply that she wished to see him as soon as his work was done.

She was unsure whether Thomas intended to consummate their new relationship that night, but in case he did, Joan washed herself with a linen cloth and dabbed rosewater on her wrists and neck and in the crevice between her breasts.

As a church bell tolled the twelfth hour, Joan heard footsteps outside the door and held her breath, her eyes fixed on the light coming through the gap at the bottom. A heartbeat later, the door opened and Thomas stood in the doorway, a candle in one hand.

Joan stood, smoothing down her nightgown. 'Here I am, Thomas,' she declared.

'Here you are.' Thomas nodded, shutting the door. 'Your journey was not too uncomfortable, I hope?'

'It had its moments.' They fell into an awkward silence, each smiling shyly at the other. 'Oh Thomas,' Joan said at last, 'this is no way to begin. We both know why I am here.' She held out her hand. 'Come to bed.'

She saw his cheeks redden in the candlelight, but he went towards her. Joan took his candle and set it on the bedside table, careful to position it away from the bed hangings lest they catch fire. She helped him to unbutton his cassock and folded it neatly over the chest at the end of the bed. She let him remove the rest of his clothing himself, aware of his embarrassment, and climbed into the bed, sitting up and pulling her nightgown over her head. She knew the sight of her naked body would quell any fears he might have, so she pushed the covers down to show more of herself. She was nervous too, but she felt he needed help more than she did, and it pleased her to feel she was the instigator of this coupling.

She lay back in the bed and looked up at the luxurious silk fabric of the tester above her. Her body was a small price to pay for such luxury, she thought as the mattress dipped beside her.

CHAPTER TWENTY-SEVEN

1511

The celebration feast was almost over, the feast to celebrate the birth of a prince. How different, Thomas thought, from his own situation with Joan. She had fallen pregnant very soon after arriving in London, perhaps from their first night together, and it had hurt him to remind her that she would not be able to be a mother to the child when it came. Joan had borne the reminder well, though he knew it pained her and was dreading the imminent birth for that reason.

Many of the diners had left their seats to talk with friends seated at other tables. As the pages cleared the plates of uneaten food away to be scraped into the broken meats bowl, the tablecloths were folded, and the trestle tables dismantled and set to the side. Those intent on remaining seated were politely asked to move because the king wanted the dancing to begin.

'Yet more dancing,' Fox murmured as he handed his

half-empty cup to a steward. 'When is enough enough, I wonder?'

Thomas grinned. 'The king is indefatigable, Your Grace. Today dancing, in the morning hunting, and at the butts in the afternoon, I believe.'

'When does he have the time to govern?' Fox asked. 'Oh, I forget, he does not. He leaves all that to his council.'

The king shouted for the musicians to play, and the hall was suddenly filled with music. Fox and Thomas watched as couples formed two lines, the dance a lively galliard.

'Is that not a good state of affairs, Your Grace?' Thomas asked, curious at the bishop's last statement.

'A king should be part of the government of the country. The late king would never have neglected business in the way his son does.'

'That sounds like a criticism, Your Grace.'

Fox raised an eyebrow at Thomas. 'It is intended to be, Master Wolsey. Do you not agree with me?'

Thomas kept his eyes on the dancers. 'I think the king is untutored in how the world of politics works. I think he shows great wisdom in leaving it to men such as yourself who do understand it.'

Mollified by this piece of blatant flattery, Fox returned his gaze to the dancers. Suddenly, there was screaming as the king left Katherine standing alone to take out the knife he kept on his belt and leap into the middle of the dance. Thomas couldn't see what he was doing, but there was laughter and girlish screeches when

336

he heard Henry give a victorious cry and emerge from the dancers, arm raised above his head. He was laughing and waved what he held, a man's purse cut from one of the courtier's belts. Henry delved into the purse and began throwing coins into the crowd. Thomas spotted the man whose purse had been cut by the king and noted his look of embarrassment and dismay. But Henry seemed to think it a fine joke.

'Never had this kind of thing in his father's day.' Fox shook his head. 'Well, I think I shall leave you to it as you seem to have a liking for it. I have work to do.'

Thomas stepped aside for Fox to pass, wondering if the bishop expected him to offer to help. But Thomas had no inclination to leave the hall. He was enjoying the music and dancing and laughter. Bishop Fox was an old man who wished Henry VII back again. Not so, Thomas. He liked this bright new court, and he had no complaint to make if Henry preferred to indulge his love of sport and fun rather than preside over council meetings. That was what kings were for, in Thomas's opinion. Let the king have his fun. Far better, he thought, to leave the business of government to men like him and Bishop Fox who knew what they were doing.

∽

Joan looked on as Thomas bent over the cot and examined its occupant. She was determined not to be sad, or at least not to show her sadness. Another child born, another child to be taken from her. She must not complain. This was what she had agreed to.

'He is rather ugly,' Thomas observed, amused.

'All babies are ugly,' Joan said, smiling despite herself. 'And he looks like you. What do you expect?'

Thomas laughed and held out his arms to her. Joan nestled against him, needing his embrace. She felt his cheek against her head and enjoyed it. It had been so long since she and Thomas had been together. He was busier than ever these days, always flitting between court and home, between court and important peoples' houses, between the city and the court. Thomas was needed everywhere, it seemed, and she had to take her share of him when she could.

'You have arranged a wet nurse?' Thomas asked.

A heartbeat passed, and Joan detached herself from Thomas. Their eyes met. 'She is down in the kitchen.' She patted his chest lightly, then stepped away.

'I am sorry, Joan,' Thomas said.

'I know you are. I know it must be so, yet… '

'I wish it were not so.'

'Do you?' she asked, looking up at him suddenly. 'Would anyone notice that little thing here?' She pointed at the cot.

'Joan,' Thomas said sadly, 'you know they would.'

She threw up her hands. 'You think it would cause such a scandal, yet I know of priests who have children. It is common knowledge, and no one bats an eyelid.'

'Tell me,' Thomas said, hands on hips, 'do these

priests you know of keep their bastards in their homes? Well, do they?'

'No,' she admitted sulkily and moved to the window seat, her gaze on the garden outside. 'Where will our son be sent?'

'Maybe it would be better if you did not know – '

'Where?'

Thomas sighed. 'To a family in Willesden.'

She heaved a great cry and Thomas took a step towards her. She held out her hand to stop him. 'Let me be, Thomas.'

''Tis not my fault, Joan, 'tis the way of the world in which we live.'

'My son is to be taken from me. You cannot imagine how hard that is for me.'

'Of course I can.'

'No, you cannot. You did not carry him within you for nine months. You did not endure pain to bring him forth. Do not tell me you understand.'

'Very well, I will not. Do you want me to stay or shall I go?'

She thought for a moment, torn between needing to be angry at someone and needing his company. 'Stay. I do need you. I will be good, I promise.' She felt his hand on her shoulder and covered it with her own.

'I do not need you to be good.'

She swivelled on the window seat and looked up at him. 'I know, I know. It is difficult, Thomas.'

'He will be well looked after, and I shall take an

interest in him. He will not be lost to us, I promise you, Joan.'

Joan did not know if Thomas was making her an empty promise. At that moment, she did not care. She wanted to believe him. It was a lie she could live with.

~

The joke King Henry had played at the feast caught on. His friends – Brandon, Compton and others of their set – were going around court blithely cutting purses from courtiers' belts. Unlike Henry, these japesters did not believe in redistribution and kept the purses for themselves instead. The desks of both Fox and Thomas were littered with complaints from courtiers who had been victims of this prank.

'It was naught but a jest.' Henry laughed when Thomas told him of the complaints at Fox's insistence. 'I never intended it to become a habit.'

'Your friends seem to have taken it as just that, Your Grace. License to behave in such a way.'

'They will soon tire of it,' Henry said, waving his hand dismissively.

'Not when they profit by it, Your Grace.'

'So, what would you have me do, Thomas?'

'Speak with your friends, Your Grace,' he suggested. 'Tell them they must stop.'

Henry looked down at the floor, his expression uncertain. Thomas understood the king's dilemma. The coterie of friends Henry had cultivated were all older than he and far more experienced in the ways of the world as well as the court. King he may be, but Henry was still desperately unsure of himself. To tell his friends to cease their japes because his ministers said he must would be humiliating.

'Would you like for me to handle this matter?' Thomas suggested carefully, keen to help Henry out of his difficulty.

Henry bit his lip and considered for a moment. 'Yes,' he said at last, 'I would. You see to it, Thomas. I do not have the time for such trifles.'

'I have your authority to say this is your command?' Henry liked that, *his command*, Thomas could tell.

'You do.' Henry nodded. 'Thank you, Thomas.'

'Just who do you think you are?'

Charles Brandon was such a ridiculous creature, Thomas thought as he roared at him. A boy in a man's body, and a rude, stupid boy at that.

'Eh, just who do you think you are to tell me to cease my antics?' Brandon said again, moving his massive body to stand before Thomas, his huge hands planted on his hips. 'I am not one of your servants, Master Wolsey.'

It took all Thomas's control not to take a step away. He stood his ground. 'No, my lord, you are a servant of the king, and it is the king's command that these pranks of yours and your companions cease immediately.'

Brandon's dark eyes glowered at him. 'The king's command! Are you saying this comes from Henry?'

'It does, my lord.'

'If that be so, then why does he not tell me himself, eh?' Brandon sneered a grin. 'This is your doing, Master Wolsey, I swear. I am the king's closest friend. Henry would tell me himself if he was displeased with me.'

'He is the king, Your Grace,' Thomas said quietly, 'and has people such as myself to manage unpleasant tasks such as this.'

'So, now I am an unpleasant task to be dealt with, am I? You butcher's son!'

Thomas's jaw clenched at the insult. He balled his hands into fists, channelling his anger into them, but kept them rigidly at his side. He was no fool. He could not beat Brandon in a fight, and even if he did, it would be he who would suffer in the aftermath.

Fortunately, Brandon appeared deflated by the lack of a response from Thomas. He shuffled his feet, flared his nostrils and ground his teeth. 'Tell Henry I will stop. I have grown bored of the joke in any case,' he growled.

Brandon slammed the door on his way out, making the portraits on the adjoining walls bang against the wood panelling.

Thomas uncurled his fists and looked down to see that his hands were shaking.

The court had become unnaturally quiet. As Thomas

walked through the corridors, there was no chatter, no laughing, no women being happily wooed. When courtiers spoke, they spoke in corners and whispered. None dared to show gaiety or joy, for that would have been unthinkable.

The prince, the little baby boy who had brought such joy to his parents at the new year, had died after only six weeks of life. Henry and Katherine – the whole court, in fact – had been fooled into believing the baby boy, having survived the birth and the first few weeks, was safe from harm, that the Tudor dynasty had been secured, that there was an heir to succeed Henry when that distant time came.

It was cruel of God, Thomas could not help thinking, to allow a woman to carry life within her for nine months, to endure the agony of childbirth and experience joy at the sight of a healthy baby, only to take that baby's life a few weeks later. He had privately prayed for Henry and Katherine when the baby died, beseeching God to take care of the little prince. And when he had been called upon to provide solace to the grieving parents, he had mouthed the usual words, told them God had wanted the prince with him, so greatly did he love the little boy. Katherine found a little comfort in those words, Thomas thought. Henry less so.

He guessed the thoughts going through Henry's mind. Henry's father had often spoken of the need for his son to produce an heir as soon as he could to preserve the Tudor line, and so far, Henry had proven unable to do so. It was not his fault, of course. Henry was capable of fathering a child. If there was any fault, it probably lay with Katherine. She had lost their first child, the girl, shortly after birth. Now this important son had been lost too. Thomas and all of England had to pray and hope that the next child would be a boy, and that he would survive.

CHAPTER TWENTY-EIGHT

Katherine was expecting her husband to come to her rooms. Henry usually spent the afternoon with her when his friends didn't persuade him away to practise his archery or play at cards. She enjoyed these long afternoons with Henry, when her ladies retreated to the corners of the room to talk amongst themselves and she had Henry all to herself. When he was alone with her, he was so different from the loud, exuberant man he became in public. With her, he was kind and quiet, sometimes showing her the latest song he had written – always dedicated to her or about her, he would say, leaning in for a kiss – or reading a passage from a book he had become interested in. Katherine loved him as she had never loved his brother Arthur, and she often felt guilty for that. But she couldn't help her heart and had convinced herself that she had been too immature when she was first wed, only a girl of sixteen, or else that she had not had enough time to fall in love with her first husband.

But enough of the past, she told herself briskly. She checked the table by the window, making sure that the wine and cakes Henry liked were there. They were. She settled herself in her chair and picked up her embroidery, a handkerchief she was decorating for Henry.

Katherine heard Henry before she saw him, his voice carried so. He entered, filling the room with his presence, and graciously said his greetings to her ladies before striding to Katherine and kissing her hand. She smiled up at him and had to stop herself from stroking his cheek. He did not like showy demonstrations of their love before others. She gestured for him to sit in the chair opposite and to help himself to the wine and cakes.

'Have you had a good morning, my lord?' she asked, returning her eyes to her work.

'I have,' Henry said, munching on a cake. 'A good ride, though I did not catch anything.'

'Never mind.'

'And you, my love?'

'I have received a letter from my father that was interesting.'

'In what way, my sweet?'

Katherine set her needlework to one side. She had introduced her father casually enough but there was intent in her words. 'He writes of the Holy League.'

The Holy League was the Pope's response to the aggressive policy of France in conquering Italy. France had just enjoyed a decisive victory over Venice, geographically part of Italy but very much her own power, and that victory had encouraged the French to march on into Italy and claim her towns as theirs. The Pope was desperate to halt their advance, but he needed help from other crown states.

Henry set down his wine cup and leant towards her. 'There is news?'

'The French are struggling,' Katherine said happily, 'but my father is concerned they may yet recover. He believes that if England were to declare war on France, they would be completely crushed, for they would be opposed on all sides.'

'Ferdinand is asking for my help?' Henry's eyes widened.

'He is, my lord. He thinks English aid will be invaluable in defeating the French.'

'To go to war,' Henry breathed, his gaze moving from Katherine to the window, his mind's eye on a battlefield somewhere, with him raising his sword aloft, victorious.

'You would look very handsome in your armour, Henry,' Katherine said softly. 'And it would please me to be able to write to my father and say my husband was willing to go to war with him.'

Henry took her hands and kissed her fingers. 'You write to him, Katherine, and you tell him Henry of England will make France bend her knee to us.'

Katherine did kiss him then and to hell with whoever saw.

Standing by the large window in his private apartments, Henry held the rose a few inches above his head, watching with undisguised delight as the sunlight caught the gold and made it glint.

'Is it not exquisite, Thomas?' Henry asked, his voice full of awe.

'Most exquisite,' Thomas agreed, pleased the king was continuing his practice of calling him by his Christian name rather than the more formal Master Wolsey. It was a sign of favour and made him a little special. Bishop Fox was never Richard. Bishop Fox was always 'Your Grace' or 'my lord', or sometimes simply 'Bishop'. But Thomas was Henry's Thomas, and sometimes, in Henry's jollier moods, just plain Tom. 'It is a gift from the Pope, I believe?'

Henry lowered his arm and cradled the golden rose in both hands. 'Yes. A gift for my help in reconciling the Venetian republicans with Rome. Speaking of the Pope, the queen has spoken to me of this Holy League he has formed. Have you heard of it?'

'I have, Your Grace.' Thomas nodded.

Thomas had heard of the Pope's new initiative long before it reached Katherine, having received a letter from one of the Pope's closest aides. The letter had suggested that Thomas, as a close and trusted acquaintance of the king of England, was in an excellent position to suggest a policy of helping the Pope take back the land the French had taken for her own. The letter had made Thomas's heart swell with pride. Thousands of miles away, the Pope believed that Thomas Wolsey, the son of a butcher, had influence over the king of England.

'What think you of it?' Henry asked.

'I think it a most noble endeavour,' Thomas said. 'What is the queen's interest in the League, if I may be so bold as to enquire?'

'King Ferdinand has written to her telling of how he has joined the League at the Pope's request. Ferdinand is eager for England to become involved.'

'And the queen – ?'

'Agrees with her father, naturally.'

Naturally, thought Thomas a little sourly. Katherine may be an English queen, but she was still at heart a Spanish princess. In his opinion, there were times it was unclear where her first loyalty lay.

'What think you?' Henry asked, falling down onto a huge pile of cushions. 'Should England become part of this Holy League?'

Thomas knew he had to tread carefully. 'Your Grace, I am flattered you ask for my opinion, but is this not a subject for all the privy council to discuss?'

'Oh, to hell with my council. I ask for your opinion, Thomas.'

Thomas considered a moment. He knew what Fox would have him say. Fox believed foreign entanglements, even those that involved the Church of Rome, only meant depletions in England's treasury and such a fate was to be avoided at all costs. But Henry was asking Thomas what he thought, and Thomas knew what Henry wanted to hear. Henry was tired of merely playing at war in court tilts and archery tournaments; he wanted to fight in one.

'In my opinion, Your Grace, and this is only my opinion, I think this is one fight England should be in.'

Henry clapped his hands joyously. 'Excellent. We must speak to the privy council at once. Thomas, you will add your voice to mine?'

'I am gratified Your Grace believes I have any influence on your council. Of course, you shall have my voice.'

Henry nodded. 'Assemble the council, then, Thomas. I want this discussed at once, you hear?'

'I will see to it immediately,' Thomas said, bowing and backing out of the room.

'Gentlemen, we are to declare war on France.'

Henry's announcement was met with silence in the council chamber. Fox and Lovell looked sideways at one another, their expressions glum. Thomas studied every man at the table, waiting to see who would break the silence.

'Ha ha, Hal,' Brandon bellowed, reaching across and thumping Henry on the shoulder. 'I knew you had it in you.'

Henry grinned at his friend. 'Will you join me in the field, Charles?'

'Anywhere you like, Hal, anywhere you like. Just give the order.'

There was a cough. 'Your Grace,' Fox said, keeping his eyes on the table before him, 'this is something that should be discussed, surely, before a decision is made.' He spread his hands, looking up at last. 'I mean, where has this idea come from?'

You had better change your tone, bishop, Thomas thought, glancing at Henry, whose neck was turning red with indignation. Fox was speaking to the king as if he was a boy who had just latched onto a new idea without any notion of what it would involve.

'Am I not the king, bishop?' Henry asked, his voice deceptively calm.

'You are, Your Grace,' Fox assured him smoothly, no doubt sensing danger.

'Then there is no need for discussion,' Henry said, his small mouth tightening. 'If I say we are to declare war against our old enemy, then that is what we will do.'

'But, Your Grace, why?' Fox asked.

'The queen has had a request from King Ferdinand,' Henry began, and Thomas saw understanding dawn on Fox's face. This wasn't going to go down well with the old man. 'He believes that with our assistance, France can be utterly crushed.'

'So, this is the queen's idea?' Warham asked, needing clarification.

'It is *my* desire,' Henry said through gritted teeth. He pointed to Thomas. 'And Master Wolsey agrees with me.'

All eyes around the council table turned on Thomas, and he felt himself grow hot. This was Henry's invitation to speak, to provide the support Henry had asked of him. He had to comply. He could not go back on his word to the king.

'It is true,' he said quietly, 'that I agree with the king and queen – and the Pope – in this mission to check the French. I believe England should join the Holy League.'

'There,' Henry declared with a decisive nod.

'Master Wolsey does not speak for the council, Your Grace,' Fox said, glaring at Thomas. 'As I said before, any decision must be a collective one, not the opinion of one very junior member.'

Thomas's stomach churned at the insult, but he held his tongue, certain he heard a snigger from Brandon's direction.

'And I must say,' Fox continued, closing his leather folder determinedly, 'your father would never have considered such a policy.'

'My father is not here,' Henry roared, jumping up from the table, forcing all the counsellors to rise. 'Are we women that we should shrink from the idea of battle?'

'Quite right, Your Grace,' George Talbot, earl of Shrewsbury said, nodding vigorously. 'Shall we all dress in our wives' skirts and handle nothing more dangerous than a distaff?'

Brandon laughed at that. His laugh served a useful purpose, for it broke the tension and calmed Henry's angry mood. Henry laughed too. But then he saw the faces of Warham and Fox and resumed his seat, waiting until all his counsellors were back in theirs.

'My good lords,' he began quietly, 'I am aware this is not a thing to decide easily. There must be discussion, and there must be diplomacy, I understand. But know this. England has a place in Europe. For so long, this island of ours has been on the outside of Continental affairs, dismissed as nothing more than an ancient outpost of Rome – useless, pointless. This is an opportunity to prove we are more and worthy of Europe's attention. And let us not forget, this is an opportunity to put down England's greatest and oldest enemy.'

Brandon and Shrewsbury clapped heartily. Warham and Fox smiled thinly and began making notes. Thomas, with a shaking hand, began to do the same.

Thomas was very nearly out of the council chamber door when Fox called him back. He turned, his papers almost slipping from beneath his arm, knowing what was coming.

'Yes, Your Grace?'

'What did you think you were doing?' Fox demanded.

'I thought I was doing my job, Your Grace,' Thomas said, not meeting Fox's eye.

'Your job is what I tell you it is,' Fox said, his voice low, almost threatening. 'And I say it is not to promote a policy of war with France.'

'The king wants – '

'What the king wants is of no consequence. The council does not exist to simply do what the king wants, but to do what is best for England.'

'The king *is* England, Your Grace,' Thomas said. 'Surely, what the king wants is the best for his realm?'

Fox shook his head in disgust. 'That is a very prettily phrased sentence, but it is hopelessly naïve of you. I had not thought you a simpleton.'

Thomas's blood boiled. 'That is an unworthy remark from you, Your Grace.'

'Oh, you think so, do you? I think it is not. I also think you forget to whom you owe your current position.'

'I do not forget it, Your Grace,' Thomas assured him. 'But you must allow me to speak my mind when I feel strongly about a matter such as this.'

Fox pouted and looked Thomas up and down. 'Be it on your own head, then,' he said. 'Here.' He thrust his papers against Thomas's chest. 'If you and the king want this war, then you can organise it.' He pushed past Thomas out of the chamber.

Thomas took a deep breath, closing his eyes. He did not like to oppose the bishop, but Thomas was his protégé no longer. He was a man of property, of some little power and, it seemed, some considerable influence, at least with the king. He stuffed his paperwork more securely beneath his arm and headed out of the door.

CHAPTER TWENTY-NINE

'Master Wolsey.' Thomas Grey closed his book. 'To what do I owe this honour?'

'May I come in, my lord?' Thomas asked.

'Of course, of course.' Grey rose and closed the door behind Thomas. 'It seems we hardly get to meet these days, you are always so busy.'

'The king keeps me so,' Thomas replied, shaking his head at the wine being offered and sitting down in the window seat. He waited until Grey was back in his chair and looking eagerly at him. 'I have come with a commission for you from the king.'

'At last,' Grey said, clapping his hands. 'Something to do.'

'Yes. I remember how you said you hoped there would be more to your court life than dice and cards.' Thomas smiled.

'Did I? I had forgotten.' Grey pointed at the roll of

parchment Thomas had produced. 'So, you have fixed this appointment for me, have you? I thank you.'

'Read it before you thank me.' Thomas handed the parchment to the marquess, aware he had not had anything to do with Grey's appointment but reasoning it did not hurt to let the marquess think he had.

Grey read the parchment. 'I am to be in command of the army.'

'Indeed, my lord. The king entrusts the command of the English army to you. You are to be responsible for the conscription of men and their equipping with arms. Once that is done, you will take the army across the Channel and join with King Ferdinand's troops on the coast of Spain to attack the French town of Guienne.'

'I see,' Grey said uncertainly.

'Is something wrong, my lord?' Thomas asked.

Grey licked his lips and looked up at Thomas, a nervousness in his eyes. 'I… I've never done anything like this before, Master Wolsey. How do I go about arranging everything?'

Thomas smiled. 'If you will allow me, my lord, I will help with the arrangements as much as I can, but I am no soldier. I have no training in arms and cannot advise on that part of your commission. But I can handle the paperwork for you if you wish.'

'Oh, would you, Master Wolsey? I would be grateful for anything you can do for me.'

'It will be my pleasure,' Thomas assured him, wondering if the marquess's gratitude would manifest in any material way.

Thomas Grey poured himself another cup of wine, emptying the jug. He knew he was making himself drunk and did not care.

Where was the glory to be had in this expedition? He had left England with so many hopes of proving himself, and it was all going to end in disaster, he could feel it.

Grey and his army had arrived at St Sebastien on the Spanish coast on the seventh of June, expecting to meet up with King Ferdinand's army. When Grey had climbed out of the boat and set his booted feet into the sand, he had looked around, his brow creasing. There was not a single Spanish soldier to be seen. Had they arrived too early, or worse, too late?

After a few days of waiting for someone to turn up, his men and officers growing ever more impatient, Grey had decided to march on to Feunterrabia twelve miles away in the hope that they would meet up with the Spanish army en route. Nothing. No army. Not knowing what else to do, Grey had ordered his army to make camp, hoping orders from King Ferdinand would soon arrive.

But the days lengthened, and orders never came. The days grew unbearably hot. Grey and his army were Englishmen, unused to the heat of a Spanish summer, and his men began to sweat and grumble. Then illness came, and men found their bowels loosening, their insides retching and their bodies growing thinner and thinner with each passing day.

Grey despatched a messenger with a letter to King Ferdinand, phrased as politely as he could manage, to ask when his army was going to turn up and reinforce the English. King Ferdinand returned a letter that made no promises and even suggested that it was better for the English if the Spanish did not join them, that it was in fact his plan to secure the territory of Navarre before they marched on Guienne together.

Three months passed before Grey angrily realised King Ferdinand had no intention of honouring the agreement he had made with King Henry. He wrote to Thomas, the one person on the council he knew he could count on to tell him what to do and be honest with him about why he and his men had been left to fester in the sun. Thomas wrote back, and Grey tore open the letter eagerly. Thomas wrote, expressing his sorrow but admitting it had become clear King Ferdinand had used the English army to pose a threat to the French so he could move on Navarre knowing that the English guarded his rear.

And so, Grey was getting drunk on the last of the wine he had brought with him from England. His officers moved amongst the men, sorting out the dead and dying and deciding who was healthy enough to return to England. Even now, graves were being dug in the hard-baked Spanish dirt. Of the ten thousand men who had sailed from England, Grey doubted whether six thousand would return.

In his desperation, Grey even began to wonder whether Henry had known this would happen all along, even whether his commission had been a punishment for his father's loyalty to Richard III before Henry VII came to the throne. He suggested this in a letter to Thomas. Thomas wrote back, furious Grey could think such a thing. He swore King Henry was incapable of such deception, and that Henry was furious with King Ferdinand for his treachery.

Grey believed Thomas, but it made his situation no better. Indeed, his situation was worsening. The English army, made up of farmers and ploughmen, shepherds and tanners, had grown discontented and began to defy Grey and his officers' authority. They were tired of Spain and waiting for a war that was nowhere near them. They told the officers they were hungry and not content to take the rations doled out to them but wanted all the food in the stores at once. The officers refused, of course, so the men knocked the store doors down and took the food, anyway. Then they found the wine and beer stores and had that too.

Grey wrote again to Thomas to tell him what was happening, hoping for help. Thomas's reply was sympathetic, but Grey was ordered to manage as best he could, for it was planned for the English army to stay put through the winter. Grey screwed up Thomas's letter in disgust, cursing him for refusing to help and expecting him to endure this misery longer.

When in his cups, Grey could be very indiscreet, and he told his officers of Thomas's letter. The officers were outraged and became as indiscreet as Grey, not caring if their men overheard their protests that England was content to let them rot. Hearing this, the men began to demand to go home. They added the threat of violence to their demands, and the officers, brave though they were, grew alarmed and found they could do nothing to calm the men. They appealed to Grey to ignore the council's orders. Even if war did come, the army was in no fit state to fight.

Believing himself abandoned by his king, Grey needed little persuading. He sat down at his camp table and wrote a final letter to Thomas to tell him he was bringing the army home.

Thomas pressed his ear to the door and listened. He heard the queen crying, but at least Henry wasn't shouting at her anymore. He felt sorry for Katherine, although he also felt she deserved Henry's anger. It had been because of her insistence that Henry could trust her father that he had agreed to send an army to Spain to support King Ferdinand. And what a disaster that had proved to be. Only that morning Thomas had received yet another letter from Thomas Grey full of complaints and declaring he was bringing the army back to England.

Thomas did not blame him. He had come to wish he had never supported this war with France. It was clear that Ferdinand had made use of Henry from the start; he had never had any intention of his army joining the English; it had merely been a ruse to distract the French. Thomas cursed himself for not having considered it possible that Ferdinand would trick them. The Spanish king had a reputation for deceit, and yet Thomas had believed his assurances without question.

Others were whispering about Thomas and his handling of the affair. Yes, he had heard the talk, the chatter, the gossip. All the nobles who hated him for being a parvenu, for being a butcher's son, were talking in loud whispers, saying the war had been a disaster from the start. It was Master Wolsey's fault, they said. It did not matter that he had worked hard to ensure its success, that the failures had been caused by factors out of his control. All the nobles cared about was that an upstart was finally getting his comeuppance.

Thomas desperately hoped that wasn't the case. He knew Henry was angry about the whole affair and that he had taken his anger out on Katherine, but he had yet to shout at Thomas. Was Henry angry with him too? Were Henry's nobles whispering in his ear that the butcher's son had overreached himself? He needed to get Henry on his own, explain all he had done and what had gone wrong, and convince Henry he was not to blame.

But he felt he *was* to blame, that was the problem. Thomas had checked the accounts and learnt just how much the expedition had cost the English throne. Two hundred thousand ducats had been spent to equip the army with food, water and arms. All that money and what had been achieved? Nothing but two thousand dead men and humiliation for Henry. He should have taken more care. He had rushed the whole enterprise, not bothering to get the best prices for goods, not allowing the officers to train their men properly, and not ensuring Ferdinand's support with clauses in the treaty that he could not back out of.

Thomas knew he had rushed everything. He had brought disgrace upon England and humiliated his king. He could only pray that Henry would treat him kindly.

Thomas knew that if there was one place he could get Henry alone, it was in the chapel. He hoped Henry would feel like praying after his quarrel with the queen and hurried to the chapel to wait for him.

Less than five minutes later, Henry arrived, storming up the aisle and kicking the front pew. It scraped against the stone floor.

'Can I help you, Your Grace?' Thomas asked, stepping out of the corner.

Henry started. 'Oh, Thomas, it's you. I did not see you there.'

'Is something wrong?'

Henry slumped down in the pew. 'It is all such a mess.'

'What is, Your Grace?'

'You can ask that?' Henry asked, incredulous. 'The war with France, Thomas, the war.'

'Ah yes, Your Grace, I understand.'

'I have been such a fool.'

Henry did not seem angry with him. Time to be self-deprecating, Thomas told himself. 'If you have been a fool, Your Grace, then I have been a greater one. You entrusted the management of it to me.'

'No, Thomas, I will not blame you. I was wrong to trust King Ferdinand.'

'He has toyed with England,' Thomas agreed.

'Toyed? He has damn well deceived me, Thomas. And not only him but K – ' Henry broke off, shaking his head. 'I should have known. Every monarch in Europe knows how sly King Ferdinand is. He has humiliated me.'

'No, not at all, Your Grace,' Thomas said quickly. 'He has dishonoured himself by proving he is untrustworthy. I think it best if we look on this as a lesson learnt. We will not allow ourselves to be deceived again.'

'But Master Wolsey, I had no choice but to return. My men were on the verge of mutinying.'

Grey was desperate, Thomas could see, and no wonder. Thomas wondered how he would feel hearing that the king was mightily displeased with him, as he had just informed the marquess. 'I fear the king does not see it that way, Your Grace. He believes that you disobeyed his direct order and wants you punished.'

Grey ran his hand through his hair. 'But can you not speak to the king, explain to him? He will listen to you. Please, Master Wolsey.'

'I will talk to the king,' Thomas pledged, 'but I promise nothing. The king is extremely sensitive about this whole affair. He has been badly mistreated by the Spanish king – the queen even bore the brunt of his anger over Ferdinand's deception. If the king can berate his own wife…' Thomas waved his hand to suggest Grey would not fare much better.

Grey fell down into the chair opposite Thomas's desk, a figure of absolute dejection. 'It was not my fault. You cannot allow the king to make a scapegoat of me. You are my friend, are you not?'

'I have long been your friend and your servant, Your Grace,' Thomas said, a little annoyed. 'I am aware of what I owe to your family. But you must realise that I am just one of the king's counsellors. There may be others who will not leap to your defence as I will.'

'But the king favours you.'

'I enjoy the king's favour, as you say, and I intend to keep doing so.'

Grey met Thomas's gaze. 'Oh, I see,' he nodded. 'What that means is you will speak for me as long as you think it safe to do so. You will not stick your neck out for a man who has done you no wrong.'

'Your Grace,' Thomas said as Grey sprung up from the chair and headed for the door, 'that is not true.'

'Is it not, Master Wolsey?' Grey halted and turned on Thomas. 'All I can say is I am glad my father is not alive to see how you repay his kindness of all those years ago.'

'Your Grace… Thomas.'

'Do not dare to call me so, Master Wolsey,' Grey yelled. 'I am your better and will be addressed as Your Grace. It is my misfortune the king's favour has so turned your head that you have forgotten your place.' He yanked the door open and strode out.

Thomas stared after him, his breath coming in shudders. He saw his secretaries peering at him, no doubt wondering what had happened. He moved as calmly as he could to the door and shut it quietly. He returned to his desk and tried to concentrate on the papers before him, but it was no use. He had handled the marquess badly, he saw that now. He had not wanted to make an enemy of Thomas Grey, just make it clear he would do what he could without damaging himself and no more. Thomas had not thought that unreasonable. But then the marquess was a noble and had not had to earn his place at court. He had no comprehension of what favour from the king meant to a man of Thomas's background. He didn't understand that Thomas could not afford to lose his privileged position.

Thomas took a deep breath. He would speak for the marquess, and he just had to hope Henry would come around and realise it was not in anyone's interest to punish him. But if the king was adamant, Thomas was not going to argue with him. And the marquess would just have to accept that.

~

'I want the marquess of Dorset put on trial for treason.' Henry thumped the table, making the pots of ink jump.

The council sitting around the table looked at one another carefully. Archbishop Warham said, 'I am not sure that would be a wise move, Your Grace.'

Henry glared at him. 'Not a wise move? Am I to let those who disobey orders act against me without fear of retribution? Dorset ignored orders to remain in Spain, and he has the audacity to present himself at court as if he has not greatly offended me.'

'I am aware of that, Your Grace,' Warham said, 'but the fact is from all reports there was nothing else the marquess could do. Had he refused, he would have had a mutiny on his hands.'

'If he could not control his men, he should never have been put in charge of the army.' No one thought it wise to remind Henry that he had chosen Dorset to command the army.

Warham opened his mouth to speak but then closed it again, seemingly at a loss to form an adequate reply to the king. In truth, the young king wearied Warham considerably. He was too old to learn how to deal with a king who was exuberant and disinclined to attend to the routine and boredom of ruling a kingdom. He missed Henry VII, who had always been at council meetings on time, always completed paperwork meticulously and rarely had time for revelry. This Henry was simply too energetic. Warham cast a sideways look at Thomas, who understood it as his cue to enter the conversation.

'Your Grace,' he said to Henry, 'if I may, the archbishop is correct in his assessment of the situation the marquess found himself in. And what is more, I believe it would look as if we cannot control our own commanders to put the marquess on trial. It would be far better to take the stance that the marquess and his army returned to England on your orders. That would be a show of strength and leadership, Your Grace.'

Everyone around the table turned to look at Henry. Henry's eyes narrowed. Thomas held his breath.

'I suppose you are right,' Henry said grudgingly. 'You usually are in such matters, Thomas. Very well, no trial for Dorset. But make it clear to him that I am greatly displeased.'

Henry rose and strode from the room. The counsellors all let out a sigh of relief.

'Congratulations,' Warham said to Thomas. 'You have worked another miracle, making the king see sense and protecting an old friend.'

'Hardly a miracle, Your Grace,' Thomas said. 'The king is a reasonable man. He would have come to the same conclusion.'

'You just helped him reach it a little sooner, eh?' Lovell raised a mocking eyebrow.

Thomas smiled thinly at him. 'Excuse me,' he said and left the room.

'There goes a fellow we should all watch carefully,'

Lovell said. 'If we are not careful, the king will listen to his advice and none of ours.'

'That is nonsense, Sir Thomas,' Fox said. 'Master Wolsey knows his place.'

'Think he is still your man, do you, bishop?' Lovell said. 'I would not be so sure if I was you.'

Lovell sloped out of the room, leaving Fox to stare after him, wondering at his words.

CHAPTER THIRTY

1512

'A letter from King Henry of England, Your Holiness.' The secretary enjoyed the look of dismay that came over Pope Leo's face. His expression was always the same when correspondence arrived from England, for Pope Leo was not fond of the tiny country across the water.

'What does he want this time?' Leo asked with a sigh.

The clerk's mouth twitched in an effort to hide his smile. 'He respectfully requests that his most beloved servant Master Thomas Wolsey be created bishop of Lincoln in recognition of his many services to his king and the church.'

Leo drummed his fingers on the desk. 'Master Wolsey seems to be making quite a name for himself in England.'

'And in Europe, Your Holiness,' the clerk said, tucking Henry's letter in between all the others he had received that day. 'Master Wolsey has built up a wide network of correspondents, from France and Spain to the Netherlands. He has a finger in every pie.'

'And you do not?' Leo raised an eyebrow at the clerk who assumed a look of innocence. 'No need to answer. I hope you do have your inky fingers in all the pies there are.'

The clerk grinned.

Leo frowned. 'But this Master Wolsey. Has he not several benefices already?'

The clerk moved to the bookcase behind the Pope. Tapping his finger along the files situated there, he gave a small, 'Ah,' and withdrew one. He flicked through the papers it contained until he found the one he sought.

'Quite a few, Your Holiness. Master Wolsey at present is the canon of Windsor, the prebend of Hereford Cathedral, and the dean of Lincoln. He is also named as the vicar of several small parishes, though I understand he has never provided pastoral care in them.'

'Well, he is not alone in that,' Leo mused.

'If I may, Your Holiness,' the clerk said, stepping back to the desk, 'in my opinion, it would be wise to grant the king this request.'

'Explain.'

'The bishopric is vacant and therefore requires someone to fill it. It is an important bishopric as far as England is concerned – not the greatest, of course, but important. And Master Wolsey has proven himself an able intermediary between King Henry and the papacy. He could be useful in such a position, and it would show King Henry that you respect his judgement.'

Leo snorted a laugh. 'After the way he was fooled by that devil Ferdinand?'

'To speak truth, Your Holiness, King Ferdinand of Spain is a great schemer, experienced in deception and subterfuge. The king of England is yet young in state-craft. And looking to the future, the wisest heads in King Henry's council are old men who may not live for much longer. Bishop Fox, Archbishop Warham. Both wrote of Master Wolsey's abilities during your predecessor's time. Bishop Fox especially thought Master Wolsey a good instrument in keeping England bound to the church. And if you are planning to continue with the Holy League your predecessor, Pope Julius, established, and wish for England to remain within it – '

Leo held up his hands to signal the clerk could stop talking. 'Very well. King Henry shall have his bishop of Lincoln. And when you write your secret letter to Master Wolsey, make it clear to whom he owes most loyalty. In return for this bishopric, I want Master Wolsey to convince his king he must go to war again. You understand?'

The clerk nodded and grinned. 'Yes, Your Holiness.'

Joan bent over the cot and pressed her lips to the rosy cheek. It was the gentlest of pressure. She did not want to wake the tiny creature that had emerged from her body screaming and bloody, the fruit of her and Thomas's love.

A tear and a wrenching sob suddenly burst forth from Joan. Covering her mouth, she quickly turned away. *Do not be a fool,* she angrily chided herself, *you knew this was going to happen. You have borne this once before. You can do it again.*

She wished Thomas was with her. He had written that he could not come to her, he was too busy. It was not a lie; she knew how much he had to do and how much he liked to do it, but still she wished for his presence.

Joan had not expected him to be with her when she had gone into labour – the birth chamber was no place for men – but she had thought he would spare a few days to visit her after the birth. In his letter, he had said he would be with her the following week, the earliest he could manage to visit. He also wrote that he trusted she and their daughter were well. The last paragraph of his letter told her he had arranged for their daughter – 'Dorothy,' she whispered as she read the word 'daughter' again – to be taken into a nunnery as the only fitting place for a bastard girl.

Joan wanted to ask Thomas whether she would ever see her daughter again. She wanted to ask him that question face to face and see his expression as he answered so she would know if he lied. She did not want half-truths or prevarications. She wanted to know, and Thomas's absence denied her that surety.

Joan cast a look over her shoulder at the cot once more. *Do not blame Thomas,* she told herself, *it is not his fault. You knew what you were getting into the moment you gave yourself to a man of the cloth. At least Dorothy* – she whimpered as she mentally said the name – *will be safe and well looked after in the nunnery.*

As the mistress of a priest and the mother of a bastard, it was the best Joan could ask for.

CHAPTER THIRTY-ONE

1514

The new bishop of Lincoln tapped the letter from the Pope against his desk, considering the words he had just read. He should not be surprised, he told himself. He had known this was coming; he had just not expected it to be so soon. When he had heard from the Pope that he was to receive the bishopric, the letter made it clear his support for war with France would be required. *Another war*, Thomas thought. *Do we never learn?*

His gaze wandered to the window. He saw the king walking in the garden, Katherine by his side. Thomas pressed his nose to the glass and squinted. Henry appeared to be in a good mood. Maybe now was as good a time as any.

Thomas made his way to the gardens and stood at the end of the path Henry and Katherine were walking along.

'Well, if it is not the bishop of Lincoln,' Henry

greeted him with a broad grin. Thomas noticed Katherine did not smile. 'What do you do here?'

'I wondered if I could talk with you, Your Grace?'

'What, now?' Henry frowned. 'The queen was going to watch me play tennis.'

'It will take but a moment, Your Grace, if the queen would be so kind as to spare you.'

Henry raised Katherine's hand to his lips. 'I will not be long, my sweet,' he said and gestured to Thomas to join him as he strolled away.

'Well, what is it?' Henry asked.

'I have received a communication from the Pope,' Thomas began. 'He would like to have your continued support in the Holy League. France is still his enemy, and Spain is proving to be a thorn in the papal side. He suggests that England could invade France and thwart Spain who is seeking an alliance with her.'

Henry looked down at his feet. 'I do not know, Thomas. I admit, there is nothing I would like more than to have my revenge on that Spanish devil Ferdinand, but… ' He looked away to where Katherine waited with her ladies.

Thomas followed his gaze. 'The Pope would be in your eternal debt, Your Grace,' he said softly.

'But after the last debacle, Thomas. I do not think I could bear such disgrace again.'

'There would be no disgrace, Your Grace,' Thomas said heatedly. 'I would see to that. We would not rely on others to make plans for us. This time, we will make our own decisions.'

Henry thought for a long moment, then cast one more look at Katherine. 'Very well. Make the arrangements.'

～

This time it was going to be perfect. Thomas would plan everything down to the last detail. Nothing would go wrong.

Thomas thought it wise to involve Henry in the plans, so at the end of every day, he would take his papers to the king's privy chamber and the two of them would sit side by side, working through the details. The council would meet and wonder what was going on, and Thomas would give them the briefest of reports, not willing to involve them and possibly delay his plans.

Nothing was too small for Thomas's consideration. One evening when he and Henry were reviewing the figures, Henry pointed to a column.

'This is a great deal of canvas, Thomas.'

'Necessary, Your Grace. One of the problems from the last campaign was that the soldiers were left to sleep out in the open. The weather was too hot, and the men were not used to it. It is my intention that every man who goes to war on England's behalf will be able to sleep under canvas. It is important for morale, in my opinion,'

Henry nodded. 'I agree. A man needs somewhere decent to lay his head.'

They moved onto the next point. Henry questioned the provision of beer. 'So much?'

'Again, Your Grace, this was one of the complaints the men serving under the marquess of Dorset made. The provision was consumed too quickly. Men cannot drink contaminated water and remain healthy. Wine is too good for them and makes them drunk. What else can they drink but beer?'

'Agreed,' Henry said.

'You note the meat provisioning?' Thomas asked, pre-empting Henry's next question.

Henry smiled. 'As the son of a butcher, I assume you know what you are about when it comes to the provision of meat, Thomas.'

Thomas smiled back. 'I know what men need to eat to be ready to put their pikes into the bellies of other men.'

'Then the meat provision is more than adequate, I am sure.'

They moved on to the men that would be sent to France. It had been estimated that England would need forty thousand men to fight her war for her, but Thomas felt even this great number would not be enough. To be on the safe side, he calculated that ten thousand merce- naries would be hired to swell the English ranks to fifty thousand. Henry approved the mercenaries' salaries, then pointed to another sum.

'What is that?'

'That is the cost of the return transport, Your Grace,'

Thomas said. 'We have to factor in how much it will cost to bring our soldiers home.'

Henry raised his eyebrows. 'We did not do that before, I think.'

'Indeed not and that was a mistake. I have also made contingency plans should foul weather or any other calamity affect the return journey.'

'And what of weaponry, Thomas?' Henry asked eagerly. 'I will not send men into battle poorly armed.'

Thomas had already thought of that. He told Henry he was arranging for foundries to be set up that would manufacture the cannon and other weaponry needed for the campaign. He noted how Henry's eyes sparkled at the mention of cannon, weapons that had the power to entirely destroy the enemy.

Henry sat back in his chair and blew out a puff of air. 'You have done well, Thomas. I thank you for all your hard work.'

'Thank you, Your Grace.'

'But you look tired, my friend,' Henry said, studying Thomas's face. 'I am told you have been working day and night on this. Why do you not delegate some of this work to your secretaries?'

'No,' Thomas said hastily. 'I would much rather manage all this myself. That way I can be sure it has been done correctly. Thank you for the suggestion, though, I do appreciate your concern.'

'Have it your way. But there will come a time when you cannot do everything yourself.'

Thomas folded up his papers. 'For the moment, Your Grace, I can manage perfectly well.'

～

The sun was warm on Katherine's face as she stood in the courtyard of Dover Castle and watched the dust kicked up by the horses preparing to leave. She was unsure what she felt, whether pleased her eager young husband was going to get the chance to show what a fine soldier he could be or worried he might come to harm and never see the child she was carrying. She smoothed her hands over her rounded belly, hoping to impart some of her strength to the child in her womb. She hoped this one would not die as the others had.

The child was the reason she was not allowed to accompany Henry to France, though she dearly wanted to. Henry had been adamant: no travelling for her. She was to do nothing that would endanger the child she carried. He was unmovable, and Katherine had to content herself with the knowledge that he trusted her enough to make her regent rather than appoint some noble, such as the duke of Buckingham, to stand in his stead. She smiled inwardly. That was how much Henry loved and trusted her; he would leave the governance of his kingdom in her capable hands.

Henry had kissed her with excessive chivalry to take his leave, and she had wished the dignity and decorum could have been dispensed with and that they could have shared a genuine kiss, one that imbued all her love in it. But that had not been permitted, nor would Henry have appreciated it.

Katherine waved to him as he boarded the launch. Henry was dressed splendidly in brand-new armour polished so highly it gleamed in the sunlight. His head-piece was polished steel topped with a rich coronal, and the crimson satin lining that cushioned his head peeped out from beneath the rim. But what made Henry truly impressive was the tunic he wore, one she knew was intended to remind the people of a crusading knight, like the Templars of old. It was a white cloth bearing a large red cross, and like those famous crusading knights, he also bore a symbol of St George on his crown.

So many men were boarding similar vessels to complete the journey to Calais. Katherine's eyes raked over the multitude before settling on Thomas Wolsey, dressed in plain robes and surveying the scene with obvious pleasure. Katherine could not understand why Wolsey was going to France. He was a priest, not a soldier. She had asked Henry what possible use could he be.

Henry had laughed, kissed her fingers and said, 'Where would I be without Thomas Wolsey?'

Katherine had not cared greatly for his response. That her husband should place so much faith and loyalty in one born so low perturbed her. She knew how much Thomas Wolsey had invested in this venture, knew how hard he had worked to make this happen, and yet she found it so very difficult to like the man. Wolsey was so obviously ambitious and so greedy. She did not hold any absurd notions about the priesthood. She knew priests were often richer than they should be. She sometimes wished it were not so, but it was the way of the world, and it was not her place to find fault with the church of Rome.

All the men and supplies had boarded the ships. The time for departure had come and one by one, the ships floated away. Katherine waited until she could make out Henry no longer, then made her way back into Dover Castle.

~

Thomas had discovered he did not like campaigning very much. Though he had done his best to ensure that not only the king had every possible comfort, but that he did also, there had nevertheless been much that he missed about a brick and mortar home. Bad weather and gale-force winds had made even Thomas's luxurious tent a cold and draughty place, and he found he missed the stoutness of four stone walls about him. He had never imagined he was made for soldiering, and this campaign had confirmed it. He hoped it would all soon be over.

Not so, Henry. For all the difficulties and discomfort, the king was enjoying himself. And with reason, because to all intents and purposes, the campaign had been entirely successful.

The English had taken the town of Thérouanne, the first French town to fall to English armies since 1453 when Guienne had been captured. The English had been proud of the battle, even to the extent of giving it a name, the Battle of the Spurs, though as Thomas found out later, that name was given because it described how quickly the French had fled the field and not because of the valour of the English soldiers.

After Thérouanne, Tournai, the wealthiest city to be found in Flanders, fell to the English army, despite the renowned thickness of its walls and its ninety-five towers that were supposed to see off even the most stubborn of attacks. Henry enjoyed his victory parade through the town's streets, wearing his richest armour and riding a magnificent courser as his henchmen walked on ahead, bearing the royal arms aloft. Henry's nobles, similarly attired, followed in his wake whilst Thomas waited in a pavilion hung with cloth of gold and purple for the king to arrive to celebrate a victory mass. It had all come about most satisfactorily, Thomas thought as the king dismounted, waved to the crowd and made his way up the wooden steps towards Thomas with a huge smile on his face.

Once back in England, Henry was determined to reward those who had made his victory possible. His closest friend Charles Brandon became the duke of Suffolk; Lord Herbert, the lord chamberlain, became earl of Worcester; and the earl of Surrey was given back his family dukedom of Norfolk, it having been taken away by Henry VII as a punishment for siding with Richard III at the Battle of Bosworth.

Thomas watched the new titles being dished out and

felt sure his time would come too. He had done so much to make Henry a victor; Henry would not forget how much of his own success he owed to his almoner.

And sure enough, before the dust of the battlefield had settled, Henry made Thomas bishop of Tournai. More titles followed: dean of St Stephen's Westminster and the precentorship of St Paul's Cathedral. There was no denying that Henry was extremely pleased with Master Wolsey.

CHAPTER THIRTY-TWO

It was one of those rare occasions when Henry attended a privy council meeting. Thomas had known he would be present, but it had been a surprise to the other counsellors to see Henry at the head of the table.

Henry began the meeting by expounding on the treacherous natures of both the Emperor Maximilian and King Ferdinand. The political world moved quickly, and the council and the king had learnt that both men had been making treaties with France whilst telling Henry they were united with him against her. Henry assured his council he was not surprised by this news, merely disappointed. And now he had his own plan to ally England with France in a surer way than any peace treaty designed by either Spain or the Netherlands. Never mind the fact that he had just waged a war against France. That was in the past. The best way to ensure amity between two nations was by marriage, he said.

King Louis of France had just buried his wife; he would be needing a new queen.

'Princess Mary?' Fox asked.

'My sister, yes,' Henry nodded.

Thomas watched as Fox, Warham and the other counsellors looked at each other, eyebrows raised.

'King Louis is over fifty years old, Your Grace,' Fox said, 'and the Princess Mary not yet eighteen. Is not that too great a disparity?'

'Nonsense,' Henry said. 'Mary must marry Louis, not love him.'

'Of course, Your Grace.' Fox nodded. 'But if I may ask, have you spoken with the princess about this matter?'

'No, why would I?'

'Why, to gain her consent,' Warham said.

'She will give her consent, do not fear,' Henry said. 'There will be no difficulty once she knows how important this is for me.'

Thomas was not so sure, nor were the others. Mary was a strong-willed creature and he doubted whether she would be as amenable as Henry seemed to think. She was young and vivacious. He understood royal marriages had nothing to do with love, but there were certain duties that required at least a liking for the other person for them to be acceptable. Louis was an old man, gouty and prone to fatigue. If the desired outcome of this proposed marriage was the getting of an heir, Thomas wondered if Louis was capable of the act itself, let alone potent. *Poor Mary,* Thomas had thought when Henry had first broached the subject with him and had wondered whether he should try to change the king's mind about his favourite sister. But Henry had changed since his return from France. Katherine had lost yet another child and Henry's heart had hardened. He was not the happy young man he had been when he first became king, and Thomas had decided to say nothing.

'Write to King Louis,' Henry said, flicking his fingers at Fox. 'Propose the match.'

Thomas straightened the cross hanging over his belly, his fingers tracking the curve of the paunch. When had he acquired such a big belly? He watched Henry on the other side of the room. Thomas knew him well enough to guess what he was thinking.

Henry was not a subtle man; his thoughts and feelings were often displayed on his face. But Thomas had sometimes been surprised by a remark that showed a direction of thought Thomas had not expected Henry to consider, a sudden change of mood from anger to calm. But this was different. This was politics, and Thomas knew Henry was trying to think of all the angles. Thomas considered telling Henry he need not bother, that Thomas had thought of everything, but he thought it would not help. In fact, Henry being on edge would probably be useful.

The door opened and Charles Brandon strode in. He was a big man, as tall and broad as Henry, and Thomas felt dwarfed by the two men.

Brandon glanced at Thomas, then looked to Henry. 'Hal?'

'We have a mission for you, Charles,' Henry said without preamble.

'A mission?' It was difficult to tell from Brandon's expression whether he was pleased or the contrary.

'Thomas.' Henry gestured for Thomas to speak.

'Your Grace,' Thomas addressed Brandon, 'the king requires you to accompany the Princess Mary to France and deliver her to King Louis as his bride.'

Brandon's mouth fell open. 'You are really going to do this, Hal?'

'She is my sister, Charles. Mine to do with as I please.'

'I know that, but – '

'And it pleases me to have an ally in the king of France.'

'Mary does not want to marry that old cripple,' Brandon cried.

'You do not tell me what my sister wants,' Henry shouted, his arm raised, finger pointing at Brandon. 'I decide who she will marry, and I have decided she will marry Louis.'

'You have decided, or he has?' Brandon jerked his head at Thomas.

Thomas was astonished to have been accused in this way. Brandon and Henry were both staring at him, and he felt the hairs on the back of his neck prickle under their glares. 'I assure you, Your Grace, the king decrees the marriage. I merely offer advice when it is asked for.'

Brandon snorted. 'Such modesty, Master Wolsey. What a change that makes.'

'Leave Thomas be, Charles,' Henry ordered. 'Listen to me. I cannot allow you to marry Mary. It simply cannot be.'

'Why can it not?'

'It cannot be,' Henry repeated emphatically. 'Tell me you understand that.'

Brandon's head was down. He did not answer.

'Charles!'

'I understand, Hal,' Brandon retorted savagely.

Thomas was beginning to think Henry had made a poor choice of envoy in Charles Brandon. He had heard vague rumours of Brandon wooing the Princess Mary, but he had dismissed them as court gossip, the boastful stories of a proud philanderer, but it seemed from Henry's words that Thomas had been wrong.

'Swear it,' Henry said.

Brandon stared at him. 'I do not need to swear. I have said I understand.'

'I need you to take an oath, Charles.' Henry snatched a book from the cupboard. 'Swear on this Bible.'

Reluctantly, Brandon took the Bible.

'Now, say you will not woo my sister in any way, from this moment onwards to the moment you hand her over to Louis. Swear it, Charles.'

'I swear I will not woo Princess Mary. There. Are you satisfied?' Brandon threw the Bible on the floor.

Henry glanced at Thomas, almost, Thomas thought, as if he was looking for confirmation that Brandon's promise was enough.

Personally, Thomas would think again about sending him, but now was not the time to question Henry's judgement. Thomas clasped his hands in front of his stomach as if to imply he had nothing more to say.

CHAPTER THIRTY-THREE

ROME, 1514

Rinaldo di Modena slammed the door of his chamber behind him, wincing as the action caused him further pain. His breath was coming fast, and his head was fit to bursting. Never before had he felt such rage. The cardinal had gone too far this time.

Di Modena willed himself to calm down as he heard the door open behind him. He did not look around, but he knew who had come in.

'Are you in pain?' Matteo asked hesitantly.

'Of course I am in pain,' di Modena snarled. 'Would you not be in pain if you had just been beaten with a cane?'

'Forgive me.' Matteo's tone was disgustingly servile. 'You should let me take a look.'

Di Modena sighed. 'I am bleeding. I can feel it.' He pulled his robe over his head, feeling the cloth catch and pull at the broken skin, making him hiss. He heard

Matteo's gasp of horror as his brutalised back was exposed to view.

'Dear God. Lie down on your bed, Rinaldo. I shall clean your cuts.'

Di Modena lowered himself onto his bed as Matteo left the room, turning his face towards the wall as he came into contact with his hard pillow. He heard Matteo return a minute or two later and set something down, then he felt the ice cold trickle of water over his back. He moaned a mixture of pain and relief as the water worked into the wounds, wondering what his back looked like.

'How bad?' he asked.

'There will be scars, I think,' Matteo said, dabbing a cloth against the welts. 'I had not thought the cardinal could become so angry.'

'You have not been here long enough,' di Modena said, accepting the pain of his friend's ministrations. 'He has always had a temper.'

'But to beat you… what had you done?'

What did I do? di Modena wondered. *What did I do that I had not done a thousand times before?* 'I think today he simply did not like my face.'

'Have you been dismissed, Rinaldo?'

'No. It is enough that I have been punished. The cardinal does not like to go to the trouble of having to train another dog to do his bidding.'

'You should complain about this treatment,' Matteo said earnestly.

Di Modena guessed Matteo was fearful for himself. He was such a mouse of a man, the perfect chaplain. It would be just like him to want others to make a complaint about Cardinal Bainbridge rather than do it himself. 'Who should I complain to? Who would listen?'

'There must be someone you could tell.'

Di Modena did not answer. He was thinking. As Matteo finished and moved away, di Modena lay still, his eyes fixed on a crack in the wall. There was no point in complaining. The cardinal was as good as untouchable. No one would listen to the complaints of a mere chaplain. But he knew he would be beaten again and that he would not be able to bear. Something had to be done. The cardinal had to be paid back for di Modena's suffering.

Later than night, when Matteo was snoring in his bed, di Modena rose and dressed and headed out of the cardinal's official residence. He was careful not to be seen as he headed into the town, not that anyone was really paying attention at that time. Those who were early risers like di Modena were too preoccupied with their own business.

He found the door he sought and knocked, pressing his ear to the wood to listen. Light footsteps came nearer, and he pulled his hood a little farther over his face.

The door opened a crack. 'What do you want?' a voice demanded.

'Hemlock,' di Modena replied.

'Wait.' The door shut and opened again a moment later, a little wider this time. The voice named a price di Modena readily agreed to, delving into his purse for the coins. He pressed them into the leathery hand that was thrust out. The hand disappeared, reappearing a moment later with a small bottle of dark liquid. 'You know what to do?'

'I know,' di Modena said, stuffing the bottle into his purse.

'There will be signs of poisoning.'

'I do not care.' Di Modena turned abruptly, heading back to the residence. He spoke the truth; he really did not care. He planned to be long gone by the time the cardinal was dead.

Thomas waved the petitioners away, gesturing for a path to be cleared for him. He had no time for these people; he needed to get to his office. An important letter was waiting for him.

He reached the outer chamber of his office, ignoring the secretaries who stood as he entered, papers in their hands, wanting his attention. He closed his office door and hurried around his desk, his eyes searching for the letter.

There it was on the far corner, Silvestro Gigli's seal in the red wax. He reached over and snatched it up, breaking the wax eagerly. He cursed Gigli's scratchy handwriting, his eager eyes too frantic to be able to decipher the words easily. He shuffled into his chair and tried again.

Master Wolsey, I have good news. As you instructed in your last letter, I applied to the Italian bankers, and they agreed to loan you the money required to aid your promotion to the archbishopric of York. I do think this was the best way to proceed, the money already being in the country rather than you arranging to send money here.

'Yes, yes,' Thomas muttered irritably, 'I know it was your idea. Well done, Silvestro. Now, get on with it.'

It was not easy to quash the rumours here in Rome surrounding Archbishop Bainbridge's murder. I am not sure how many of them reached your ears – in truth, I did not think it worthy of your notice to inform you of them – but it was said that you had a hand in Bainbridge's murder, having suborned the murderer, di Modena, to poison him, you and Bainbridge having so great a dislike for one another, and you coveting his seat of York.

Thomas snarled. How dare people say he was involved in Bainbridge's death? He had disliked Christopher Bainbridge intensely, it was true, for the man was an arrogant bastard who took every opportunity to abuse him, but that Thomas would stoop to murder was a foul idea. How much more evidence did they need than the body of the executed di Modena, his torso bearing the scars of Bainbridge's frequent and terrible anger? Even Bainbridge's other servants had testified to how they were beaten and abused by the dead archbishop. Thomas took a deep, calming breath and returned his attention to the letter.

It was thought in certain circles that you applied for the archbishopric of York with unseemly haste, but I did my best to assure my colleagues in the church here that your haste was borne out of a desire to serve both the Pope and your king to the best of your abilities rather than to any personal advantage. King Henry's request to the Pope that you be given the seat helped immeasurably, I am sure, and I do not think I lie when I write that the archbishopric is as good as yours. I am sure that your letter of confirmation is not far behind this one you hold in your hands.

So, I will end this letter with my congratulations, and trust that the new archbishop of York will not be forgetful of what his most loyal servant has done for him in Rome.

Silvestro Gigli

Thomas put down Gigli's letter and reached out a shaking hand to take up the cup of wine set out for him by his page. The cup's rim knocked against his teeth as he took a mouthful. He had it, he had the archbishopric of York. He had been sure his money would swing the vote in his favour, but even so, there had been a kernel of doubt in the back of his mind that he would be dismissed as an upstart by the Vatican. But no, he had it.

Once he had been confirmed in the seat, there would be only one churchman higher than him in England, and that was William Warham, archbishop of Canterbury.

He raised his cup in the air and laughed. 'Not bad for the son of a butcher.'

CHAPTER THIRTY-FOUR

1515

'Ruined. All ruined.' Henry screwed up the letter from his sister and threw it across the table to Thomas.

Thomas picked it up and smoothed it out, meaning to file it later. 'It is a great shame, Your Grace. No one could have foreseen that King Louis would die so soon. Is your sister very upset?'

'What? No, of course she is not,' Henry said scornfully. 'Mary hated being married to him. She is overjoyed he is dead, never mind what it means for me. Read for yourself.'

Thomas read the letter from Henry's sister. It was clear that Henry was correct. Mary was not at all dismayed to find herself a widow. Her life as queen of France, though brief, had been miserable. Her ladies and other servants who had journeyed from England with her had been dismissed almost at once, a dismissal she had blamed the duke of Norfolk for, claiming he had done so because all her servants had been chosen by Thomas Wolsey and it was well known how greatly Norfolk hated Thomas. Mary may have been right about her servants' dismissal. Thomas did not know.

His eyebrow rose as he carried on reading and discovered that Mary had had to fend off the attentions of the new king, King Francis. Francis had a reputation for being a rake, and Thomas wondered if Mary had mistaken his amorous advances for serious intent, her sense of superiority naturally assuming he wanted to make her his wife rather than his mistress. Whatever he wanted, Mary made it clear in her letter that she was having none of it. She ended by reminding Henry of the promise he had made her – that her second husband would be of her choosing, not of his.

'What does the dowager queen mean by this sentence, Your Grace?' Thomas pointed his finger to the line, holding the letter up to Henry.

Henry had been resting his head on his hand whilst Thomas had been reading. He had complained of a headache earlier, and Thomas thought he was still suffering. Henry opened a bloodshot eye to see what Thomas was pointing at.

He sighed. 'She made me promise she could marry whoever she liked when Louis was dead.'

'You gave her that promise?' Thomas asked in surprise.

'I did not know Louis would die so soon,' Henry said, exasperatedly. 'Mary kept on at me. She said she would not marry Louis if I did not promise her.'

'And now she intends to hold you to it,' Thomas said. 'What will you do?'

'She cannot expect me to keep that promise,' Henry said, wincing as his voice got loud. 'I will need her again.'

'To marry to another king?'

'Maybe.'

'Will she be returning to England?'

'Yes, she will. I will not leave her there for Francis to do with as he pleases. She must be brought back and swiftly.'

'Who shall you send to escort her? It must be someone of suitable rank.'

'Brandon can go.' Henry closed his eyes and rubbed his temples.

'Is that wise, Your Grace?' Thomas asked carefully. 'Knowing the duke and your sister once had an understanding?'

Henry peered at him. 'Brandon swore an oath. Remember, Thomas? He promised not to woo my sister. That oath binds him still.'

'I trust you will remind him, Your Grace,' Thomas said, rising from his chair. 'The duke may feel that his oath was not to woo Mary whilst she was a maid. As a widow, he may feel he has license to try again.'

'He has not,' Henry said decisively, 'and I do not need him to swear again. You do not understand such matters, Thomas, you are of too low birth. An oath is an oath.'

Thomas nodded. 'If you say so, Your Grace.'

Thomas glanced out of the window. The sky was darkening; it was getting late. The council had been sitting at the table for more than three hours, by his reckoning, and he sensed his fellow counsellors' restlessness. The pile of papers before him was almost done, just a couple more. He slid the top paper towards himself and noticed with surprise that it was addressed to him directly, not to the privy council. He turned it over to inspect the seal. It was the seal of the duke of Suffolk. With a great sense of foreboding, he opened the letter and read.

'Ill news, Master Wolsey?' Fox asked.

Thomas held the letter up. 'I fear the king will think it ill. The duke has married the dowager queen of France.'

'He's what?' Lovell burst out. 'He's married the king's sister?'

'He has,' Thomas said, tapping his fingers against the table, thinking. 'Against the king's express command.'

'The king must be told, Master Wolsey,' Fox said solemnly, his expression making it clear he had no intention of doing so himself.

Thomas nodded resignedly and clicked his fingers at the clerk. 'Send a message to the king requesting he come to the privy council urgently.'

The clerk disappeared from the room. A silence fell upon the counsellors. Fox broke it.

'The duke has committed treason by marrying the king's sister without his consent,' he said.

'Treason?' Lovell echoed. 'Do you really think we should call it so to the king?'

'What else can we call it?'

'The duke is a great friend of the king's.'

'I doubt if the king will think of him so kindly once he hears what the duke has done, Sir Thomas.'

'Who will tell him?' Lovell looked around the table.

'The letter was addressed to Master Wolsey,' Fox pointed out, casually reaching for his cup of wine.

Thomas cast a sideways glance at him, knowing Fox was enjoying this situation.

There was a commotion in the corridor outside, and the counsellors got hurriedly to their feet in expectation of the king's arrival.

'What is all this?' Henry asked, waving them all to be seated and dropping down into the chair by Thomas. 'I was winning my game of bowls.'

'We are sorry to have disturbed you, Your Grace,' Thomas said, remaining standing. 'But we have had a communication from the duke of Suffolk that cannot remain unanswered.'

'What is it?' Henry asked, his face suddenly serious.

'It transpires that the duke has broken his oath to you, Your Grace, and married the dowager queen.'

Henry's mouth fell open. 'He has broken his oath?'

'He has, Your Grace.' Thomas reopened the letter, knowing that Henry's sense of the chivalric code of honour was deeply offended. 'He writes, "The queen would never let me rest till I had agreed to marry her. And so, to be plain with you, I have married her secretly and have lain with her in so much as I fear that she is with child."' Thomas closed the letter. 'If that be the case, Your Grace, I fear the marriage cannot be annulled.'

'My sister with child by him!' Henry murmured. 'But could it not be the child of King Louis?'

Thomas shook his head. 'The dowager queen told King Francis she was not with child by the late king. Had she been, King Francis would not have been crowned, as the unborn child would have been next in line to the throne. And in any case, it is doubtful whether the late king was capable of fathering a child, he being of advanced years and a partial invalid. The child, if there be a child, must be the duke's.'

'But he swore he would not woo her,' Henry snarled, stabbing the table with his forefinger. 'He made me a promise. He made a promise to God.'

'It is reprehensible, Your Grace,' Fox said. 'We were saying before you arrived that the duke's actions are treasonous. He must be punished.'

'The duke does say that he would rather be dead than have Your Grace discontented,' Thomas said, glancing from Fox to Henry. 'He is aware of the offence he will cause.'

'Perhaps the duke should have thought about displeasing the king before marrying the dowager queen,' Fox suggested.

'It seems the dowager queen gave him little choice,'

Thomas said, wondering, even as he spoke, why he was sticking up for Charles Brandon, a man who had never liked him and who had gone out of his way to insult him.

'He had a choice,' Henry snarled. 'And what makes my sister think she can choose her husband?'

'There is a rumour, Your Grace, that you promised her second husband could be of her choosing,' Lovell said.

'She had no right to marry without my permission,' Henry glared at Lovell, who dropped his eyes, and Thomas knew he wished he had kept his mouth shut.

'What punishment, then, Your Grace?' Fox asked eagerly. Too eagerly, Thomas thought. Everyone, including Henry, knew that Fox disliked Brandon. 'The duke should, at the very least, be taken prisoner.'

'At the very least?' Henry queried.

Fox stared straight back at Henry daringly. 'If not executed, Your Grace.'

The council held their breath, all eyes on Henry. Henry's eyes were on the tabletop as he considered. Then he sat back in his chair, decision made.

'They will not be allowed to come to court. And my sister must pay back the cost of her marriage to King Louis. How much is that, Master Wolsey?'

Thomas had to think and think quickly. 'Around twenty-four thousand pounds, I believe, Your Highness, not including her dowry.'

'I shall have that too.' Henry nodded. 'My sister's marriage to King Louis has yielded me nothing. I want my money back. You will write to the duke and my sister, Thomas, and tell them.'

'Of course, Your Grace,' Thomas said, pleased to see Fox disappointed that there would be no execution for Charles Brandon.

~

Thomas expected Henry's anger at Brandon and Mary to fizzle out. Henry had a good heart, and Thomas doubted whether it could remain hardened against his closest friend and his beloved sister for long.

But it was taking too long and Brandon and Mary were growing tired of waiting for Henry to relent. It had been months since they had returned to England and Thomas suspected that young Mary missed the hustle and bustle of court life and was sniping at her husband to do something about it. And so Brandon had written a letter to Thomas begging him to persuade Henry to let bygones be bygones and allow him and his wife back to court.

Thomas allowed himself a little smile. Brandon was all humility now he needed something from the mighty Thomas Wolsey. Where was the bravado of only a few years before when Thomas had been nothing but a chaplain in the king's service and Brandon had scorned him for being the son of a butcher? Oh, this was delicious. Should he please the duke by agreeing to speak with the king? Or should he keep him hanging on, wondering if Thomas Wolsey was going to do the mighty duke a good service? Thomas thought about it for a long while and decided it would only increase his standing with both the king and the duke and duchess of Suffolk if he could arrange a reconciliation.

And Thomas did not doubt he could do so. For the king trusted his Thomas wholeheartedly, implicitly. Yes, Thomas decided, he would speak to the king on Brandon's behalf. And enjoy every single minute of it.

CHAPTER THIRTY-FIVE

'Ah, Polydore, there you are.' Thomas did not bother to smile at his fellow clergyman. He had sent for him more than four hours ago – what had the man been doing all this time? 'Take a seat. I will be with you in a moment.'

Thomas bent his head back to his work. Polydore Vergil slipped into the chair on the other side of the desk, and Thomas heard the older man's rather laboured breathing. Thomas scrawled his name at the bottom of the page and set down his quill, wiping his inky fingers on a cloth. As he wiped, he noticed that the skin on his right thumb and forefinger was deeply ingrained with ink, a stain of many years of writing; it would never wash off completely.

'I would like you to go to Rome,' he announced to Vergil.

'To Rome, Master Wolsey?' Vergil's expression was more one of dismay than pleasure.

'Why, Polydore, would you not like to return to your

home country? I would have thought you would wish to visit your old home and perhaps even kiss the feet of the new Pope. Does that hold no appeal?'

'Well, yes, a little,' Vergil said, his eyes dropping away to inspect the floor. 'Although, I must confess that England has become my home. I have been here twelve years now.'

'You are an Italian, Polydore. Rome is in your blood and will never leave you. Now, when you arrive in Rome, I would like you to do something for me.'

'Anything, Master Wolsey,' Vergil said in a resigned tone.

'Do you know Cardinal Hadrian?'

'I have heard of him, though I have not had the pleasure of his acquaintance.'

'I have corresponded with him frequently over the years. I pledged my support to him when Pope Julius died. If he chose to stand for election to the papacy, I promised he would have my support. That never happened, of course. Pope Leo was elected, but still, I gave him my word, and he was pleased to accept it.'

'And now you want the favour returned.' Vergil nodded knowingly.

Thomas's jaw tightened. 'If you care to phrase it so, yes. Although I do not intend to insist on Hadrian's support. This is a very delicate mission I am trusting you with, Polydore.'

'I understand,' Vergil said hastily. 'Complete discretion.'

'Exactly. You are to present yourself to Cardinal

Hadrian and pass on my good wishes. He will enquire of you how I do, and you will tell him how close to the king I am. If he seems interested, you can then take the matter further.'

'So, I am not to ask him directly if he will vote for you?'

'No, you are not. I would not have you be so vulgar as to do that. You are to sound him out. If he seems amenable, that is the time to press him on pledging his vote for me.'

Vergil laughed a little uncertainly. 'Forgive me, Master Wolsey, but would it not be simpler to ask the king to speak for you?'

Stop trying to wriggle out of going, Thomas thought with irritation. He suspected Vergil was far too comfortable in his home to view the journey to Rome with anything but dread. Thomas understood his reluctance; he was not a happy traveller either, but he understood the necessity of travel to achieve one's ends and was prepared to do it. It was true, of course, that for Thomas a journey these days was not simply a journey; it was an opportunity to go on a procession, to be seen, for wherever Thomas went, he now went with an entourage of upwards of one hundred servants, all decked out in his own livery. Vergil, when he went to Rome, would travel with only one servant.

'This is a church matter, not a sovereign one,' Thomas said. 'I cannot and will not ask the king to become involved. I am asking you, Polydore, as a friend.'

Thomas knew that last remark would work. Vergil visibly swelled with pride at being called a friend of Thomas Wolsey.

'Of course, Master Wolsey,' he said. 'I shall go to Rome with pleasure. I am sure, though, my presence will not be necessary. I am certain you are already at the forefront of all the cardinals' minds in Rome. Your election to the College of Cardinals is assured.'

'I would like to think so.' Thomas smiled. 'But you know me, Polydore, I like to leave nothing to chance. Thank you for this. I am sure you know how much I appreciate your efforts. How soon can you leave?'

'Well, let me see.' Polydore began counting off on his fingers. 'I will need to book passage to Calais, find a suitable lodging – '

'All done,' Thomas cut him off. 'There is a ship leaving from Dover for Calais in three days. I have written to the lieutenant of the Port of Calais and he will provide you with a bed for the night.' Thomas rattled off the detailed itinerary he had arranged, amused that Vergil listened to him open-mouthed.

'But you did not know I would agree to go, Master Wolsey,' Vergil pointed out when he finished.

Thomas smiled and shook his head. 'Oh Polydore, as if you would dare say no to me.'

~

Thomas had thought it better to deliver a two-pronged assault on the papal authority in his ambition to become a cardinal. Whilst Vergil's mission was a very real one, Thomas had also engaged Sylvester de Gigli, still in Italy, to test the waters of papal feeling towards him and promote his cause whenever he thought best.

But there was one person who could perhaps tip the balance in Thomas's favour, and, as Vergil had suggested, that was Henry. He had told Vergil his promotion to the College of Cardinals was not a sovereign matter, but that was not entirely true. It was true Henry could not make Thomas a cardinal in the same way he had appointed him royal almoner or royal chaplain, or even arranged for him to become the bishop of Lincoln or Hereford, but Henry could petition the Pope on Thomas's behalf, just as he had done when Cardinal Bainbridge had died and the archbishopric of York stood vacant.

As soon as Vergil began his journey to Rome, Thomas sent a request to Henry for an audience. Word came back that the king would see him at Eltham Palace. This was one occasion Thomas thought not ripe for his usual procession, and so he boarded his barge with only his secretary and a page for company, save for the twelve oarsmen who propelled the barge through the muddy Thames.

Henry was pacing up and down when Thomas arrived. 'Thomas, what is it? I am supposed to be playing bowls. Compton is due a thrashing. He has beaten me the last three games.'

'I am sure you will win this time,' Thomas replied dutifully. 'I promise not to delay you long, Your Grace.'

Henry settled into a chair, hooking his right leg over the arm. 'Speak on, then.'

Still standing, Thomas held his hands in front of his belly. 'I am sure Your Grace is aware that England has had no cardinal since the death of Cardinal Morton. I think it is time for that to be rectified. To that end, I would like to ask if you could recommend me to the Pope.'

'You mean ask Leo if he will make *you* a cardinal?' Henry asked doubtfully. 'Is that not a bit ambitious of you, Thomas?'

'I do not think so, Your Grace,' Thomas said, not daring to look Henry in the eye. 'And if I may, following your commitment to the Holy League and your successes in France, the Pope will pay great attention to anything you may request of him.' He took a deep breath. 'Also, I believe not having a cardinal in England reflects poorly on you. It is almost as if the Pope is saying England is not worth a cardinal.'

Henry sat up. 'By God, you are right, Thomas. After all I have done for the Pope, I should have a cardinal here.'

Thomas relaxed. 'My secretary is just outside if you would like to dictate your letter to him, Your Grace,' he offered helpfully, not wanting to waste any time.

'Yes, yes, bring him in.'

The secretary was brought in, and Thomas gestured him towards the small table by the window upon which sat a writing slope complete with paper and ink. 'Write what the king tells you,' he said in a low voice, and the secretary nodded.

Henry stood, hands on his hips, his eyes on the ceiling as he constructed his letter in his mind. The secretary had already started writing the customary greetings and was waiting for the king to begin.

'"I would like for my beloved counsellor to be honoured and supported by the church. I do not embellish the truth when I say that I can do nothing of any importance without Thomas Wolsey; he is my most secret and trusted servant. To this end, I humbly request that Master Thomas Wolsey be appointed to the College of Cardinals without delay." There, how does that sound, Thomas?'

Thomas blinked away the tears that had begun to prick at his eyes as the king spoke. 'I am humbled by your faith in me, Your Grace. You do me too much kindness.'

'Nonsense, Tom,' Henry said, clapping him heartily on the shoulder. 'It is no more than the truth. You are my right hand. Never think I do not know it. Now, may I go and play my game of bowls and thrash Compton?'

'Of course, Your Grace.' Thomas grinned and stepped away, leaving room for Henry to pass. To his secretary, he said, 'Have that letter despatched at once.'

◈

Pope Leo drummed his fingers upon the table, thinking. His secretary had just finished reading out King Henry of England's letter asking that his beloved counsellor be made a cardinal, and Leo was in two minds what to do about it.

On the one hand, Leo was willing to grant King Henry his request, mindful of how loyal the young king had been to him, joining him in his Holy League and winning victories, however insignificant, against the French. On the other, it was not long since Thomas Wolsey had been made archbishop of York, one of the highest church positions in England, not to mention all the other benefices Thomas had acquired over the years since becoming a priest.

Wolsey, and Leo had no doubt that it was Wolsey who was seeking the cardinalate, was so nakedly ambitious, it irked Leo. Did Wolsey think he only had to ask and Leo would be forthcoming? There was also the matter of the gossip attached to Wolsey's name. The murder of Bainbridge had not been forgotten. Although Rinaldo di Modena had confessed to administering the poison, the suggestion that it had been at the behest of Wolsey, a man Bainbridge had openly detested, was still fresh in Rome. Should such a man be made a cardinal? And what then? Would that be the end of Wolsey's ambitions? Leo doubted it. He had no doubt that once made cardinal, Thomas Wolsey would be angling to be made *legate a latere*. This was a title that made the bearer the Pope's representative for life and would give Thomas Wolsey the power to make church reforms and decisions about the church in England without referring them to Rome.

'No answer for the time being,' Leo told his secretary. 'I need to think about this matter before deciding.'

The secretary tucked Henry's letter into a folder stuffed with unanswered correspondence and opened the next paper on his pile.

CHAPTER THIRTY-SIX

1515

It had taken almost a year for Pope Leo to make up his mind, but he had done so at last. Thomas was to be England's first cardinal in fourteen years, and he had jumped for joy when the letter arrived from Rome confirming his appointment.

There was no time to waste, he thought; he must begin the arrangements for his elevation at once. He left his suite of offices and headed for the offices of Bishop Fox. Fox's secretary showed him in.

'Oh, 'tis you, Master Wolsey,' Fox said, turning his attention back to the Bible in his hand. 'Come and sit down.'

Thomas drew a chair up to the desk. 'I wanted to talk to you about my hat, Your Grace.'

Fox closed his Bible with a sigh. With eyebrows raised, he asked, 'Is it on its way?'

'It will be very soon, I am told,' Thomas said.

'Well, you have worked hard for it.'

Not 'You have earned your cardinal's hat', Thomas thought resentfully. 'Yes, I have,' he said, determined not to let Fox spoil his good mood. 'As England does not get a cardinal every day, I thought it would be a good idea to make an occasion of it when it arrives.'

Fox frowned. 'For a hat?'

'No ordinary hat, Your Grace,' Thomas insisted. 'After all, I will be the first cardinal in England since Cardinal Morton.' *And then you will have to bend your knee to me,* he thought savagely. 'The Holy Father has bestowed this honour upon England and the king as much as myself. I am sure the king would agree that the occasion should be marked with a ceremony.'

Fox opened his Bible again. 'Well, you always know what the king wants, Thomas, so I must believe you are right.'

'There is another reason why I thought you might agree, Your Grace. The hat is a symbol of the church's authority. It would not hurt to use the ceremony to remind the people of how great the Church of Rome is. You will remember you were once very keen on re-establishing the church's authority in this land, and you told me I would be integral to that goal. I believe I have fulfilled my duty in that regard – more, in fact, than you ever believed I could.'

Fox's nostrils flared. 'I remember.'

Thomas smiled. 'Then look on the arrival of my cardinal's hat as an opportunity.' He kept the smile on his face as he watched Fox consider his words.

'Very well, Master Wolsey. Myself and Warham

shall make the arrangements to receive your hat with the utmost ceremony. Will that satisfy you?'

'Indeed, Your Grace, my thanks.' Thomas stood and turned to go. He paused and looked down at Fox, who was staring at the floor, his mouth pursing and relaxing, pursing and relaxing. 'Are you not pleased for me?'

Fox looked up at him. 'I am pleased for the church that there will be a cardinal once again in England. The truth is I worry for you, Master Wolsey. You have risen so high, so far from your beginnings, that I worry how far you have to fall.'

Thomas frowned. 'Why talk you of falling?'

'To fall is almost inevitable in this world. We are at the mercy of kings. We are safe as long as we continue to please, but if one day we no longer please, what then will become of us?'

'You talk of ifs and maybes, Your Grace,' Thomas said. 'None of us can know what lies ahead.'

'You do not think about the future?'

'I do my job as best I can, Your Grace, and trust the future will take care of itself.'

Fox crossed himself. 'Amen to that.'

The hat had arrived in England.

To Thomas's annoyance, it had not arrived without its problems. The red silk hat with its wide brim and heavy, elaborate tassels was being conveyed from Rome to England by Cardinal Gambara. Thomas had only heard of Gambara, never having met him, and he had expected that a papal envoy on so important a mission as the deliverance of a cardinal's hat would be appropriate to the occasion. But not so. The servant Thomas had sent to receive Gambara when he arrived at Dover reported back that the cardinal was dressed extremely poorly, wearing shabby travelling clothes and having none of much better quality to change into for the procession to London that had been arranged. Not only that, Thomas read with increasing outrage, his cardinal's hat had been stuffed into a linen bag where it was no doubt becoming creased and dirty.

By the time Thomas received this news, Cardinal Gambara had already begun his journey to London. Thomas despatched a messenger at once to his servant, instructing him to catch up with Gambara and stop him before he took another step. Gambara, Thomas instructed, must order himself new clothing from a local tailor, having the bill sent on to London if necessary, and a wooden box lined with silk must be procured for his hat. Thomas would not have Gambara disgracing him in public. He could already imagine the whispers and jeers every time Gambara stopped at one of the churches Thomas had specified, the people saying the Pope must have a very poor opinion of Thomas Wolsey if this was how his cardinal's hat was delivered.

Meanwhile, Thomas wrote to Elizabeth, Henry and Richard, inviting them to London to witness his investiture at Westminster Abbey. It was heavy on his mind how he had been selfish in the past about his achievements, not wanting his family to be a part of them, and he was eager now to make amends. He did wonder where to put them, though, for he knew the abbey was already filled to bursting because of all the nobles and peers, as well as the members of Parliament he had invited to attend. He would find a space for them, he resolved, as he studied a plan of the abbey. Perhaps there at the back, near the corner. He shrugged. It would have to do, he decided, then moved on to the next item on his investiture agenda.

And then, suddenly, the day was upon him. Unable to eat, his hands shaking, Thomas had kissed Joan goodbye and left York Place, the large house he had only recently acquired as the archbishop of York. He made his way in a closed coach to Westminster Abbey, not wanting to be stopped by the people who would reach out their hands for a blessing or beg money from him. At the abbey, his chaplains and secretaries were waiting in the room set aside for him, and as they dressed him in his robes and copes, Thomas ordered his clerks to run through the details of the ceremony. He had planned everything down to the last detail, and the event, he was certain, would run smoothly.

The next few hours passed in something of a blur. When he had time to reflect, Thomas could remember hearing the abbey fill up with spectators, could remember walking out into the abbey to be greeted by Archbishop Warham, who was to perform the investiture, flanked by two Irish archbishops, eight abbots and eight senior bishops. He vaguely remembered seeing

Bishop Fisher's grim face, his hand curled around a crosier.

And then he could remember nothing until he found himself kneeling before Warham and feeling the heavy triangular tassels knock against his shoulders as the hat was lowered onto his head.

Thomas got to his feet, and Warham gestured for him to process down the nave. Two crucifers each lifted an enormous gold cross into the air and stepped in front of Thomas. Waiting for confirmation, they began to walk before him, and Thomas followed immediately behind. He was tempted to look over his shoulder but knew he should not. It struck him then that for the first time in his life, he was the first person in a church procession. Before, he had always followed senior bishops or archbishops. Now, they had to fall in step behind him.

I am unique in England, Thomas thought, forcing his lips not to curl in a smile as he walked past the pews crammed with dukes and earls, duchesses and countesses. *There is no other churchman in the land that holds the power I do now, not Fox, not Fisher, not Warham. Let people say of me what they will. I am Master Wolsey no longer, the butcher's son raised above his station.*

I am Cardinal Wolsey.

PLEASE LEAVE A REVIEW

If you have enjoyed this book, it would be wonderful if you could spare the time to post an honest review on whichever book platforms you use.

Reviews are incredibly important to authors. Your review will help bring my books to the attention of other readers who may enjoy them.

Thank you so much.

JOIN MY MAILING LIST

Join my mailing list to stay up-to-date with my writing news, new releases and more, and receive a FREE and EXCLUSIVE eBook, *The Queen's Poet*, a short story featuring Sir Philip Sidney and Penelope Devereux and one of the greatest love poems of Queen Elizabeth I's reign.

It is completely free to join and I promise I won't bombard you with emails. You can easily unsubscribe at any time.

You can join here: www.lauradowers.com

ALSO BY LAURA DOWERS

THE TUDOR COURT

The Queen's Favourite

The Queen's Rebel

The Queen's Spymaster

The Queen's Poet: A Short Story (*Exclusive to subscribers*)

The Tudor Court: Books I—III (Boxset Edition)

THE RISE OF ROME

The Last King of Rome (Book I)

STANDALONE NOVELS

When the Siren Sings

COMING SOON

The Eagle in the Dovecote (The Rise of Rome, Book II)

CONTACT

I'd love to hear from you. If would like to comment or ask a question about one of my books, then get in touch. You can find me at:

www.lauradowers.com

Made in the USA
Middletown, DE
22 May 2020

95568150R00257